THE LOST MARBLES STORY

A Novel written by **THOMAS F. RUKAS**

Copyright 2017

Edition - 2

THE LOST MARBLES STORY

This book is Dedicated to the memory of

Gary Mosier.

Cover art Concept by Thomas F. Rukas

Cover art design by Tesia Barone

REVIEWS:

"Reading this novel was like watching a movie. The author really places the reader into the story." – Anna A.

"I couldn't put it down. The characters were colorful and defined and I felt like I knew them." - Denise A.

"'Nick' was my favorite character because he was a badass. The women were exotic, some downright evil. The whole book was good. I can't wait for the next one." – Zemo.

TABLE OF CONTENTS

Introduction...5
Chapter 1- The Lost Marbles in 1998......................7
Chapter 2- Woodstock..11
Chapter 3- The Band Forms................................28
Chapter 4- Tightening up our Act.........................38
Chapter 5- The Big Show...................................52
Chapter 6- The Record Deal................................62
Chapter 7- The Siren's Coast...............................76
Chapter 8- Tripping with a Witch.........................91
Chapter 9- Crooks and Deviates..........................112
Chapter 10- Chaos and Readjustment...................129
Chapter 11- New Management...........................134
Chapter 12- We're on a Roll..............................147
Chapter 13- The Plot Deepens............................166
Chapter 14- Winslow, Arizona............................178
Chapter 15- Taken, in Flagstaff, Az. 200
Chapter 16- Back in Pennsylvania........................221
Chapter 17- Heading Out of the Country...............232
Chapter 18- The Island's Story............................245
Chapter 19- The Island Mansion..........................257
Chapter 20- Ladies Night..................................272
Chapter 21- Nancy and Me................................296
Chapter 22- Intervention and Togetherness............303
Chapter 23- Lost Marbles are Back......................312
Chapter 24- Catching up, 1998...........................324
Chapter 25- Epilogue.......................................336
ABOUT THE AUTHOR...................................344

Introduction

There's an old expression regarding destiny, comparing it to the way a bed is made, and how well we'll sleep. Some believe that we all have some spiritual protection, of some sort, that guides us to our destiny, and that our destiny lies within the way we make our beds, or more specifically, our lives. Angels are miracles. Miracles are angels. Some believe, and others don't. Those who believe know that they are without beginning and without end, and appear in many forms such as human, which is rare; and to be frank, rather dramatic. I myself believe they also appear in quiet, or subtle, unannounced and overlooked forms such as a moon shadow, a sunrise, a warm memory, or something as simple as the shape of an oak leaf.

Though not a religious person by any means, I do consider myself spiritual to some degree, believing that a destiny could be a choice . . . if our eyes are opened wide enough to see it, our arms are opened wide enough to receive it, and that everyone's guided to it by faith, hope, love, and sometimes a miracle.

This story of The Lost Marbles is purely fiction, and the characters portrayed in this book are, likewise fictional. It is about a man at a turning point; reflecting back on how his life, ranging from the pinnacle of the bizarre to the depths of despair, has lead him to a fork in the road of his destiny. His reflection on how the uncomplicated beginnings, leading to a full and sometimes outrageous life, brought him back to face the solemn reality that is nothing more than hesitant, and nothing less than a nightmare. Through all of his challenges of the lows, unpredictable mayhem, and glorious highs in life; In the end, Stan will find that his original goal as a successful musician in a moderately successful band won't fail; but will be eclipsed by something far greater than he could have ever imagined or hoped for. He will find that his sincere love and respect for women, primarily one in particular, will end up being the very life force saving him from dissolution, and possibly his own demise. This is the story of The Lost Marbles.

Thomas F. Rukas - Author

c. 2017

NOTE:
This is a work of fiction. Names, characters, businesses, places, events and incidents are either the products of the author's imagination or used in a fictitious manner. Any resemblance to actual persons, living or dead, or actual events is purely coincidental.

THE LOST MARBLES STORY

PART ONE

Chapter 1

The Lost Marbles in 1998

    The smoke-filled room was alive with cigarettes and the sound of screaming voices, trying to be heard over the loud music coming from the stage. . . or rather cheap platform, where our band was playing; as we were all squeezed tightly together in an area no bigger than a jail cell, between microphone stands, drums and amplifiers.
    All in all, it was a good night of jamming; as we were playing our usual classic rock, with hearty jazz overtones. Everyone seemed to be happy, except for me. I can't explain it, but I wanted to be anywhere else, as this life I've presently honed from years of draft ale backwash, lousy pay, and conversing with drunken strangers, was as stale as the smoky air, and as dull as the empty beer glasses. The broad excitement that once was, playing the bars and generating intoxicating energy to help please the local patrons, grew as thin as the greying hair on my aging head. My drinking days were finished many years ago, and that might be the proverbial weight tipping the balance of my direction the other way, thus keeping me no longer from sitting on the fence of this dead-end circus, but I don't really know.
    'Can't explain it? I think I just did.

As I ride the strings on my Fender P-Bass, I'm also on what seems to be a brain auto-pilot, guiding me through the last song of the night as these thoughts dictate an ominous feeling of "What the hell am I doing here?" Then "Cousin Benny's" amazing guitar riff diverts my attention to the song we're playing, as I continue to ride the bass, smiling and listening to those high and low notes he creates on his Stratocaster guitar, blending and bending so easily and freely, engorging the song with the breath of life itself, as we breathe it into our instruments, then out again, just like we did in the earlier and younger years of our lives. The jamming is an intense communion, making us laugh and smile with approval. As I weave in and out of the melodious string of notes, I'll add a syncopation that gets a hard-lined definition by "Flash" the drummer, and "Nick" on the rhythm guitar. Our music is a well-tuned, sweet sounding conversation about how we all got here in the first place. We call ourselves "The Lost Marbles," and I used to never want it to end, but that's all appearing to be changing now.

Anyway, soon the song takes its original structure and we find our places back in the routine, or on auto pilot. As the song ends and the applause dies away, I put my bass in its case and lose myself in the bland ritual wrapping of the cords and taking down the equipment.

We all take our parts in packing up, ambling quietly past each other barely uttering a word. Occasionally from the bar, a couple will come up and say, "Good job! You guys sound great! 'Real tight'."
"Thanks," one of us will say.
"What's the name of the band?"
"The Lost Marbles."
Another guy would say, "Where are you playing next? "You guys are tight."

Another lady comes up and says, "He's right. You guys play like you are best friends. I can see you all really like each other."

BAM!! That really hit me! I just nodded and kept to myself.

The truth is, it seems, we really 'don't' like each other. We used to, really, since we've known each other for many years and now have virtually nothing to say to each other unless we're playing. . . or better yet, jamming together. We're all good musicians, and time and tide along with life . . . and a touch of fate, brought us all together; And also, the fact that we *did* used to really like each other. At this moment in time there's a dark cloud looming that I can't explain nor vanquish. It's just there, and as it looms, I purposely try not to think about it, as I've been mildly successful in forcing this darkness away from me. . . so far.

I actually love these guys, and have great memories with them, and I'm sure the feeling is mutual, but "Love" and "like", although a fine line, is very different.

We all have our nicknames; For instance, "Cousin Benny" is our lead guitarist, Benjamin Unkelheyer. Although he's also known as "Cuz" or "Benny", he's no relation to anyone in the band. There's "Nick", our rhythm guitarist Frank Nichols, who sometimes plays the lead, but overall funks out the band with his strong chops. There's our drummer 'Flash', whose real name is Henry (Hank) Zeke. In the early days, someone saw the heat he generated with a lady, as she came up to him with a long, thin silk handkerchief, and waved it around and around his head from behind him as he played within the rhythm of the song. Hank was trying to down a lit, flaming shot of 151 proof rum in one hand, while drumming with the other, and he and the girl's hanky both caught on fire. Fortunately, no one was hurt, other than Hank's ego, pride, and most of his beard. Nick started calling him "Flaming Flash Hanky," which stuck, but it was much easier to say "Flash". It's a good thing too, Hank wasn't fond of "Flaming Flash Hanky" and although there are other versions of that story, that's the story I remember.

I'm Stan. My given name is Tom Stephens, named after one of my dad's army buddies. I've been called "Stan" since I can remember, but I have no idea where it came from. Rumor has it that my brother Paul gave it to me, when we were kids about 5 and 6 years old, drawing and coloring together. Since we were catholic, we were morbidly fascinated within our parochial youth, by the institution's canonized martyrs, and how they died so brutally for their faith, as illustrated pictures had displayed in our catechisms, or as graphically described by our first and second grade nuns. My brother was artfully drawing people getting their heads chopped off and guillotines chopping bodies in half, while I was into outlining a man tied to a pole and having arrows shot into his chest, arms, eyes, mouth, ears, etc. This particular portrait, crowded with the arrows, cost me the rest of the heavily used red crayon. My brother and I supposedly argued over which martyr mine was; and whose body was consuming my carefully placed projectiles. I said, "Saint Stanislaus" and he said it should be "Saint Stephen," and added the reminder that he was older, which makes him a good deal smarter. Although he was right, at least that time, I still stuck to my arrows, and he reportedly started calling me "Stanislaus" instead of Tom, and eventually shortened it to Stan. Most people, I think, assumed it was my real name, or better yet, confirmation name.

Nonetheless, as I continue tonight in helping with the packing up of the gear from the evening's performance, we're all continuing our somewhat awkward silence, and my mind wanders, between an apparent break in the dark fog of depression, and through to the brighter thoughts of the earlier years; Days when we laughed together and were much happier, and how it all came together. It seems like yesterday, but it was a long, long time ago. . .

Chapter 2

Woodstock

It was in the summer of '69, a very warm and humid summer night as delivered by the dog days of August. We were on a double date at the Bucks County Drive-in movie theater in my '65 Ford Falcon. I was with Mae, and Cousin Benny was with Nancy, who liked calling him 'Cuz.' Nancy was a sweet thing, who was short, loud, had dark brown hair and was well built, and was courageously outspoken with an obvious New York accent. Mae was soft spoken with a slight sexy rasp in her voice, and her blonde wavy hair would lay nicely on her skin, soft and milky white, as I gently nibbled on her ear. Both girls wore short slinky summer dresses that night while Cuz and I wore our standard summer attire; jeans and tie died tee-shirts. Mae loved and shared my British Sterling cologne, and also shared my Southern Comfort and my Banaca breath freshener, along with her tongue. The movie, to the best of my knowledge was "The Love Bug," about Herbie the Volkswagon bug, but we weren't really watching. After what seemed to be a long time of necking and making out, we got into a discussion about a happening festival, which we had heard about that day. Woodstock, N.Y. was featuring a 3-day concert with the best of the best bands in the line-up.

"Let's go," Nancy said after talking about it.

"It already started, and it's all the way up in New York," I answered.

"Yeah," Mae followed, "but if we left now, we could get there by 3:00am and enjoy two days' worth."

"That's crazy," Cuz said. "We only have a couple bucks between us. How much is it?"

"Who cares?" Nancy shouts, "Maybe we can sneak in, and I have my dad's company credit card for gas."

"That's probably between 150 and 200 miles!" says Cuz, "If we're really going to drive that far, there's no maybe about it." Cuz took a sip of the Southern Comfort. Then he said with commitment, "Driving a distance like that means we ARE going to get in." There was a slight pause before he said, "Period."

That was the spoken word that put us over the top, and we all knew then we were definitely going! We left the movie before it ended and took route 611 north through the Delaware water gap to Scranton, then interstate 81. The ride was pleasant and quiet as Cuz and I shared the driving responsibilities while the girls slept most of the way. Cuz and I talked and bonded like we have before on long drives, especially since we both love music. He was already an excellent guitar player at 16, a year younger than me. I was in and out of high school rock bands as he was, and he and I spent many a loose weekend jamming together with different drummers, keyboardists, and other guitarists, but the most creative times we had together was playing one on one with each other. This was the second trip he and I have taken together, considering earlier this summer just he and

I drove to California and back, and it was the best adventure we'd ever had; To this date anyway.
"Stan, 'you think we can pull this off?" he blatantly asks.
"If, and only if we can find it," I say.
"I'm humbled. 'Lots of great musicians up here; lots of great bands," Cuz said, with almost pretentious nervous overtones in his voice.
"I know. We wouldn't be here otherwise," I answer.
"Nancy turns 17 tomorrow. Do you think she'll still like younger men?" He asks me.
"She'll always like younger men, and older men," I said, "but it's Mae who's 17 tomorrow. Nancy was 17 last May, remember? She's a 'Taurus'. How the hell did you forget that?"
"I think it's funny," Cuz smiles, totally disregarding forgetting which girl was having the upcoming birthday, "it's funny how we just did this drive without telling our folks about it. How and why did we do that?"
"'Mom always thinks if I'm not home in the summer for days, I'm down at the shore," I tell him.
Cuz doesn't like to talk much about his family. They don't seem to miss him too much.

We were both limited on our knowledge about marijuana, but we enjoyed drinking when we had the chance, and the first time we'll ever try pot will be at Woodstock.

We were in the vicinity of Max Yasgur's property where the event was, driving down country roads that were backed up with traffic and parked cars, and we lucked into what seemed to be a nice area to park our car. We got out, locked it up, and pointed ourselves in the direction that everyone else we saw was going. It was very dark as we walked along, with a thin herd of what sounded to us like young adult hippies with flashlights, including lots of talking and laughing, along with the smell of marijuana. A joint was handed to me by a very strange girl, and her beautiful eyes looked right through me while I shined the light on her face.

"Do I know you?" I asked her, but she smiled a captivating smile and winked, and said collectively,

"Someday you'll know, and you and I will be together when the universe calls us together."

A chill went through me, but by then Mae pulled me away and said, "Can't you see she's on something? Just stay away from her."

I shrugged my shoulders, shaking off the chill, and I took a long toke and held it in my lungs. (I pretended I wasn't that limited on my knowledge of pot). I handed it to Mae who passed, then I was handing it to Cuz, but Nancy snatched it from my fingers and took a long, long toke. Cuz, the whole time, holding the flashlight beam on Nancy's face reached with his other hand. She smiled and closed her eyes as she placed it in his waiting fingertips. I looked around for the strange girl who handed it to us, but she had disappeared into the growing crowd of people.

We heard a distant muddled roar coming from the direction we were headed, mixed with an occasional screech of microphone feedback. There was a female voice talking over a PA system, but we couldn't really understand her words. It was a sound that reminded me of summer camp, and the camp's PA system echoing through the dark night.

We ended up walking over an embankment and over two weighted down wire cattle fences, through tall weeds and grass until we heard the female voice clearer and now singing,

"Swing low, sweet chariot,
comin' for to carry me home . . . ".

As we got closer and closer to the music with the crowd singing along, the crowd grew denser and there was an almost constant smell of pot. As the crowd finished a chorus of "We Shall Overcome," The roar of the applause was real. They said the woman's name, but we couldn't hear it over the applause.

I heard some guy yell behind me to another person, "It's after two, we better get to the tents." Then another female voice yelled back, "We'll see you back there Franky."
"It's only after two o' clock and the show's over?" I asked the guy.
The man said, "Hell no, we're gonna rest for tomorrow. It's a long weekend ahead. I'm just keeping tabs on my little sister. Where you guys from."
"Pennsylvania," Cuz answered.
"Me too, where at in Pa?"
"Furlong," I say.
"No Shit? I'm from Warminster," he says.
"Small world for sure," Cuz said, "I'm Benny but you can call me Cuz like everyone else. This is Stan, Mae and Nancy."
"Glad to meet you. I'm Nick, but you can all call me Nick."
I overheard Nancy say to Mae "'Sounds to me like we should all call him 'ass'."
"I heard that," Nick said, "Just don't call me late to 'The Dead'."
I said, "Nick? I thought I heard that girl back there call you Franky."
"That was my little sister," Nick said. "My given name is Frank Nichols. She's the only one in my family to ever call me Franky. Don't you ever call me Franky!" Then he looked at Nancy, regarding her sly comment to Mae and said, "I'd even prefer 'ass' over 'Franky'.
"You got it," she responded with a smile.

THE LOST MARBLES STORY

Now Nick was about our age, in a tie died shirt, with a sparse, thin beard with no mustache and long brown hair, that flowed clean down his back about half way to the top of his hip-hugger jeans. He kept throwing and flipping it back over his shoulders as he felt he needed to. He was tall and lean, with a great sense of humor, and was walking with a big black dude whose head was shaved, and whom he introduced to me as "Derek." Derek was still in the marines and was just back from a tour in Vietnam, but he's now in special forces and is presently on leave and headed back to Nam next week on some secret assignment. Derek was pretty quiet while Nick did the talking for him, but then Nick started chatting with us about more interesting matters.

"Where are you guys stayin'? You are staying, aren't you?" Nick inquired.

"We have no plans. We're playing it by ear," I say.

"'Playing it by ear' you say?" continued Nick, "You don't happen to be musicians too?"

Just then, Derek laughed at Nick and just shook his head, rolling his eyes at Nick's candor as we continued walking and talking, meandering toward their campsite.

"As a matter of fact," Cuz responded, "Stan here is a great bass player and I play electric guitar."

"I play guitar too", Nick replied with a big smile, grandstanding his perfect teeth, then adding, "I have a Les Paul".

"If I had the money to get a Les Paul I'd buy a Stratocaster," said Cuz.

Nick, a talker, shifted the conversation to talking about his present line, some home realtor work and house inspections he did with his father, as he then glanced over at the girls without their awareness.

"Your girlfriends are pretty nice, and I think I know who Nancy is. She lives just around the corner from me," Nick said with a sly grin.

"She does?" Cuz responded surprised.

"Yeah, she has a nice house," Nick remarked taking a toke off of the joint.

Now maybe it was the way Nick was pronouncing the word 'house', or the weed we were on, or the wine, or the combination of everything that caused this conversation to take an interesting turn. Cuz thought that Nick said, 'nice ass' instead of 'nice house' and he tried not to take it personal, and like the Cuz I know, he rolled right past it and took it with a grain of salt. Then he just patiently responded in kind.

"Yeah," Cuz grumbled, "I guess it's alright."

"Alright? It's beautiful!" Nick continued, "But I guess you've been up there many times."

"Excuse me?" Cuz said getting pissed.

"Sorry, Cuz, I didn't mean anything by it." Nick said as he picked up on the fact that maybe Cuz was bothered about something he said as Nick continued:

"I was just assuming that since you're both together, I figured you've spent some time inside of that fine spread of hers."

Cuz just shook his head, biting his tongue in frustration, but remained silent while Nick continued talking. I took the joint from him, not picking up on it yet, that Nick was only talking about her house and yard, while Cuz continued thinking he was talking about Nancy's ass. I took a toke on the joint, trying to follow this entertaining conversation, and handed it back to Nick as he continued:

"But on the flip side of that," Nick said, "in the front she should manicure that big bush, which would add value to that whole spread." Nick took another toke off of the joint saying, "All in all, it's certainly a tasty gem, but I could certainly do without that untrimmed bush."

By now, Cuz was turning red, fuming, and trembling at what he was hearing, maybe even thinking Nick was some sort of pervert by this time, and tried to maintain self-control, until Nick uttered, "No, shit, if she was my girlfriend Cuz, I too would probably spend most of my time in THAT spread. Hell, I'll admit, I wouldn't mind even buying something like that if I could afford it".

"WHAT??" Cuz said aloud.

Then he finally snapped, "Well she's not your girl, and she's not a 'spread' as you say, 'for sale'! Stop making her out to be some sleazy hooker!

"What the fu- ?" Nick chimed in, confused, but Cuz cut him off continuing his rant:

"Who the hell do you think you're talking to, punk? You don't know me, and what I do with Nancy's 'ass' is between her and me, and nobody else! You're talkin' about my girl dude, and you're really cruisin' for a fuckin' bruisin'."

"WHOA there, champ!" Nick replied, "Who on this holy planet earth of ours is talking about her ass? I never even mentioned her ass!"

Cuz answered, "I'm standing right here! I heard you say, 'she's got a nice 'ass'? Right Stan?" he asked, directing the attention toward me.

"I didn't hear anything," I safely said, taking another toke.

"And you also suggested that I've been 'up there many times'?" Cuz said with his face redder than I've ever seen.

"'HOUSE'," Nick was shouting, "'H-O-U-S-E', Mister Jackass, I said "House'. Not 'ass'. That's the 'layout' or 'spread' I was talking about! I can only imagine what you were thinking when I mentioned her bush! Maybe you should switch over to cigarettes and water, friend, and while you're at it clean the shit out of your ears!"

Everyone broke into hysterical laughter, even Cuz, that is everyone except for Nancy and Mae, because believe it or not, they were already talking in a separate universe about going home.

"Mae's parents are going to worry about her," Nancy said.

I believe to this day that they both got cold feet about staying the weekend and decided to simply leave because it was too much of a hassle for them.

"You've got to be fuckin' kidding me!" I said.

Nick said, "There's supposed to be a half million people coming here by tonight. Good luck getting out of here this morning."

He started strumming his acoustic guitar as his scruffy looking buddy, with the long dark frizzy hair, was already hammering on the congas to a song that I was told was played early in the show. "Freedom, freedom . . ."

We decided altogether that if we didn't leave now, we wouldn't get home by Sunday night as originally planned, but maybe Tuesday, so we said our goodbyes while they were playing.

"Oh", Nick said, this guy over here jamming with me on the congas is Hank Zeke. But you can still call me 'Nick'"

We were getting too anxious to leave at that moment and fell just short of snubbing Hank, who was busy anyway, grinning and pointing at some topless chicks who were dancing by flashlight to their energetic rhythms.

"Do it baby! Yeah! I'm in love!" he was yelling.

"Nice meeting you all, and take it easy," we said as we left.

"I'll take it any way I can get it, and Good Luck," Nick said, shaking his head at Hank's juvenile outbursts.

Our girls walked ahead of us, but Cuz and I turned around to listen to Hank and Nick jam for a bit, and it was captivating. Besides the dancers, there were sit-in people on harmonica, and a tin can, and another guitar, but the solidarity was clearly Nick and Hank, as they were very tight. Our girls came back realizing we weren't behind them, and Mae's unmistakable voice whispered in my ear a familiar phrase, "Are you coming?" "Yes."

The four of us walked for what seemed to be hours while we stumbled through groves of people, hippies half naked, and some completely naked, but fortunately, daylight was breaking. I drank some wine that was laced with what was called, "Magic Mushrooms," and was feeling so strange that I couldn't tell if some of the things I believed I was seeing were real or not; and seemed to be having a momentary lapse of reason, time, and reality in general. I was also hearing echoes, reverberating everything anyone was saying.

I began experiencing mild hallucinations, and it took some effort to distinguish those from reality, so I felt the need to walk away. I had to pee, and I temporarily lost Cuz, Nancy and Mae, as I wandered into a field of tall grass that seemed to be barren of people. I wandered down a hill and while answering the call of nature I was startled by a vision; was it real? It was a beautiful topless redheaded girl, knee deep in a pond and bending over as if looking for something. She had creamy white skin and her long red hair was fixed up off of her shoulders with a beret. The only thing she wore was what looked like the bottom of a G-string bikini around her perfect ass, and on her ass, was some writing, apparently in lipstick, which read,

"Happy Birthday Sweet 18."

I couldn't resist as I said, "Happy Birthday!" She looked at me, and then looked back down, waving me away, and continued to bend over, seemingly searching, with her bare breasts almost touching the water. "Did you lose something in there?" I asked.

"Shhh! I'm catching my breakfast." she said in a loud whisper.

She slowly moved forward and lowered her hands and forearms into the water deeper; when all of a sudden there was a splash! She wrestled with something under the water, almost going under herself. She then pulled up a large catfish, that was about 30 inches long!
"Gotcha!" she said aloud.

She cradled his wriggling body under her bosom and walked to shore and up the weeded hill toward me while the fanning fish was slapping at her breast. I was trying to look at her eyes, but the fish kept moving, diverting my attention downward. "I'm up here, look at me," she said.
"I know," I said embarrassed, and added "I wasn't looking at your boobs."
"I wasn't talking to you!" she said to me shaking her head, "I was talking to mister catfish here. I want to see his pretty face."
Now, I was really embarrassed but tried not to show it.

"He's a biggie," I said, as I still wasn't sure if she was real. She had the prettiest blue-green eyes, a very pretty face, like a dream, and when she smiled, her perfectly white teeth almost glowed against her face, which seemed slightly tinted pink from the sun, which is a redhead thing, I guess. She was able to raise the head of the slimy, wiggling catfish high enough to say, "That's right, keep squirming mister, it won't do you any good."
I told her, "He doesn't seem to want to go."
"Ohh, he'll go. I'm making him an offer he can't refuse, I'm inviting him to breakfast," she said. This dreamlike goddess then looked at me and continued talking.
"By the way, I'm Eve," she said, "and you are? . . . "

I figured by this time she was definitely talking to me and figured I'd better respond.

"Stan," I said nervously, "Nice to meet you."

I watched her slowly squat down with the wriggling catfish and set him on the dry padded down grass. And holding him down, pulled out a sharp, threatening looking hunting knife from her G-string. She started, easily and without remorse, cutting and skinning his still gyrating body as she spoke collectively, "Stan, you're invited to breakfast too, but I'll understand if you say no on such short notice."

She turned and looked up at me with hopeful eyes, while not missing a single cut on skinning her writhing prisoner and she continued talking,
"This is my property you're on now, but we're gonna walk over to Yazgur's to see the show later. We're camping out this weekend like everyone else."

Suddenly the fish slipped away, and she turned her head downward to quickly pull his slimy tail back, saying,
"Oops. Oh no you don't, mister! I wasn't talking to you. Get over here!" Then added, "Catfish can be so stubborn."

Her looking away gave me the chance to check her nude body out again, (What can I say? I was a young red blooded American boy!) and gripping the quivering fish firm, she returned to her pitiless skinning and looked up at me again, awaiting my response.
"I can't," I said, "I have people waiting for me."

Just then I heard Mae calling my name. Eve looked in the direction of Mae's voice and said, "I understand."

Then we heard another female voice.
"Well Eve, did you get him?" Looking in the direction of the second voice Eve said, "Come here Lila!"

From the direction of that voice came another beautiful woman. As she got closer I thought I was seeing double, as it was the perfect image of Eve, except her hair was down, long and beautiful. She too, was topless, and in one hand, she was carrying small fur pelts, in the other a hunting knife. As she neared, I noticed she was wearing nothing covering her bottom but a belt; and attached to it on her left side was something dangling.

"Yeah, He's here." Eve said.

Were they talking about me? This mushroom concoction I'm tripping on was getting me paranoid enough, and then I heard squealing coming from Lila's belt as she stood in front of me. It was two squirrels, alive, and dangling upside down against her left hip, wiggling, squirming and chittering, and they were apparently included in their breakfast feast. Lila had bloody pelts in her right hand from two other squirrels and with her knife in her left hand gave me a soft poke, and playfully said, "Mmm yummy. Who's this?"

Eve looked up at me and said, "Stan, this is my twin sister, Lila, but I call her my evil twin. Lila, meet 'Stan'. . . and stop poking him with that!"

I inadvertently said, "Pleased to '*eat*' you," then wondered what was going on with my poor disintegrating brain for saying that. I've never tripped before, or smoked pot for that matter, and I've always been a bit squeamish about seeing anything being killed. Lila leaned into me and I felt her warm breath as she softly and slowly ran her hot wet tongue from my neck up and into my ear, and twirling it, repeated my exact greeting, whispering: "Pleased to '*eat*' you too!"

I was stunned, and almost melted right there, along with my brain; right on that spot. I couldn't move, and deduced that she knew I was tripping, and was just goofing on me; fucking with my head! But now everything was very wavy, like I was seeing things through a tunnel, or like being under water with my eyes open. . . but still breathing . . . I think.

"Lila, stop flirting with him" Eve said, "he says he can't stay for breakfast."

Then she looked at Lila's two squirrels and said, "So we got the little bastards. Good. I can't wait to eat them too; Surf and turf!"

Lila looked deeply into my eyes and said, "Yep, hell is coming to breakfast." Then she looked away from me.

"There were four of these critters, stealing baby robins right out of the mother bird's nest, eating them alive. They certainly won't be doing that again," Lila said, slowly and seductively licking her lips.

She then walked to the pond's edge and bending ever so provocatively, rinsed the fur pelts while her kicking, squealing victims that were tied to her belt, still try hopelessly to free themselves, but she ignores their efforts. Then standing tall, and voluptuous, ties the pelts together around her back from the front, making a revealing top for herself while supporting some nice cleavage. And unhooking the pitiful squirrels she lifts them to see her new fur top she skinned from their two buddies saying,
"What do you think boys? I think these look good on me."

Lila and Eve broke into laughter and I began to wonder if they're just purposely freaking on me or if they're just plain ass crazy people. They're talking to squirrels and fish for God's sake; Could I be in danger here?

Their laughter was now in complete unison, as if they were one person, and everything I saw started to become like moving picture illustrations, erotic and mystifying. The two women, twins, appeared to come together becoming one person, then separated into two again, with colorful trails as this seemed to happen again and again. There were also geometric lines exploding everywhere, crisscrossing with strange colors I've never seen before. With this mushroom, or maybe LSD high, or whatever this feeling may be, who can tell if any of this is real? However, in the midst of the chaotic high there was something warm and comforting, at least with Eve.

Then she told Lila, "Really, we shouldn't torture them like this. That's bad karma."
"So is eating baby chicks out of the nest," she said, "I'm only returning the karma."

Lila was close enough to me that I could hear her stomach growling, as she directed her attention once again to the squirrels saying:
"Oops! Can you hear that you two?" as she humorously pulled the two creatures up and pressed them together with her thin fingers to her tight belly, so they too could hear the growl.
"That's the dinner bell," she said, "We have to get back to your friends in our little frying pan and flip them over." Then with a sexy evil glare at her two unfortunate victims added, "Then it's your turn to fry," and hooked them back to her belt and slowly sashayed over the hill to her campfire.

As I watched her walk away, the hill seemed to be melting, and I was again seeing those geometrical lines, bending and crisscrossing, distorting my thinking and my vision. The sky around her goddess-like figure was exploding with an endless changing of colors, liquefying the hill with the tall grass around her, lighting up like flames of fire in the first hint of sunrise. I shook my head in a real, quick fashion to try to realign myself.

"Like I said, she's my evil twin," Eve said with her bright smile and her captivating eyes, "Right now, she's on her way to skin and cook them, like the others. When she's pissed at someone, animal or human, she's merciless; You don't ever want to cross her."
Then she added:

"She's crazy, but she's my sister, and I love her no matter what. You don't know what you're missing here, Stan, I'm sorry you can't stay."

She winked at me and said, "'See you around.'"

I watched her carrying that gutted catfish in one hand and the hunting knife in the other walking very provocatively up and over the same hill, melting in an abstract work of art. I was still hearing and seeing everything distorted because of those magic mushrooms, so I have to figure out in my head if that whole episode of Eve and Lila really occurred. I'm thinking that I may never do this kind of hallucinogen again. I'll find out later that it was all some sort of premonition of things to come, mixed with a taste of reality.

I met up with Mae, Cuz, and Nancy; Actually, truth be told, they were picking me up from the ground saying, "Wake up Stan," and all I remember after that was we continued on our quest of trying to find the car. On the way, I realized that I was entirely naked; It had just come to me.

"Where's my clothes? My wallet?" I asked. Mae was carrying my pants and shirt while Nancy held up my wallet saying, "You don't get this back until you put your clothes back on."

Cuz was carrying my sneakers, but my socks and underwear were history. Fortunately for us we did find the car, where I dressed into what was salvaged of my attire. I didn't even realize I was nude, and I guess still tripping. The car, my '65 Ford Falcon, was still intact and there was room ahead for us to drive out and down the country road and eventually gravitating toward interstate 81.

We were pretty quiet on the way home while my brain was still a little fuzzy from those mushrooms; but feeling closer to normal (I think). The girls slept most of the way and Cuz was driving as we were chatting about life, the road, and the people we saw at the festival, especially the ones we met.

"That 'Nick' was sure an interesting individual", Cuz was saying, "Did you listen to his guitar playing?"

"Where was he getting the energy to play like that?" I asked.

"'Acid', maybe 'speed'", Cuz said.

"No, I don't think so" I rambled on, "I think he was high, or maybe some of that, I don't know . . . but it all seemed so naturally aggressive, especially the way Hank and he played together. The timing was right on for a loose jam".

"I know, I did take notice to that," Cuz grinned, "I couldn't tell though if he was generally a good person or a complete asshole until he started jamming."

"There's that 'ass' word again", I said, "so what did you finally decide?"

"I don't know, the jury's still out on that one," was his reply.

"Well," I noted, "in my opinion I think he's a good guy who's a creative musician; And as an older musician once told me, 'Musicians are generally assholes.'"

"Well in my opinion," Cuz summarized, "let's stop for breakfast".

I've never mentioned at that time, my encounter with that mysterious redhead Eve, or her sister to anyone because they'd think I was crazier than I already am. That was one moment of Woodstock I've kept to myself.

We pulled into a diner just south of the Delaware Water Gap. I don't know what time we left the festival grounds, but it was now 9:35 am, and we had a nice breakfast, took the girls to Mae's, and dropped off Cuz. I slept into Sunday.

Chapter 3

The Band Forms

Summer went by quickly after Woodstock and I continued through my senior year at Central Bucks High School. I was the only one I'd ever heard of, besides Mae, Nancy, and Cuz, to have been at the Woodstock festival and not stay for any of the entertainment, since we had missed the entire first day, and left long before Saturday's show started. It almost got embarrassing to talk to my friends about it, but high school was just a drag anymore anyway.

I wasn't seeing Mae anymore, and Cuz and Nancy also went their separate ways, as he and I simply continued cutting our teeth through the local music scene together, playing in and out of bands at sock dances, private parties, . . . and even one night at a 'Del Val mixer' (they were called), where a lot of college girls lined the stage to see and hear, and dance to covers of the music by Sly, Cream, Iron Butterfly, Motown, Hendrix, and Stax, done locally by Cuz, me, and a few college-going musicians; Who incidentally got us in with them because they thought we sounded great together, and told us we made them sound better. (Plus, their bassist and lead guitarist were coincidentally busted that week for dealing pot.)

Anyway, my music pulled me through the hard times with teachers, high school crushes, and break-ups, but my grades were at average and I finally graduated. With another break from school to look forward to, Cuz and I continued to play with assorted musicians while having another great summer. I had no plans for college and once again, I didn't know where I was going. Neither of us worried too much about Vietnam or the draft, since Cuz and I both had very high draft lottery numbers. I got a day job in a shipping and receiving department for two dollars and hour and eventually rented an apartment, while Cuz worked at a place where they made urethane foam cushions. That place was like the proverbial salt mines from what his stories about the plant revealed. In the next 4 years, we developed our skills together in music, partying, and life, continuing as adult teenagers into our 20's.

My 23rd birthday party in the early January winter of '75 was a stepping stone for the future to come. The weather was mild for this time of the year and in the 40's tonight. Cuz and I had just finished setting up our amplifiers and PA system in the big room at the farmhouse, that we were now renting together with two of our female roommates. He was with Jenny; a tall blonde with long straight hair and a curvaceous slender figure and I was now with Barbara, who had the prettiest strawberry blonde hair, also curvaceous and tall, but not quite as tall as me. She pushed the hair away from her face, exposing her faint pink freckles and stood on her toes to kiss me, saying, "Who's coming tonight to jam?"
"I'm not sure," I said, "But the word is out that it'll be some quality players."
I tell her this because I had heard, through the grapevine, that some cracker musicians are coming tonight, not just some of the regular drunks, and I'm told by some folks this is a birthday special. We're expecting around 20 to 30 people for this birthday shindig, along with the players.
First arriving is 'Zemo', an Afro-American harmonica player who can only play when he's either drunk or stoned, or both, and no one's ever seen him any other way. Anoth-

er player walks in giving a big holler: "HRAAAAAAAAAAAAH!!" It's 'Bird', with his one conga, ready for anything. No one's ever known these fellows' real names, since they've always been known solely as 'Zemo' and 'Bird' and they're regulars at our jams. We've never seen them any other time, and never hang out otherwise, although Bird did give us his card, which read, 'Bird', with his address and phone number and invited us to come over anytime. All that's stated on his calling card besides, the above mentioned is his business, which reads: 'Self Employed', that's it! We have no idea what he does, besides playing a conga, but he's a character alright, which adds to the energy of the evening.

Next was our friend Adam Crank, with his axe; an alto saxophone. His pet name is "Bloody Reeds" but Cuz and I are the only ones that'll ever call him that. The nickname came from him jamming on a solo for about 15 minutes, non-stop, and when he was finished, he was wiping the reed on his mouthpiece revealing the rag was red from his own blood. We like Adam and his playing, but he's only a sit-in because he's got too many other bands going. He's only here tonight for my birthday, God bless him.

After a few more people and three or four more couples, the door opens again and in walked Cuz's old girlfriend Nancy. Neither Cuz nor I have seen her in years, so she looked a little older than the Woodstock days, but she looked very good, and even better than I remembered, as she was a bit thinner and more voluptuous; and very sexy for a person of her short stature. Behind her was a tall man in a muscle shirt with his muscles flexing, as he carried a guitar case and an amp. With his relatively short hair, and being clean shaven, with the exception of a perfectly trimmed mustache, and with a strong jawline, he looked like one of those male porn stars. He had a wide captivating grin, and as he smiled and reached out his hand, he looked hauntingly familiar. Then he said, "Happy Birthday Stan . . . Hi, I'm Frank, Frank Nichols, but you can call me 'Nick'".

I was completely taken aback, because I didn't recognize him, but he seemed to have the same gleam as when I met him at Woodstock, except his long hair was now short, and he was clean shaven; except he now sported that mustache. He was a little more filled out now too, in a good way, and we laughed, because he knew who we were and intentionally greeted us like strangers.

"What's happenin' Captain?", he said with that grin.

"I had no Idea", I said while he greeted Cuz.

Cuz told Nick to put his amp down beside his own while leaning his head, as if pointing it toward Nancy said to him, "She's got a nice house," . . . remembering the near scuffle at Woodstock over a similar innocent comment, back when Cuz was still dating Nancy.

"You damn right, real nice, and I'm still paying for it", Nick said. We all broke into laughter at Nancy's expense, but she didn't mind, as she commented,

"He still can't afford all of that happiness."

"I can't tell you how good it is to see the both of you again," I said.

We continued to set up microphones and kept on talking to catch up.

"What's new with you Nick?", Cuz asked, "What have you been up to since the summer of '69?"

"Ohh, up to about 10,000 feet or so, over in 'Nam."

Cuz looked at Nick as I did, in shock. We both stood there silent and curious, waiting for the rest of it; but Nick said nothing more, so we had to ask.

"So, you went to Vietnam? Were you drafted?" Cuz asked him.

"Nah, I enlisted when I saw my draft lottery number, you see; My birthday's September 14. I'm a lucky guy; I was number one".
"You're still number one," Nancy chimed in.

Nancy and Nick are apparently together, an item, and have been for a while. I don't know what ever happened between her and Cuz, but it's all water under the bridge now.
"What ever happened to Mae?" I asked Nancy. "Do you ever see or hear from her?"
Nancy's pretty face dropped a little as she paused before responding;
"You haven't heard? She was killed in an automobile accident", Nancy told us.
"No!" Cuz said.
I asked, "When?"
"The following spring after you two broke up," She said. "She and her boyfriend were on there way to the prom when a drunk driver T-Boned them in an intersection and she was killed instantly. Everyone else survived with minor injuries." She continued,

"The drunk driver got out of the other car, and immediately started complaining and aggressively approaching her date, 'Phil', who was the one driving. Phil ignored him and was in the process of trying to revive Mae, not realizing she was already gone. The drunk man grabbed Phil by the neck and started punching him in his back and side while he was still leaning over and tending to Mae, but Phil turned around and punched him over and over again until the couple he and Mae were with, were able pull him off. Phil had injured that man badly. It was an awful night hearing about the whole incident!"

"I'm very sorry to hear that," I told her with a hug and a tear. "I know you and Mae were very close." I couldn't believe my ears when Nancy told me. Someone that young; Someone I knew, of whom at one time was very close and dear to me.

Something else hard to believe for me is something I never told anyone. I had a dream about Mae during prom season that year. One Friday night, I was thinking a lot about her before I went to bed and couldn't get her out of my mind as I fell asleep. In my dream, I was at some outdoor event where there were a lot of people; and was walking in one direction where I saw Mae with a group of folks, who were walking the other way, passing me. We recognized each other, so she walked up to me and gave me a wet kiss, but the kiss was icy cold, as if she just drank from an icy drink, and she smiled and said, "Good Bye Stan," and kept walking. I never again gave the dream much thought until now. A slight chill went through me as I snapped out of my daze and gave my condolences to Nancy.

In a change of mood, I went up to Nick to ask him about his Vietnam adventure, but he wasn't really into talking about it, other than he told me he was in the paratroopers. That's what he meant before, when I asked him what he was up to, saying 'Ohh, about 10,000 feet or so, over in Nam'. He liked making light of his tour of duty, but I think it must have been something else, although I'm not sure why, it's just something I'm sensing as I talk to him. Paratroopers are a tough group of soldiers, and it's hard to believe that someone I knew from the Woodstock weekend could become a soldier, much less a paratrooper.

The night went on as we all set up the rest of the equipment, food, and of course the beer. Our friend Runx showed up eventually to wish me a happy birthday, and also because he likes being around free beer. . . and loose women. Runx writes and arranges songs, great songs, and we're going to be doing a few of them. He said he wanted us to perform his songs but just to call them "original compositions." He has them all copyrighted but said if we ever make lots of money off of them he'll be glad to take some of the credit then.

Runx loves Cuz and I, and our ambition, and swears we'll make it big someday, and even wants to start writing a book about it. He also said that he senses this to be a good night of playing and feels it in his bones. I hope he's right.

I then looked around the room and asked the inevitable question:
"Is anyone going to play drums tonight?" I was curious about the rhythm section.
"I don't know who all's coming," Cuz answered, "I just heard the word that there's likely to be all-star musicians." The term: 'All-star musicians' usually means the best of the best from our locals, and always a good prospect for a great jam. We never know who'll show.

Just then a bearded man with frizzy black hair entered the room, looking a little lost.
"'Nick here?" He asked.
"Yes, you play the drums I hope", I asked.
"I have them in the truck. I'm Hank. And who are you?"
"Stan," I said, "I'm Stan, and I remember you! We met at Woodstock."
"Oh yeah, you're the pussy whipped dude who left early with the broads. . ." he paused with an evil laugh, checked himself and then said:
"'Just kiddin' witcha' . . . 'How's it slidin' Sam? "
"*STAN*", I belted back.
Just then Nick walked into the room.
"HEEEEEY HEEEEEYYYY!!!! How the hell are ya doin' there, Mr. Henry Zeke!! 'You meet everyone?"
"Just Sam," Hank said, still nervously laughing.

Nick looks at me, winks, then corrects Hank again regarding my name, and introduces him around.
It turns out that Hank enlisted in the marines and was also in Nam. They didn't see each other over there, although they were there at about the same time.

After Hank loaded in his drums, we all tuned up and began to jam. Cuz started it off with a blues progression in the key of A. I fell into it, as Nick watched, until the turnaround, so When Nick came in on the A, strumming the rhythmic power chords, Cuz took off on the lead guitar, ascending the notes and the energy of the movement. With the strong rhythm of Nick's playing, I easily weaved within the melody on the bass while keeping the song's form, raising a genuine original and interesting composition by the three of us. Hank was not playing yet; but was sitting behind his full set of drums with closed eyes, bobbing his frizzy head to the rhythm, seemingly feeling it out and listening.

At that point, I couldn't imagine what he could add, playing drums, and I almost felt sorry for him, because it was almost as if we didn't need him, as this was already the most solid sounding and tightest jam or band I've ever been in; I was totally impressed. Nick carried the titanic solid rhythm so well that I've never heard a combination of three players, two guitars and one bass, sound so solid and complete, and without drums. When the next turnaround came, Hank started playing right on the 'A' chord. UNBELIEVABLE!!

You'd have to hear it, and words can't describe what I felt! "Orgasmic" was the closest I can come to description. Hank's drumming, although nothing complicated, centered it all, while filling in the gaps. It was the most solid thing musically I've ever experienced, jamming or playing, ever! When Hank began playing, it was like another band sat in.

THE LOST MARBLES STORY

The others came up, Zemo and Bird, and the night and the party were cruising with a lot of jamming, drinking, smoking, and too much fun. We all had the best time. The solid tight core was Cuz, Hank, Nick, and me. No one else was really needed; but were welcome sit-ins as the movement continued as a colorful, melodious funk configuration. I was also trying to get used to Hank calling me 'Sam' most of the night.

This was the night that Hank got his new nickname "Flash". We don't know who she came with, but this red headed woman, very pretty, was drunk (like everyone else) and decided to flirt with Hank. She walked past me, where we were playing on our makeshift stage, and she had a long thin scarf, or handkerchief. Hank was impressing everyone with his playing, but mostly with his antics; drinking lit, flaming shots of 151 rum while continuing his rolling rhythms on the snare and double basses. I believe it was during a solo where he was telling the girl, who we were all unfamiliar with, that she had nice tomatoes. (The front of her T-shirt was silk screened with a portrait of ripe tomatoes).

The girl swirled the handkerchief around and around his head as he played. He tried to down his 3rd fiery lit shot, when the handkerchief caught on fire, along with his crotch and facial hair, in a bright blue and orange flash! The panicked girl ran with the flaming 'hanky' because she was, how Hank put it, too 'stupid drunk' to let go. Someone threw a pitcher of beer on her, putting the flame out, and luckily, she was alright.

Fortunately, no one was hurt, other than Hank's ego, pride, and most of his beard. Nick started calling him "Flaming Flash Hanky" after that and it started to stick. Hank did not like that at all, since every drunk at the party, which entailed everybody at the party, was now calling him

Flaming Flash Hanky. Soon after that, I shortened it to "Flash," and it caught on. He was actually alright with that, and from then on, for some reason, finally remembered that my name was 'Stan'. Go Figure.

That night, the band to beat all bands was formed, and minus the sit in extras, we had the four of us. Cuz, Nick, Flash, and myself were were all in agreement immediately that we should pursue the potential; Vow to persevere; Consolidate our energies and talents; Form a combo.

Chapter 4

Tightening Up Our Act

We scheduled rehearsals Tuesdays and Thursdays, while Cuz and I used our house as the place for practice. Over a period of a year or more, we practiced without booking any gigs or talking much to any outsiders of our project. The band was getting tighter than we could have ever imagined, as we were working on covers of old blues tunes in the beginning but branched out into original compositions combining blues, rock and fusion. We had about 10 songs we composed ourselves; group effort, and a few that I had written on my own and with Cuz a few years back. We were also doing about 15 or so tunes by our friend Runx, which were the best ones, and we respected his secrecy about them; calling them, as he requested, "original compositions." We were ready, as that year was full of learning, bonding, and partying, plus we've kept the band to ourselves with closed rehearsals. We didn't even want to expose the band gradually, like playing at parties etc. because it was all kind of secretive. Our intention was to pounce on the music scene like a lion.

The past year or so wasn't without some adventuresome stories though. Cuz was almost killed, or at least beat up pretty bad at a bar one night. Some drunk construction

workers from out of town showed up while he was doing an acoustic thing for free beer and a dinner. They wanted him to play some Deep Purple and he declined. The bully then walked up to him and cold cocked him, knocking him off of his stool, then laughed along with the other construction jerks. They walked out leaving Cuz on his ass, and the bartender furious. Cuz had a swollen jaw and a bloody nose, but fortunately nothing broken. Nick wanted to know who they were but we had nothing to go on, other that their red Chevy four-door pickup. A week later, that pickup was spotted around dinner time at a burger place in Doylestown. Nick got a hold of Cuz right away and drove him over, and I'll tell it the way Cuz saw it.
"That looks like it," Cuz said, regarding the pick-up, then Nick and Cuz walked inside to check it out. Nick walked in first and sat at one table while Cuz walked in a few minutes later, then walked past the men and saw it was the same three guys that were in the bar a week ago.
"Hey, remember me?" Cuz asked, as he looked him right in the eye. The bozo was the same guy who had punched him that night. He was a big stocky oaf with large biceps, making his flannel shirt cling tight around his upper arms as he sat and then looked away, then continued eating his French fries.
"You want something?" asked the other dude sitting across from him.

All three were a good size, all ranging from six two, to six five. The one who delivered the blow to Cuz last week was the biggest. They were carpenters from upstate, working on new townhouses going up across town. Cuz looked at the dude who asked if he wanted something, and then looked away, snubbing him.

Looking back again at the biggest guy, he repeated, "Remember me?"

The guy just kept eating his French fries with a grin, then said:
"We were drunk the other night, 'twinkie', you won't like me sober, so go lay down and be a good little fairy."

That was all Nick needed to hear, as he strolled nonchalantly up to the table looking at the three of them. Nick pointed to Cuz, and asked the three of them jokingly,
"Is this man giving you a hard time?"

The big guy held a French fry and said: "
"Yeah, he's giving us a hard time. Why don't you give him a blow job and mellow him out?"
The other two laughed aloud, and Nick started to laugh too.

Now, the guy with the French fry was sitting opposite the other two. Nick said to him:
"I only know one way to give a blow job, and I'd like to give you one, if you know what I mean."

The guy dropped his French fry and started to stand when, "Pow!"

Nick hit him in the jaw so hard, that he flew completely over the adjoining booth. As the other two stood to his aid, Nick grabbed them both and kept punching them, like an out of control windmill, until they both went flying through the plate glass window, shattering it onto the pavement outside. Nick turned to the first one again, who instantly got up and jumped through the new opening in an attempt to escape Nick's wrath. Nick chased him out to his truck and upon catching him, started pounding and pounding at his face. Blood and teeth were flying as he held his head by the hair, banging it on the truck, and made him apologize to Cuz directly. His bloody, toothless mouth managed to squeeze out an "I'm sorry" before Nick let go and said to Cuz, "We'd better beat it" as they heard sirens. I don't know how, but Cuz and Nick made it out of there ahead of the law, and needless to say, they avoided that place from then on.

Nick drove Cuz home while Cuz complained of not being able to get a shot in of his own.

"Why didn't you let me take a crack at him?"

"Because they were all too big. Did you see the tattoo? He was a marine."

"But I feel like you did all the work", Cuz said bummed out.

"I enjoyed it. They were cowards, marines or not", Nick said. "I can't stand bullies, cowards". . .

I had my adventures too, as I was now working at trimming trees during the days. It was for a local tree trimming company that was sub-contracting for the electric company. In layman's terms, we were clearing up the wires from overgrown branches. I was not comfortable with heights, but I needed to make a living somehow, and I lucked into a trade I could fall back on (no pun intended); which was actually something that could be called 'substantially unfulfilling and mildly treacherous'. In the mornings, I would meet the crew at the electric company sub-station, then the crew of four would drive to the job. We would get to the section of trees we were trimming for the day and unload the tools we would need from the truck. Chain saws, ropes, saddles, pole clips, bull poles, ladders, and a canister of ice cold tea in the summertime. We would strap on our saddles, hook on the 120-foot rope, chainsaw, and a hand saw, then put the extension ladder up to the first branch to begin our climb. After a few months of this I was climbing the trees satisfactorily but still afraid of, and stayed away from the Tulip Poplars, which were wide with virtually no branches until you reached twenty feet. The foreman told me he'll let me know when he feels I'm ready for those, so 'Pete', the 'top climber' usually jumped on the big ones.

I've never seen anybody climb trees and trim them like Pete, since he was a regular acrobat and totally fit. I've never seen him eat any food either, as he drank milk all day and snorted methedrine; or methamphetamine while the others only drank beer, except maybe the foreman, Ed. Although I never saw him drink anything, he always smelled like a distillery; and when I rode with him to dump the wood chips, that we derived from the wood brush chipper, I could hear whiskey bottles clanking around under the seats, which is probably why we ended up taking our lunch breaks at the nearest bar without him. He had cases of beer in the back of his pick-up truck which he, at the end of the day and an hour before quitting time, would sell individual cans for fifty cents apiece to any of us who were interested.

    One day, trimming trees down near Glenside, I was climbing up an oak tree which was topped off (which means cut back to being just beneath the three phase electrical wires a few years ago) about twenty-five feet up. It was a White Oak. The leaves on the White Oak are rounded at the edges, which makes them not as pointed as the Pin Oaks, the Red Oaks, or the Black Oaks in this area of Pennsylvania. For me, it's an easy tree to identify because of this shape. Like any other oak tree, the torso, or main body of the tree and its branches are a very hard wood. Climbing it is hard on the legs and knees, since the hard wood is not as forgiving as, say the Willow Tree.

    Anyway, I was told to always know where the wires are at all times during climbing. Due to the oak's full foliage of summer I didn't realize how high I had climbed. I was at the top of the tree with my head, unbeknownst to me, 12 inches below the wires carrying 13.2k volts while I was tying in my rope from my saddle to the highest tree crotch beneath me. The oak's vertical shoots surrounding me had grown straight up past my face and very tall. They were actually through and between the phases. I was at this time getting some occasional shocks, still not looking up like I should have been. I was once told to be careful when I begin to feel these electrical pulses, meaning I was too close.

Well, I didn't think I was anywhere near the electric cables, and I thought I had some head clearance, for some reason. I went to stand on the crotch without looking up, and now noticing the singed, dead black birds laying around me on the smaller horizontal tree shoots. Then by chance, or rather luck, my two- half hitch knot was too tight, not allowing me slack for the freedom of standing. There was a single, perfect oak leaf jammed in the knot. I removed it, loosened the knot, then thought I'd look up, this time before standing. My plastic hard hat brim clipped the live wire, startling me, as I honestly didn't know I was that close to it. In other words, if I had freely stood up without looking, my head would have gone between two phases and both of my shoulders would have been touching two of the three phase cables. Therefore, in the midst of the leafy oak foliage, I would have completed a circuit of about 13,200 volts, give or take a few ohms of resistance, and I would have had the misfortune of being fried like those feathered corpses laying tattered around me. That one, single oak leaf stuck in the knot saved my life.

So, with great mental fortitude I realigned my thoughts, grabbed my tools, checked my pants (fortunately they were clean), then trimmed the tree as I had originally planned. Using the chainsaw and the pole clip, I made it look like a masterpiece right out of Home and Gardens.

I finished out the day alive, bought and drank two dollars' worth of beer from the back of Ed's pick-up, hung up my saddle, and went home. That was my last day as a tree trimmer. I'm not cut out for dangerous work, and realized I wanted to live to play music, not live to see if I can die sooner than I wish.

"Here lies a man, who had the nerve to do a job he didn't want in the first place."

I ended up getting work immediately anyway, as a mason's laborer. Harder work, but a with reasonably longer life span.

Another great story was with Hank, or now known as Flash. He had gotten a new apartment, or rather shared a house with two or three other tenants. Nick and I dropped him off, and I'll tell the story the way he told me. He was loaded, smashed on rum and beer. He started walking up to the porch of the house we were in front of.

"You gonna be OK?" We asked him as he staggered.

"I'm fine", he said.

He continued up the steps as we drove off, and he tried to stick his key into the lock on the door, but it wasn't working. He was thinking that this is a brand, new place for him to live, and maybe there's another key he forgot about, or it's maybe the wrong key. He also knew that there are other roomers he shared the house with, one of the other tenants who might happily let him in, even though it's late. He started banging on the door; No response; He banged again fruitlessly; Silence. He then walked down the stairs and looked above the porch to where his room should be, and he thought of climbing up the pillar and drainpipe to his window, but realized how drunk he was and how embarrassing, if not fatal, the fall would be. He went to the back door, but it too was locked, so he kicked the basement window open and climbed in. "This will get me in the house if I can find the stairs," he thought. He walked through the pitch black, stepping onto something that crunches, like breaking of glass beneath his feet. "Oh no," he thought. "My new roommate Ted just took all of those storm windows down, he's going to be pissed."

He continued to walk in the darkness of the basement, with his hands in front of him feeling his way but could not find the stairs. He turned around and back tracked in the same manner, through the darkness, crunching a few more alleged storm windows as he felt his way, like a bull in a china shop.

He reached the basement window and climbed out; and scratching the top of his head in inebriated thought, wondered how he could get into his house and finally into bed. He walked up the porch steps one more time, and considered sleeping on one of the porch chairs, but then tried the lock again, banging on the door at the same time. He heard the door knob jiggling from the inside and thought "It's about time!" The door swings open and an unfamiliar face greets him. "What the hell are you doing? What do you want?"

Now, an unfamiliar face is common in Flash's new place, due to friends of his roommates occasionally sleeping over as guests on the couch, and that's all this person was to Flash. "You don't know me, but I live upstairs," Flash said, trying not to slur his words. The man at the door said, "Yeah, you live upstairs alright, and *TWO DOORS DOWN!*"

Flash nodded his head to the affirmative at the gentleman, and meandered humbly and guiltily to the correct house, recalling the sound of crushing glass coming from: Not his own basement, but apparently someone else's.

That proved to be embarrassing to Flash, since it was a new neighbor, and he later said that when those neighbors were sitting out that summer he could never look at them again. Nothing was ever mentioned about the storm windows. "Maybe they were unaware they had them", he

thought, with more rationalization. We found out later that those were not storm windows Flash inadvertently busted up, but very expensive stained-glass windows that were apparently stolen from a construction site of a nearby church and hidden within that basement by that same neighbor who had told Flash he was at the wrong house.
Bad karma cancels out bad karma . . . I guess . . .

Anyway, Flash, needless to say, had developed a drinking habit over the years but insists that other than some mild skirmishes with the law, or a fistfight or two, he has it under control. There was the time he ran into an old female friend at a local bar next to the Willow Grove Naval Base called the "Porthole". He said 'hi', she said 'hi', and he immediately started making out with her. . . tongue and all; then as he was nonchalantly asking her if she knew where he could get his hands on some quaaludes, he saw sparks! A fist from the lady's boyfriend knocked him clear across a table and onto the floor. The guy was about the 'size of a house', according to what the patrons said that saw him connect with Flash's jaw. The big guy then mumbled the word "asshole," then just shuffled his way out the bar room door. The guy's girl, Flash's female friend from the past, 'Debbie', leaned over him and held his face, "I'm sorry for that, are you going to be OK?"
"Why did he hit me?" Flash asked in his clearly honest stupidity.
"He's always been a jealous shit head. I don't want to be with him anymore tonight. He's drunk and I'm tired of this shit from him," she said, then asked Flash for a ride home.
"Where did he go? I want to find out why he hit me."
Flash was committed, and intent on a mission to talk to him. He wandered outside, against the wishes of Debbie and the others with them, and saw the big guy getting into a car across the dimly lit parking lot, who then observed

Flash approaching him. He got out of his car and aggressively came at Flash, waving his hands; "C'mon, you wanna fuck with me?" he was yelling.
"I just want to know why you hit me," Flash shouted.
"You were fuckin' with my chick! You were kissing my girl, slipping her the tongue right in front of me, and feeling her up! That's why!"
They were at arms-length when Flash answered him with his drunken dim wit, "There must be some misunderstanding, you see she and I are just friends!"
Then Flash said something imbecilic that, just might put a boyfriend over the edge:
"I haven't fucked her in years."
"POW", right in Flash's kisser, with more sparks, as Flash went down like a ton of bricks right onto his back. The guy then sat on him and wheeled a few more punches to his face before saying, "'You give up? You gonna stop being ignorant?"
"YES!" Flash yelled and the guy went back into his car. Flash walked up to the car once again and this time went to open the door. The guy saw Flash's bloody face and must have felt sorry for him, because he just yelled, "Fuck off," and pushed the lock button down.

Flash walked back inside, past Debbie who asked again, "Can I go home with you?" But it fell on deaf ears, as Flash walked to the bar, finished his beer, walked through the front door onto the front lot and across HWY 611, trying to avoid traffic. Then to a phone booth to call Nick to come and get him.

Nick drove him home to his and Nancy's place because it was closer, and because they wanted to keep an eye on him. He didn't really need a Doctor but they were concerned about a possible concussion. "I got worse from the priests at Archbishop Wood high school," Flash said with a

grin. He fortunately survived the rest of night without incident, and in the morning, he did want to know why his jaw was swollen and his lips stuck together with blood. He had to be reminded about the bar room scuffle. "Oh yeah," he remembered.
"I like Debbie, she's always been a good kisser. 'Nice tits too"
Nick just shook his head, as he usually does to Flash's ignorant sexual comments.

Nick always treated Flash like a kid brother, but I guess he was that way with all of us; even though he was about a year younger, he always seemed older and more together, and for the most part, wiser than the rest of us. He avoided fights unless he saw some degree of unfairness or bullying, but he thought Flash got everything he deserved in this case.

Cuz and I continued living where we rehearsed in the same farmhouse, the only change was that our girls moved out. They headed westward to Colorado with a brown haired, attractive girl named 'Ginger', to find the new 'California', or so was our opinion. That's what they called Colorado back then, but they will eventually find their way to the real California. Now Ginger was a beautiful woman, well-endowed, if you know what I mean. She had a nice figure and usually dressed suggestively, enjoying the display of those assets she had, without any shame. Ginger even had the same pentagram and spider tattoo on her belly as Barbara, and was always getting Barb to try new things. Once, Ginger's attire really caught my eye. One summer day, wearing a very low cut tight blouse and very short denim shorts, she brought to our house two large bullfrogs, holding them by a leg in each hand as they kicked. Barbara asked, "What are you going to do with them?" Ginger politely responded, "I'm going to show you some survival skills in case we're living in a commune someday. I'm going to show you how to skin them and cook them, like I learned from the people in the bayou down south."

They both walked into the kitchen with the poor victims, and while getting him ready for dinner, Ginger's frog, suspecting her intent I guess, leaped in desperation from under her hands and off of the countertop, directly into the opening in the front of her blouse. However, this reprieve from his inevitable fate was short lived, for as she leaned back, her top tightened, trapping the poor thing within her busty cleavage, showing only his poor pathetic kicking legs. Barbara's face turned bright red, as did Ginger's, as they both went into a fit of laughter. Her hand wrapped around both legs as she pulled him out from between her breasts, and held him up very close to her face. Then Ginger mellowed and said, "You're a bad, bad boy." Then she examined him momentarily before jokingly asking the amphibian,
"Let's see if you're a Prince." Then humorously giving him a kiss just in case said, "Well, I guess you're not a Prince, but you *are* good enough to eat."

Ginger smiled, then laid him down calmly, and held him on the counter with those slender fingers, with the painted black, long fingernails. With a sharp kitchen knife, she began cutting and skinning him alive, unmoved, and sporting an evil grin, as the creature kicked frantically.

Poor bastard, I thought, it's the way of the bayou, their culture I guess, and I read that people have been doing this down there for years. I also watched Barb for a minute, following Ginger's lead and skinning her own frog, however, she was really getting into it, a little too much for my liking. She seemed to be enjoying it even more as her condemned victim squirmed! The smile on her sadistic pretty face was priceless, as well as bone chilling and down-

THE LOST MARBLES STORY

right sickening. She frightened me, especially since they were both doing this without killing them first and I left the house, feeling nauseous. The only good news was that they both at least ate every bit of it, and enjoyed it; More power to them.

Anyway, Barbara even had an idea that she wanted to be an aviation pilot after taking a plane ride with Nick and Nancy. She said she was going to take flying lessons when she got to the Golden State. She's a dreamer and I hope everything always works out for her. We loved them, truly, but they were not ready to be tied down, nor were we. They wanted the freedom of bean sprouts, yogurt, keifer (a yogurt like drink), and good pot. Besides, the Grateful Dead were playing at Red Rocks and it was the perfect excuse for them to exodus now.

Our rehearsals with the band, as I said earlier, got tighter than we could ever imagine. We were ready to do something, ready to explode. We set up a concert at the old County Theater in Doylestown. A local promoter, for a minimal fee promoted the show, and we worked with him on the selling of tickets.

Someone had to be billed as the main feature to draw a crowd, but since no one ever heard of us, we had to get somebody who people would have known, somebody with a name, somebody who people would say, "Hey, 'so and so' is playing in Doylestown tonight, let's all go and see that show!"

But nobody was available for top billing, at least no one with any kind of fame. After searching, the agency, and with Nick's help, we finally came up with something. A local yokel who was in the area for about 3 years seemed like a logical candidate. His band was long disbanded, but he

was doing solo shows with some mediocre success, and the locals still remember his name.
'Jackie Clark'.

Will he draw? Who knows for sure, but just in case, we put the word out strong since we wanted as many people as we could possibly get, to come to the show. Jackie was from a rich family, from what we heard, and that his father was Jonathan Clark, a CEO and a salesman at a pharmaceutical company, with a somewhat sleazy reputation from what I heard, and who pretty much gave Jackie anything he wanted growing-up, such as the best guitars, amplifiers, and drugs. He was spoiled rotten, also from what I've heard, but he was also able to develop his talent without any financial obstacles. He never worked a full-time job growing up, or ever, but was able to band musicians together in his basement for practices. Due to his exposure, and I'm sure some influence from his father's wealthy contacts, had gotten noticed a few years back by a major record label with his band, and the word was out that their might be some of those scouts in the audience for the upcoming show.

This was a very exciting prospect for us, and we were aware of three things: One, we had to have a full house; Two, we had to sound original and creative in our original material; and Three, we had to sound our tightest, and had to be at our absolute best!

We continued to rehearse and tighten up our show material. We were to play for 45 minutes, then Jackie Clark would come up for his show. He was of course top billing, but at the time we didn't mind. We had to come up with a name for the band pretty fast. We agreed to call it 'The Marvels', but we added an ethnic twist for classiness (in our own minds).

We unanimously decided that the band will be called: "LOS MARVELS".

Chapter 5

The Big Show

On a warm Saturday night in June, 1977, the show was on, and it was a packed house. It turns out that most of the people arriving for the show were there because we had put the word out and they were there to see our band; our friends, and friends of friends of friends. Also, the advertisement for the show featured the new, upcoming blues fusion band, with the added, "Dead Heads Welcome". There were people also showing for Jackie Clark; since Jackie had a hit record on the local stations. Back then, local radio DJ's played 45 rpm records and the Jackie Clark Band had a lot of airplay locally with his single. Side A, was a cover of "Kansas City" and the B side, was a blues standard called "The Hunter". Both songs were pretty decent recordings and he had intentions of using his full band, which he recently reformed for this show upon hearing from our friends that we'd be a tough act to follow. They were almost on their way tonight when, while packing up their equipment their bassist and saxophone player got into a heated argument over drugs, women, and paranoia. The bass player shot the saxophonist in the neck with a .22 caliber. The sax player survived but was temporarily paralyzed. The cops locked up the bassist and the other musicians called it a night by going to the bar, that is, all but Jackie, who showed up here as a solo act once again.

Now Jackie was what some folks called a 'face', meaning he had good looks, appealing to the ladies. His prominent cheek bones, blue eyes, and long straight blond hair seemed to melt women's hearts, well, some women anyway. Nick's girl Nancy, thought of him as just another pompous 'ass'. Jackie looked at us, as he strolled in with his acoustic Martin guitar, like he was questioning us, and we had all of our equipment ready to go as he went over to Cuz, to ask him if we could back him up on a couple of songs. To everyone's amazement, Cuz said, "Sure, why not?" This pissed off Flash, Nick, and me. "Cuz", Nick said, "What are you doing?"

"I just wanted to help him out because he's in a bind," Cuz said.

Jackie then chimed in, "I just need some backup band strength for a couple of my songs, you guys understand. You're all pretty damn good from what I hear, I just need some help, that's all."

I looked at Nick, then Cuz. "Cuz, we're a band, and we work well together in our democratic realm. We have no leaders, which is why we work well together, so next time, run it past the rest of us before volunteering our services, that's all," I told him with my best shot of diplomacy.

THE LOST MARBLES STORY

"Understood", he said.

Nick looked at Jackie and asked what songs, keys, and what his plan was as we all listened. He guided us quietly through the changes of three of his songs in two minutes of cramming. The lights in the house started to dim and the crowd began their pre-show applause knowing it was starting any minute now. "Good Luck," Jackie said to us, as he walked into the wings behind curtains.

We stood nervous, but ever so confident, holding our guitars in the now dim lights as Flash sat down at his drums. We watched the curtains slowly open with the spotlight on a man standing front and center, holding a microphone. The audience couldn't see us yet. Our nervousness was growing just a little more.

"Good evening ladies and gentlemen and welcome to the County Theater".

"Please join me in welcoming one of the best local acts you've yet to hear:

Ladies and Gentlemen, 'THE LOST MARBLES'!!"

This, apparently, was how our band was billed here, and without our knowing, I might add. It turns out that this was our name on the tickets. The marquee on the front even read "THE LOST MARBLES". At this point, I don't believe any of us noticed. We were too psyched up for the night ahead of us. (We found out later that Jackie purposely sabotaged our name for this show, due to some kind of arrogant jealousy trip he was on, or something of that sort, I was told later. He had his hand in the tickets being printed up.)

Nevertheless, the lights went very bright on us as the applause roared like a thunder I've never heard! The drums started into one of the 'original compositions', called "Sing Those Blues". After a few measures of the drum lead in, Cuz, Nick, and I came in with the two guitars and bass for

the lead in melody. After two measures Cuz and Nick split into the harmony for two more measures, then the singing started with Nick playing the driving rhythm and Cuz playing lead riffs around my singing,
"She keep's knockin' on my door,
I don't want to let her in no more 'cause you know. She's been here before.
And, I don't want to . . . Sing those blues anymore . . . "
"If she's left me once, she's left me twice.
Every time she's left the place was full of ice and you know, I'll be on them rocks like before . . . and . . .
I don't want to . . . Sing the blues anymore."

    The audience was going wild, and we were hotter than ever! We were like a miniature form of the Beatles, well anyway, to our own selves we were. The energy was unending, as Nick was jumping around, Cuz was twisting and bending to his guitar riffs, and I was bouncing, when I wasn't singing. Flash was pounding the drums like Moon and Baker rolled into one. He was singing backup and not missing a note, as if it was like all of our biorhythms were in synch; I never wanted it to end.

    Our friend Zemo had stood up on the corner of the stage, barely in sight of us and the audience, with his new dread locks in front of his face, and his mouth cupped with a handful of his harmonica as he aggressively, and without distain, played his heart out . . . even though no one could hear him over our loud stage volume.

    Cuz was looking over at me with an eternal grin as we neared the end of the first song, and like myself, he was probably remembering our early days when we wished something like this could happen but never seemed to come to pass, despite our continuous efforts. It was a good feeling to see all of it coming to fruition tonight!

We went into the next song, a complicated instrumental, and another 'original composition called "Zenith". Once again, it started with Flash's full thunderous drums, with his double basses, then the two 'Cuz and Nick' melodic guitar melodies with my bass guitar's 16th notes, running up and down the neck and scales before it stops, except for the bass itself setting the beat and groove. The other instruments come in likewise, as the song is a combination of Latin, rock, fusion, and a mystic core of new age.

Our surprise 'ace up our sleeve' for this composition was the three girls, friends of Runx's, we had at one microphone singing harmony for sections of this song, and only this song. It was Runx's own idea for producing the song better live. It was risky, but it ended up sounding great, as they sang in unison with a rising minor scale twice in the song. Once in a mellow passage with Cuz playing minor and major pentatonic modes in a fugue, where they would rise within the minor scale continuing in unison, then ended in a crescendo of dominant 3-part harmonies, then the same way again later in the song; This time, over a rhythm of Flash's rolling drums and Nick's and Cuz's strong guitar riffs and rhythms. The song raises and lowers the energy of the crowd, just within limits of tolerance and just before it goes back into the driving rhythm of the composition itself, bringing out the thunderous applause of the audience as they actually stood on their feet for the last two minutes of the song.

You almost couldn't hear the coda over the screams and applause, and thunderous foot stomping! A pair of skimpy lady's panties flew over my head from the audience and made a perfect ringer on the high-hat cymbal of Flash's drum kit.

With these first two songs alone, we were already twenty minutes into the show, due to the length of "Zen-

ith". We did a few more songs, keeping the audience sitting and applauding until our final 'original composition, "Rock and Roll Radio". This one had them on their feet cheering the whole song through. I began the vocal with Nick playing the rhythm,
"I don't want to work my job no more.
It gets too hard when the weekends are buried below.
I don't want to go outside the door.
I just want to be on the rock and roll radio".
Cuz, Nick and I kick in with the signature melody line as Flash pounds in the undeniable groove.
"The room seems to be so lonesome, so quiet and calm.
Except for the loud, loud thunder 'cause the radio's on.
It puts me in such a peaceful frame of mind.
If the peace ain't yours the rock and roll radio is mine. . .
Turn it on . . ."
"Rock and roll . . . radio . . . " The harmonies from Flash, Cuz, and Nick kick in over me singing, "Turn it up", "Turn it on . . . "

    A standing ovation at the end of that song almost brought me to tears, which was technically the end of our set of tunes. We wanted to do an encore, but we were not permitted, due to the second act; 'Jackie Clark'.

    Unknown to us, he had it in his 'contract' that the opening act will not play past their designated set of songs. In other words, 'No Encores' for 'Lost Marbles'. If I say we were pissed, that would be the understatement of the year, and now it was time for the 'Jackie Clark Show', and he's going to need our help. . . and we're going to *give it to him*.

    The curtain had closed for us and we were told to keep everything as it is in our set-up. Jackie immediately walked out with his acoustic guitar, as a stage hand brought him over two microphones with boom stands. He was set up in about 45 seconds flat, as a shot of feedback alerted the audience, and he said, "I wanted to make sure people were still out there after that last show", and he giggled. There was a "Booo", followed by two or three more boos. He retracted with, "What? I was just kidding, and I was hoping no one left, because those guys are a tough act to follow!" Then he said aloud, "Let's give those guys a hand, let's hear it for 'The Lost Marbles'".

The crowd roared a mighty two minutes or so of applause before Jackie was finally successful in calming them down. Our name has been "The Lost Marbles" ever since. We actually liked it better. (Thanks Jackie).

Jackie started with a strumming in the key of A to an 'original composition', a tune called "Loralee". It was almost kind of a folk rock. I liked the poetic lyrics and the rhythm, and it was a good change of pace from what we were doing. The house had a spotlight on him and the audience was in the dark, except where the spot reflected off of the stage in the front rows. They were bobbing to the rhythm and open to him singing the lyrics:
"You float through the window like an angel,
On a broken wing, with phrases on your tongue.
Licking my wounds with a passion
Draws me to the heat, as I caress your song."

It turns out that this song "Loralee" is also written by our friend Runx. He ran into Jackie some time ago gave him a few of his tunes with the same direction he gave us, that he wants some credit if the songs ever become anything of substance or ever go anywhere. He has copyrights on everything and doesn't worry, but Jackie is too stubborn and too egotistical to record them. At least that was always our theory even though the record company suggested them (Runx's songs) over his own original material, but Jackie went with the covers and blues standards instead. He did OK locally with them I might add, and he gets the gigs.

The record company is supposedly here tonight for him, and they want to see what he can do, so they can back him on a nationwide album for him which they've been considering.

This acoustic version of 'Loralee' seemed to go over pretty good tonight because at the coda and the last minor chord, there was a polite round of applause. But despite the positive response, we started hearing, "Where's the 'Lost Marbles'"? Then some more . . .
"We want Lost Marbles". Jackie kept his composure but added, "They went home".
"BOOOOoooo" said an audience heckler. Jackie turned around to us.

We were standing in the wings, and to this day, I swear I didn't understand where he was going, or what he wanted to do. The other guys picked up from this, that he meant for them to grab their instruments.

Flash sat down at his drum kit and started pounding out the drum beat to "Kansas City," while Nick grabbed his Les Paul, and with a loud volume, started strumming the 'A' chord for the beginning of "Kansas City," in the key of A. Cuz, and then I jumped in. Jackie had a very crazy look on his face,
the look that was a cross between excitement, anger, and fear! We were also not playing in his normal key for the song . . . which was supposed to be the key of 'E'. For Jackie to sing the song he had to shout, scream, yell, and growl. Whether he liked it or not, it sounded almost soulful. The bearings within his voice box were grinding like they needed to be lubed. His face was beet red, as he belted out the lyrics, "Going to Kansas City, Kansas City here I come".

We went through the progression once, twice, then the solos. Cuz took a burning hot slide guitar solo like I've never heard him do, but maybe it was the combination of his own anger towards Jackie misconstruing our band name, or just his self-centered remarks that put Cuz over the top. Or maybe it was just that Cuz was feeling great about playing to a crazy full house yelling for our band to keep on playing because Cuz took a second, then a third solo, and each time the audience yelled and screamed louder.

Jackie started to sing, but unfortunately his voice was buried in Nick's beginning of his own solo. Nick's guitar was loud, and cutting-edge quality as Jackie stopped trying, and Nick continued with his hot licks until the turnaround of the progression. That's when Cuz kicked back in, and they both started playing off of each other. Their notes intertwined within each other and within the song as Flash and I carried the bass and drums to the hypnotic pulsing and thumping of the songs' boots, Lost Marbles style, stepping all the way to and from Kansas City. The combination of all this throbbing energy dominating the stage, beat our audience into an ever loving and inevitable submission. They were ours and we were theirs as there was no escape, for anybody.

Jackie just let the powers that be, just be for now, and there was nothing he could do but watch, as we played our hearts out to this long version of "Kansas City". He would make up verses of the song over Cuz and Nick's solos and growl the lyrics out loud into the mike, and at the audience as he walked along the edge of the stage.

Now, in the corner of the stage by the curtains, was a silhouette of a man standing with a flute held up with his hands stretched out from past the side of his head to his mouth. He couldn't be heard from where I was standing, but he was apparently jamming to our output of stage energy and sound, as he bounced around like pan, or like a character out of a storybook.

Jackie walked over to his direction, and upon reaching him, gave him a shove in an obvious effort to remove him, and the silhouette just stumbled back toward the curtains. As the character disappeared, falling through the curtain, Jackie turned around towards us and it was then that the flute player's head, and only his head, popped through the curtain with his flute in his mouth as if antagonizing him with his flute playing. Jackie heard it and turned toward him again, and once again, the flautist disappeared behind the curtain. The spotlight operator, thinking that this was part of the show, turned his attention, and the spotlight, onto Jackie and the flute players' head popping in and out of the curtains as our band carried on our prolonged and hot sounding high energy solos, still playing 'Kansas City'. Jackie would walk back toward us and the flautist would follow him, mimicking his steps directly behind him, like a clown would do to a ring leader at a circus, then retreat back under the curtain upon Jackie's turning around to chase him.

I was in stitches laughing; but managed to pump out the bottom end sounds on my bass, weaving between the melodies of the slide guitar, the guitar, and the driving drums. The flute player popped his head in and out again and again, while Cuz and Nick and I started to actually play accents to it, followed by staccato stops and rolls by Flash on the drums. It was like a comedy routine. A live, living vaudeville show once again at the county theater but instead of Jackie Gleason, it was with Jackie Clark. Jackie eventually picked up on the comedy of it, but had a hard time maintaining his own sense of humor about it.

We let Jackie sing the last verse, still having to stretch his voice with inhuman sound and force to its limits, finally ending the song, procuring and enormous thundering applause from our faithful fans. The power behind Jackie's voice in this new key, for him, added an unexplainable energy to the verses he sang, but almost made him hoarse. The audience ate it up, along with the driving solos, and also when the flute player came from behind the curtain to take a bow, who himself got a standing ovation.

Oddly enough, I never even heard his flute over the loudness of the band, and I have no clue if he can even play well. We just know the audience enjoyed the shenanigans, as we all did, all except Jackie that is.

We did one more song with Jackie which was the flip side of his record, "The Hunter." A blues standard in the key of E. We started it in the key of A, and Jackie's face immediately turned beet red again. Once again, he was driving his voice hoarse, and once again, we were doing the driving solos, but this time, the flautist just walked off of the stage and we were on our own. Once again, we got a standing ovation and we did our time. . . the show was over.

Chapter 6

The Record Deal

The curtain closed for the last time, and we were safely secluded from the view of the audience. The backstage lights came on, and through the curtain, we could hear the sound of mumbling, talking, and people slowly leaving. We talked about the show, as we began packing up the equipment while two men, dressed in classy three-piece suits

walked up to Jackie, and after a whisper the three of them walked out of sight. Behind me I heard a voice say, "Nice show"! It was our illustrious and comical flute player, holding his hand out with a big smile.
"Hey", I said, and stood up to shake his hand.
"I'm Gus", he said. "Jackie knows me, but I really don't think he likes me," he said, volunteering this comment with a smile. Gus was a bearded fellow, with brown hair and very white teeth that showed like the Cheshire cat when he smiled and continued about Jackie, "He and I graduated same year from Upper Moreland High. We used to hang out together".

Hearing this, I assumed they were probably good friends, but I assumed wrong. "Jackie and I used to jam and hang out at his place," he continued, "I have a funny story about Jackie, which might explain why, I think, he has a hair up his ass about me." Nick and Cuz crowded around to listen. Gus began his story:

"Jackie used to travel up to New York state, in his new BMW, to get guitar lessons off of Jimmy Summers.

"Wait a minute," Flash chimed in, "Theee Jimmy Summers?"

"YES! Theee Jimmy Summers," he repeated, and continued, "His dad knew him somehow, and had lessons set up for him. Anyhow one time he asked me and these two chicks to go with him. We got to New York to a hotel where we met Jimmy and had a beer with him. Jackie then gave me the keys to his BMW, and asked me to stop back, in a couple of hours, while he took his lesson. He even gave me a one-hundred-dollar bill, to get some gas and some beers at a 'beef and beer' he knew of."

Gus, in telling the story, then sat and looked around to see if Jackie was around, like this was a big secret. But seeing he wasn't, he continued, "Jackie slipped me the owners' card and his drivers' license, telling me to be cool. He remembered my drivers' license was suspended at the time. Anyway, good to my word, I put gas, but only a dollar's worth into the vehicle and drove the ladies to the bar. I parked out front in the loading zone because, well, it was the only space I could find, and I could keep an eye on it through the bar room window. Anyway, I figured we wouldn't be long. Unfortunately, we got involved in a game of pool, and I was doing pretty good too, damn good. Then I noticed that there was flashing lights outside the window, and saw a cop standing there, looking at my car, or rather Jackie's BMW. I finished my pool shot, my bourbon shot, and my beer, then me and the girls stepped outside to see what was going on. There was a tow truck hooking up Jackie's BMW to take it away. The cop looked at me and asked, "Do you know who owns this car?"

'I own it sir', I told him.
'Did you know you parked it in the loading zone?'
'Yes, I did officer'
'Why would you intentionally park it in the loading zone?'
'I was getting loaded' I told him.
'What?'
'I mean I thought I could park there for takeout,' I said.
'What is your name boy?'
'Jackie Clark'
'Let me see your license and registration', he said. 'You're Jonathan Clark Jr?'
'Yes, I am, just call me Jackie'.
'Sure, mister Clark', he answered.
'Look, don't tow it away', I said, 'I'm standing right here, just give me the damn ticket and I'll be on my way'."

Gus, telling us the story started laughing, causing us to do the same, then said, "Wait, let me finish the story. So, the officer looked at me and said, 'You're a little too drunk to drive, aren't you?'

He smelled my breath and wrote me another ticket for public drunkenness.

He gave me another for indecent exposure when I started urinating on the sidewalk in front of him."

Cuz, Nick, Flash, and I were in stitches by this time, listening to this unbelievable 'Jackie' story as Gus continued:

"Fortunately, one of the girls sweet talked him into letting her drive me and the other girl home so the car wouldn't get towed, but I still got the three tickets.

'Here you go mister Clark', the officer handed them to me.

'Enjoy your day', he said.

'This'll help', I said.

When we were finally out of the officer's sight, I ripped up the tickets and threw them out of the BMW window, and I was done with being Jackie for the day. It was sure fun while it lasted, but I believe that's why Jackie doesn't care much for me," Gus said finishing his story.

"I believe you've got a valid point," Cuz said.

"Plus, he doesn't like gay people," he added. "I'm 'bisexual and he knows it. Jackie's disgustingly heterosexual, and homophobic, and doesn't want people to know he's linked to me."

"That would make for another great story," Flash said smiling.

Jackie returned with the two well-dressed men and walking up to us, Jackie said, "We have a proposition for you guys."

"I'm not that kind of guy," Nick said, reflecting on what Gus just told us.

In adding to Nick's candor, I stated, "We're cheap, but we're not easy."

"Stan?" The one well-dressed man asked.

"I'm Stan", I said. "And this is Nick, Hank, but we call him 'Flash, and over here's Benny".
Cuz said, "Don't call me Benny. Just call me Cuz. Everyone else does", and gave me a wink, then patted me on the back.
Gus chimed in, "I'm Gus."
Jackie responded, "Get lost."
Gus smiled, then pinched Jackie's ass, causing him to jump, then played his flute to "Stars and Stripes Forever" as he marched comically into the darkness from whence he came.

"I'm Walter Hahn from Bobcat Records and this is my partner Robert DeMos. We're looking for a new backup band for Jackie Clark and we believe we've found them", he said.
"Why tell us?", Flash asked. "We're not his managers, he can do whatever he wants".
"You don't understand," he continued, "Bob and I believe we can put you together with him and we can all make some serious money!"
"What?"
"Yes, you guys up there tonight made this whole Jackie show come together with your musicianship, humor, and with your following of people, even though Jackie did say he brought the majority of the crowd".
"Now wait a minute, he didn't . . . " Cuz began but Jackie cut him off.
"You guys were phenomenal up there, that's a fact," Jackie added, "I would like to do my show on the road as 'The Jackie Clark Show' with you guys as my band".
"Get lost scum", Nick said with a confident smile, "We're good enough as is, we don't need any two-bit jackass as a front man." Nick continued, "Let me tell you something Jackie, you were good tonight because *we made* you good. And THAT'S a fact. Now be a good little ass kisser and get

on your way, and take these two, three pieced, well suited for gold digging con-men with you, before I get angry and personally escort the three of you off of the end of stage left myself".

We were flabbergasted and in awe at the same time, since we were all in agreement with his words. Nick spoke for us with the exact thoughts we all had, only he put them together so eloquently in words everyone could understand and with the utmost impact they so deserved. I felt proud to know him.

Mr. Hahn and Mr. DeMos said nothing, as they turned and voluntarily exited stage left without any personal escort from Nick or anyone. Jackie glared at us with fiery daggers coming from his eyes, and said with a voice, not unlike a little spoiled child, and a bit gravelly sounding, from the stretch put on his vocal cords from our changing the key of his songs for him tonight:
"You guys are FOOLS! ASSHOLES! I'll that see you never play this town, or state ever again!" Then he added, "and when you pack my stuff up, you better not scratch anything!"
"Pack his stuff up?" Flash said confused.
"Rich kids", Nick said shaking his head, "You can't live with them and you can't shoot 'em".

Jackie stomped like a little boy off of stage right, and into the darkness of the now empty room. We saw his equipment there all set up, and we left it as it was, as we smiled and packed up our own before we loaded up the van and went guiltlessly to breakfast at Don's all-night diner.

Pancho the cook, and sometimes waiter, came over to our booth and threw down the menus at us. There were other booths taken, along with some stools at the counter, and we imagined some of them were probably folks from

THE LOST MARBLES STORY

tonight's show, since by this time, it was 1:22am going by one of the diner clocks.

Nancy sat, as usual, next to Nick in the booth, and stroking the hair from his forehead said, "You guys were all tremendous tonight, including that 'ass'."
"Don't call Flash that", Cuz said, "He's alright". Flash just looked up from the menu not really listening, then Nancy said, "You know perfectly well I was referring to Jackie."
"Do we have to talk about the show right now? Can't we talk about the weather or something?" Nick seemed perturbed.
"I think you were right Nick, telling that maroon what for," I told him. "Anyway, I heard it was supposed to rain, since you asked." Nick half smiled and yelled to Pancho, "Panch, can I get a plate of French fries and gravy, and a plate of onion rings?"

We all had gotten our food, a mixture between us of burgers, eggs, bacon, fried chicken, and of course the French fries, gravy and those deep-fried onion rings that bounce when inadvertently dropped on the floor.

Eventually, about half way through our meals, from around the corner came two familiar faces. It was the faces of the 'three pieced well suited for gold digging con-men', as Nick put it hours ago, the Bobcat record company executives we were just previously acquainted with. They were at the register, paying for their meals and they noticed us, and instead of walking out, to our surprise they actually approached us smiling. "Hey, 'nice place to eat after a tight gig, huh?" Walter Hahn asked us. Flash mumbled under his breath, "Now his sorry, stuffed, fat ass is ready to shit".

"Come again?", Mr. Hahn asks. I interjected while kicking Flash under the table, "He said 'sorry, it's tough that when asked, there's no place to sit'".

Mr. DeMos said, "I just wanted you boys to know we really enjoyed your separate act as well. Walt and I think that with the right management you can really go places."

"Yeah," Walt started in, "You presented a tightness that we've almost never seen in a local act. You really had the crowd going with the music."

"But it wasn't as good as 'Jackie'", Nick said.

"You were right about one thing Nick", Mr. DeMos said, "You made Jackie's act good tonight. I don't ever remember him sounding better, even in the studio. What you guys did behind him was accent his potential. He was glowing, but that's not taking away from your talent as a band at all. If anything, we emulate it, however, we're in the market of selling, hitting dead center if we can, the streamline of what people will buy which is what is called 'pop', or to be more conservative, a popular sound that appeals to all. We want it to be less of a crap shoot, virtually no risks and more of a sure thing. That's why we think the combination you have, with Jackie, provided we can get his voice to that same dynamic he had with you tonight, and with the easy jamming behind him, we feel we all can make millions.

"It's not going to be easy with that clown," I told him. 'If you're good businessmen, you should be able to notice that his personality alone is a high risk; Are you sure you're ready to bank on something as volatile as that?"

"I don't think he's as bad as all that," Walter said. "He has his quirks as we all do, but off the record, (no pun intended) I believe if he sees the potential of his own fame, he'll kiss your ass as he does ours to make it work".

"There will need to be a contract that all of us can unanimously agree on of course," Cuz said.

"Of course," Mr. DeMos chimed in.

THE LOST MARBLES STORY

Nick, sopping up the rest of his gravy with his last French fry said, "Give us a week to think about it and we'll get back to you".

"Of course," Walt said, then we shook hands and the two record businessmen left the diner.

Nick got up to walk to the bathroom, mainly to wash his hands along with taking care of business. He passes Pancho, who was saying his habitual, "Everybody chewing, 'dats good," in his Spanish accent. We all left tired, fulfilled, and wondering what was going to happen next. Is there really going to be some kind of legitimate record deal for us? If nothing else, this is all pretty exciting and the next week will tell all.

I went back to work the following Monday. At 7am I was on the job carrying 12"x16"x8" cinderblock and stacking them on scaffolding for the block layers. Then mixing lime, cement, and 35 shovels of sand per batch in the cement mixer, I made the mortar for the crew. I dumped this blend into full wheelbarrows and wheeled it to the pans next to the block layers and shoveled them full. I repeated this until I'm caught up enough to grab my bag of tools; then join them in laying block on the wall using my trowel, brick hammer and striker. I have to be careful with my back, and with this kind of work, but it keeps me in great shape. It's beautiful work for this time of year, as long as we don't get rained out. Rob, one of the block layers, who's completely bald, and built like a weight lifter, is the fastest brick and block layer I've ever seen. He's the one I have to keep my eye on the most, since he runs out of mortar and block faster. As long as he has stacks of cinderblock and a full pan of mortar, I'm good to go with my laying of the block. I'm the only laborer though, so when any of them, (and there's 3 of them), are getting near empty I have to have them supplied. I don't know how Rob does it though because he's supporting, not just a family, but a genuine habit with hemp; or marijuana.

He told me that when he gets up in the morning, he smokes a joint, then he has breakfast and coffee, then smokes a joint, with another coffee from his thermos on the way into work. He works from 7am to 10am break, eats a sandwich, drinks coffee, and smokes a joint. He lays block from 10:20 until noon, smokes a joint, eats a couple sandwiches for lunch, drinks coffee, smokes another joint, then lays block from 12:30 'til the 2:00 joint break, where he doesn't stop working but the guys pass a joint to each other on the wall. At 3:30pm, we pack it in, and he lights up a joint and finishes his thermos of coffee on the way home. He does this five days a week, but I don't know what he does on the weekends, however, this past weekend he told me he was at our show, which explains why I thought I smelled pot there.

"I had no idea you were in something like that,", he said as he buttered the ears on another block with mortar. "My wife and I really had a good time".

"Thanks, I didn't see you there," I said.

"Oh, we were in the eighth row around the middle. 'Lots of screaming folks behind us too. My wife and I really liked the 'Rock and Roll Radio' song."

"That's one of my favorites too", I told him.

"That Jackie Clark guy was around the area for a while," Rob continued, "I hear him on the radio. He sounded different Saturday night. I think he sounded a lot better live than on the radio."

Rob picked up his brick hammer and gave the new cinderblock he was holding a single swipe with the head, making it a three-quarter size to fit the end of the run.

"See that?" He said, wanting me to observe how perfectly cut the three quarter was. I acknowledged him as he confidently said, "You could be as good as me someday, with some of the same qualities I have."

I responded, "You mean like, humility?"

"What?" his face went blank before I could quickly ask another question.

"Do you think we were as good as Jackie?" I asked him to be honest.

"I'm familiar with Jackie's songs on the radio. I'm not crazy one way or another about that stuff. You surprised me because I didn't know you were that good. The whole combination of that made the show interesting to me. Would I come see Jackie again? Probably not. Would I come out to see you guys again? In a heartbeat. I don't know if I answered your question."

"You did." I muttered as I dropped my trowel hoping Rob didn't notice. "Oooops", he said, "I saw that. I have eyes in the back of my head."

Then I mumbled jokingly, "But your heads up your ass."

"My hearing is good today too," he said laughing. I'm lucky Rob has a good sense of humor.

"Is playing music something that you really want to do for a living?" he asked me.

"Eventually, I would like to do nothing else," I told him, "I wouldn't mind traveling on the road, writing and playing songs, meeting new people, and just having a life of fun, but without any complications."

Rob puts up his line and makes it taut for laying another course of the 12" block. He takes his trowel and with quick swipes butters the one side of the newly laid blocks on this length of wall then the other with the mortar up to where I was working so yet another course can be applied, doing it much faster than I could ever do it. "Just think," he says, "You could be doing this for a living if you really want! You see, you have potential here!"

Now did he mean block layer or musician? Rob has always been funny that way; Accidentally deep! That was enough to make me think deeper on what I need to do this coming week with this whole band and recording thing.

As for his pot habit, I asked him how he can afford it, and he answered, "I can't, that's why I'm dealing it on the side, this way, most of it is free." Then he butters another cinderblock, telling me, "Stan, come on, I need some more mud here."

I leave my tools and jump down to get another batch of mortar mixed, so I get the mixer running, throw in two buckets of water, lift an 80-pound bag of cement and place it on the mixer grid, stab it in half with the shovel then flip it over to empty it into the mixer, then a 50-pound bag of lime and do the same, then 35 more shovels of sand, adding water as needed, and presto, another batch of mortar. My new realization, thanks to Rob, is I don't particularly want to do this masonry job for a living, much less for the rest of my life.

Cuz was in the same kind of bind as me, as he was working at a carpet place by now. His job was "Toe Motor Operator," which is a corporate classy name for a fork lift operator, only at a carpet warehouse, instead of forks on the front the machine, it has a long pole for sliding into the cardboard roll at the center and lifting the carpets for either the storage racks or onto the truck trailers. It was interesting enough for a job and a nice paycheck, but a dead-end future for someone who wants to be a musician.

Nick was in a rut too, as he had training from the VA and was doing some welding at a local shop. It wasn't exactly what he wanted to do forever but it was alright for now, and he was still involved with the service somehow, special forces or something, but it wasn't full time. Him being a paratrooper and being involved in some secret missions in Nam, somehow keeps him connected to them, but he never talks about it, ever. He's also having bad dream issues about Vietnam, but he never discussed any of that with us. Nancy, being our friend, told us he'd rather keep that stuff to himself. Nick treats her like gold, and she respects him highly. I do believe that if anyone ever spoke ill of Nick in front of Nancy, she would stand up to them for him . . . and probably rip their throats out. That's at least what I believe, knowing what I know about Nancy. She is, and always has been a trooper, and I envy their relationship. I think to myself, if I could ever have something like that in a relationship, I'd be very happy and fulfilled in my life. They're so right for each other and they seem to keep each other centered, stabilized, but all I can do for myself is to keep on dreaming, for now anyway.

Flash is also in the same boat as us. He's had lots of jobs but at this time he was working on a farm in Bedminster. They raise horses, goats and other animals, and they're also building a new barn, so he helps with the goats, horses, chickens, then labors with the crew up there, doing construction, and running farm equipment for cutting alfalfa and baling hay. It's certainly a clean living for someone who likes that sort of thing, and most of them do.

Flash has grown accustomed to his own free spirit and partying though, and doesn't care one way or another about, pretty much anything. He's grown unreliable at these kinds of jobs and wants something with more substance in his life, like we all do I guess. He's been trying to keep his drinking contained and has had some success, but it still rears its ugly head from time to time. Like Nick, he's dealing with memories of the Vietnam war zones. He had experienced hand to hand combat to the death over there; and saw some of his friends get killed right in front of him.

Even though he, like Nick, does not talk about it, it weighs heavy on his heart and sometimes comes out with excessive drinking.

    We had a rehearsal Thursday night at our house as usual, the house Cuz and I have been renting. As usual we were getting a lot done and we can feel how tight we're getting as a unit. There was a knock at the door, and it was Walter Hahn and Robert DeMos, the record company scouts, who wanted to discuss further, about our thoughts and their possible interests and outlook on what can happen and what they can potentially offer us. We were all ears, interested as well and open to everything they had to say. They want us to be the band behind Jackie Clark, and Jackie had already given his approval of the idea. We will have an album and a record deal, a national tour lined up with 55 cities, a steady weekly paycheck of $300 each for 1977 through 1978, but we'd have to play as the Lost Marbles exclusively for Jackie. The contract would keep us as a band with him, but we couldn't play on our own or with anyone else without permission. We can only play songs Jackie selects, in other words, we were his gelded helpers.

    Needless to say, some more negotiations were in order and they lasted through the night and into the morning, without any lawyers. There was a lot more involved than I can say here but I can give the bare facts. What we finally worked out was we, as a band, will cut our own album with material we choose, separate from another album we would cut with Jackie. We'll use a sub-label and they'll market it separate from the album with Jackie Clark. We will tour that album separate from Jackie Clark the following fall of 1978 right after our tour with Jackie.

We were all, for the most part in agreement with this new negotiation as we still get our tour with Jackie with the $300 each a week. The deal was signed, and we were on our way to becoming the closest we've ever been to being rock stars.

Chapter 7

The Sirens Coast
(A Club of Strange Seductive Witches)

The first recordings with Jackie Clark were tough to get started. He told us he was engaged to be married with a girl he'd been seeing for over a year. He was sometimes in a fog, or daze, but we still were able to get a couple of songs in the can. He actually used one of Runx's songs "Loralee" on the album, and we did a good job backing him up on that one. We really went all out, because it's a great tune, but along with that there were also some more standard covers, including 'Kansas City' and 'The Hunter', the two on the single 45 he put out a year ago locally. The record company was still against him using any songs he wrote, but in all honesty, I heard a few of his songs and I'd have to agree with the record company on this one. Jackie is not a song writer, but he has good looks and some personality, and can play acoustic and electric guitar with some flash.

He's not a bad singer either when he puts his mind to it, but this bizarre escapade of grandstanding Jackie Clark was sometimes hard to bear for us Lost Marbles, even though we were tolerant knowing we were getting our own professional recording out of it. After a few more painstaking hours we were done with the session, but we still have a long way to go though I know we'll get it all done. Mr. Hahn and some others from Bobcat said they'd like to see it in the can and ready for mixing by the end of the Month. The pressure's on.

I headed out to what used to be a local bar but is now a club, which Jackie had recommended. It is presently under new ownership and of course new management, and also near home so it was convenient for a nightcap. Jackie said he knows people there and handed me a card that said "SIREN-V.I.P." It's for the bar, or rather club which is now called 'The Siren's Coast', changed from years of being called 'Uncle Sammy's Bar and Grill'. I entered, and I was amazed at the change made to the place.

I'll admit, it's pretty classy, and not what you'd call your typical shot and beer bar. It's entirely all coastal seashore décor, with nets on the walls, with the fake lobsters and crabs in them, the pictures of sailboats and beaches with the sand dunes, and tanks of water containing live lobsters, live crabs, and live fish and eels. There was the regular bar to get drinks, and a cooking bar where Japanese style cooking was a show performance.

There was a big banquet room where the stylish tables and chairs could seat over a hundred people if they wanted. The people working were all women; Attractive women that were scantily clad, some in bikini tops and see through waist sarongs, showing off their well contoured hips. Some were wearing nothing but an apron, barely covering their otherwise naked breasts. Some were dressed in grass skirts and belly dancer style attire. I sat at the bar, ordered a shot and a beer, and while thinking about how to quit my day job since I really don't need it anymore, as I panned my eyes around to check the place out.

There was a feeling like we were on some island somewhere, with some, not only white, but Asian and Caribbean looking women. One blonde Caucasian girl, a cook, short but with a sensual build, wearing only a skimpy black apron pulled a squirming eel out of the live tank and laying it onto the cooks' counter, methodically started skinning it alive; like I've seen in one of those Chinese street markets on TV. It continued to squirm and make farting noises while she grinned heartlessly, chopping it up into pieces and let it fry right there on the bar grill plate in front of the customers; One which was a woman crying on her boyfriend's shoulder at the violence of the cooking process she just witnessed.

I looked across the way at how this place changed from the way it was. Everything was new to me here. The new bar, the new people. . . and the new, very tall, about 7', and thin; curvaceous, attractive exotic belly dancer on an adjoining bar over by the new lobster claw machine, where it looked like you pay only a dollar to try your luck at grabbing, (with the small crane and claw), a live lobster for dinner if you wanted. The woman was doing a belly dance to 'Witch Queen of New Orleans" and was bending over for her only customers in that area; four glassy eyed guys in expensive three-piece suits staring lustfully up at her soft sensual moves.

The two lobsters in the claw machine tank back themselves into the farthest corner from her as she kept licking her lips and snapping her teeth at them as part of her hedonic show. She was a very mildly dark-complexioned woman with commanding features, that to me resembled a young Elizabeth Taylor. She had beautiful light green or hazel eyes under those long dark eyebrows that added a wicked leer of determination. She emanated an imperiously controlling aura about her that was not to be denied; Brilliantly spellbinding.

Her tongue was unusually long, no kidding, at about 6" and she waved it up and down, fast and then slow at the glass tank, putting the lobsters, and the glassy eyed patrons sitting at the bar beneath her into a trance. The crustaceans are huge four-pounders, with what look like piles of barnacles and darkened coral that glistened like glass on their shells, and it's certainly like nothing I've ever seen before on lobsters.

The gorgeous dancer also had layered shoulder length black hair and was wearing only a thong and pasties with thin golden chains, as she gyrates her beautiful derriere, belly, and figure. Her breasts are full but not too large, certainly not small. There's a tattoo of a black widow spider within a pentagram on her belly, reminding me of my old flame Barbara, who had one exactly like it.

This dancer also had one of a rattlesnake on her lower back and her long legs had what looked like snake scales painted on them, but I'll bet my beer that's all a tattoo. She was a beautiful circus-like freak and had a real island like look about her as she'd bend and move like her back had no bone. She ignored, almost as if to snub the patrons ogling her from that area bar; but kept her attention on the lobsters who appeared to be looking at her, and probably shitting themselves as she rotated her long, wet tongue at them.

Then there was the hostess, who wore her hair up, and I could tell it must have been very long by the excess of curly locks. She was perfect, and well out of my league, as she too was tall; at about six feet, a reddish brown haired gorgeous lady with creamy white skin, orange freckles on her back, her chest, and on her cheek bones. I'm guessing she's probably Irish or Scottish decent; And she was blessed with the figure of a supermodel, and like I said, out of my league.

As I watch her jotting down something onto a notepad, her eyes looked up and right into mine as I looked away nervously. I felt an instant connection, like I already knew her, but I didn't have the nerve to follow through. When I tried to subtly glance back she was still looking at me with a smile then back down into her writing, as I felt her glance pierce my soul. She was like no one I've ever encountered anywhere, and I couldn't take my eyes off of her this time. Like the man sitting next to me said, she was like a witch drawing me into her or something, but he was actually watching and referring to that belly dancer, who was finishing up the dance.

As the song finished, the dancer got down off of the platform, put down her castanets, picked up her drink and slowly, still clad in her chains, pasties and thong, walked over to the lobster claw tank game. The way the game works is if you are able to pick one up out of the water and put it into the basket, you win the lobster. You can either take the lobster home for dinner; or have them cook it here for you. If it was me, I would probably feel sorry for it and take it to Jersey and let it go into the ocean, at least that's what Nancy asked me to do when she heard I was coming here tonight. She told me she thought this was a cruel game, and those lobsters in the tank were actually in there all week. I just now remembered she asked me to grab them for her and release them in the ocean, but I'll wait my turn.

Anyway, I watched this sexy, almost naked belly dancer secretly, as she placed her dollar in the pay tray and was bending over, cursing at the poor crustaceans softly and sure of herself, even talking to them, and telling them things like, "It's all over boys, I see you looking at my boobs. Don't worry, I'm only going to smother your sorry asses in butter and suck on you 'til there's nothing left of you but your useless and pathetic shells."

I immediately thought she was psycho, or somewhat crazy as she continued:
"Fuck! It's time to give it up you tasty little bastards," she said, as she turned the crank and was trying in vain to lift them out to their inevitable doom. To me, she sounded a little off her gourd; talking to those lobsters the way she was, and I was starting to really wonder about this new place.

She was also very aware that some guy, half her size, was standing immediately behind her, with his chest at her butt, watching, sweating and absorbing her sensuous moves as she swayed from side to side, like a Cobra, hypnotically mesmerizing its prey, and listening intently to her erotic phrasing of her words.

Apparently, I finally figured, that it seems she was only 'performing' this erotic display for this short guy's benefit, as some service to him for a tip, maybe, and as a hedonistic show exclusively for him, a paying customer. Anyway, she soon gave it up, and walked into her dressing room, followed by that same dwarfed man wearing an expensive suit yelling about something.

The man sitting next to me laughed and said, "That short dude has really got the 'hots' bad for her. He's actually friends, or some kind of partner with some of the owners, who are affiliated with organized crime, I think, and he 'got solid gold teeth too . . . did ya see that?"

Then my bar friend leaned over to me and with his breath of stale beer whispered, "I believe his name is Marco. Somebody told me that they were married; or used to be . . . but you know how those stories go, and I heard that she's an honest to goodness witch! A real life, witch, from a mysterious island somewhere! All of these women are witches." On that note, I was thinking that my bar buddy has had enough of the brew.

Anyway, this fellow he called Marco, is a man in his late fifties, maybe, and only about four, maybe four and a half feet tall, salt and pepper hair, but is physically almost perfectly proportioned except for being a little pudgy. He's considered a dwarf I guess, or little person who looked like he lived a rich life of spending and eating. He had an attitude with her, and he really wanted those lobsters, but she failed, seemingly intentionally, on trying to nab them.

That pretty hostess who I was eyeing, interrupted his harassments by grabbing him from behind like a wrestler, and keeping him in a choke hold said, "Time to mellow, boy!" Just then the dancer came back into view as if on cue. She walked tall toward him with her near naked chest straight out and demanded him to leave. As he was hopelessly trying to break free from the hostess's hold, he told her she was supposed to cook those lobsters for him. The dancer then told him, "If you don't leave, I'm going to enjoy cooking you!" Then gave him a long evil leer and continued, "Like the shrimp that you are!"

Before he could say another word, the dancer took his head in her hands, cupping his mouth with one and the other on the back of his head, then twisted it to the side as he moaned while the redheaded hostess holding him laughed. Then the dancer stuck her long tongue out like a snake, vibrating the tip of it dead center into his ear and tickled with the very end of it until the man actually wet his pants. Letting go of his head, the dancer laughed and sensuously sashayed away, walking tall and proud to her dressing room as he cussed and tried to break away from the hostess's restraint.

His friend, a big guy in a suit, black hair and mustache, who had been sitting with him quietly this whole time before his initial pursuit of the voluptuous dancer, quickly came over to the hostess and grabbed him from her, pushing her away, then told him to 'forget about it'.

"That guy's name's 'Tony'," said my bar buddy who's still sitting next to me and catching me up on the goings on at this establishment.

"Them two's inseparable and Tony watches out for Marco. Either the dancer or the hostess could have beat little Marco to a pulp," he said as he took a gulp of his beer and continued, "The dancer's known as 'Snake'. She's even tougher than Cookie the hostess there." Then he kind of halfway mumble whispered, "Witches." Fortunately for me, my buddy went back to paying attention to his beer.

Anyway, it looks like this 'Tony and Marco' left quietly after the confrontation, so I thought I'd try my luck, and asked that same pretty red headed hostess about the lobster claw machine, and she asked me to show her the VIP card, and handing me the card back said, "Good luck," and I walked up to the machine with my dollar. There were only the two lobsters in the tank and I really started to feel sorry for them. I decided I'd try my luck catching them, and if I did I'd set them free like Nancy had asked. I'd set them free in Jersey; And at the same time maybe impress the attractive hostess.

With all my skills and concentration, I was able to grab and place them both into the slot, winning them both. There was a thunderous applause from the patrons as one of the bar owners herself, Erin, handed them to me. Erin was dressed scantily like all of the other women working in this place, wearing only a white apron that barely covered her front and exposing her entire naked back and legs. She was a beautifully tall and slender, full breasted blonde in her thirties. The only other garment she wore besides the skimpy apron was a revealing florescent orange lacy thong, and she was already busy and in the middle of steaming a bushel of Maryland crabs.

"Do you want me to cook those here for you while you watch? It's usually the custom here," she said pointing at one of the steaming pots right behind her.

"No thank you," I said shyly, "I'll take them home as is."

Although I told the pretty gal I'd take them home, I left out the fact that I was going to put them in our salt water fish tank at home until tomorrow, and drive to the Jersey shore to set them free.

"Suit yourself," she said with a smile, as she went about her business. I watched her for a bit, sensually bending and grasping those treacherous lively crabs fearlessly, one in each bare hand, and toss them savagely into one of the steaming pots.

"Your thong glows in the dark," I told her, but she just ignored me as she continued emptying the bushel basket of critters in the same ruthless manner, two by two; into the steamy caldron that she towered over, occasionally preventing a few renegade crabs from escaping their inevitable and grisly fate by fiendishly nabbing the desperate defectors as they climbed out, or bravely batting them back into the pot using her one hand while seasoning them confidently with the other. I couldn't help noticing that she too had a tattoo of a coiled rattlesnake on her lower back. What can I say? I notice these things.

    I went and sat once again next to the guy I was drinking with when first I came in. "No one here but Snake or Cookie has ever been successful at nabbing one of those lobsters from the tank, much less what you did, capturing two of them," my bar buddy told me, and added, "People even started thinking that the claw machine was rigged."

    I sat with my live lobsters in the container and my beer and watched the TV for a while, a late movie was on with Barbara Stanwyck and Clifton Webb. In the movie Barbara was kissing him goodbye while she was getting into the last of the lifeboats on the Titanic. I was thinking what a poor bastard Clifton was when I looked away towards the bar area hoping to catch another glimpse of my newly found muse, Cookie, the hostess, when all of a sudden, she was gone, disappeared before my eyes. I started to look around in a panic but immediately caught myself and thought, "oh well . . . " Then, from behind me a soft voice in my ear said, "What are we watching? Is this seat taken?" Turning around, and to my surprise, the voice was Cookie's.
"No, this seat is yours if you want it", I said.

    Her eyes were a hypnotic greenish blue and she was one of the most beautiful women I have ever met, and I couldn't believe she was here, and talking to me. She wore a low-cut blouse that was generously showing her abundant cleavage, and I'm being honest when I say she wasn't inten-

THE LOST MARBLES STORY

tionally flaunting it, it just looked ravishingly natural for her.

"You took my lobsters," she said with a pout. "My friend, 'Snake' the dancer, and I were trying for them all day. I even named them, 'Tony' and 'Marco'."

"Wait a minute," I dubiously asked, "you 'named' them?"

"Yes," she replied, "I always name the lobsters I'm going to eat after someone I don't like. You see, I'm a witch, and it's a curse I bestow on them."

Right away, a red flag went up for me regarding this chick, and my now quizzical opinion of her sanity, like maybe she's a nut.

"That's . . . weird!" I said taking a long sip of my beer. I then realized my lobsters were named after those two dudes who just left following the commotion. "Well," I told her, "You're not eating these. I won your 'Tony and Marco' fair and square, and they're going to be freed into the ocean tomorrow. I'm keeping them in our salt water fish tank at home until then." I felt just as crazy as her, saying that.

"That's noble of you. 'You're a vegan?" she asked.

I told her 'no' but I wanted to give them another chance at life.

She thought for a moment, and looked into my eyes, and with a slow lick of her full lips leaned her breasts directly into my upper arm and her pretty mouth into my ear and asked in a soft whisper, "Can I have the chance to win them back off of you?"

What an original pick-up line, I thought, as her hand pressed lightly onto my belly, giving me an immediate sensation that something was very familiar about her. I was smitten, despite her crazy witch talk, but I tried to be cool and blew her obsession with my crustaceans off; for now.

"I'm sorry," I told her, "I didn't get your name. I'm Stan".

"I'm pleased to meet you Stan. I'm Angeline, but you can call me 'Cookie'. Everyone else does". She raised her empty mug to the bartender getting his attention for another draft. "Take that out of this," I said to the bartender sliding her a ten. "Not to sound cliché," I told Cookie, "but are you new around here? I see you're associated with this bar and the new management, but I've never seen you here before."

"No, I don't usually come here. Actually, this week is my first time as hostess here. I'm new to this area and I was doing this as, well, pretty much a favor to the owners. I've lived in New York for most of my life and now I'm in Lambertville, New Jersey, just across the bridge from New Hope, Pa."

"Yeah, I know where Lambertville is," I said, "That was the drinking place a few years back when Jersey changed their drinking age to 18. This place ain't bad though, and it's all newly remodeled. Plus, I live around the corner so this is easy for me."

"Oh yeah? Where? 'You have your own place?"

"I share it with a friend".

"Oh. You're with somebody?"

I laugh, "No, no, nothing like that. My friend and I rent it. His name's Benny, he's like a cousin to me. I even call him 'Cuz'."

"That's nice," she said slowly sipping her beer.

"So, I take it you're single?" I asked.

"I'm on a rebound, fresh out of a relationship".

"I'm sorry to hear that". I said downing a shot of bourbon.

"Don't be," she said, "I'm happier at this moment than I've ever been. I've never felt this free. I even get to talk to strangers." We both laughed.

I looked right at her as she took the last gulp of her mug. She raised it again, and again I got her another. I was completely smitten. Was I drunk? No. Was I high? No. Was I in love? That can't be, I didn't even know her. But somehow, looking at her, and talking to her, I felt like we've always known each other, so, what is it?

Just then, coincidently, she glanced back at me saying, "Did you ever look at someone and feel like you've known them in a past life? Or a thousand years? So where are you from Stan?"

"Originally from Philly, but you don't know me," I told her.

"You're funny," she said, "That's not where I was going with this."

After a few more beers and some more sharing about the universe, astrology (She said she was a Leo), witchcraft, and past lives, I had her follow me in her Jeep wrangler home to my place. As we were pulling away from the club, we saw a slew of cop cars pulling into its parking lot. When we got to the house I asked her about it.

"What was that, a raid? Or a bust?" I asked her.

"The place has been under surveillance by the feds for a week. It's something about stolen jewelry, or diamonds they're looking for. They won't find anything though," she told me as we walked through my front door.

      I put the two lobsters, 'Tony and Marco'; covered with those strange barnacles on their shells, safely into the fish tank. "I've never seen these barnacle like things on lobsters before," I said to Cookie, or rather 'Angeline' I decided to call her, "Have you?" She answered, "Sometimes." and immediately changed the subject, "This is nice here Stan."

"Thank you," I said.

      I grabbed some wine and we went outside where we talked under the stars, totally naked in the back yard. "Why do they call you Cookie? Angeline is such a pretty name."

"I cook for a living," she said, "When I'm not at the club or home I'm actually a chef at a restaurant in Lahaska"

"Wow", I said, "I would have never guessed."
'Yeah," she added, "I also studied psychology, hypnosis, witchcraft, sorcery, and the powers of the human mind. I can actually hypnotize anyone into imagining anything I want them to, especially if they're under a hallucinogenic. It's part of my hobby of witchcraft."

After saying that, I thought she might have been just a little crazy, but I kind of liked that. She then told me that there's an island of witches in the south pacific that uses cannibalism as a cleansing punishment for their civilization. They also sacrifice small sea creatures to perform voodoo type sorcery on their proposed victims. I told her that I wouldn't consider something like that as 'civilized'.
What exactly is 'civilized'?" she asked. I had no answer for that one.

We watched the fireflies, and I asked her if she knew if it was the females or the males that light up. She said that they both do, and added that she has a passion for research. She said she read that there's a particular species of firefly where a female blinks and glows for the sole purpose of luring the male of a completely different species, then when the male arrives, thinking he's going to have a night of sex, she simply abducts him, peels him, and eats him alive. Once again, I was at a loss for words.

She then handed me a small white tab of mescaline and asked me to pop it into my mouth tomorrow night.
"Why tomorrow night?" I asked, but she ignored my question and continued talking about herself.
"But besides all of that, my real passion is for cooking. Maybe I'll cook you a nice dinner sometime soon if you're a good boy", she said.
"That would be great", I told her pouring some wine. "What would you cook?" I asked.
"Anything you'd like. I can cook anything".

"Surf and turf featuring filet mignon and lobster," I said totally kidding with her because of the lobsters I caught. "You're on", she said adding, "For you, I'll even cook in the nude, but it has to be those two lobsters you have there, Tony and Marco." I just shook my head no, then she said, "I'll tell you what. I'll cook those two up for myself, but I'll buy two extra lobsters to cook for you. I really need 'Tony and Marco'. It's part of a spell I'm dying to show you.

She was insistent, but I told her 'no' and repeated my quest about releasing them in the ocean. She pouted that sexy pout again, as her eyes looked deep into my soul and I felt myself getting hot. Her predominant way of wanting to cook and eat my two buddies against my wishes got me eerily excited, even though I know she had to be fooling around with me. At least I think she was fooling around.

'Part of a spell' I thought. It's hard to tell if she's kidding or serious since there's a lot of mystery behind this seductive woman. Her perfect face; Her beautiful green eyes, and our genuine interesting conversation, even her dark talk of witchcraft. I feel the spell may have been cast already!

She let her long reddish-brown hair down to lay across her soft, white back and shoulders as she rested on her belly. We drank some wine, then turning on our backs facing the stars we mapped out the milky way, shed our view on life in other solar systems, wondered about God and the universe, then we slid into each other's tender universe as we made love like I've never made love before. We stayed entwined and rolled all night in naked ecstasy and sweat, and into the morning light of sunrise.

The whole night through, I never mentioned the band or the music, for we were too busy looking into each other. Even before we made love, we sat for about 10 minutes quietly, without a word, as we stared into each other's eyes, then after making love, I nodded out for a bit. When I awoke, Angeline was gone, as quickly as she came into my life, like a provocative dream untold. The first selfish thought on my mind was of my lobsters, as I immediately checked the tank; but they were still in there milling around. 'At least she's not a thief' was my next thought, as I then surrendered to reflecting on the previous evening of lust and decadence.

She appeared in my life like a revealed secret of the universe then disappeared as if it never happened. But it did, most certainly, happen. Hell, I need some coffee.

Chapter 8

Tripping with a Witch
(A Surreal Adventure of Lust and Love)

I went to the recording studio at Noon as planned, meeting up with everyone there. Jackie was a no show, but we didn't need him for what we were recording. We were doing rhythm and lead guitar tracks today for most of the songs, and going over some mistakes using the punch in, punch out method. Nick, as usual, was at the top of his game, and I know his stability and confidence has a lot to do with his tight relationship with Nancy. That's my opinion at this moment anyway. I'm thinking that way about Nick because I myself was with someone last night, whom I'll probably never ever see again, and I'm a little envious of him. He laid down the rhythms like a brick layer, which reminds me, I forgot to call my boss to say I got another job.

We were all psyched up about this new record contract and it showed. We were all in synch and getting in the groove, not even concerned about the absent Jackie Clark. He'll be here to do his part later tonight or tomorrow Mr. DeMos said.

We got our first paychecks too. A whopping $300! I'm usually used to seeing no more than $175 maybe sometimes $200 a week, but that was following hard labor and over 40 hours of working. This $300 for playing music was a treat. Someday there will be royalties too, but that won't be for a while, I'm told by Walter Hahn. Anyway, at the end of this month, when the record is finished, we're supposed to get the touring schedule for the upcoming tour.

The day is done here, and I head home to unwind. Cuz told me he won't be coming straight home because his new girlfriend and he are having issues, and he'll be spending the night at her place. Apparently, his new girl Stephanie is bummed out about this whole record deal, and him leaving to travel on the road with the band, which is perfectly understandable, and hopefully they'll be able to work it out. Although it's not effecting Cuz's playing yet, I can see where it could, because he gets sentimental, and sometimes emotional about these things.

So, it's getting near dinner time and I'm hungry, and I'm getting into the mood for laying back, and being on my own again tonight. I've decided to take the two lobsters that I freed last night from their doom, over to the Jersey shore tomorrow, instead of tonight to put them back into the ocean. I had some supposedly mild mescaline from Angeline which I popped into my mouth, thinking it may keep me awake for a while, but it will also expand my creativity, causing my imagination to run wild; but instead of writing songs or poetry, I rest my eyes and think mellow thoughts. I think about last night and imagine Angeline and me alone, on a deserted island, while the radio is playing classical music, Handel, and I'm in a good state.

There's a knock at the door, and to my complete surprise, it's Angeline; and wow, she looks rather stunning! She had her long, now even redder hair, full and down on her shoulders, and was wearing skin tight sweat pants hugging every curve, with a short, thin sleeveless top. Not that it matters, but I don't think she was wearing anything at all underneath that top.

"Could you please help me with some of these groceries Stan?" she asks.
"What's all this? You totally took me by surprise here," I asked her, shaking my head from my fuzziness.
"Why?' she asked, "I said I'd cook you a dinner. I've got filet mignon, two fresh lobsters, all the herbs I'll need, white wine, I hope you have garlic and butter here".
"We have that, yeah." I was at a loss for words trying to adjust to the reality of her being here.
"You can't have Tony and Marco, I told you that before," I said regarding my two new pet lobsters in my fish tank.
"You will eventually hand them over to me, tonight." she said, then added, "I brought two extra lobsters anyway, but your two, Tony and Marco, are special to me. They're going to be mine."
'She *is* crazy; a loose nut' I thought, and she spoke like she wasn't hearing a word I said.

"By the way," she added, "how is that mescaline? I'm assuming you popped it already?"

I was still too busy wondering what her endless obsession was with those two lobsters I rescued from the Siren's Coast, and why she was so engrossed with wanting to eat them. I was now totally tripping on the mescaline high as she took over the kitchen, familiarizing herself with everything, as I kept my guard on the 'Tony and Marco' lobsters in my fish tank. She pulled the meat out, (I'm talking about the fresh filets of mignon,) and showed me how lean they were at about a pound apiece. She took them out of a plastic bag with a marinade and placed them into a pan. Angeline then took her plastic bag with her two live lobsters, dumping them into the sink saying, "Here you go boys, last stop, everybody out!" I appreciated her jovial candor with the doomed, very fresh, and very much alive sea creatures.
"Be careful," she told me, "like Tony and Marco, they don't have the protective bands on them," and started to fill the large pot with water. Then eying me she said, "I'm reading your mind Stan," she continued with her slow drawl that wasn't southern, but very sexy and articulated, "I can see your thoughts. I didn't tell you I was clairvoyant." Then she asked in her soft-spoken, serene tone, "Who's Mary? In the red bikini?"

That scared me, when she said that. How does she know about Mary? I never told anyone about this woman from my childhood, and I thought I was hearing things.
"Well?" She said, "What was your attraction to her? Something she was cooking?"
I shook my head as I tried to rid myself of a chill. She read my mind? I immediately changed the subject:
"Where did you get all of this?" I asked.
"She then gave me a smile and winked, as if she knew something I didn't, then she put the pot of water on the burner.

"Don't worry about it", she said, "I told you I'm a chef. We're going to eat good tonight and I promised you a great dinner." She put her arms around me and gave me a long soft kiss and a big hug. I knew then for sure she had nothing on underneath. I did not want to let her go . . . ever. "I always keep my promises," she said. Then she glanced her pretty eyes at my two lobsters inside my fish tank, and then back, staring directly through me whispered, " I won't have to steal them from you, I promise I'll be sucking them both down into my belly before daylight."

"As I told you before," I said, "I've gotten attached to those guys and I'm setting them free." She softly kissed me and we shared our tongues for a moment, and I was hypnotized . . . as she softly whispered into my ear, "Setting them free, inside me."

She snuck away and into the kitchen to the ones she brought, and slowly slipped off her shoes, her sweat pants and her shirt. She was now totally buck naked in my kitchen, standing tall against and over the sink with her arms up behind her head putting her hair up. The tattoo of a black widow spider within the pentagram on her tight belly, similar to the one I saw on the dancer at the club, loomed over the sink like an omen of death for the lobsters as Angeline herself glared downward, past her milky white breasts into the basin at them, saying, "Look, this one's trying to get out." She fearlessly bumps him with her spider tattooed abs backwards, preventing his progress while grabbing him by the back, placing him onto the counter, "So," she said, slowly bending over to address him, and looking the poor creature directly in the face as it backs away from her with his claws up in protest, "You're telling me you want to be first?"

She is crazy!! She's talking to them, and my imagination is going wild, as this mescaline kicks in even more. I'm thinking crazy thoughts, but I don't say anything to her about it. Just then, she pointed to a large insect on the outside of the kitchen window. "That's a Praying Mantis," she said, then continued, "Did you know that besides eating other insects, the females tempt and lure in their male counterparts, who are fully aware of their own impending doom but approach her anyway; then she devours them while mating with them? I find that very erotic!"

My whole being was just looking at her and listening, but I didn't have a single reply to her comment. It reminded me of her other haunting commentary on the fireflies the other night.

She then bent down again to her bag and pulled out a black, sheer, skimpy, lacey peek a boo teddy with a cute little apron attached. All of her movements were slow, and seductive. She pulled it over her head and stretched the see-through mesh straps across her front and her back, leaving virtually nothing, and I mean nothing hidden. Even the black widow spider was peering menacingly through the near invisible mesh. A small heart on the skimpy apron by her crotch had letters that read, "Kiss the cook".

"You weren't kidding about cooking in the nude," I said. She had me so shocked, and at the same time excited to be with her, that nothing at this point seemed to surprise me. Anyone else, I would have thought 'plain ass crazy', and I did for a brief moment, but I also felt like we were connected, and that I knew her. It's very scary; but after all, we bared our souls to each other last night, didn't we? Why should anything about her shock me? The fact that she says she's a witch actually makes her all the more enticing. Maybe I'm the one who's crazy.

"While the filets are cooking I'll get these lobsters started," she said. With the pot of water now heating, she told me,

"I'm going to bake one and boil one. You tell me which one you like better."

She takes the first protesting critter and holds it firmly on the counter, directly beneath her spider tattooed tummy, with her soft hands and gentle fingers, slowly and calculated, then with a big sharp knife to its back, she splits it down the middle. "Scrunch."

"Can you get me that spoon over there darling?" she asked me rather serenely as her thumbs were delicately but mercilessly ripping the still squirming shellfish apart. Her calm expression with a smile never changed as she was as cool as a Swedish masseuse, while she flips it over and spreading it, showing me the insides as she held its legs down to stop them from moving.
"He's dead, it's just reflexes," she said.
"Yeah, right", I said sarcastically, and we both ignorantly laughed.

I would have left the room if this was anyone else doing this, since I'm not a strong person in this way, but she has a way about her that draws me to her, almost as if it's turning her on, or maybe it's the mescaline. Truth be told; I've never been comfortable with killing things, or as I've said before, watching animals being killed . . . even for food; but I have done so, although reluctantly. Also, I can't take my eyes off of her, due to some crazy magnetic appeal.

Anyway, as she's scooping with the spoon she wedges between her finger and thumb what she said was his heart, and popping it sensuously into her mouth remarked, "Mmm, I always suck this down for good luck."
"Better you than me," I said, but I was still trying to stop the room's walls from melting into the floors during another of these many mescaline aberrational mirages.
"I'm glad you like lobster," She said, interrupting my hallucination while smiling and sucking on her lobster heart,

"Some people are allergic to shellfish and can actually die from eating it, but I can eat it forever."
"I'm not allergic at all," I said, "I like lobster, crab, scallops; all seafood".
She then interrupted me by saying, "Now, I want you to watch me very closely, and take notes if you have to so you can make this on your own sometime."
"Okay," I said looking her voluptuous figure over, "no problem Angeline, I'm going to watch you very, very closely."
(How could I not?)

My mind was reeling with the drug effects; hallucinating, and fantasies of sex with Angeline; and despite all of this, I was clearly focused; tuned into her every move. It was like watching a motion picture of colorful outbursts and poetry in erotic ambulation. Because she asked, I watched as she took the garlic and butter mix and slowly and meticulously rubbed it all up and down the still fidgeting meaty tail and insides of the creature, with her dainty hands and fingers; with those black painted fingernails, and she perceived me watching her. Her peek a boo teddy was so sheer, I could see everything from her soft, resilient breasts to her thong exposed perfect derriere. I wondered how the garment could even stay on her without falling off. Simple physics I guess. Watching her took the edge off of the tripping.

"Hold still you," she said softly in her same commanding tone to the still moving doomed creature beneath her powerful fingers, as she packed and patted the empty torso with her homemade potato and garlic stuffing. The final touches were done on the first crustacean, and good to my word, I'm still watching her closely, as she had asked, while she bent over and put it onto the oven tray, still kicking believe it or not. While bending over top of it, she gave it a slow rub with butter sauce, seemingly putting it to sleep, using her fingers fastidiously with one hand and pulling her sliding peignoir top back up with the other. "Ooops," she said smiling over at me, making sure I'm still watching, "I'm still getting used to wearing this thin teddy. I'm popping out again," she said, as she shoved the tray into the pre-heated oven.

The large pot is now coming to a rolling boil.
"Boy, you're not at all squeamish, are you?" I said, as she delicately grabbed the second feisty lobster, holding him firm in her gentle fingertips just under her bosom, waving the poor thing as she spoke in her delicate soft voice, enunciating every word.

"Most men think women are the squeamish of the sexes," she said, and continued, "and some say that it comes from the history of the Garden of Eden, and the serpent, and that the woman was cursed to be this way because of giving the apple to the man. But I have absolutely no fears here, and I can't be squeamish in my business. I grew up near Long Island, up in New York, so I was used to being around seafood, working on lobster boats and fishing boats, putting the men to shame."

She continued waving the defiant creature around in gesture as she spoke:
"It's not that I enjoy killing so much, although it *is* an erotic turn on for me, sometimes, like tonight, but it's an inexorable requirement for survival," she said.

The lobster started flapping its tail in a panic, startling me, but she held it firm, ignoring it as if nothing was happening, and continued her soap box documentary. To someone tripping, this was nothing short of comical.

"People in society as we know it generally have grown soft. They eat meat, but they're against killing. When they see meat in a wrapper in the store they have to realize that someone had to kill it first."

"I know", I tell her, "I run into them all the time when I talk about fishing."

"The biggest hypocrites", she adds, "are the ones condemning those who kill fish, lobsters, chickens, or other animals; but those same people order it at restaurants; or buy it from the frozen food section of the local market."

Just then, the lobster quickly fanned its tail and did a back-flip, spinning towards the floor, but Angeline's quick reflexes bounced him up with her bare knee like a trained juggler and she lifted her tiny apron to catch him. We laughed, as that was one of the funniest things I'd ever seen tripping. With this hallucinogenic high, I saw solid, colorful trails behind him when he was being juggled, as if she was performing a cartoon like magical trick.

"Nice try mister," she said addressing the shellfish in the same low, almost a whispering sexy voice.

The next few seconds seemed to last forever as these feelings were all too familiar to me, like I've lived them before. This mescaline high I'm experiencing was deep, profound and scary, but just as equally provocative and fascinating. Everything was like watching a real to life cartoon, and I could tell now she was actually playing, not just with the lobster; but playing with me.

She knew I was a bit queasy about killing anything, although I knew it was inevitable that it has to be done in order to eat tonight. At that moment, I sort of envied the lobster, as she had the most devious grin with that dark lipstick and very white, perfect teeth, looking hungrily down at him through her cleavage as he lay in the web of the black widow tattoo, helplessly trapped in that tiny apron. As I said, those few seconds seemed to last forever, and as I watched her, she reminded me of someone she mentioned; Mary, my babysitter from my childhood, as I had watched Mary cook live lobsters when I was a child. How the hell could Angeline have known about that? Did I say something to her under the influence of this hallucinogenic? I actually felt a shiver, then my grip on that thought diminished as I broke away, back to the present cooking situation where I continued to watch, as visuals kept distorting to the beating vibrations of mescaline.

    She casually flipped the lobster from her apron to the counter, closer to its impending fate. Then she placed her delicate fingers and thumb around its back and lifted it, positioning its face an inch from her mouth as she playfully spoke in a soft whisper to it once again, as if directing her words metaphorically at me. "Give it up, your ass is mine now," she said lifting the lid from the boiling pot with her other hand, releasing the steam which plumed upward and surrounded her in a mysterious aura of unearthly mist. She held the objecting crustacean over the cauldron, with its last-ditch efforts of spreading its arms in defiance; And with her callous but victoriously sexy smile, overruled him; lowering him diabolically, and head first into his boiling demise. His tail curled, hooking himself onto the brim in one last effort to escape, but she daintily grasped his tail through the steam, lifting him from his last hopeful plea, and pushed him down unmoved, into the abyss. She looked down into the pot at him for a second then returned the lid. Her face was a little flush as she peered directly into my eyes and said, "What a rush, that always gets me fucking hot, boiling a live lobster. It's so lasciviously and amorously erotic, and downright obscene."

    Then keeping her eyes fixed on mine, she slowly, like a constricting snake, wrapped her arms, and then her long legs around me tightly, causing me to completely support her as I walked her into the other room. As tall as she was, she was as light as a feather, especially being near naked.

It was all so seductive to me that it was frightening! With my now completely crazy and ethereal high, I was imagining how that lobster must have felt, as I put myself in the poor critter's place for a brief moment; and she knew it, as in my mind I was vicariously looking at Angeline from his perspective, and how that must have felt for him being dominated, then boiled alive by this beautiful siren for dinner; but then, I quickly bounced back to reality.

With her tightening hold on me she smiled, her nose touching mine, and reading my mind once again whispered, "Don't worry Stan, I have different plans for you!"
That too was eerie, that she said that, being a very powerful presence, yet very feminine at the same time, the ultimate turn-on for me.

She gave me a long hug, with her arms and legs still wrapped around me, and was trying to stop herself from laughing. I felt so embarrassed at my thoughts and visions but comforted at the same time from her hug.
"I'm sorry," she said to me, "I realize you're tripping, I'll try to be cool."

She slowly released me, and turning the meat temperature down low, on the stove, led me to the living room where we sat on the couch with a glass of wine, and talked while dinner was cooking. I held her hands in mine, and they were very soft, and I couldn't believe she's done the work she's said she's done with these hands. But she did.

"I don't believe you ever told me what you did for a living," she said.
"I lay block and I labor for a local masonry contractor."

I didn't want to tell her yet about the recording contract. I still felt like I might jinx the whole project if I talked about it.

"That's really hard work," she said. She reaches over to feel my muscle as I said, "Cooking is really hard work too. I don't know how people can do that for a living."
"Take off your shirt," she said.

Looking and talking to her I can feel her heart and her soul. I feel like I just want to please her.
I pull my shirt over my head and she said, "You have a really nice build, I know I told you that last night in the heat of the moment but God, you really do!"

I just gleamed at her sitting crossed legged in her sexy teddy and I couldn't hold back. I began kissing her uncontrollably. She returned the passion and we were in the very long moment of luscious petting until we heard the timer. Unfortunately, the food was ready before we could get too intimate.

We got our table set and we served ourselves. Everything was laid out with a touch of class and it was all delicious. We sat across the table looking into each other's eyes enjoying the food. The garlic butter was running down her chin at each succulent bite and licking of her lobster. If she only knew what she was doing to me, wearing that see through nighty and wow, those bedroom eyes. Something tells me she knows. "Here," she says holding a juicy piece of lobster tail up to my watering mouth. I suck it down.
"So, I see that you're a musician, what do you play?" She was referring to the amps, the guitars, and drums across the room in the practice area.
"I play bass. Cuz, my roommate plays guitar."

She held another tender piece of the delicious filet mignon to my lips. I held a juicy, dripping piece of lobster tail to her mouth and she slowly and suggestively licked and bit at it until her whole mouth opened, engulfing the morsel and sucking it halfway in before biting it in half. She and I were feeding each other like this through most of the din-

ner. It was the best tasting meal I've had in a while, but definitely the best supper engagement I've ever had.
"Do you guys play out anywhere?"
This inquiry was getting dangerously close for me. I really don't want her to know right now about the recording contract or the upcoming tour. I can still be truthful. "No, not yet. We're still in the developing stage."
"I love music, she said, "I've dated some musicians. I can listen to jazz in the evening, you know, the sound of the extended style piano chords across the syncopated off beat of the drums against the bass, with tenor sax on top. Then there's classical, with Chopin, Mozart, Schubert, and let's not forget to mention Beethoven. I know his fifth and ninth are the most popular but I'm partial to the third symphony. And how about Leonard Cohen? "Iodine." "Hallelujah!"
"He wrote a song called 'Hallelujah'?"
"Not yet," she said, "But I love the song 'Iodine'. It's dark."
    I was impressed at her broad knowledge of music and the arts, and told her so, as she handed me a small plate of dark green leaves and asked me to finish it.
"This is a special salad I made," she said, "Tell me what you think of it."
    I started it and realized it was pretty good.
"Not bad. What is it?" I asked as I was finishing it. She smiled and just said it was her own special recipe.
"You're an interesting person Cookie," I said, "But can I just call you Angeline? It feels better to me."
"Sure," she said, "That's fine."
    I stood and leaned over to kiss her and fell over into the table knocking us both to the floor.
"You alright?", I ask.

"Sure, I guess we're finished eating," she said. "There's some filet mignon left," I told her.

"Put it in the fridge. You can eat it tomorrow," she said, "I'm still hungry for lobster." She looked at me licking her lips.

"Oh no you don't," I said. "I told you they're mine. I've become attached to them." She started breathing in my ear and whispered, "I want to eat themmm."

I laid down on the floor with her and just shook my head 'no' as she began kissing and licking me all over. Now I was tripping out of my mind and was ready to explode. I was out of control as she rolled around with me on the floor, but only teasing me; torturing me savagely with her tongue, and lust. I couldn't get away from her, not that I really wanted to. She teased me and teased me to the brink, until I gave in and said, "OKAY! TAKE THEM, for crying out loud." I couldn't help feeling I was now letting Nancy down, since she's the one who asked me to free them.

Angeline then stood up, calmly and completely composed, walked languidly over to the tank in her bewitching soft gate, and in her thin see through chemise, or teddy if you will, towering tall and victorious over her victims. The both lobsters, Tony and Marco, immediately threw their claws up in defiance, as if to defend themselves.

"Look at them," she said, "They know! They know I'm going to cook them."

Angeline reached in and pulled them out of the tank in each hand, saying:

"So, Stan, are you ready to take these two guys and some wine and go to the beach?"

"What?" I asked. I wasn't ready for a drive to the beach tonight.

"I mean, you have no choice," she commanded.

"Are you out of your mind?" I asked.

"Yes," she said, "Out of my mind with hunger. Let's go!"

She put my two, now condemned lobsters, into the cooler and also a bottle of wine. She loaded it into the Jeep with some more wine and a five-gallon cooking pot. She threw a long flannel shirt on, covering her lacey teddy and we were off to LBI.

It was a very warm and humid night, and as she drove I realized that there certainly was something special alright, as she had previously told me, within that leafy salad concoction she made and fed to me. Whatever it was made my hallucinations increase! She was bewitching me!

We arrived at her favorite night beach by 10 pm. It was very secluded, and the ocean was rolling its waves as we felt the misty, refreshing spray of the salt water. The moon was full and bright on this clear night, and over the dunes, we could see the beam of the lighthouse. We laid down some blankets and set a couple beach chairs. I saw her starting to scoop a pit for a fire and I felt a force from somewhere compelling me to gather some dry drift wood. "Can you fill this up with some sea water?" she asked, holding the pot out to me. "Make it three quarters full."

I couldn't stop myself from occasionally turning to see her soft glow in the moon's shadow, as I walked down to the surf. She was taking off the flannel shirt then slipped out of her teddy, rendering her completely nude in the moonlight. Her long wavy reddish hair was glowing against the shadows, and she was a sight to behold, as she continued bending to tend to the fire which made her bare figure look incandescent against the dark background.

I brought the pot of sea water up to the fire and she took it from me, mounting it onto a place she had made in the fire itself.

"Take your clothes off." she commanded, and I obliged.

I stood with my bare skin feeling the mist and breeze off of the ocean. She had me sit crossed legged with her, and silent as we waited for the water in the pot to boil. Angeline kept humming a haunting melody I've never heard, and kept it resonating until the water in the cauldron reached the boiling point.
"It's time," she said.
While she was reaching into the cooler for one of the sea creatures, it pinched her, drawing blood, which ran down her arm.
"Shit!" she said, "Oh, he's gonna' get his."
She tended to her wound while I myself tried to corner the varmint. I peered at the lobsters within the cooler and wondered about their unusual covering of barnacles. I never noticed it before, but in the moonlight, they looked more and more like real diamonds. When I reached in to touch the back of one of them, the crazy crustacean reached up and pinched my hand too! I pulled my hand out with him hanging onto it. I wasn't seeing reality anymore at this point, and everything was seemingly growing bigger, and bigger. The fire, the beach, and especially Angeline! I felt like I was on a different planet; another universe entirely! Then I realized nothing was getting bigger, an aberration I was shrinking, as if I was in some story book fantasy. I was now at about one fifth the size of Angeline, and I was feeling like I was in a dream that wouldn't allow me to wake up, no matter how I tried. Something else as crazy, was that these lobsters were now appearing as people; the same size as me!

My hallucinating had put me in some kind of dream sequence, because the damn lobsters appeared as those two characters that Angeline named them after, the ones she didn't care for at that bar; Tony and Marco; with Tony clutching my hand and pulling his other arm back to hit me.

But these guys were not wearing their three-piece suits. They were wearing clothes made of diamonds from neck to toe.

Tony had grabbed me and pushed me away, because they were both cornering a woman our same size. The woman looked just like Angeline, and helpless, and they were both getting on top of her, apparently trying to rape her as she screamed. I tried to pull one of them off, but he grabbed my arm again, pushing me away, as they both laughed and were taking turns with her. Mysteriously, the bars of some cage came down over top of them, separating them from me and the very woman they were harming. They were befuddled, until they looked up and saw the giantess Angeline, naked and towering over them through the cage bars above.

They became frightened and were now crying like babies, and asked me to free them, as they ran desperately in circles and climbed within the cage, pointlessly searching for an opening. Of course, I thought I was losing my mind, and then I realized it must be the mescaline and that leafy salad potion that Angeline fed me; which brought on a nightmare I'll hopefully awaken from. I had to keep reminding myself it wasn't real, it couldn't be.

The two men kept pleading with me, but I wanted to run, or do something, anything, I couldn't move. I felt like some force was freezing me in place; completely motionless. Angeline, naked as the seductive giant goddess she was, and standing five or six times taller than us in the moonlight, bent over top of the cage, slowly and provocatively opened the top.

She pulled Tony out, screaming his head off while she nonchalantly hummed a melody that drowned out his pitiful cries, as she walked over to the pot and held him down on the sand, crouching over him. She took her fingernails and scraped the diamond clothing off of him like she was scaling a fish, flipping him over and over, slowly and carefully ripping and tearing, as he kicked and squirmed frantically.

Then she picked him up by his legs and lowered his bleeding naked form into the boiling pot without changing her smiling, euphoric expression, still humming in ecstasy.

Then her flawless form approached us again. Her hair blowing in the breeze and nude body, both glowing off of the flames and moon against the night sky gave her an aura of fire as she mercilessly clutched Marco, like a hawk after a rat, who screamed the loudest, but it didn't break her concentration as she did the same, held him down by one hand, peeling the diamond attire from him in spite of his squirming, and lowered him feet first kicking and squealing like a pig, into his boiling perdition. He even tried to leap back out of the pot but her soft hand was right there to catch him and almost tenderly push him back in, as she continued her humming and grinning. The wind kicked up and sounded like it was resonating the same melodious tune as she was, blowing her hair wildly until it looked like flames against the night sky as she stirred the large pot containing her still squealing victims, like an alluring redheaded witch she continued to purr her haunting assonance into the morning hours.

To me she was now a giant, sultry demoness that horrified me in her erotic evil form, as she resembled the legendary siren witches I had heard of and read about, as she leaned over and stirred the brewing pot. In my racing mind I thought, 'I didn't want to be the next victim', and I lost it completely! I felt was able to finally run and decided to do so. I ran, and I ran, as I heard my heart beating like it was going to come out of my chest! My legs had the energy to keep on going. I heard Angeline's voice, "Stan! Wait!" But I kept running.

Just then, I was tackled to the ground by a normal sized naked woman running faster than me. It was Angeline. "You're freaking out!" she said, "They're only lobsters! You've seen me cook lobsters before. Remember; you're only tripping!"

Then she hugged me, as I continued to cry in disbelief of the superior hallucinations I had just witnessed.
"They're only lobsters," she repeated in a whisper, "I cooked them, Stan, they can't hurt us anymore."

I was shivering as she started kissing me all over, and then we laid naked in the sand, rolling around as we made love, right there into what seemed to be oblivion. We walked back to the fire hand in hand and I watched her go ballistic on eating the two lobsters, Tony and Marco, like there was something personal she was settling with them. I asked her what it was in the bucket beside them, but she didn't say anything. A chill went through me as thought I saw diamonds, in the bucket, glistening in the moonlight. I remind myself again that I'm still tripping, as she said nothing while she continued slurping and eating. I didn't feel afraid of her anymore as we were somehow feeling hopelessly one with each other after this. She asked me if I was having premonitions of the future, regarding my freaking out, but I didn't answer. Then she told me that I was reading her mind, and that we were spiritually connected for a few hours. She said that I witnessed her past, and also her future through the hallucinations, which was why she asked me about the premonitions. I told her I couldn't tell what I saw, and that I didn't want to think about it anymore.

I can honestly say I never once tonight really thought about the band and the recording project. That was all buried under my fears and hallucinations in the moonlight, and her bewitching presence.

    We drank our wine, then I stayed naked with her in our sleeping bag under the stars as we watched the moon slowly move westward and once again, we made love; into the crack of morning light. Sometimes, she was like an animal with her sexual drive and stamina, and I was fortunately able to match her.

    I drove her Jeep back to my house after we loaded everything up. She slept on my lap most of the way and it was then, while driving and looking down at her pretty hair that I realized that I had not a stitch of clothing on my entire body; I'd forgotten my damn clothes at the beach, and lucky for me, my wallet was left at home. "I hope a cop doesn't stop me," I thought, as that would have been one for the books, trying to explain my way out of my driving in the nude. Anyway, a new day had started, and I wondered what it would bring, since I've had nothing but surprises in the past few days. I wish I knew what Angeline meant by me being able to see into her past, and her future; and if I did, I wish I could decipher what it was I had seen. I don't know what that concoction was she made for me with the leaves, but I've sworn off of anything hallucinogenic forever! . . . once again!

Chapter 9

Crooks and Deviates

I was getting ready to go to another recording session as I cleaned up the kitchen somewhat, and I'm echoing last night through my tired brain. I'm pleased to have found someone like Angeline, but I must now concentrate on the reality at hand, such as focusing my energies on this whole Bobcat Records deal and the band. Cuz isn't back yet and I'm hoping everything is alright with him, and that he and Stephanie have it all worked out one way or another, so he too can concentrate on the music we're trying to accomplish. It's absurd to think that we're only considered as a backup band for Jackie Clark, and that's always bothered me. It's been an underlying thorn in my side, irritating me like an annoying hangnail. The time I just spent away with Angeline, even though the time was short, helped me to clear out some of the cobwebs in my brain. I want to be happy where I am at all costs, but I don't want to hurt anybody doing it.

My creative juices were flowing, even during the recording session at Bobcat, and I was glad to see Cuz was at the top of his form, as was everyone else, even me, surprising enough, even though I was a bit drained, but the creative energy was carrying me through. The session, although musically tight, was repetitive and boring, since we were still coloring up new blues cover tunes for Jackie and had put Runx's "Loralee" on the back burner for now. They've decided not to use it on this LP, but it's a possibility for ours, if we ever get to making our promised album. We'd just cut out Jackie and redo the vocals, since all of the rest of the song is us, and our own arrangement anyway. We had Jackie's acoustic guitar on it originally, but his strumming didn't cut it, so Nick went in and redid it without Jackie knowing it, but some say he found out and that his ego decided to cause him to shelf the tune, which is only hearsay for now.

All we know for sure is that we're replacing it with yet another boring blues standard. We continued into the evening, and by midnight we were all exhausted and played out. We've managed to get all tracks for the album in the can, and ready for his vocal dubs. I set my bass into the case and stood up to stretch my back, remembering that I've had a creative melody and lyrics going through my head the entire night, bouncing around in there like ping pong balls in a lottery machine. I feel a headache coming on, and the only way to prevent it is to empty what I have going on in my head. "If you guys don't need me anymore I think I'm going to bow out," I said.
After I said this Cuz looked at me and said, "You look tired. 'Must have been a good night last night."
"I just want to go home. I'll be sitting up for a while unwinding," I told him.
"That's alright, I'm off to Stephanie's for the night. She's making a late dessert,"
I was glad to hear that, then I told him, Nick, and Hank that I thought everyone was in form, and that they all did a good job. That's the thing with us, we all complement each

other after sessions, bringing out the outstanding points of musical achievement in each riff and/or song. I left with my fender bass in my carrying case and went home to mellow and write down what was in my head.

I sat out on a lawn chair in my backyard on this clear night under the still full moon, looking at it and the shadows it was casting. I sat with a large cup of chamomile tea and my Ovation acoustic guitar and started playing and writing chords and lyrics that were within my head. It all started to flow like water from a breeched levee:
"She walks the night, tonight she's beaming
Reflections of her day.
She feels secure within her dreaming
Which guides her friends to say;
"She has no life. Look at her lonely as
She pretends to smile".
Her eerie glow shows this world of her own.
They try to guess the unfigured style."

I was taking sips of my tea and writing with a trembling hand thinking of her. I'm comparing her to the mystery of the moonlight itself. The thought of her is overwhelming and I remember her in my words, trying to paint a picture. I continue:

"In the wake of her moves she is self-assured.
In the realm of her thoughts she's been here before.
Through the deep in her eyes she's an opened door.
From her head to her toes she is often more."

I play the easy but perfectly aligned chords on the acoustic guitar with the melody that I whisper-sing. I embellish the song with a repeating chorus which seems to tie the song up with an opinion. My opinion of someone I might or might not know.

Chorus:
"Don't try to count her out, she's a mystery.
She'll start you thinking.
This world won't keep her down, she will rise again.
She's only sleeping."

I then compare her once again to the moonlight and its shadows. I remember holding her close, a long moment that had me not even wanting to try to figure her out, but I was feeling imprisoned and free all at once. A moment I wanted to last an eternity.

"You feel her heart, but you can't know it
As you recognize it's beat.
It doesn't change, although she's different
Each time your feelings meet.
Pretend to know, while she's relating then,
You might understand.
What she's about, 'cause what she's saying is:
'Catch me if you can'."

I was beaming like the full moon, thinking, "Did she write this, or did I?" I can feel her here but I can't see her. I was ecstatic, and don't remember writing lyrics this deep in such a short period of time. Come to think of it, I don't remember ever writing lyrics this good! Chords, melody, lyrics, the song is complete. I'm missing her tonight, but writing this has eased that pain, but in truth, I'm not sure I was thinking about only her. This was the first night since we've met that I haven't seen her, although it was only two nights ago that we were first acquainted. There's yet another woman that comes to mind with these same feelings, only with her they're more abysmal, or profound. Spell or no spell, I feel like I must be truly in love, with somebody. I know that when I'm with her I feel like I've always been with her. This is an awesome feeling and I don't want it to ever end.

Nick, Nancy, Flash and I went to the recording studio for the mix down, while Cuz would stop by later after his make-up dinner with Stephanie. It was a Tuesday, and I tried in vain not to think about Angeline. I haven't heard from her, and I have no way of contacting her, and needless to say, I'm missing her, but as they say, 'life goes on.'

We arrived at the studio, and Flash, Nancy and I walked in while Nick parked the van. We heard the tunes playing in the room while they were at the sound board in the sound proof room mixing. Two of the engineers were there, sitting with Jackie, and his fiance. Not being able to see clearly through the window I walked in, and it was a complete shocker to me as Jackie stood up and said, "Stan, I'd like you to meet my fiance Angeline. But you can call her Cookie. Everyone else does."

It was her! My Angeline! Only Angeline was wearing sunglasses and sporting a shiner, a black eye! She just looked down, instead of acknowledging me. I couldn't see those eyes.

Jackie finishes the intros as the others walked in. "Nancy, Hank, meet my gorgeous fiance, Cookie. Angeline was wearing the sunglasses to try to cover the bruise, but Nancy picked up on it right away, as she reached and removed them from her face. Nancy, not one for discretion, asked Angeline, "Who did this to you?" Then she looked over at Jackie and said louder, "Did *YOU* do this to her?"

You see, we had heard through Gus, the flute player who knew him and had told stories about Jackie, that Jackie's been known to punch, kick, and even push women he involves himself with, down stairs, and on one occasion, off of a balcony into a swimming pool. His women show up places bruised and on crutches. Then they sometimes disappear, never to be heard from again. I took these stories in stride at the time, not giving them much credit; until now. I just looked at Angeline in total disbelief and anger because I didn't want to believe she was engaged to this fucking asshole! I didn't say a word, because I didn't get the chance.

Nancy repeated herself, louder, "DID *YOU* DO THIS TO HER?"

Not one for conversing with women on any kind of intelligent level, Jackie took his hand and placed the whole thing palm first, fingers and all, over Nancy's face and said, "Why don't you fuck off!" and shoved her face and head backwards knocking her into me, and we both went tumbling back. Luckily for us, Nick had arrived to break mine and Nancy's fall. However, this proved to be unlucky for Jackie Clark . . . very unlucky!

Nick pushed me aside and went right to Nancy.
"Are you OK?" he asked, gently stroking her face.
"Yes", she said, "But it looks like Jackie hit his . . ."

Nancy never got the chance to finish, as Nick turned and dove into Jackie, and started pounding the living daylights out of him. Angeline, crying, walked up to my side and just stood there with me watching the slaughter, neither of us lifting a hand to try and stop it. I'll even say, due to the circumstances I was kind of enjoying it. I've broken up every other fight I've ever seen, and being in construction, there were a lot of fights. Call me ignorant if you will, but I just didn't feel compelled in any way, to try to stop this one. As odd as it sounds, I was mostly enjoying feeling Angeline's warmth on my right as she just stood quietly next to me.

Nick was eventually pulled off by the engineer and Walter Hahn, as they told him and us to get out, and said something about a breach of contract. Why not? They have their material now, only it looks like Jackie will need dental work, a face lift, and a walker for a while. Too bad.

I left the studio with a hole in my heart, as Angeline just stood there. 'Who was this person?' I thought, and still felt her inside me, and that didn't go away, as I was somehow still smitten. I was really beginning to believe in sorcery, or whatever this hold was she had on me.

Flash drove the van because Nick was too upset, though I really think he was just tired from all of that punching. Flash hit me with another bombshell, saying, "I had no idea that girl was his fiance," he said, "I was with her for a couple of dates a few months back. She had the other eye black then. She said she got it from a fishing pole or something."

"What do you mean you were with her? 'You went out with her too?"

I was starting to wonder where this girl's head was. "Yeah," Flash went on, "I had no idea about her and fuckhead. I just liked her. We shot pool and I took her home. I thought I was out of my league with her, but she pretty much dumped me anyway."

"Why did she dump you?" I asked.

"She said she wasn't my type, after she dressed like wonder woman for me." Flash just smiled and said, "But look at the type of assholes she prefers!"

I never told a soul about Angeline and me. That's a part of my life that would always be a secret, at least at that moment in time. Nancy said, "I doubt she prefers him. Something must be going on there, for her to stay with that piece of shit."

"Leave it alone Nancy," Nick said as she held him.

"No, I won't leave it alone," she slammed back; "I'm afraid that all of this is going to come to a head real soon. I think it's best if we . . ."

Nick cut her off once again, "Leave it alone Nancy!"

She kept quiet and we just all rode in silence for a while until Flash said, "I guess this means we need day jobs again."

The next day I drove out to Long Beach Island to walk the sandy beach and the edge of the surf. I wandered and did a lot of thinking and wondering. I even thought I'd somehow run into her if I walked far enough, but I didn't. I must have walked ten miles up and down the Jersey coast. I got back into my car and drove home, looking at every Jeep wrangler that passed me, and I made it home by nightfall.

That night a knock came to the door, and it was Runx, who had Gus with him, carrying his flute as usual. Runx was sorry to hear about the whole misfortune, regarding the studio and record company. "I heard he blackened Angeline's eye again. Boy, that asshole doesn't deserve her," Runx said, "So Nick lit into him because of that?"

"No," I told him, "Nick ripped him up because of him hitting Nancy."

"Hitting Nancy? Wow, I'm surprised Jackie's still alive," Gus said.

Runx then said, "I can tell you now, I've been having an affair with Angeline for the longest time during her and Jackie's entire engagement period."

Once again, I'm hit hard with a surprising statement, wondering if anything in the universe was sacred.

"Really? 'You're still involved with her?" I asked.

"No, not really, not now. About a week ago I tried to have a rendezvous with her and she shot me down. She said she found her soul mate, or something of that sort; go figure, look at the asshole she chose." Runx shook his head and continued, "She only came on to me because she needed something else, and I obliged. I really liked her too, except that I wouldn't fall for her, fall under her spell. I even wrote a song about her, about a witch on a sea shore calling out to men, only to take, then break their hearts and spirits," Runx said, smiling an evil grin.

Confused, I kept everything to myself, and ask him, "So you think that Angeline's a witch?"

"No Stan," he said, "it's just a figure of speech within the song. Artistic license. She has some very strange ideas regarding sex though, I loved it."

"Strange ideas?" Gus asked.

"Yeah, she wore a chef's hat, and forced me to lay naked on her kitchen counter, buttering me up like a roasted..."

"Alright," I said interrupting him, "too much information!"

After that ridiculous revelation by Runx, Gus said that he too was dating her, despite her being engaged, and that about a week ago, she told him the same thing, that she found her soul mate.

"I was pretty broken up about it," Gus said, "but I respected her decision good or bad. I just think it's too bad it's Jackie."

"How do you know it's Jackie she's talking about?" I bellowed, "I mean that if she was engaged to him for over a year, and you both were dating her then, why in hell would she discover him as a soul mate now?"

"Easy there chief," Gus said smiling. "Don't get your bowels in an uproar. Why would you care one way or another? Anyway, I heard he's home from the hospital and she's making him a nice dinner tonight to ease the pain that Nick fed to him last night."

They both laughed and I'm sorry to say, it got me laughing and crying at the same time. Fortunately, no one noticed the crying, and Gus as Runx were now heading out the door. To hear she was making him a nice dinner was too much for me to take in right now, especially after hearing about her sexcapades with these guys.

"So, I guess all of you guys were laid off?" Runx asked grinning.

"We're in disposal I guess." I told them.

"You guys will find something." Runx said, "You're pretty good."

"Hey," Gus said, "Why don't you get a lawyer and take Bobcat Records to court?" Runx then looked at Gus with a sneer, and backtracking the conversation said, "I didn't know you were seeing her too, you slime dog".

"See ya'" I told them, shutting the door, and went to the kitchen, putting on a teapot to fix myself some chamomile. I fed my cat 'Mr. Charlie' and I sat down to look once again at the lyrics of my newly written song without a name, then there was another knock at the door. Thinking it's probably those two again I opened it up saying, "What did you forget?"

To my surprise, it was Angeline.

"I want to explain," she said crying. She didn't have her sun glasses this time and she just leaned her head on my shoulder and I held it firm, as she sobbed like a little baby. We went in to sit down and I offered her a cup of tea. She said she meant to tell me about Jackie, but she wanted to end it with him first. She also said she had no idea that I was in his band.

"I just don't understand how you could lead me on and deceive me without any kind of remorse and do it so well without me even picking up on it," I told her.

"I didn't lie about my feelings," She said, "I was genuine in revealing my feelings for you. I'm going to end it with him, but it's all very complicated," she said.

"You get up and you leave! How complicated is that?" I asked, and continued, "I just don't know if I can believe you, finding out tonight that not only did you cheat on him, with me, but you were even having affairs with Hank, and Runx, and even that fuckin' Gus! Gus and Runx said you stopped seeing them just last week because you finally found your soul mate. . . 'your soul mate Jackie?"

Angeline was now totally composed, and asserted, "My soul mate is whoever I feel comfortable with at the time!" she said with a soft confident smile; and looking through me once again with those blue-green eyes continued, "Last weekend with you was the best of times. I enjoyed every minute of it because we were in synch spiritually and emotionally that night, and I believed our souls touched, actually touched"

"Hogwash," I said aggravated.

"Tell me something Stan, do you remember meeting me at Woodstock?"

"Woodstock?" I asked. "We met at Woodstock?"

"Yes," she continued, "don't you remember? I handed you a joint while walking in during Joan Baez . . . You were with a young hottie, and when I handed you the joint, you asked me if you knew me." Angeline kept trying to jolt my memory; "I also caught a catfish with you that following morning."

"You were that girl?" I asked surprised, "That same girl I saw that morning catching the catfish?"
"By the way," she said, "That catfish was as stubborn as you. I wish you would have joined me for breakfast back then."
"Your twin sister was too scary for me," I told her.
"Twin?" She looked at me with an uncomfortable glare, then lightened up her stare and said, "Lila's still crazy, but I haven't seen much of her."
"So, you're Eve?" I asked.
"Short for 'Evangeline'", she said. " I was tired of 'Eve' and I just liked 'Angeline' better."
She took my hand and told me to look into her eyes, "You can see me now can't you Stan? You know I would never intentionally hurt you. Knowing you from Woodstock was what made me choose you for the full moon ritual. No one else would have been sufficient."
"What full moon ritual?" I asked.
Ignoring me, she said, "You have to promise me something. You have to promise me you won't say a word to anyone what I'm about to tell you."
I was getting nervous because this could be anything at this point, but being stupid, I wanted to know.
"I promise. What's the next big mystery?" I asked sarcastically.
She began to tell me an unbelievable story, but true enough in her eyes for me to believe.

"The Bobcat Record Company is not just a record company, Stan, it's a front for an operation that's into smuggling and selling drugs, and other narcotics. Jackie's dad is a top sales rep for a big pharmaceutical company, and he's also a wheeler dealer, or rather 'pusher' for the oxycodone, hydrocodone, pharmaceutical cocaine, and codeine, to name just a few. They sell it on the black market, and in the streets, and have an army of people working for them; a mob, if you will. There have been hits made; murders, directed at anyone who puts their secret operation in jeopardy. Jackie's previous girlfriends have not just been beaten, but have mysteriously disappeared, and Jackie's own father is one of the ones butchering them and disposing of them. It's something his father actually gets off on, as Jackie once told me. Hell, I've seen it first hand when I was younger."

"When you were younger?" I asked, "How long have you. . . ?"

"Never mind," she cut me off keeping her train of thought, "I was afraid I'd be next if I didn't take the steps I took tonight."

"What steps were those?"

"You'll see by tomorrow."

"How the hell did you get caught up in this in the first place?" I asked her.

"Innocently enough. I knew him since I was a teenager. I went out with him on a date. He was good looking, charming, and I just kind of liked him. Then I found out he was well-to-do so it kind of made the pot sweeter and kept me away from very bad things happening to me in my life at that time. I knew I didn't love him but as most people do in relationships, I settled. I'm ashamed to say that I fell for the tempting free ride, as it were."

"You were a gold digger."

"No, not at all, but I wasn't completely happy with him. I only went back to him recently and he asked me to marry him. It's always been hard for me to commit to any relationship. Thus, entered the sideline flings. You know; Hank, and the Runx, and Gus . . . "

"OK, OK, I get it," I interrupted, "So how did you find out about the illegal goings on in the realm of Jackie?"

"It wasn't just Jackie, it was important for the Bobcat people to be closer to Jackie's father, and that's where Jackie comes in, with the recording and the bands. You guys, the Lost Marbles, must have been another attached modification for them, making for a better cover, and they could also make money off of the recordings. It all had to look legitimate and they only have three or four 'name' acts for recording, while the rest is small potatoes like Jackie."
"Or us", I said.
"No," she said, "I heard that you guys weren't ever going to make a record, or if you did, they were going to simply shelve it."
"And you never knew I was part of the band, until, maybe . . ."
"Yesterday," she said, "when I saw you come into the control room," she said, with a tear.
Jackie, Walter Hahn, Robert DeMos, the engineers, they're all very bad people and need to be stopped," she said, and added, "I'm sorry you were involved in this way, Stan."
I gave her a hug, and I asked if she was going to go home to Jackie tonight.
"I still live in Lambertville, and that's where I'm going tonight," she told me, "Jackie's done, from now on, as far as I'm concerned."
She sat and after a pause softly spoke,
"I made him a dinner of fresh Dungeness crab soup tonight, and now I'm leaving, and you won't be seeing me for a while."
She gave me a long hug and said, "You won't be able to find me if I make it out of this crap alive."
'What the hell are you talking about?" I asked, still confused.
 She pulled me over and sat me down and said, continuing in her slowly spoken soft tone, "If anything happens

to me you need to go to this place. It's in this area right in Lake Nockamixon," showing me a map drawn of a path to a secluded cove along the lake. "There's a weighed down, sealed chest that is in about 20 feet of water, containing 7 million dollars in cash. Jackie has it hidden from his father and the rest of them, money skimmed off of the top of their profits, and I'm not supposed to know about it. His father knows it's missing but has an idea I might know about it so I want you to recover it, if anything happens to me. I don't want his father ever finding it. The case also has a patent or something he had stolen from another pharmaceutical group, and evidence of murder, that would put him away for life. He was ruthless in murdering four innocent people for this, and he stands to make billions, if he finds the chest. Jackie always had and held this over him, for some control... like a form of blackmail I suppose." Then she said, "Jackie also mentioned something about sorcery, and a wedding ring hidden in there, but that's another story for another time."

She gave me a big hug, and she said something to me before she left. "Remember this?" And pulling open her blouse, she revealed she was wearing that very sexy teddy, the one she wore while cooking last week. In a few moves that could only be matched by Houdini, she had the nighty off, and in her hand. She put it in mine and said, "I want you to keep this for me. Give it to me when you see me next time." Within the garment was a sack of tiny rocks.
"Diamonds," she said, "Don't let anything happen to them, please! I trust you!" She gave me another hug and kiss, then she was gone. I was remembering my hallucinating evening with her, and the diamonds I saw, or thought I saw? I wondered if these were those alleged peculiar diamond like barnacles that were attached to the shells of those creatures she had eaten. Were diamonds being smuggled into that

Siren's club on those lobsters? My imagination? . . . stupidity? . . . or both?

I kept thinking about all of this mob-like jargon, 'contracts', assassinations, witness protection, and lifestyles of the rich and devious, and I seriously wondered if this was really reality, and how the hell did I ever get to this place in my life?

Everything seemed to be going very well for a while, and then, Pow, one fight from Nick and everything is knocked down like a stack of dominoes. I felt like I was in the midst of chaos, confusion, love, hate, and corruption. This pandemonium cluttered my disorganized turmoil with a disarray of lawlessness and anarchy. What was once, supposed to be a musician's dream, with a potential forthcoming of an impending and promising future, turned out to be a nightmare of bedlam. I could go on, but this would only drive me further into insanity. So, for now, I'm going to do what any red-blooded American would do in a situation such as this, I'm going to get drunk!

I headed out to a bar by the river, and as I walked in I saw that the pool table was taken and the bar was full, except for one stool, which I immediately occupied. It was between two women, who's faces I couldn't see since they were facing away from me. One of them had long light brown hair, pulled to the side and over her shoulder laying across the front of a fishnet top with nothing underneath. I tried not to look at it when she leaned into me to say 'hi', with breath that smelled like she had been there all day. I heard the brown-haired girl on the other side of me say "Say, tall dark and lonely, can I buy you a drink?" It was Nancy, without Nick.

"Sure," I said, "if you let me buy you one." She and I talked about what just happened, but she changed the subject before I could elaborate.

"I think you guys could do well with the right management," she said abruptly.

"Who did you have in mind?" I asked her suggestively raising a brow toward her.

"No, not me," she said and continued, "I'm more of a farm girl. I want to be a homebody for my man."

She took a sip of wine and added, "whoever that might be."

I was surprised at her statement and repeated it, "Whoever that might be?" She glanced at me and changed the subject, "This place was here for years, and I bet that these patrons around us had parents that stood on this same floor, under this same roof, doing exactly what they're doing now." I was quiet as she took another sip saying, "Did you know that the mule barges used to have layovers at this very bar over two hundred years ago?" I looked her in her pretty brown eyes and said, "No, I did not. Are you a history buff?"

"No," she said, "I just like to read about things like that."

She and I talked for a while and I didn't want to get drunk anymore. We hugged, then went our separate ways, into the dark night.

PART TWO

Chapter 10

Chaos and Readjustment

I was awakened by my hysterical room-mate, as Cousin Benny was freaking out. He was first upset about finding out about all of the Bobcat studio fighting and firing the other night, now he hits me with yet another bomb.
"Stan, Stan, wake up! Holy shit!
"What's up Cuz?"
"It's Jackie Clark. Jackie Clark is dead!"
"Dead?"
"Dead! He was found in his home. He suffocated, or choked, or something like that."
I was really curious now after what I heard last night but I promised confidentiality.
"Was it, murder?"
"They're not sure, it's under investigation. They say it might have been some kind of food poisoning. He was allergic to some seafood. They say that's what he ate last night."
"Oh . . . Oooohhhhh . . . " I said with another oh. I think I understand now. "Somebody said that it may be because of his bruises from getting beat up the other night and they might indict Nick for manslaughter."

"That's ridiculous," I said.
"That's just what I heard." And he walked out the door.

I got dressed and put on a pot of 100% Columbian coffee. Then I thought, "Good. The Lord giveth, the Lord taketh awayeth." That's all of the praying he deserves from me, the murdering fiance beater. There was a knock at the door. It was Nick and Nancy. I offered them some coffee.
"Did you hear?" Nick asked. "Yes," I said, "You guys want cream and sugar?"
"No sugar for me," Nancy said. Nick said, "Cream and sugar for me please."
"I have to tell you something Stan, and I don't want you to get upset, OK?"
"What is it Nick?"
"This whole Bobcat deal, you don't know the half of it."
"Then why don't you tell me the half of it?"
"He's going to tell you the whole thing," Nancy said gloating.
"Let me talk Nancy"
"OK, Talk."
"Bobcat is a shady outfit. They're into a lot of crooked shit. They're full of bad, bad people and they're in a position where they're very dangerous, only because their operation is about to blow wide open."
Nick continued to tell me pretty much what Angeline had told me last night. He told me about the music end of it and how that's a cover for the real operation which was the narcotics, and other shady pharmaceuticals. He added a few more things which I didn't hear, like how his position in this is part of a government sting operation and how we all played a part so far in it, unbeknownst to us! I'd be lying if I said I wasn't upset; I sure was. I knew Nick was affiliated with the government somehow since his paratrooper days, but I didn't know how involved, since he and Nancy were

always tight about it. How could he drag us all into this operation without us knowing, like playing us as pawns in a chess game.

"It wasn't like that at all," he said. "You were all into the music like I was. We were going to make albums. That would have all come to pass if . . . "

"If you didn't fuck up and pummel that asshole Jackie," I told him.

"No, something else happened," he said. "He was killed last night by his fiance Angeline. She fed him shellfish knowing he was allergic to it."

"If he knew he himself was allergic to it, why did he eat it? He's not stupid," I said.

"She got him drunk," he said, "fed him Dungeness crab soup and he, stupid drunk, and high on pain killers ate it."

"That's not murder, is it? She can just say she didn't know."

Nick nodded his head and said, "Yes she can, but they have a million dollars and lawyers that will contest that. They want heads to roll and they're coming after me too."

"If they're a mob, do you think there's a contract out on you?" I asked him.

"No doubt. But this whole sting is going to come down before that, I hope. I'm telling you about all of this because I'm closer to you than the others, and I trust you. Do me a favor, don't mention anything of what I just told you to anyone".

I had to ask him, "Is Angeline in on this sting operation too?"

"No, she's just his fiance, or was. Now the law will indict her too."

"Nick, I have to tell you something. Angeline and I have been seeing each other."

I told Nick about the shore, the dinner, the time we spent together, and how I feel about her and her feelings for me. Then I asked him if there's any way, her knowing what she probably knows about them, that she could be granted some kind of immunity and maybe testify; and be put into a witness protection program.

"That's always a possibility and I shouldn't be telling you this, but I think they're actually counting on her doing that. I hope she's aware of that too." he told me. "Are you absolutely sure she feels the same way about you?"
I looked at him and said, "Absolutely!"

He and Nancy both finished their coffee, gave me a hug, and left, but Nancy came back once more to tell me not to worry about anything, and that everything will be alright. She looked into my eyes, and I felt her right in my soul, as she softly said, "Make sure you know what you want in your heart."

Then she hugged me again, and slowly walked away. I realized what a lucky man Nick was, to have Nancy, and for a moment I envied him, as I watched her walk out the door.

Before the fall of 1977 I found another job. The masonry company wouldn't take me back until they had an opening, so I got into the drywall business. I linked up with a guy who was sub-contracting for a drywall company. Alex Hopper was about my height and age and lived with a girlfriend who used to come to the farmhouse for our parties. He was looking for a helper when he ran into me at the convenience store, where he was covered with spackle and I coincidently asked if he's hiring. He told me he'd pay me $3.00 an hour to start, so I told him to count me in!

He's going to train me on the production tools, and basics of drywall finishing, so now I have a job, some income, and now all I need is for the band to get back together.

We were rehearsing our Tuesdays and Thursdays again, and everything seemed like it was rolling along smoothly as time passed. A lot has happened, such as, the Bobcat Record Company had folded, and Jackie's father, Walter Hahn, Robert DeMos, and some of the engineers, along with about 20 others nationwide, were now doing time, big time, thanks to Angeline's testimony.

There was also a rumor that she herself, had murdered three of the bigtime dealers connected to the corporation, for brutally killing one of her girlfriends, right in front of her, but the lawyers could supply no proof. That particular story had Angeline luring them in for sex, doping these proposed victims up, stripping them naked, tying them to chairs facing each other, and then, naked herself, flayed the skin off of them in front of each other while they watched, then beheaded them like fish, one at a time while they were still alive. At least that's what Bobcat's defense attorneys came up with to discredit her testimony as a witness. The word is out now that she was killed, murdered by a hit man, but I didn't believe it. I know it sounds corny, but I can feel her in me, and I knew she was alive somewhere, but I kept that thought to myself.

Chapter 11

Lost Marbles New Management

It was now 1979, and Nick met up with me at Sally's Bar in Lansdale, where we were talking to the owner about us playing a gig within that establishment. Nick was still very calm, despite the rumors that there was a contract out on him, but we haven't seen anything yet that might lead us to believe that these rumors are true. We were still a band, playing now at local bars, performing what the people wanted to hear, which was classic rock and blues standards.

We were staying away from the original songs for now, doing standard classics and blues, and although we had day jobs and were getting by, we were still young, and in being young we wanted a little more than just this. We were not ready to settle as a local band playing local taprooms, and there was a thought that we might be able to record our own songs, push them ourselves with our own promoting, and maybe set up an east coast tour at bars and other venues as a new original act. That was the main reason that Nick wanted to meet up with me, having this idea that we can do it on our own, without record companies and with a lot of hard work and sacrifice on our parts.

Cuz walked in the door and sat down next to me, so I bought him a shot and a beer and had the same. Nick was quiet while I unraveled the idea to Cuz about the band and what Nick's idea was, but Nick just kind of looking down, and I thought something was up.

A man at the end of the bar was getting up, paying for his drinks, and with a six pack under his arm was walking out, having to pass Nick, Cuz and me to get to the door. I wasn't paying him much mind but I sensed something with Nick, and as this man was passing us, he pulled a switch blade out from under the six pack he was carrying, and before it could be buried into Nick's back, Nick had a hold of his forearm, and I could hear the snap as he broke it in half, pulling it down over his head. The man screamed in pain until Nick plunged the knife into his temple, shutting him up instantly. Cuz and I were up on our feet by this time in shock, but Nick, who barely stood during the whole encounter, if he stood at all, downed his beer almost like nothing had happened and said, "We'd better go."

We all left, without saying a word to each other, in separate vehicles and I was on my way home, not knowing what the hell was behind any of that skirmish we just witnessed. I watched Nick actually kill somebody and now I'm on my way home.

At home Cuz met me at our front door and asked, "What the fuck was that? What the hell is going on with him? Should we call the police?"
"I wouldn't, but I'm sure someone already did," I told him, "I'm as taken aback as you are about all of this."

I put on some tea, took off my shoes, and tried to relax for an hour in solitude while Cuz went to bed. I finally stopped shaking; and wondered to myself if I should be doing anything now, regarding tonight's episode. I couldn't come up with anything, other than turning off the lights and going into a sound, well deserved sleep.

There was a knock at the door first thing in the morning. It was Nick. "Have you guys seen Nancy?" he asked in a desperate tone.
"Why? What's up?" Cuz asked.
"She wasn't home when I went to sleep last night, and she wasn't there this morning."

Just then there was a knock, and the door flew open. It was Nancy.

"Nick!" she said, "Are you alright?"

Nick gave her a hug and said, "Where were you?"

"I left before you got up, and you didn't hear me come in last night because I didn't want to wake you. I just found out about Sally's. What happened?"

"The old man, Mr. Clark. He's reaching out from prison. 'Tried to give me a calling card last night but his goon's contract was terminated."

"So that was someone with a 'contract'?" I asked.

"Is this stuff over now that you snuffed him?" Cuz asked.

"I don't want to talk about that." Nick said.

"Far from over," Nancy added.

"We won't talk about it," Nick said. "There's bigger fish to fry," he said.

"There is a guy from the Philadelphia radio station that was playing some of our stuff on the air," Nick told us changing the subject.

"What stuff? We didn't record any stuff," Cuz said. Just then Flash walked in holding a new set of drumsticks tapping them in triple paradiddles on our shoulders and backs as he walked by.

"We didn't, but remember the stuff we did at the theater? The stuff before the asshole, I mean before Jackie came up to play?"

"You were right the first time," Flash said grinning, "And yeah, that whole show was tight. It's a shame we didn't record it." Then Flash pointed with his drumstick at a spot, on Nancy's shirt, right at her breast, and asked her if she was leaking.

"You're a pig," was Nancy's response.

"That's what I'm trying to say," Nick responded.

"That I'm a pig?" Flash asked.

"No, that someone *did* record it, the show at the theater, and it sounds great! That's the stuff that's getting played on that station. I opened a letter from the guy this morning."
Nick looked over at Nancy, handing her the letter that was in his hand while he continued telling us about it.
"And I was looking to tell you, Nancy, but you were nowhere to be found." Nick continued directing his attention to Nancy.
"With what happened last night at the bar, I became worried about you," he told her.

Nancy started reading the letter as I kept shaking my head.
I said to Nick, "I want to talk about the letter, but really Nick, what's going on with you?" I asked firmly. "Cuz and I were a little devastated about what we saw at Sally's last night."
"I took care of it," Nick said, "Don't worry. The cops already know and I'm going down there now for an interrogation, so they can investigate."
"What songs are being played on the radio?" Flash asked.
"'Rock and Roll Radio' and 'Sing those Blues'," Nancy said reading the letter.
"They actually made a single with side A and side B," Nick said. "It's been getting airplay in Philadelphia and now they're playing it on New York stations. They want the band to perform it live, but they want to know who our agent is."
"Our agents are in jail," I said.
"They are NOT our agents anymore. Technically we own the rights, whether they think so or not, right Nick?" Cuz said.
"Right as rain," Nick said. "Just because we were under the now liquidated Bobcat company for the performance doesn't make them the owners of this so called 'bootleg'

they're playing on the radio now. The musicians and songwriters have full legal jurisdiction over the material as far as we're concerned."
"So, what's our next step?" Flash asked.
"I'll get 'hold of the people," Nancy chimed in with a serious and determined tone, "I'm declaring myself the agent."
"I was hoping you would." Nick said with a smile. "Anybody have any objections to Nancy taking care of this for us? As our agent?"

There were no objections since we all knew Nancy would be the perfect agent for the band. She's intelligent, level headed, assertive, attractive, and also Nick's better half, making us all confident with that in itself. Someone has to push us forward, and the best person for the job just volunteered, so what more could we want right now?

Nick was cleared by the law, as expected, and was aware that these attempts on his life could happen again. Like Vietnam all over again, he was always looking over his shoulder, only now it was in the land of the free, his homeland, by a 'so called' American who's doing time, apparently seeking revenge over the death of his moron son, Jackie Clark.

The police are unable to prove anything, but we all knew, and Nick handled all of this pretty well. This was no surprise to Flash, Cuz, or I as we all knew him as solid and stable, and although this looked like a present threat to him, we all still felt that because this was 'Nick', we knew he seemed to have some kind of an invisible shield protecting him and anyone around him.

Nancy, feeling the same way of course, was unmoved by any of the supposed threat and pursued our careers with her calls and meetings with the Philadelphia and New York radio stations that were interested, and her goal of making us famous.

The Lost Marbles had put together a package containing pictures, a bio, and of course the 45-rpm record containing 'Rock and Roll Radio', and Sing Those Blues'. We had Nancy take charge of shipping them and doing the interviews for now, as more and more radio stations were becoming interested in finding out who these 'Lost Marbles' were. We also continued our present gigs at the local bars, which were Sally's, The Sport's Castle, Brick Oven, and Paul's Place. There were also new venues now in Philadelphia on Market and South Streets where the newly recorded single was now apparently in demand. After a month of playing and doing the day jobs we were all ready for the first of the South Street gigs in Philly. We were also asking for more money and playing four nights a week. Cuz, Nick, Flash, and I had quit our day jobs again, because of exhaustion and irresponsible episodes by some of us.

Flash was drunk after a South street gig at Dapper Dan's, a club that had name acts from time to time. They'd have everyone from the nationally known artists to local acts, and we were trying to get into the loop, since we were sounding great; actually, having an encore that particular night.

The way the place was set up was, you walk right into the bar off of South street and the band would set up about 100 feet toward the back, down a 30 feet wide corridor that has the bar on one side and tables and chairs on the other. The walls were full of pictures of bands and artists who have played here. Dead Kennedys, Elvis, Jerry Garcia, Gary Mosier, Strange Death, Robert Hazzard, and even a picture of Jackie Clark. The bands would load in from the street and walked the equipment through the people to the band stand. There was an alley in the back, but with no room for vehicles to pull in and load.

Anyway, it was a royal pain in the ass, and even the bigger name acts were subject to this, only they had roadies doing the bull work. Once the place was packed with people, the door man would cut people off from coming in due to a fire safety hazard.

After having a great gig, and a packed house, and after we were all loaded up, we were on our way north. Flash downed a double shot of bourbon and a mug of draft at the bar then a quart of beer on the sidewalk before entering his Buick Skylark. He was off before anyone could say anything to him, and fortunately, he didn't have any band equipment or instruments with him. What happened next was sketchy but as I recall the story as Flash told it to me, it was this:

He was driving north on Route 611 and made a right onto Cheltenham Avenue. Coming down the ramp, he dodged a Dodge and then jockeyed his way into the center lane, which came to an abrupt end, and his car was now stopped, resting on a concrete medial wall. He opened another quart of Schmidt's beer, guzzled it down, and went to sleep. A police officer pulled up next to the vehicle, and with a flashlight looked inside. He somehow overlooked Flaming Hank in the back seat on the floor under a blanket, so the officer put a sticker on the car and called a tow truck to remove and impound the vehicle. Flash heard the officer leaving and got out of the car, resting on the medial wall, and scratching his head, wondered what he could do about his predicament, when he saw three big dudes coming over to see if he was alright.

"Hey man! 'You OK?" one of them asked. He was a large, big built Afro-American man with a billowing afro haircut and a full beard. They all appeared to be very friendly while

another, a big lean, clean shaven white dude with an Elvis style haircut, sideburns and all, said:
"Yeah, 'you need any help?" The third guy, with dark hair and a goatee, who was a bit smaller and looked Hispanic remained quiet.
"Ohh, I'm alright," Flash said. "I might need help in getting this here automobile off of this wall though."

They surrounded the front bumper and with Flash's help, they managed to lift the front of the car off of the wall.

Being grateful, Flash shook their hands and gave them his last $20 as a tip for helping him, but they shoved him over the concrete median and laughing aloud, jumped into poor Hank's car that they just freed from the concrete guard rail. They spun out and up Cheltenham Avenue, disappearing quickly with his Buick, into the smoke and the smell of burning rubber.

"I'll be a son of a bitch! They just stole my car, and I gave them my last $20.00!"

Flash was pissed, but at least he still had some small change on him, because there just happened to be a phone booth on the corner where he immediately made a dime call to the police reporting his car stolen. He of course lied, told them it was stolen by carjackers at 611 and Cheltenham avenue an hour or so earlier, thus covering the time when the cop was putting the abandoned sticker on the car. A different cop came by to pick Flash up and take him down to the police station where he finished the story, covering his bases. Flaming Hank called me, but by that time I was home in bed sleeping my own exhausting night off. When I answered the phone, he told me the whole stupid story and added that he needed a ride.

His Buick was found by the Delaware river without the mag wheels and the chrome steering wheel. His insurance company gave him the money to buy a brand, new vehicle, which he used it to restore his 1970 VW Bug. His resourcefulness was commendable but didn't change the fact that the band was getting pissed at these drunken excursions.

Another time, shortly following his break up with a young lady named Katie who he was seeing for about a year, he ended up at Rocky's Bar, one of his favorite watering holes near Lake Nockamixon. He was sitting alone, brooding and talking about how fucked up women are and asserting this to anyone who would listen. The bartender kept serving him shots and beers and was consoling him with free hardboiled eggs.

Soon, his ex, Katie, walked into the bar with her new boyfriend, waved and introduced the big man to Flash, "Bert, this is my friend I was telling you about, Hank. Hank, this is Bert," then she leaned on Bert, kissing his cheek and whispering something in his ear causing Bert to break out with a laugh as he looked right at Flash saying nothing, and shaking his head.

Flash peered down into his own beer and just sulked, and next time he looked up he witnessed them arm in arm, walking out the door. He ordered another shot and beer and revealed out loud for anyone to hear, "I think that's fucked up that my ex can just stroll in here like she owns the place. She has a lot of nerve coming in here, period! Let alone with that asshole!"

The bartender brought him his order and he downed his shot like a cowboy and started drinking his beer. There was a couple sitting across the bar looking at him and the woman eventually commented to Flash, "It's a free country. She can do what she wants, 'go where she wants. . . "

The woman had short blonde hair and a round face, was a bit stocky, but seemed small and younger in comparison to her boyfriend who looked like a weight lifter. He was in his 30's and thinning up top and sported a full beard beneath a permanent frown. He was quiet, but attentive and glaring at Hank now, with frown turning to a derisive grin.

"I know it's a free country," Flash said, "but we have an unwritten rule since we broke up. That rule is that she doesn't come into the bars I go to, and I won't go to the bars she goes to."

"I didn't think that there were any rules once a relationship is done," she said. "It sounds like you're trying to control her. I think it's time for you to let go of her."

"You don't know what the hell you're talking about, "Flash said.

"That's what you think," She said taking a sip of her drink.

"You know what I think?" Flash said.

"What do you think," the woman answered.

Flash, mockingly holding his head high with pride, glared with a smile right into the woman's eyes; and with a drunken slur, the pompously half-witted and thoroughly inebriated ex-marine proudly quipped:

"I think you're a lesbian!"

The man sitting next to her slammed his beer mug down breaking the handle and Flash pointed to him and still looking at her added,

"And your little dog too, Dorothy."

"That did it," the bearded man said, "You and me, are stepping outside right now!"

Flash said, "Two things; number one, you're right, 'Toto', we are stepping outside, and number two, I still think she's a lesbian!" He was apparently into a 'Wizard of Oz' drunk, where he gets into naming his surrounding rabble after the movie's characters.

Flash walked out of the bar's front door first and headed out back, with the big guy following right behind him. In his mind, he heard the guy creeping ever closer while he continued moving his way into the darkness. Flash swung his arm around hoping to catch the big guy in the jaw with his elbow but actually lost his balance and fell down. When he stood up the man cold cocked him in the jaw sending him right back down on his ass. He stood up but got a punch to the ribs, and another in the face giving him a black eye as he laid curled up on the ground. After a few seconds of peace, he felt sharp kicks to the ribs and groin area. He looked up to see that it was the girl he labeled as 'lesbian', doing the kicking and now cleaning the bottoms of her shoes on his face.

The big guy said to his girlfriend, "Stop, he's had enough I think." They both started laughing and he said to Flash, "That's for calling my girlfriend a lesbian, and for insulting my best friend 'Bert,' who was actually that guy you saw with your ex-girlfriend 'Katie'."
"Well, I hope they're very happy together," Flash said.

The couple who just kicked his ass walked away, leaving him there, and he literally slept there until daylight, and called me to come get him. "This can't go on," I told him. I arrived at Rocky's after only one cup of coffee and four hours sleep, but it was a Monday morning, and we had just had Sunday off to catch up on some well-needed rest. I drove him to his house where he was staying and they told me they didn't want him there anymore, and were coincidentally putting his clothes and other belongings onto the porch as we arrived.
"This is what's been bumming me out lately," he told me. "I just didn't want to say anything and bring you guys down. We've been doing well with the gigs and,"
"Enough!" I bellowed.
"What's the matter with you?" he asked me.

"What's the matter? I'll tell you 'what's the matter'! The matter is we HAVE been doing well and we want to keep on doing well! Tell me something Hank; where are you going to live now? You've been drinking yourself into oblivion on what appears to be a daily basis, and we've got important gigs coming up, and frankly, you're not participating as a team player any more. Flaming Hank seems to be on a separate team, the Flaming Hank narcissistic team!"

I guess I've been holding back for a long time, regarding Flash's escapades with drinking. Nick's been sticking up for him, enabling him to carry on, like it was meant to be part of our existence. I know I drink too, and I drink to excess when I feel the time is right, but so far it hasn't interfered with the function of the band and hasn't posed a threat to 'The Lost Marbles' teamwork.
"What the hell does 'narcissistic' mean?" he asked.
"It means you!" I told him.
"Look," Flash said, "Have I ever let you down with delivering a good drum groove?"
"No," I said.
"Have I ever missed a gig?"
"No".
"Have I ever missed a rehearsal?"
"No," I told him. But then I asked him, "What if we all did what you did?"
"What do you mean?" he asked.
"We're supposed to be a team and you should think of us like we think of you, all for one, one for all. But you don't think of anyone else, or how it affects us when you go off into these binges and self-centered tirades and we have to bail you out or take care of you." As I was talking to him I was beginning to think he was really listening and I took it a step further:

"Now imagine this for a minute Hank. What if we all got drunk where we lost our living space? Or our vehicles? Who would take care of us?"
"Nick would," he said.
"No Hank!" I belted out to him continuing, "I'm saying all of us. That means Nick, you, me, and Cuz. Where would we all go if we ALL started getting irresponsible, loaded, and not giving a shit, losing our apartments? house? vans? cars? Where would we go? Where would we rehearse? Do you see what I'm getting at? What do you think would happen to us if we were all selfish and didn't care about the other guy on the team? Who would take care of us then?"

Flash paused, and seemed to be actually thinking about what I had just said, with a deep look in his eyes, which were transfixed on something that wasn't there. Presented with the quandary, a mystery, as if soul searching the depths of life itself, and as if answering the age old mystic timeless conundrum, or an ancient riddle, he looked at me and then answered confidently without hesitation, "Nancy."
"You are without a doubt the most hopeless case I've ever seen!" I said. "You are the ultimate project for the beloved Saint Jude! Maybe he can help you. I sure as hell can't!"

Flaming Hank came to our house and crashed for now, since Nick told us to roll with it for the time being. Honestly, this will need to change soon or it will be the death of us as a band, or at least that's my present feelings.

Chapter 12

We're on A Roll

The gigs kept rolling in, one after another, as Nancy was managing us out of her new office over at her and Nick's place. We were booked all over the southeast corner of Pennsylvania and New Jersey, and were ready for the clubs in New York, but before we elevate ourselves to Manhattan, Nancy said we needed to make an album.

We've decided to use the same idea as the 45 'single', since we had the live recording from the County Theater gig. Cuz, Flash, Nick and I listened to it and decided unanimously that as a live recording it was flawless, so Nancy set us up with a guy who had the equipment and technology to make EP's and regular 33 rpm vinyl cuts. We fit all of the songs on both sides and called it "Lost Marbles Found Live," and were printing out 1000 copies at a time, selling them at the shows. Nancy hired people to sell the albums and T-Shirts wherever we had room at the gigs, and placing them in local record stores in Doylestown, Willow Grove, Glenside, Jenkintown, and as far north as Allentown.

By 1980 we were playing four to seven nights a week, and graduated to having equipment managers, who would load in and load out everything except our own guitars, which we insisted on carrying ourselves. The band started staying at hotels and motels, and eventually ending up moving entirely into Nancy's and Nick's house, which was big enough to accommodate all of us and our equipment for rehearsals, that is, when we could rehearse. We seldom practiced anymore, and their house was more of a layover place for us when we weren't playing out of town, which was rare anymore.

We also had the groupies, who were not only at the gigs, but they started coming by the house. Every night we played, us single guys knew we were going to get laid, but we weren't sure who, since it was always a trap shoot, for lack of better terminology. If by some chance we didn't want to get laid some night, we'd literally have to work at not making it happen, since there was always a lady for each of us who were single, ready to buy a drink, or turn us on to a line or two or three or four or more of cocaine, speed, or just a joint or two.

Cuz, was trying to be discrete in his flings, and coined the phrase, "Don't tell Steph," while I was ready to say the proverbial phrase we were in 'hog heaven', but that line can't be used for how pretty and sexy most of these women were. The 'hog heaven' phrase can however be used to describe the availability of the drugs and alcohol surrounding us all of the time those days. This availability also did not do anything to improve the situation or issues we were having with Flash. Cuz and I were also dabbling a bit too much in the extra fringe benefits, but for the most part, we felt we were on top of things. The thing with Cuz, was that I didn't want the 'baggage' of trying to remember what, and what not to say around Stephanie. Steph is considered part of the family, and I wasn't crazy about Cuz's timid deceit, and dragging us into it, regarding his own dealings with the women and the drugs. He's however a good guy otherwise, and a great guitar player, and I don't want to jeopardize our friendship; so, I remain quiet.

Nick was as stable as ever, as his rhythm with Hank's drumming is like a solid rock, but I sometimes think that Nick's solid playing is the only thing holding that poor guy's drumming together. No matter how drunk or incorrigible Flaming Flash Hanky seemed to be at a gig, he's as tight as a drum (no pun intended) when he and Nick were playing together. As a bassist, I can say it's the strongest rhythm section I've ever experienced, and sometimes wished his timing would go off, just so I can use it in my arguments with him regarding his drinking, but it never happened.

I was hoping he had a strong liver, but unfortunately for now, we're all young and like myself, we all think we're going to live forever. We're going to keep playing and rocking right into our future, never going to die, because we're indestructible! Yeah, right. Talking about all of this, and narrating our story from the future, I know better.

Everything seems to be happening so fast now, as Nancy was in full control, like she's the mom, and she has become the boss of the band. Nick is still the quiet balanced protector of us and Nancy, and still has Hank's back as far as the drinking, but he has gotten impatient with him on occasion. Technically, there is no real leaders here in the band democracy, since Nick looks to me for approval on everything, as opposed to Cuz or Flash, but Flash is still his boy, his best friend. Cuz is laid back in respect to the way the band is managed but when we're within the music or in the show, he'll take the creative lead roll and I'll mesh with him on that angle as he and I'll look to each other and Nick and Flash will follow suit. I look to Nick for overall confidence, and to get things done, while we all look to Nancy.

I talked to Nick after a rehearsal one night and asked him to meet me, one on one, to discuss a few issues. I did not mention wanting to talk with him about Hank's drinking. He and I had a night to kill with just him and me, so we drove separate vehicles to Molly's bar, over in Bedminster.

Nick took his knapsack with a change of clothes for later, and he and I entered the pub, and were the only ones in there at this time, except for Molly. Molly is the owner and bartender, who's short, plump, and friendly, and smiling as we walked in. It's a very small bar, and the patrons are usually the locals, within a 5-mile radius or passers by stopping in for quarts or six packs to go. The bar's length is about 15 feet at best, with the whiskey bottles of choice within arms-length across the bar between us and the full-length mirror and of course this is all directly in back of Molly standing right in front of us asking for our order. We order a beer apiece and lay our cash on the counter, while Molly takes it and makes change. She says she'll be mopping around back and to call her when we're empty, as we quietly sip our beers and look at mirror's reflection of ourselves, and the backward neon lights from immediately behind us on the picture window, calling out to route 113; which sits only 10 feet away, and any passersby who feel free to stop in. Nick sets his mug on the coaster and says, "Did you hear we're playing in Manhattan next month?"

"I heard 'Asbury Park' next month," I said, "first the 'Stone Pony' and then 'Convention Hall' warming up some name act."

"We're doing Asbury Park first," was Nick's response, "and the following weeks in Manhattan. We won't have time to shit." He takes another sip of his beer. "In the middle of the summer we're doing a tour in Arizona!"

"Arizona? What's out there?" I asked.

"There's a pocket of people from the college stations that are playing our songs out there. We're supposedly in demand and Nancy says we have to go. We'll be there through the month of August."

Nick thinks for a second then downs the beer and calls Molly. Molly pours us a pitcher, takes a few more dollars, and returns to her mopping in the back.

"I really like Hank, or Flash, as you guys call him," Nick says with a contagious smile, "but I can see there's a potential problem."

"That's why I wanted to talk," I told him.

"He gets a little weird, a little paranoid," Nick states.

"A little drunk," I add.

"Yeah, a little drunk," says Nick.

"He's a great drummer, especially with you at his back," I told Nick affirmatively.

"I'll always be at his back," Nick added. He then said, "I wasn't with him when we were in Nam but I know his story. Have you ever heard his story?"

"No," I told him, "but I'd like to hear it."

"Well then," Nick begins, "You know of course that Hank was in the marines and he and I won't talk much because there's a lot we want to forget."

"I respect that'" I said, "and you don't have to . . . "

Nick interrupted, "It's important that you know and what I'm telling you doesn't leave this room. Hank is a hero, but in some ways, he thinks himself a coward. There are people he knows that have no idea he was even in the service, much less in the midst of the Vietnam war; And also, a sharp shooter prodigy comparable to Annie Oakley.

Hank was in from the end of '69, right after we saw you guys at Woodstock, until '72. He was in the Cambodian mess and Ho Chi Minh trail. He was on a patrol one day, and was already callous to the seeing of blood, but never got over the killing at that time. Every time he buddied up with someone, they were killed, it seemed to him, right next to him in the same hole. He was known by some as the 'trap' and some were superstitious about being with him. Anyway, like I was saying they were on a patrol with nine G.I. grunts when they were ambushed. The Vietcong had built tunnels everywhere and that's where they came from. They were immediately surrounded and seemingly shot at from all sides. The Lieutenant was walking up front, beforehand, and telling the guys this was his last patrol, as he was going home to his wife, and his new daughter whom he hadn't seen yet other than pictures. He was smiling and having the men try to guess what the baby's name was. They were telling him one by one what they thought.
"Megan?"
"No."
"Rachel?"
"No."
"Sue?"
"No, besides, Sue's a boy's name."

There was laughter because they were all thinking of that 'Boy named Sue' Johnny Cash tune, popular there at the time. It was then that the enemy opened up on them, even though alert and looking, they were still ambushed. They all laid down for cover except the lieutenant, who stood up and yelled something they all couldn't understand due to all of the enemy gunfire. Hank was looking right at him when the lieutenant's face seemed to explode, propelling him backward and flat on his back, motionless, with blood pumping in a morbid rhythm from a large hole where his face used to be. He and his G.I. buddies were pinned down, frozen in fear, time, and uncertainty after that; unable to fire back, just waiting for death.

Hank told me he went blank, then saw red. Maybe it was the red blood from the hole in the lieutenant's face, or maybe just the complete reversal of fear which is a very fine line between bravery and insanity. Out of the blue and into the red, he stood up and was screaming with a blood curdling yell, running like there was no tomorrow, transfixed and straight at one of the Vietcong.

He had lots of ammo and he simply shot the poor bastard's face off, avenging his lieutenant. He then dove, with his bayonet right onto and into the next goon in that same fox hole then continued his crazy rampage to another, at 10 feet away, firing and stabbing. The GI's Hank was with followed suit, doing what Hank was doing. They really had nothing to lose, as they were not fearing death anymore within this new found crazy rage of theirs, and it seemed as if the bullets from the Vietcong were doing nothing, like they were shooting blanks or something, because these eight men felt invincible. They ended up killing about 14 of the Cong, wiping out that whole tunnel patrol. I think only the one American Lieutenant was killed, and only one other GI was grazed. Hank never got anything from the brass, you know, like a medal or a promotion regarding that attack . . . except the privilege of living another day there."

Nick took another sip and continued, "Oh, and he got the respect of the guys he was with, which was the most important reassurance to him. Hank was only a private at the time, and him going crazy drove the fear out of everyone around him and into the Vietcong. The men with him were not pinned down in fear anymore. The one witness I talked to told me the whole story, saying he never saw anything like it. I had run into him during a layover in Hanoi. Hank told me the same thing word for word after I had to pry it out of him. But Hank told me another story, about another earlier patrol, before that one." Nick took a sip of beer, then continued telling the story.

"When Hank first got to be 'in country' he was one of the FNG's (fuckin' new guy) like quite a few others. His good friend Patrick Boyle was with him from boot camp and Pat was getting married to a girl named Patricia Hendricks. On the helicopter on the way in to Vietnam, he rolled up his pant leg and showed Hank the tattoo, "Pat and Patty Forever". He wanted Hank to be his best man and that gave them both reason for staying alive in the jungle, as they went on a patrol, his first one, out into the jungle. He was a marine, but had not seen action yet, being 'fresh off the boat' and looking for an interesting adventure, you know, loyal to 'God and Country' and being with the American boys. They were all grouped together re-cutting a trail using their machetes when they spotted a kid, looking about 12 years old, come walking to them through the trees and vines. They went through the routine of aiming the guns and addressing him. The kid was Vietnamese, but you can't tell by looking if it's North or South Vietnamese, they're all the same, and he was just a kid for Christ's sake.

Hank and Pat stood aside while some of the others pushed the kid around in their raw interrogating ways, uttering what little of the language they knew, trying to get from him where the hell he was going and what it was he was doing out there, until the Lieutenant broke it up and the boy fell to his knees weeping. The kid spoke in broken

English, something about his mama and pointed in the direction he came.

The Lieutenant tapped two of Hanks buddies he arrived with, one of them was Pat and just missing Hank. He ordered them to be careful and see what the boy was concerned about. The two marines, FNGs, with a corporal, walked slow through the jungle brush. They only got about 10 yards in and there was an explosion. Hank dropped to the ground with everyone else and felt something land on his helmet. It was his friend, Pat's shredded lower leg, bloody with only the boot still on. He recognized the tattoo with his and his girlfriend's name, "Pat and Patty Forever". The team of men stood looking at the kid who smiled and started shooting at them with a pistol he must have had stashed nearby. It was obviously a mine or some kind of booby trap that killed Pat and his buddy, and the kid set them up, or so it seemed. The one sergeant put the kid away in one shot between his eyes with his M14 and all hell broke loose, as shots were firing off everywhere; a real live ambush. Hank said he fired into the jungle even though he couldn't see anyone, just smoke from rifles, and thought he got at least a few of them but he'll never know for sure as he made it out of that one; but he'll never forget his buddy Pat, who didn't."

Nick looked at me and said, "I know Hank has a problem, but we'll handle it."
"I know you will, and I'm sorry for the shit he's been through. I just don't want any of us to become an enabler for his problem. Just think about that Nick."
"I think about that all the time," he said. "Any one of those bar fights where he got the shit kicked out of him he could have won sober. He may drink because he wants a reason to lose." Nick dropped his head, then raised it to take another sip of his brew and said, "I have to take a leak, and

I've got to change these clothes." I watched him meander to the men's room with his knapsack.

I ordered another pitcher and poured myself a mug with a cold delicious foaming head. I looked up and into the bar mirror while sipping my brew and was startled by what I saw. It was Angeline's reflection! It was from the other side of the window on the outside, in back of me! Her beautiful red hair and smile peering directly at me. I set my beer down, almost dropping it and turned around, but there was no one there. I was just thinking of her, and now I'm hallucinating, watching my hand tremble as I took another sip, and I felt two soft hands on my shoulders. I'm afraid to look up into the bar mirror in front of me again but I do, and there she is.

"I missed you terribly," she said.

"Angeline!" I said . . .

"Shhhh!!" she said, "Don't say my name so loud, I'm supposed to be in 'hiding'."

She was wearing a very thin blue chiffon top that was low cut to her navel and loose, leaving nothing to the imagination regarding her perky naked body underneath. The soft slinky top and her breasts pressed warmly against my upper arm as she leaned in to give me a warm soft kiss, and we caressed for what seemed to be forever.

"You're not going to tell me where you've been?" I asked gazing into those beautiful green eyes. "That's not important now, is it? I'm sure you've got better questions than that."

"Well then," I asked, "How long are you here for? Are you planning on disappearing again?"

"I can't even answer that," she said looking down, "but I'm here now, aren't I?"

"Are you?" I asked. I was distracted by a couple drops of what looked like blood on her bare cleavage. She noticed me looking, then wiped it off with a napkin. She put her napkin over her nose and as if to answer my unasked question said, "I know, nose bleed. It's better now." She sat on the stool, put her hands on my lap and asked me if I missed her. I answered her with yet another embrace and a kiss.

Just then Nick came back from the men's room, nodded his head at her, and calmly sat down. It was then I realized that Nick knew all along she would show up here tonight. Nick downed a beer and stood up, stretched, and said, "It's time for me to go; you kids have a good night." And with that he was out the door. I remember I thought it was kind of weird him leaving like that. Angeline had one of her hands in my back pants pocket and placed her other hand softly on my shoulder then glided it down to my chest and said, "I have my car. Why don't we leave here so we can talk some more? I've got a lot of things to tell you."

I agreed and finished my beer, and leaving a few bucks on the bar, I rose and with my arm around her waist, we started walking through the door. We barely got through the door when Molly ran from the back room screaming, "Oh My God! Oh My God!" She grabbed the telephone from the bar and dialed. "Police? There's a dead man in the men's room here at my bar. . . Huh? . . . I said, 'Molly's Bar', here at the Highway 113 crossroad in downtown Bedminster! It looks like his throat was slashed! There's blood on the wall, the toilet, all over the floor! I don't know the man. 'Never seen him before!"

During the graphic description Angeline was tugging at my arm, pulling me away and further through the door. "Come On!" she told me, "We can't stay around here!"

Because of that bad news, and with my hands shaking, I took my car and she followed me, as we drove to an old cemetery I knew of, where we could sit together and talk. As I drove carefully so she wouldn't lose me, I thought about Molly's horrifying find in the men's room and why Nick did what he did. I'm assuming Nick did this because this man must have attacked him, like the guy in Lansdale at Sally's bar. I'm wondering how long this kind of stuff will be going on? And is our band in danger? I've never dealt with this kind of lifestyle and I can't see ever getting used to it, then I start to wonder on how the hell did I ever get involved in any of this?

Anyway, we drove with our lights off into the cemetery and parked, then got out of the car, immediately handing her a paper bag I've been holding onto since I last time saw her.

"What's this?" she asked me.

"The last time I saw you, you asked to give this back, the next time we see each other. It's the teddy, with the sack of diamonds, and I also included your precious secret so called treasure map," I said, then opened up, saying, "After what just went down at the bar tonight, and after all of the crap that's been going on these days that have nothing to do with playing music, I prefer not to be part of any of it," I told her as she intently seemed to be listening, and I continued, "I'm glad you're OK, and it's good to see you alive again, but please keep me out of the surrounding evil rat race. I have enough trouble watching my back as it is, without your bullshit, plus these undesirables, seemingly still coming after Nick."

Angeline just gave a blank stare while I was talking, and peered into the bag silently, like she didn't know what I was talking about. I added that I've just kept that bag in the car for luck since we last saw each other, but I don't know if I need that kind of luck with what's been going on lately, but at least the band is playing out a lot.

She just put the bag in her car and we walked.

"This is nice back here," Angeline tells me, as she squats to pee in the grass right next to me, away from the nearest grave.
"I hope I don't make you too comfortable around me", I said sarcastically.
"Not at all," she says facetiously, as she farts aloud, before pulling up her slacks.
"Just like old times," I said grinning, as she seemed a bit looser than I remember.
"The best," she said popping open a cold Michelob bottle and handing it to me.
"I wonder what happened back there at the bar." I asked, knowing she might think Nick had something to do with that whole bar scene.
"A man was killed," she said and took a big swig from her beer.
I changed the subject and asked her about Bobcat Records and about some of the things that went down. At first, she was a bit reserved and unapproachable, but after her second beer she was opening up.
"Do you remember Lila?" she asked me, as she leaned back on a tombstone.
"Your so called 'evil twin' from Woodstock?" I asked laughing.
"Yes, of course. She's heavily involved with the bad things that happened to those jerks at Bobcat. It was her way of watching out for me. She was angry and of course she got carried away. She's sick, and a pretty unforgiving being."
"Well," I added, "she's pretty. I'll give her that."
Angeline gives me a punch in my shoulder and then agreed.
"So," I continued, "was Lila the one who supposedly tortured those three men I heard about? Those three men from 'Bobcat' studios? Did that really happen or was that just a lying lawyer rambling to discredit you as a witness?"

"She skinned them alive." Angeline said, "Literally!"
The hairs stood up on my neck, as her eyes seemed to pierce right into me when she said that. "Lila has no heart and takes no shit from anyone," Angeline added, "They simply messed with the wrong person. She was coerced by a woman they call 'Snake' who was there with her."
"I remember seeing 'Snake' at the club," I told her.
 "Lila is a saint compared to Snake. Just the sight of that woman makes any of those bobcat guys tremble because of what Marco did."
"What did Marco do?" I asked.
"The story I heard was Marco was pissed because she embarrassed him in front of his friends. I was holding him when she did the tongue thing on his ear making him pee himself the night you and I met. Her tongue is very long, and she flutters it fast like a snake. Anyway, when the whole shakedown and sting was happening, Marco slipped into the dressing room at the club and stuck a big kitchen knife up her best friend Erin's ass, then slit her throat with it."
 'Holy shit!" I said with a shiver as Angeline continued:
"Snake had her mind set on getting even with him anyway, for something else that I can't say right now, but murdering Erin, the way he did, put her further over the edge. Marco hasn't a clue, and he might even think Snake's dead, but I do know he's deathly afraid of her."

Angeline took a sip of her beer, and leaning into me started kissing me passionately, as we slid down the tombstone and undressed each other, caressing in a seductive ball of rhythm, as we made love on that warm spring night beneath the stars and the stone etched names of Alexander and Dorthea Zilley.

Something was different though, something about Angeline made me think this was not the Angeline that I remember. She looks like Angeline, smells like Angeline, and even tastes like Angeline, but she's not meshing with the inner center of my being. This person I'm making love to is not the woman I was in love with at the beach once upon a time ago! I kept my feelings to myself when she asked, "What? Is something wrong, Stan?"

"No, absolutely not," I lied, "I'm just thinking about tonight." The love making was passionate, but almost empty at the same time, and I was suspicious that she was feeling the same way, whoever this was.

We stood up and got dressed, and meandered through the tombstones and graves when Angeline asked, "Are you aware that Nick's been fucking Lila?"

"WHAT?"

"Nick's been fucking Lila!"

"I heard you, and I don't believe that for a second."

"Believe it," she said opening another beer, "They've been getting together off and on for some time now, ever since before Jackie Clark was killed."

"But," I said, absolutely devastated, "he's been so happy with Nancy."

"Yes," she said," and he's been just as happy with Lila."

"Where the hell have you heard that?" I demanded.

"I didn't just hear, I see." Angeline took another sip off of her beer as she leaned her head to one side, letting her red hair down over her shoulder while she scratched the back of her head.

I didn't want to know anything more about it for now. But I did ask her about Jackie, because she brought his name up.

"So, it's true about you slipping Jackie the seafood he was allergic to?"

She smiled at me, then looked at me with a kind of distant stare, avoiding my question, and said, "Stan, you're the only

THE LOST MARBLES STORY

one who knows I'm alive. Everyone else thinks I'm dead; That I was done in by a man known as 'Balance'."

"Balance?" I glared at her trying to believe this shit. Then I said quickly,

"Nick knows you're alive."

"No", she said.

"Come On! He saw you sitting with me at the bar just now!"

"Yes, and he thought I was Lila because Lila is stalking him.

"She's stalking him? I thought you said they were getting it on."

"He keeps avoiding her," she said, "but they're still engaging when the mood's right for both of them. So yeah, no one knows I'm alive but you."

I take a swig of my beer, and I continue to wonder about all of this. She peaked my curiosity about the guy that was supposed to have done her in.

"So'" I ask, "Who's this 'Balance' character you've mentioned?"

Angeline squinted her eyes at me and tilting her head to one side again said, "It's short for Balancia. Antonio Balancia. He's a very bad man, a true seed of pure evil, and I have a story for you which you may find hard to believe."

"I'm all ears" I told her. At this point, with all that's been going on, and as before with her stories, I consider myself stupid enough to believe anything.

"My mom died a long time ago, while giving birth to Lila and me. When we were 10 or so, my father bought that land near Woodstock, where you and I first met. That was our property you saw us on during the concert, and it still is, which is a very small ranch house and about 40 acres.

One day, a couple years later, at a time when my dad was down on his luck, a man approached him and asked him if he could rent about two acres off of him. My dad asked him what it was for, and he told him he worked for a pharmaceutical company and they were experimenting with marijuana. Daddy ignorantly OK'd the land, and the greenhouses they built, and was paid well for it.

The man that approached him with this deal was Antonio Balancia; or better known as 'Balance'. Although to keep himself under the radar, he had people call him 'Tony'. He himself took care of the greenhouses and harvesting. My dad was then able to financially raise us the way he wanted to, with our mom being gone.

Something else my dad was ignorant of, was how Balance sexually abused my sister and I since we were 13, as we were raped and sodomized regularly. He threatened to kill my father if we ever said anything about it. Lila got it the worst, but as we got older, we were able to avoid being around when he came around, and we've never spoken about it.

As it turned out, Jackie Clark's father was the one running the deals and business transactions regarding the greenhouse. He came out from time to time, and could be a predator on some occasions, as I've seen what he did with, not just us, but to one of the girls at the Woodstock festival. I tried to stop him, and I promised someone I'd never mention that incident.

Anyhow, because he ran things is how I met Jackie in the first place. He used to come out and tend to the crop and the greenhouses with a few others after the first few years, and he seemed nice. The work became too much for just one asshole (Balance) to take care of. Jackie and I used to talk and I was free from Balance after that, but Lila wasn't."

"So, you weren't lying when you told me you started dating him," I mentioned.

THE LOST MARBLES STORY

"Well, I was kind of sucked into all of it, in keeping everything quiet. I was never OK with it, so some of what I told you is correct. All I know is, that I fear that asshole 'Balance", but I know for a fact that Lila does not, and she's going to kill him. This man, Balance, is the person they call to eliminate someone. He's also sadistic in his methods and lives for murdering, like Jackie's dad. He does have a weakness though, a fear. He is claustrophobic, as Lila found that out about him when she was 14 years old. That's all I'm going to say."

Then she took a sip and said, "His partner, who is a shrimp, a midget sized guy who's a coward and just as much a barbarian in his own methods, is the guy who hired Balance, and that's actually Jackie's father Jonathan. He keeps himself incognito under the name of Marco."

"You mean they're like Tony and Marco, the name of those two lobsters?" I asked.

"What? Two lobsters? I don't remember . . . "

"The two lobsters I fished out of the tank. The ones with the shiny barnacles."

"Oh, those weren't barnacles," she said laughing, "those was actually diamonds, glued to the shells." Then she held up the bag of diamonds.

I do remember seeing the diamonds, following my weird hallucinations on the beach with Angeline. She continued, "That club, 'Siren's Coast', was a high-class whorehouse and smuggling ring cover-up. Also, lots of narcotics went through that place. The ladies there finally turned on the establishment once they found out how the owners and their connections were torturing and killing people.

The women working there were essential in that sting operation. Truthfully, I wouldn't want to be in the shoes of Marco, Balance (Tony), or any one of those animals belonging to the center of that Bobcat group. Some good friends and family were brutally murdered, and the women working there want restitution. They really have their sights set on 'Marco'. They'll literally skin him alive if they ever get hold of him. Right now, he's safe from their clutches in his prison cell."

    She dropped her head and started peeling the label off of her Michelob bottle with her long fingernails and sporting an evil grin. We were both quiet for a moment. Frankly, I now know for sure that this person who has been talking to me all night is not Angeline, but her twin sister Lila. I don't let on. I had just made love to her; a strange woman, tonight in the cemetery, and I was now a little bit frightened of being with her. Why was she pretending to be Angeline? And what happened to Angeline? I'm worried that she may really be dead.

    My brain was on overload and detecting what I knew was dishonesty on Lila's part with all of her incognito, wondered what the hell was fucking going on. I felt a chill of deceit, or at the very least, I felt I was going crazy. That's the only way I can describe it for now. I just wanted to get away from her, but I do believe her story about them growing up, and I'm saddened.

    I kept my cool and my crazy thoughts to myself, as I got into my car and just drove off. I drove for a long time before getting home, and didn't seem to care about the map, diamonds and the teddy that I handed her. All I know is this was not Angeline who I just gave them to, and just wanted to be home where I felt safe. . . and sane.

Chapter 13

The Plot Deepens

Oddly enough, Nancy was still up and asked if Nick was with me.
"Didn't he come home yet?" I asked.
"No, detective Stan. That's why I asked you first. You guys realize this week is booked, starting tomorrow night in Philly; and a rehearsal before the gig."
"Shit," I said wearily, "I'd better get some sleep." I took a half of a quaalude from Nancy (she was holding it out with a pretty smile). "Tell Nick, if he ever comes home, that I need to talk to him first thing in the morning," I told her, as I swallowed the half tab, and then retired to my bed. I tossed and turned at first but just as quickly nodded off to dreamland.

I dreamed I was in a cage in some wilderness surrounded by trees and tall grass. There was another cage, that looked empty, and was right across from me about 100 feet or so. Everything around me looked big, the trees, the grass, but the cages and I seemed small in context to everything surrounding me, like I was tiny. Just then, I heard footsteps getting louder and louder, coming from behind me and as I turned, it was unbelievable! It was Angeline's twin sister Lila, only she was about 20 feet tall, was naked, like I remembered her from Woodstock, and her long red hair reminded me of Angeline, but she was obviously different, although I can't explain how, other than in spirit or personality, and the fact that she was now 20 feet tall; similar to my hallucinating scenario with Angeline a while back. She walked right past me, to the other cage, and she stood over it as I heard a man and a woman screaming from inside. She bent over and opened the cage from the top and reached in. She pulled upwards, with her hand what appeared to be a man, about 12 inches in comparison to her. The man looked like Nick, although it couldn't be, because I couldn't imagine Nick screaming and carrying on like that, even with a gigantic evil woman towering over him. She held him in the air by his legs upside down in front of her face with one hand and ripping the clothes off of him with the other. She held him like a plucked chicken, waiting for slaughter, then lowering him to her side, she slowly walked into the forest, with him in one hand and firmly gripping a butcher knife in the other. The woman she left in the cage looked like Nancy, and she too was screaming, while watching Lila walk away with her 'Nick'. Then she slowly mellowed and looked right at me and asked me if I'm alright. She kept asking, "Stan, are you alright?" My heart was beating so fast by then that I awoke from the dream. As I did, I saw Nancy was standing over me shaking her head. "Stan, are you alright? You're having a nightmare."

"I was? Yes, I believe I was . . . I guess . . . "

I wiped the sleep from my eyes and with both hands, roughly scratched the sides of my head above my ears trying to erase what I envisioned as morbidly real, only moments ago.

"You were screaming something about Nick", she added. "Are you sure he's alright? It's getting light out and he's not home yet."

Nancy seemed more than a little concerned, so we made some coffee and I shared the evening's adventure at Molly's Bar with her. She listened, shuddering at times like me telling her about Molly finding the poor guy dead in the bathroom with his throat slashed.

THE LOST MARBLES STORY

"What makes you think Nick had anything to do with that dead guy in the bathroom?" she asked me, "Did you see the guy dead or did you just hear Molly saying it?"
"Why the hell would Molly make it up?"
"I'm not saying she made it up. I asked if you saw the guy?"
"No. I did not".
Nancy had a point, and who the hell would want to stick around there after hearing someone saying someone's dead in the men's room?
"You saw Nick leave the bar . . . right?" Nancy asked.
"Nick left just before that", I told her, "It was not Nick dead in the toilet!"

We took sips of our coffees and sat quietly for a few minutes. When she was looking away from me, I secretly stared at her in the new morning sunlight, at the beautifully feminine contours of her face. I've known Nancy for years and as time goes by, and life moves forward, I realize how much looks are sometimes taken for granted. She's actually a very beautiful woman.
"You really love him, I can see that," I told her as I placed my hand onto hers.
"You can see what you think you see," she said, "I've known Nick for a long time, and of course I care about him." She was quiet for a few moments while sipping some coffee. Then surprisingly said, "I don't care so much for the cheating as long as it's not obvious."

I was taken aback, since it was beyond belief to me that Nick could ever cheat, much less cheat on someone as bright and attractive as Nancy.
"He cheats?"
Nancy just looked at me as if I asked, "The Pope's catholic?"

"You don't have to cover up for him. Don't insult my intelligence."

"Honestly," I told her, "On my mother, I have, or rather had no idea!"

She laughed. "You didn't know this whole time? I find that hard to believe!"

I was honest with her and told her that I would have felt very uncomfortable about knowing he was doing this because I'm friends with both her and Nick, and I believed in them as a couple. I'm also feeling just a hair stupid now. Now, if it was Cuz, it's blatantly out front, and I thought of his catch phrase, "Don't tell Steph."

"Gosh Nancy," I said, "I always thought of you two as the ultimate couple."

"We're a couple alright," she said, "And although I still love him, I sometimes wonder why I'm still with him."

She started telling me about Lila, and about their affair.

"Lila and Nick met at Woodstock, and they were tripping on the same stuff you were. It was a combination of mushrooms laced with LSD . . . or at least that's how it was explained to me. Lila had pot she simply stole from the greenhouse, and was turning people on, as was your friend Eve, or better known to friends these days as Angeline. Anyway, he fell for her and they hung out all weekend. They stayed in touch and they were fuck buddies until I started dating Nick. He and I hit it off pretty well, and I'll admit, he knocked my socks off, and I fell in love. So, Nick went into the service, and eventually so did Lila."

Nancy took a sip of coffee and with her steady hand, pushed her hair back and continued.

"She actually made it into the special services and learned all of the things paratroopers and seals learn. She never made it to Vietnam, but was stationed stateside, while he, however, was fully involved with what was going on over there; and Nick and Lila were, of course, never in contact that whole time, but got back in touch sometime afterward. He tells me they're just friends, but I know better."

Her eyes went into a momentary glassy stare, out towards the door, as if expecting it to never open again for Nick. "As I said, I love him," her eyes slowly shift back and stare with meaning this time, into mine, "but I really don't know if I'm 'in' love with him anymore." Silence fills the air, as she takes another sip, and then says, "Maybe I never was."

I asked her what she knew about Angeline and told her about the night she and I had; cooking at home, then at the beach. Nancy asked me about the two lobsters that were in the tank, and if I ever freed them. When I told her Angeline ended up cooking them she said, "Oh no, did she eat them?"

"Both of them, ruthlessly" I said . . . why?"

"That's like the kiss of death if she named the creatures. I just heard that those women working at that club were part of some witch cult. Legend has it that they curse certain people with the sacrifice of small animals. Did you know that those lobsters may have had over a couple of million dollars' worth of diamonds planted in them stolen from Jackie's dad and Balance?"

"No, I didn't," I answered.

She continued, "They were never found in the raid. I of course didn't know that when I asked if you could let them go. I'm finding this out only now, through Nick. He has his ways of finding out these things."

As she said that, I concluded that he found out these things by sleeping with Lila, but I was silent. "Do you know if Angeline named them?" Nancy asked.

"Named who?"

"I know this sonnds silly, but did she give names to those lobsters?"
"She named them 'Tony' and 'Marco,'" I said.
"'Tony and Marco', Hoooh boy . . . That's 'Balance' and Jackie's dad Jonathan, A.K.A. 'Marco'," Nancy said shaking her head, "I wouldn't want to be in their evil shoes for all the money in the world."
"That's what . . . " I started to tell her about my meeting with Lila (who was seemingly pretending for some reason to be Angeline), and her saying the same thing, but I thought better of it.
"What's what?" she asked. To cover it I just said, "Brain fart, never mind."
"I just hope Nick is alright, and Stan, I'm really glad you are, and I enjoy your company, especially right now."

She rose from her seat and calmly walked over to turn up the radio to a familiar song by The Temptations, "'Just my Imagination" and started to sway to it.
"This is one of my favorites," she said, swaying and pointing her finger at me and beckoning me to join her in her moment, "Come on and dance, with me Stan, I can use a hug," she asked me with that pretty smile of hers, with those white teeth lighting up her perfect face. How could I resist?

We held onto each other in the moment of the song, swaying and turning to the melodic voice of Eddie Kendricks against the background vocals of the rest of the Temps, with the musical flavor of the Funk brothers. As we did, I lived for the proverbial moment, and my mind wandered to another place I haven't been before. A place where nothing else in the world existed. A place where there was only Nancy and me, barefoot and naked on a sandy beach under a moonbeam.

I started thinking about the time we all went to Woodstock, and before that, those days she was with Cuz and I was with Mae. Nancy and I had always flirted with each other, but never crossed any lines. I guess it's safe to say I've always had what is called a mild crush on this fine lady. She's not just physically attractive and sexy, but she's got a good head on her shoulders and keeps her feet on the ground.

"You're stepping on my toes," she whispered loudly into my ear, causing me to stumble back a bit to refocus.

I embraced her again, and we continued as another song started, "Dream," by the Everly Brothers. Then she surprised me by saying, "I've always wanted to slow dance naked on a beach in the moonlight."

I was at a loss for words because I felt she read my mind, and the only thing I could think of was to hug her tighter, because she was hugging me tighter. The song reminded me of the beach, as a boy, and my teenage babysitter with her bikini in 1958. But it just made me hug Nancy even tighter.

'She would look great in a red bikini', I thought, but I certainly didn't want to impose a bikini on her volunteered image of dancing naked.

The thought of Nick never entered my mind, until the door opened behind me. Nancy immediately hugged me into herself, and tighter, as to not break our stride, and assured me that it was alright to keep on swaying to the music with her.

"You two look cozy," Nick said in a slightly sarcastic tone, "Did you get any sleep?"

"Did you?" replied Nancy.

The song was over, and Nancy and I let go of the moment, sitting down with Nick on the couch. Nick got up and sat across from us in the easy chair and pulled a can of

Schmidt's out of his knapsack offering me one. I declined and looked at Nancy, as she shrugged her shoulders looking at me, then looking back at Nick asked, "So, what happened last night dear?"

I got up and switched my seat to a chair where I could see them both.

"If you only knew," he said looking right at me. Nancy looked at me again and once again with a sharper tone addressed Nick, "SO, what HAPPENED last night . . . DEAR?!"

I asked Nick, "What the hell happened at the bar, Nick?"

Just then Cuz walked in with Stephanie. Cuz and Stephanie have been off and on for the past year, regarding their relationship, but they've been apparently working at it. They seem to be getting pretty tight lately; Or at least we've been seeing them together more and more. Steph is a very attractive, dark haired woman, and what most people would consider 'big boned' in her physical stature but not overweight. She certainly carries it well, as she does with her strong personality, though it's hard to tell if she's mad sometimes, at us, or if she's just on edge. Anyway, she seems good for Cuz.

Cuz said, "Hey, we got some news for everyone. Steph and I are going to have a baby!"

Now, you know that expression people use about news knocking you off your chair? This literally caused me to fall backwards, on the chair I was already leaning back on.

"Come again?" I asked.

Stephanie said, " 'Come again' you say? No thanks, that's how I got pregnant in the first place."

I guess I'm the only one in the room *not* thinking what she said was funny, because everyone else laughed, and began congratulating them. In the midst of all this I didn't want to lose my original directive, which was to grill Nick a

THE LOST MARBLES STORY

little about last night's episode at Molly's bar. I'm going to have to get him alone somewhere, and I really want Nancy to be there, since the issue is that we're performers in the public eye, and there are these murders happening all around us, and God forbid, 'seemingly' directed at us.

Now Cuz, our lead guitar player, is going to be a father, and this whole house has sure gone crazy!
"How far along Steph?" Nancy asks with her captivating smile and speaking as if everything is peaches and cream.
"Oh, about eight weeks. I'm due January 13th next year."
"Well, congratulations to both of you," Nancy gleamed, and turning to Cuz added, "Cuz, this is a new page for you, being a father. I hope you're ready to give it you're all."

"I'm ready," he said, sharing her smile. Before I could say anything, Nick spoke up and said facetiously, "Congratulations Cuz, are you ready to work this into our upcoming busy touring schedule?"

Nick, could be as quiet as can be at times, but this wasn't one of those times. He, probably unknowingly or unaware, spoke for me and the band. It was exactly what I was thinking but was not quick enough to respond. Cousin Benny just looked down, but Stephanie said, "Benny is going to be a good daddy and is also very aware of his commitments. You don't have to worry about the gigs or the band. He'll be there."

Nick smirked and glared at a quiet Cuz. Then maintaining his fixed look, still on Cuz, asked Stephanie, "Can he still talk?"
"Like she said," Cuz glared right back, "I'm fine with it. Are we rehearsing today? Or are we supposed to cower once again, from the goons who are stalking you Nick?"

Now some folks, including Cuz, might expect the receiving end of this question to incite anger, or in some cases violence. But those folks don't know Nick and of course, are a hundred percent wrong.

"Touche," Nick responded, relaxing his face with a smile, and we set up to practice some of the new arrangements. Flash soon came by and we rehearsed for the next three hours while Nancy and Steph had a nice 'girl talk' session. For those three hours, we were all one again, working on song breaks and chord changes and harmonies while the world was at peace, for now.

Afterwards, Cuz and Stephanie left, Flash opened another beer and sat on the couch, and Nick, Nancy and I sat out on the porch with coolers as I opened up the conversation.

"So, Nick, what happened at the bar last night?"
"Oh, not too much. You were there."
"NICK!" Nancy belted out. Nick looked at her and pursed his lips as if saying, "ooooo", then he stated, "Someone died. Someone who needed to die I guess."
He opened his wine cooler, drank half of it, then said, "That Lila is pure hell on some people. All the guy was attempting to do was cut my throat. I could have handled it, but somehow, I don't know how . . . she was there. She calmly slit his throat like some kind of merciless naked witch." Nick grinned and shook his head, continuing to relive the scenario saying, "That's right! She distracted him by walking up to him totally naked. He just stood there like he was in a trance, as she pulled his pants down to his knees, and punched him square in the nose, then cut his throat in a quick slash; then, while he fell to the floor coughing and bleeding to death, she calmly slid the knife right up his ass before she went back out the window. What a show! . . . What a mess!"
"Eww, Good Christ Nick! Thanks for the graphics," Nancy said shaking her head.

"Hey, you asked, you wanted to know. Anyway," He continued, "I guess she put on her clothes out there, and that's when you saw her Stan." As he said that, I remembered seeing a couple drops of blood on her cleavage that she said was from a nose bleed, and I now know who's nose. Nick then said, "I was left there with this bleeding guy slumped over on the floor. I just picked him up and placed him on the toilet in the stall, knife and all, and shut the door. There was blood and shit all over everything. Fortunately, I had a change of clothes with me."

He finished his cooler and reached into the ice to grab another. I grabbed another cooler also and asked, "How did Lila end up in the men's room, at that time, and 'naked'?"
Nick shrugged his shoulders and said, "Search me. She took care of this poor idiot coming at me. I could have handled it but she took care of it. I guess she didn't like him, or she felt she was protecting me."
"She was stalking you again wasn't she Nick?" Nancy asked with an assuring smile.
"She was there to meet Stan," Nick said, "but Lila has a sixth sense about these things. She's got an evil streak, and I'm glad she's on my side."
"So, Nick," I asked, "why was she pretending to be Angeline to me?"
"See, you're not supposed to know that I knew that. She wanted something from you that only Angeline knew. Whatever it was, I think she got it."
I had to ask Nick, "Tell me the truth. Is Angeline dead?"
"I'm afraid so. And if you don't already know, Lila is on a personal rampage about that. She has a vendetta against everyone involved."

Nick picked up his cooler and continued, "Ok, I may as well tell you. The man dead in the bathroom tonight was sometimes Balance's partner in their constant sodomizing of her and her sister. Lila, I guess, was sending a message to Balance that she's coming for him, or maybe she was simply blood thirsty for revenge for her and her sister."

I dropped my head for a moment, as I was just entering a deep thought, remembering Angeline and the good times, however few, that we shared. Nancy sat next to me and stroked my back and said, "Stan? Are you alright?"
"I'm alright." I then walked to my room and slept for what seemed to be an eternity.

Chapter 14

Winslow, Arizona

The Convention Hall gig was fun. With just a simple show of 5 songs with the 4 of us, we opened up for The Titanics, who have 4 songs in the top 40, and for The Bolts, who have two songs in the top ten. We got ovations for both "Sing Those Blues" and "Rock and Roll Radio", even though the songs are barely in the top 40. We've developed a strong cult following, but we're not the stars yet. We then did a few nights at the Stone Pony, and then The Mainpoint, in Philadelphia. Then we packed up the dodge van with the trailer and headed west toward Arizona.

Our new equipment managers comprised of Nick's old friend Derek Gale, whom I last saw at the Woodstock festival, and another big, white guy called Al Finny, drove on ahead of us with the equipment in a box truck. They've kept themselves separate from us offstage, so on the road, it was just the five of us, including Nancy, who hung out together with the band, unless there were groupies involved.

On the way to Arizona we did a few gigs along the way, playing a club just outside of Nashville, in Murfreesboro, Tn. and also spent a few days in the Smokey Mountains camping and whitewater rafting, all five of us in a single raft, down the Ocoee River. Flash was once again almost killed by bad luck when he fell out of the raft into a # 5 rated rapids. Nick, of course, jumped in to pull him free from the under tow. We camped there in those woods and sat by the fire that night reflecting.

The five of us, Nick, Flash, Cuz, Nancy, and I, were passing a joint and a gallon bottle of burgundy. Flash told us he was sorry for the trouble, while Cuz just sat looking into the fire, no doubt wondering what his Stephanie was doing at this very moment back in Warminster Pa. I looked at all of them one by one, quietly, first at Cuz, then Flash in a glassy eyed daze next to Cuz, then across the fire at Nick throwing another log onto the sparks and flame. The log fell towards me so I leaned forward to remount the wood onto the glowing heat while I shifted my glance across to Nancy, who I caught looking right at me. I was a little embarrassed and looked away, but returned my eyes to hers. She was smiling now and winked. It gave me a warm feeling. . . or maybe it was just the wood on the fire heating up, or maybe it was the wine. In any case, she and I looked at each other until we fell asleep sitting up, along with everyone else.

In the morning we awoke, fire already out, we climbed directly into our single raft and finished our whitewater rafting journey. We packed everything in, took a shower in the outside showers the rafting rental place provided (like down at the seashore) and we stopped for a breakfast of eggs, onions and grits at the local diner. We were then on our way on highway 40 westward again.

We all took turns driving and napping through Arkansas, Oklahoma, the Texas panhandle, New Mexico, and then Arizona, non-stop. We stopped in Winslow at what's called the Meteor Club and Bar. We're scheduled to play tomorrow night and Saturday night and have two rooms reserved for three nights in their motel as part of the deal; Nancy booked us right.

THE LOST MARBLES STORY

Winslow is a town along Interstate 40, which is the old Route 66. It's a long thin town with Hwy 40 separating into two one way streets through Winslow proper; The business district. Outside of the bar on the marquee is our name in lights - "The Lost Marbles". Supposedly, we have a following out here because of KAFF Radio out of Phoenix, who even have a transmitter tower on top of Mount Elden in Flagstaff. Speaking of which, as we look to the west from our motel, we can see the Mount Elden foothills at the base of the snowcapped San Francisco peaks that are located just north of Flagstaff only 60 or so miles away. We'll be heading there by next weekend.

Today, we loaded into the two rooms at the club's motel and we all head south to a place called Clear Creek. Nick stayed behind to nap some more. Flash drove and Cuz, Nancy and I were the navigators guiding us to this beautiful swimming hole. Cuz and I had found it a few years back one summer, the summer of Woodstock, when we were in between 11th and 12th grade. We took a late June driving trip, just the two of us, across country and miraculously stumbled onto this gem.

When we arrive today, I see that it's just as pretty as I remembered, with the white sandstone diving cliffs, the deep clear water, and the carving on one sandstone slope that read, "Stan + Nancy". I had secretly carved that there when Cuz began dating a girl that he unknowingly didn't realize, nor did she, that I had a crush on. That girl of course was Nancy. I started dating Mae when Cuz began his relationship with Nancy, but I was originally smitten, or rather developed a mild crush on his girlfriend. The more he talked about her on that trip, the more I felt a growing flame for her. I felt I had to mark my feelings somewhere or I'd go crazy. I had no pen or paper at the time, just an ancient rusty cut-nail in my pocket that I found in the desert. But I respected Cuz's and my friendship, so the closest I came to betraying him was secretly writing Nancy's name somewhere. I had honestly forgotten about it until just now. I can't believe the sandstone held up, and that it's still there, a bit faded, but still deep in the stone.

I walked ahead of everyone, past the etching and heard directly behind me, "Hey! Look at this! 'Stan + Nancy', " Flash said. Nancy and Cuz stopped to look and moved on. Cuz never flinched, so I knew we were still friends, I jokingly thought. There were also lots of other rock etchings, "Bob and Carol", "Ted and Alice", and my favorite, "I WISH I WAS HERE". The rest of them were rather faded and old.

We stood on a tall cliff, maybe 40 feet above the deep creek, and quietly looked around in awe of the spectacle. Nancy didn't hesitate in taking off all of her clothes and being the first one to dive into Clear Creek from a lower 10-foot cliff. The rest of us stripped and followed closely behind her, and we were all in. The water was warm where you swim on the top but almost freezing when you dive down to 8 feet or more. Notwithstanding the story yarn Cuz was feeding to those who would listen, what he heard about the water snakes in this creek that could and would drown unsuspecting skinny-dipping swimmers, it was the beginnings of a great day. I of course swam out to the center and down a way, only to see that about twenty feet behind me was Nancy. I continued my swimming until the cliffs, jutting out into the water hid me and Nancy from the rest of our crew.

Nancy was closer to me now, and I could hear her breaths between her strokes, which she mellowed with using the side stroke as she came nearer to where I was. I was treading water at this point, looking up at the sparse plant life on the rocky cliffs, which were shear, and beautifully majestic.

I heard a short scream behind me, and turned around to see where Nancy was, but she was gone. I spun myself completely around while treading the deep water and still hadn't seen her, anywhere! Nancy had vanished! After a slight panic, and remembering Cuz's snake story, I shouted her name and heard nothing, except my lonesome voice echoing off of the canyon walls. Just then I felt a strong sharp grasp tightening around my kicking feet, and was then propelled upward and out of the water upside down, totally disorienting me as I plunged back into the creek head first. I pulled my head above the water, and wiping the drips from my eyes I see Nancy's smiling face laughing at me, saying, "GOTCHA!"

"How the hell did you do that?" I asked her. She's such a small person, yet she lifted me above the water.

"Don't underestimate the power of a woman . . . ever," she said still laughing. She and I continued to side stroke our way to a ledge area just above the water's edge where we climbed and sat. This was the sunny side of the creek and there was enough room for us to lay out on the dry sandstone and sun ourselves in the nude, and talk. We were real comfortable with each other.

"I'm impressed," she said.

"At what?"

"At what you chiseled into the sandstone years ago, 'Stan and Nancy'," she said with a cute shy smile.

"You would have been more impressed if I had put your name first," I said.

"Nah," she said, "If it was 'Nancy and Stan' written in stone, with my name first, it would have seemed you were too presumptuous. Now 'Stan and Nancy' in stone, is al-

most like 'Hey, I'm Stan, I'm here, but you can be here too if you want, Nancy'. 'You know, second billing. It's cute."
"That's . . . pretty deep . . . " I said almost sardonically, then I looked into the water.

We were quiet for a while looking up at the cliffs, and the sparse vegetation hanging off of the sides. The calming water ripples were occasionally lapping at the sandstone ledge we rested on. Nancy yawned then said, "Wake me up when the band's ready to go on. I could sleep here all day." I agreed with her, as this place was absolutely beautiful, but too beautiful for sleeping. Then I caught myself nodding out within this peace and quiet.

When I awoke, my arms and legs were totally entwined within Nancy's. We somehow did this in our sleep, so when we awoke at the same time we were hugging each other . . . totally naked. We were only napping for about 10 minutes, maybe, before we became aware of our predicament.
"Who's going to let go first?" Nancy asked smiling.
"Not me," I say.
Somehow, after a while, we mutually rolled apart and lay looking upward to the blue sky, observing a single cumulous cloud.
"I hope there are no surprises out here in these upcoming Arizona gigs," I said to Nancy.
"That's why I booked us away from the New York and east coast scene," she said, knowing I was talking about the attempted violent hits on Nick's life by these undesirables. Then she said, "See that cloud? I can make it disappear."
I guess she was trying to change the subject by this soliloquy into the cloud, or maybe this will be some profound and artistic vignette of hers, about life.
"The cloud's not bothering me," I say.

She giggled and said, "No silly, I mean I can make it disappear by just concentrating. You know what I'm talking about?"

"Not a clue."

Nancy laid back and kept her eyes transfixed on the cloud. In a few minutes, I couldn't believe my eyes. It was evaporating!

"See?" she said. "I'll get rid of it totally if you wish."

"I like clouds, they make the sky appear bluer," I said, and we started talking, still laying back and looking up.

"Why do men cheat?" Nancy asked, out of the blue, with a sigh.

"I don't know," I answered with the same kind of question, "Why do women cheat?"

"But men cheat more."

"I disagree." There was a pause, then she said, "Let's talk about something else."

I said, "Pick a subject."

"OK," she said, "What's the funniest first date with someone you've ever had?"

I had to think for a while, as it made me realize that I had a lot of first dates, more than I'd ever care to think about and to be honest, quite a few were one night stands. I was able to remember one first date though with a breath of laughter.

"Kristen."

"Kristen?"

"You don't know her." I told Nancy. "I met her at one of our early gigs. We went to the shore, rode bicycles on the boardwalk, and we hung out for days. Well, on the first day, we stopped at a place with our bicycles on the boardwalk in Wildwood, New Jersey to pick up you know, sodas, sandwiches and some trail mix for a small picnic. Anyway, we sat on a bench overlooking the Atlantic waves and we were

making out. She was taking sips of her ice, cold soda and when we kissed, she squirted the soda into my mouth. I thought it was kind of neat."
"That's . . . kind of gross. . . " Nancy said squinting her eyes and turning her head to the side.
"So, I took a sip of the soda and kissed her back, sharing the icy cola with her once again in a French kiss."
"I thought this was supposed to be funny," Nancy mumbled.
"Wait," I told her. "So, a few minutes later Kristen was facing me once again with her lips pursed and her eyes closed. I leaned over for another kiss expecting to dip my tongue into her mouth of ice cold soda, and she slowly filled my mouth up with chewed up trail mix and raisins!"

Nancy burst into her irrepressible laughter, holding onto her stomach and turning onto her side as I continued the story, "I gagged, and immediately turned my head to the ground and started spitting it all out and then started a reflux of dry heaving!"
Nancy said, "Stop!" as she still couldn't catch her breath, and laughing as I continued, "Kristen just looked at me surprised and was saying, 'What? What's the matter?' I could only look into her spacey eyes and ask, 'What the hell's the matter with you?'"

Nancy laughed so hard she rolled herself off the rock and right into the creek. While I was reaching for her hand, and helping her out onto the ledge, her face was inches from mine with her lips puckered. I felt the urge to lean in for a kiss but just then a spray of creek water from her lips dowsed my face causing me to let go of her hand, sending her back into the water with a splash. She laughingly helped herself out of the water and back onto the ledge as we returned to our original resting positions.
"So, what was your funny first date?" I asked her.

She laid back on the flat rock with a sigh and looking up at the cloud, disappearing over the cliffs started her story. "It was just before I started dating Nick, right after Cuz. There was this boy Freddie. He was from Willow Grove. He said his car was in the shop, and I picked him up in my mom's car. We went to a dance and had a relatively good time. He was sweet, but he liked to drink. Anyway, after the dance we went to the ice cream parlor in Newtown where he almost got into a fight. I ended up breaking them apart. I felt responsible since the fight was over me anyway."

"Over you?"

"Yeah, I winked at the guy across the counter. I know, it was an asshole thing to do. The guy came walking around and right up to us, totally ignoring Freddie, and the big dope started talking to me.

Anyhow, Freddie didn't say a word, he punched him in the stomach and the guy went down."

"I thought you said they almost got into a fight and you broke them apart."

"Not them. The guy had two friends who came over immediately and I stepped between them saying, "ENOUGH!"

"That's not a funny first date," I said.

"I'm not finished. After that we left and headed home down a dark route 413. Along the way we saw something run out but it was too late to avoid hitting it. We both got out to see that it was a skunk. It wasn't dead, but moving around, and it really stank too. I didn't want to drive after that so Freddie took the wheel, but he backed up over it again to put the poor thing out of its misery, then we headed to his house.

After we drove a few miles in the summer air with the windows down, we didn't smell the skunk anymore. He got out at his house in Willow Grove, kissed me good night, and I headed home. I parked the car and headed into the house."

"Really? That's all of it? Poor skunk," I said sympathetically.

"No, that's not all. My father woke up before I could get to my room, and he was screaming his head off about the pungent odor, marinating the rooms of his house! I'm serious when I say I didn't smell a thing!"

"The skunk must have neutralized your sense of smell," I told her, "those things do happen."

"I guess," she said, "Anyway, he was yelling and I told him about the skunk. He went outside in his boxer shorts to smell the car then stomped back into the house. Now he was really pissed! 'That's bad, that's really bad' he kept repeating. He wanted to know if we brought the 'damn' thing home with us, or if it was still in the car. That's how bad it must have smelled to him, but I couldn't detect anything with my senseless nostrils.

He wanted to know who did it, if it was me or Freddie who was driving when we killed the skunk. I did leave out the fact that I was the one who first hit the poor thing, and told dad that Freddie was the one who ran over it and killed it. He called Freddie's parents to let them know that Freddie's going to clean and detail my mom's car."

"Amazing."

"I'm not finished. The very next day Freddie came by to give the car a cleaning, detailing and wax job. When he asked me to help him while he was scrubbing and sweating his ass off I told him I couldn't. Just then my other date showed up."

"No, don't tell me. . . 'Nick'?"

"In his brand-new full-dress uniform!"

"You. . . my lady, are evil!" I told her while we both broke into laughter.

THE LOST MARBLES STORY

I never met this 'Freddie' guy but I could picture the poor bastard's forlorn look when he saw Nick pull up in his new uniform with the stiff hat and the shiny buttons to take off with this girl who could step in shit and come up smelling like roses.

We laid back in the sun and Nancy asked me to open up to her. She wanted me to reveal something that I've never told anyone. She said to trust her and that she would do the same. I told her I have nothing.

"Try again." she said with a determined, yet mellow trusting look.

"Look," she said, "I'll tell you something I've kept to myself for years. Something that if I tell, I might die. But I need you to trust me. That's why I want you to go first."

"Alright," I said.

Nancy sat her naked body up and crossed her legs and looked directly into my eyes with those pretty brown eyes of hers . . . very attentive.

"When I was about five or so, I had a babysitter who I had a crush on. Her name was Mary. She was about 18 or 19 and she told me I was so cute that she could eat me up, and said I was her boyfriend. I took it seriously of course. She was very pretty, with flowing dark red hair, blue eyes, and very well built."

"Yeah, here we go . . . " Nancy said sarcastically.

"No, I noticed things like that back then. Anyway, she took me with her one day to the store because she wanted to buy a new bikini for the summer. While we were out, she said she was in a beach cookout mood, and also took me to the seafood market to pick out two fresh lobsters that were on sale that day only. She saw me looking at them in the tank and had me pick them out, but I did not know this was for dinner, as I thought they were going to be pets.

When we got them home, I wasn't afraid of handling them and I put them in the tub. She put ice cubes in with them and said that it keeps them fresh. She went to put on her new bikini and sun herself out on the deck. I didn't see that she also put on big pot of water to boil because I was too busy playing with my new pets. When she came to get them for cooking, she was wearing the bikini and asked me how I liked the bright red color. I told her it was pretty, since even back then, cleavage and belly buttons caught my eye."

"You're bad," Nancy said.

"No, really," I said, "she told me 'Thank you love', then gave me a big white toothy smile with those perfect white teeth of hers, and then a big hug. She stood straight, put her hands on her hips and looking at the lobsters in the tub said, 'Come with me boys, fortunately for me it's dinnertime, unfortunately for you, you're my dinner. Mmmmm.'

'What are you going to do with them?' I asked worried.

'I'm going to cook them and eat them,' She said. Then slowly bending over, as not to pop anything out of her bikini top, and reaching into the tub she grabbed them both with her long fingers, and newly painted fingernails, and carried the doomed crustaceans to the kitchen. That's when I saw the big pot with the steam billowing from it. As she held them both over the heat wearing her red bikini, and her big smile, I yelled, 'NOOO.' She looked at me, then back at them and yelled, 'YESSS,' and plunged my two pets slowly into the pot head first, savagely, with no remorse, laughing like some wicked witch I heard once in a cartoon, and pushing them mercilessly against their will into the steaming pot of water with both hands as they struggled, splashed and flipped their tails, while she continued to smile fiendishly. They must have been real fresh because one even climbed right out of the pot at her, and grabbed the strap on her bikini top, pulling it completely off, but she just nabbed the bikini bra in a tug of war with him, topless, and held it high, with him hanging off of it, over the pot until he let go, then flicked him backwards with her fingernail into the scalding water before tying her top back on. It all looked pretty dangerous, and horrifying at the same time."

"Oh my Gosh!!" Nancy said looking terrified, but with a smile and shaking her head, "Stan, You poor thing!"

"Yeah, I was devastated," I said, "and in love at the same time. But I thought she was going to cook me next, because she used to tell me I was so cute she could just eat me up. I didn't know what was happening with me, but if Mary wasn't as pretty as she was, I probably would have run away screaming but I stood in awe, continuing to watch her smiling her evil grin, looking down into the pot, fixing that slinky bikini with one hand, and the other poking at them with a fork, and talking to them saying stuff like, "Down boy, there's no point . . . " She wouldn't even put the lid on right away, watching them squirm. 'Look Stan,' she said, 'They're still moving, and they're already almost as red as my new bikini, see?" She picked me up with the strength of wonder woman and held me under her forearm, hugging me at her side so I could look and compare, and I did. I thought I fell in love right there and then, with her in that overflowing red bikini top."

Nancy let out a screaming laugh and said, "You are funny!"

"Anyway," I continued, "when Angeline was cooking the lobsters for our 'dinner night' together, I was totally tripping my ass off, and maybe that's why I was fascinated by her cooking them; her being a near naked woman, telling me that boiling live lobsters always turns her on. I didn't know why, but I was imagining I was the lobster, and worried that she was going to cook me. Sometimes when I think of it, I think I might be crazy, even though I was tripping."

Nancy and I sat for a bit before she asked me about Angeline. She wanted to know if I still had feelings for her.
"You and Angeline had some memorable times together," she said, "Do you still think about her?"
"I think about her a lot," I told her. "It seems though, every time we were together I was on some hallucinogenic. The night she cooked those crustaceans, I was doing mescaline, and she said she was a witch, telling me she could make me think anything she wants, controlling my mind. Angeline said she could read minds, and she actually asked me who Mary was; Mary in the red bikini. Something else she told me that night, was that she insisted that I could see her past, and witnessed also her future, but I couldn't decipher any of that."

Nancy broke into a fit of laugher again, then said, "That's almost . . . spooky."
I continued, "At Woodstock, I was doing that mushroom shit, and when she was gutting this fish she caught, I was hallucinating, and imagining I was the fish."
"You were high as a kite though," Nancy said, ". . . that's why. You were feeling bad for the creature, while at the same time, fulfilling your deepest fantasy of wanting to be dominated by a woman. Your babysitter 'Mary' was where this may have originated. It took the mushrooms and mescaline to make it surface in its surreal way. All of those details, distorted as they are, is how you remembered it, and it's nothing to be ashamed of, as you're not hurting anyone with your fantasy, except maybe the lobster."
"But," I said, "was it my fantasy or hers?"
"Good question, I'd say 'both', but I'm no psychologist."

Nancy stretched her arms and leaned back with a devious smile and continued, "I think your story's kind of cute. It makes me want to cook you a lobster dinner with live lobsters right now . . . in a red bikini." Nancy then looked into my unsure eyes, and my now blushing face, then slowly and sensuously licked her lips, and with conviction gave a long, but soft and sexy, "mmmmmmmmmm, I'm hungry . . . " she said, mimicking Mary in the story I told her.
"Stop that," I told her.
She laughed and said, "I'm sorry, it *is* a cute story though."
I jumped into the water to cool off and I told her it was her turn to unveil this secret of hers.
Nancy said, "You'll never believe it, even when I tell you."
"Go on, what is it?" I said as I climbed back onto the ledge with her.
"Here goes . . . Angeline and Lila are one in the same."
"What??"
"Angeline and Lila are the same person. She has what psychiatrists call a split personality. Her real name is Evangeline Helwig."
I paused and thought for a minute, then I was pissed.
"You are out of your mind to try and tell me something like that. I know that's bullshit. I've seen them both."
"When did you ever see them together?"
"When I met them at the Woodstock festival," I said. "They were both talking to each other and everything. I saw them as plain as day. Angeline called herself 'Eve' and while she was cleaning a fish Lila came over with the squirrels on her belt. I saw them both together talking to me and to each other. Somebody's pulling your leg Nancy. Sorry to burst your bubble."
"I told you that you wouldn't believe it," she said. "Do you remember you were tripping on a strong mushroom mixture when we found you after you wandered off? And you

just told me a few minutes ago you were hallucinating when you were with her."
"So?"
"So, you were on a strong hallucinogen. What you really saw was Evangeline Helwig all by herself, with the fish, and probably with the squirrels. . . and she was probably back and forth talking to her own personalities or just telling you about her phantom sister because she was tripping too. You envisioned both of her personalities at once. Either way, I'm telling you, she's just one in the same, and like I said before, on a hallucinogenic it's just how you remember it . . . even after you come down. Only you and Nick know this about her."
"Nick's aware of this too? Nick knew this the whole time?" I asked.
"Nick already knew them, or rather 'her' back then, since Evangeline was actually the one who got him into the paratroopers," Nancy said very confidently; and that scared me. "Evangeline, or Angeline if you wish, was in training in the service and was into the martial arts. She was as good, if not better than any man, but they wouldn't take her in the paratroopers. So, because she was such a bad ass; a killing machine; the government found another field for her.
"But I saw them both! At the same time!"
Nancy smiled and reminded me once again, "You were doing those magic mushrooms. Evangeline told me all about it. She was Lila and Angeline. And you, in your state of hallucinating saw them both. Those mushrooms were laced with LSD. Your mind, being very creative made you see what she was telling you"
"All bullshit. I don't believe it."
"Believe it. Angeline has DID, or Dissociative Identity Disorder. She's Lila when she wants her very dark side, and Angeline otherwise. They are so separate that one personal-

ity is unaware of what the other does . . . or remembers. That's why Lila would come to you for something that maybe you and Angeline would know about."

I immediately thought about the time I returned the diamonds with the map to the chest of money to her, not knowing if it was Lila or Angeline that night, but kept it to myself.

Then I degenerated to something a bit less mature. "So'" I said, "That means Nick has been with . . . or rather fucking ANGELINE!?"

"Evangeline Helwig," Nancy said raising her finger like a school teacher correcting me. "By the way Stan, if you ever run into Angeline or Lila, it's not a good idea to confront her with her DID issues. She herself is very aware of it of course, but it's not a good idea to mention it unless she brings it up."

Nancy and I laid in the sun for a while until there was a yell, "Snake! snake!" It was Cuz swimming to us from around the cliffs, and laughing and said, "So are you guys coming or not? We're leaving. Remember, we've got to play tonight." Nancy and I poured ourselves into the water and swam back to the others and we headed back to the motel.

As I watched Nancy climb out of the creek and walk up to where her clothes were, I once again realized how lucky Nick was to have her, even though I now knew he wasn't true to her, and if he's deserving of her, only time will tell.

I got back to the room first, because Nancy, Cuz and Flash went to the hall to check things out. Before I could reach the door knob, the door opened and Lila stepped out, wearing skin tight jean shorts and a flimsy halter top. She kissed me on the side of the face, winked, and continued walking past me. I watched her walk to a Jeep rag top wrangler and drive off. I entered our room and Nick was

writing out a set list for tomorrow. "Hey'" he chimed, "did you get wet in the hole?" He was referring to the Clear Creek swimming hole. I said, "Yeah. And how about you?" He continued writing and was quiet for a few seconds with his eyes occasionally glancing up from his writing at me. Then he said, "I don't know what you mean."
I just left it lie, and I looked at the songs with him until Nancy came back with food and beer and we all chowed down. For the rest of the night and into the morning hours we sat up and sang songs together, as even Nancy joined in heartily, getting to sleep just before daylight.

We all slept in until about 2 PM. We got a late breakfast, which was lunch, and headed to see the famous Meteor Crater. By the time we got back we saw our loyal equipment managers relaxing on the deck with a pitcher of beer, and thanks to them we were already set up in the hall. My Fender bass amp and the Marshall amps were previously carried onto the stage area and set up by Derek and Al, along with the Peavey PA system. Derek is so strong, he can carry two speaker cabinets at once, one on each shoulder. He's also as trained in the martial arts as Nick, since they were both in special forces during their Nam days. Al is also huge, and solid as a rock, spending some time in the marines but never made it past his boot camp training, although he did complete about five weeks of it. He was awarded an undesirable discharge for inadvertently killing a drill sergeant, but was acquitted for the alleged murder under the condition he agreed to the discharge. Al could be incorrigible sometimes, and the story I heard was he was bad mouthing the drill sergeant, who subsequently handed a bayonet over to Al, and the drill sergeant gave Al an order:

"Here! . . . You, big mouth pig fucker, I'm ordering you to kill me. . . but only if you think you've got the balls big enough to do it" The instructor's intention was to either shut Al up, or be ready to put Al down physically and in embarrassment in front of his troops. Al ran the bayonet, without hesitation, right into the sergeant's chest, of course killing him instantly. Al's lawyer argued that he was following orders, which was the defense that got him off easy.

Anyway, Al's with us now, and we call him 'crazy Al' when he's not within ear shot, but even when he is, he doesn't care. Now Derek, who was a Green Beret, has been AWOL since Nam, since after his 3rd tour of Vietnam, when he deserted. He saw so much of the war, the endless killing, and the murdering of innocent people by his own troops, that he felt he had enough. When they called on him for a 4th tour in the jungles, he split for Canada, and believes that, himself being black, had something to do with his 4th (and third) tours. His four years were already up when they gave him his new orders, but there were no lawyers that wanted to defend his objection to go, even though he was decorated as a hero. Derek is not afraid of anything, but he does have Post Traumatic Stress Disorder, or PTSD. I only saw him close to being violent one time, when he grabbed a guy by his lapels and threw him firm against a wall saying, "I almost died for you, countless number of times, you piece of shit. You need to learn some respect for your fellow man!" Then Derek let go of him and the man quietly walked out of the bar. All this man did to originally instigate trouble with Derek was to buy the bar a round, then looked at Derek and said, "Buy the 'coon' one too. It's on me." Derek actually did, in my opinion, keep his temperament in check, considering. Anyway, we were immediately flagged from that bar, and it was no big loss.

So, the Meteor Club room was a big room, full of many people who have heard of us in these parts. I'm told by the owner that we have a full house, people from all over. Folks in the room are from Winona, Flagstaff, Seligman, Page, Prescott, Sedona, and even a crowd from Phoenix, Scottsdale, Tempe and Mesa. I even heard that there was a group of people from Albuquerque, New Mexico. There's a crowd outside who couldn't get in tonight buying tickets from some of our staff for the show tomorrow, and for next week's outdoor concert at Buffalo Park.

At eight o' clock we were ready, as Cuz had his tuner unplugged, and his amp set. Flash had the drums in front of him like a bomb waiting for detonation, while Nick, with his guitar strapped to him, looked like the soldier that he once was, armed and going into battle. I looked at him, then right past him I saw Nancy's smiling face, and with her wink, I had to look away to concentrate on the upcoming bass lines. We started with John Lee Hooker's "Boom Boom," then we went into the originals, like "Now You're Back." The crowd was going wild and insane, even though I didn't think anyone this far west ever heard of us, but I was apparently wrong. We continued song after song with thunderous applause after each and every one. We saved "Sing Those Blues" and Rock and Roll Radio" until the end of course. They wanted more! We mellowed them out with a very well-structured version of "Loralee." The owner demanded we get off of the stage and out of the building after that, but what a crazy night!

The following night was more of the same with a new audience, and again we played our hearts out, as Flash let loose with a ten-minute drum solo, while we did a few lines of cocaine, generously given to us by someone who partied with us since last night. The man called himself "Dallas," and said this coke was pure, and flown straight to Texas from Columbia. It was very good, and so was the pot, as we all got a nice buzz from the coke in time to come back on stage after Flash's solo, and we jammed for about a half hour on the rest of the song, the song being "Zenith." Women in the front were taking their tops off and Flash, with a permanent grin, would yell, "Look at them bounce!" A pair of panties would fly past, just missing me and land on Cuz's shoulder, and slide lazily down onto the floor. People would come up and dance on the stage area while Big Al escorted them politely off, and as we finished, it was another night to remember.

We finished up and headed back to the room, letting Derek and Al pack up, while we stayed up all night drinking with a few invited women without their boyfriends, and about four couples looking to party with us. Dallas continued to serve what seemed to be mountains of cocaine, but as a few of us lost interest, the hangers on hung on. The beer flowed with the whiskey, but I limited myself to the fringe benefits and jammed on the acoustic Martin guitar with Nick and Cuz, and Flash on the congas. There was a harp player and one of the groupie girls had a great voice, with Cuz once again using his proverbial catch phrase, "Don't tell Steph," before the end of the night.

There was a beautiful woman leaning over my back as I strummed the rhythm of the songs. Her tube topped breasts were at my back while her hair was across my neck and shoulders, and I still kept to the beat. I looked up and saw Nancy, sitting next to Nick, but she leered at me with a cold stare as I rocked this pretty lady on my back, while we all played on. The night soon turned to daylight again as I don't remember drifting off; come to think of it, I don't even remember daylight happening.

All of a sudden, I woke up in one of the beds alone, and just knew that somehow, in some port of time during my inebriation, although I don't know who she was, I do, most certainly remember getting laid.

Chapter 15

Taken, in Flagstaff Arizona

We got to Flagstaff Sunday night and set ourselves up at the KOA campsite, which was in a great location on the east side of Flagstaff, where we could see the east side of the slightly snow-capped San Francisco Peaks (yes, even in the summer) and its foothills which has Mount Elden. Mount Elden has no snow this time of year but supports a radio transmitter tower that we could see at its highest crest peeking out over the city. This hill stands about 2400 ft. above Flagstaff and can be seen from anywhere in town. It's also 9301 ft. above sea level so we're already near a 7,000 ft., elevation here in town. We also had facilities like bathrooms and showers, so for a week's stay it was pretty nice, and like being on vacation. We took day trips to see the sights; going to Sunset Crater, Walnut Canyon, Oak Creek Canyon, the Grand Canyon, Painted Desert, and the Wapatki National Monument, which was one of the most interesting places to me, being built by ancient pueblo people, the Anasazi. We also took a ride on the ski lift and hiked to the top of Mount Agassiz, the second highest peak in Arizona at 12,360 ft.

Mt. Humphreys, which we didn't get to, is the highest in this same range of the San Francisco Peaks at 12,637 ft.

By Friday, we were beat, and the concert was to be Saturday, during the day at Buffalo Park, at the base of

Mount Elden, and we're to play last, after the Yippi-i-Odelers. The Paradise Dance Band is before them, and an act called 'Billy and Debbie' are before them. We did a rehearsal to tighten up our set, and to get some of the rust and cobwebs out of our bones from taking it easy all week.

We were taking a break outside of the small shelter we rented at the facility, all except Nick, who drove off for some beer. Then all of a sudden, a man in plain clothes walks up to Derek, who was standing next to his van and shows him a badge. Four more dudes, looking almost the same, with jackets and ties and those brimmed hats grabbed Derek, Al, Nancy, and Cuz, then handcuffed them and put them into their unmarked cars. "Possession of cocaine," we heard one of them say.

I saw our cocaine friend, Dallas, sitting in one of the cars these dicks were driving and wondered if he was busted too, or might this 'Dallas' 'character' be a narc? Since none of us knew or met him until we played Winslow, we don't know.

"You're also wanted by the military authorities for being a deserter," I heard one guy say to Derek.

After they were loaded into the two vehicles, they drove off, leaving Flash and I waiting for Nick to return. Usually Nancy would take care of these kind of things but without her, Nick was our next choice, so when Nick came back with the beer minutes later, we told him the story.

"Where did they take them?" he asked.

"I guess to the police station," Flash said.

Nick and Flash took off together in our van leaving me to lock everything up, then I'm to take Derek and Al's van to meet them at the Flagstaff police station.

Once again, everything gets weird for our band, meaning just when you think the dust settles, something bizarre happens to kick things up again. I figured that Nick and

THE LOST MARBLES STORY

Flash would go downtown, post bail, and we'd bring everybody back here so Nancy could get the ball rolling on lawyers and such, to get everything settled, but as luck would have it, nothing is ever as it seems. A black Jeep Wrangler pulls into the KOA and the dark tinted window rolls down, revealing the familiar face of Lila. "Where are you going?" she asked me as I was getting into the van to meet Nick and Flash downtown.

"You wouldn't believe what just happened," I told her.

"Try me."

"Derek, Al, Nancy and Cuz just got busted. We're going downtown to bail them out."

Lila paused and said, "They're not downtown, and they're not busted."

"What? I was here Lila, I saw them. I saw them get taken away," I told her.

"What you saw was them being kidnapped," she added, "Those weren't cops. Those were those bad fucking people from Bobcat, working for Jackie's dad, and 'Balance' was one of them."

It's been as confusing a life for me as it was exciting from time to time, ever since the inception of this band, the 'Lost Marbles', but now I'm off the charts confused. Especially when she corrects me, saying: "Besides, I'm not Lila, I'm Angeline." And then walks over and gives me a hug and a big wet kiss. . . I rest my case!

"I don't have time to explain," she said grabbing my arm rather firmly, "We have to leave now. You need to come with me."

"Where are we going?"

"See that tower on Mt. Elden?

"Yeah, so?"

"That's where they're going, and that's where we're going. We're going to do some climbing."

I was a little confused once again, "Why don't we drive? There's a dirt road that goes directly to the tower."
"Trust me," she said, "If we go via the dirt road, they'll see us coming, besides, Balance and I have a new understanding, of sorts, and I have a plan."
So, I walked with her to the base boulders of Mt. Elden to start our climb. Angeline was wearing very short, terry cloth tight shorts, revealing her muscular legs, and a thin halter top. And flinging a small backpack onto her bare shoulders she preceded before me as I followed. "I hope these old sneakers I'm wearing hold up," she said establishing the pace. We got to the base and we began our climb up the stacked boulders of Mount Elden, which were rounded and appeared to be 5 feet to 8 feet high. Some were 12 feet but we climbed around them, using our hands, feet, knees and chest to mount these suckers and then onto the next round of them. Angeline was climbing them like a mountain goat, in her athletic gate and had to occasionally stop and wait for me. I was sometimes watching her moves, not just to learn from them on this climb, but it's hard not to watch a perfectly toned body like that, in terry cloth.
"Concentration Stan," she yelled to me, "It's the key."

Anyway, we were probably a quarter of the way up before we started encountering shrubs and some juniper trees, and to this point it had been all boulders.
"Do you want to rest?" she asked standing on a rock with her hands on her hips, looking directly down at me. Looking up I saw her bare, sweaty belly and belly button, while her nipples looked like they were going to pop through, and escape from her soaking wet paper-thin halter top any second, and I had to look away from her.
"Do you?" I returned the question. She laughed and turned around saying, "I asked you first." Then she continued

climbing. Eventually my ego gave in to my weariness and I said, "Yeah."

"Yeah what?"

"Yeah, I want to rest," I told her, sighing between my deep breaths, as she flung her backpack off and handed me a canteen with water. "We'll stop for a few minutes before we continue," she said taking a swig from it, then squatted down on the rock above me. It's like a constant 45-degree grade boulder slope we're climbing, as we're using not only our legs but our arms and hands as well. After about 5 minutes we continued, at her insistence, and we started seeing more and more twisty junipers and other trees, although still sparse. I looked down and saw the city of Flagstaff, Arizona below, with the houses and church steeples getting smaller with our increasing altitude, as we were at about 1000 feet above it by now. To the southwest horizon, we saw storm clouds with what looked like precipitation coming from them, and they appeared to be moving this way.

"We'd better keep moving," Angeline said, "That's coming this way."

We climbed just a little higher when she said, "Whoa, see that?" I turned around to look at what she saw. "What?" I said. She turned and pointed saying, "Lightning!"

It was frightful and unnerving to see electrical bolts gyrating through the threatening and darkened sky headed our way. It's not above us either, as it appears to be a low storm, at the level of this mountain we're scaling, and we were just getting to the giant pines' tree line.

As we continued to climb, the storm was so fast, it was on us now, with lightning bolts hitting as close as 40 feet away. "Over there," Angeline said as she grabbed my arm and pulled me with her, to a trench surrounded by rocks, and we leaped into it. "Keep your head down," she said as we laid down together and waited the storm out. I had hurt my foot jumping into this little ravine and I came to the conclusion that it felt sprained. It's cold enough at this altitude that the precipitation became snow and sleet mixed, a big difference from a few hours ago.

"Here," she said, "Huddle up against me to keep us both warm."

She pulled off her backpack and her sheer top came off with it, exposing her naked breasts, and she pulled my shirt off also, for the warmth of the body heat contact. I didn't mind, after all, we've been intimate before, and I'm not shy with her; Maybe just a little wary of her mental multi-personality issues, but I'm alright with it in this storm.

The thunder and lightning were simultaneous with each other now, meaning that we were directly within the storm. Some of the lightning was below us and some of it was at our height to our left and right. We held each other shivering from the chill, but some of that was sheer fear, at least on my end. I don't think there's a timid bone in this woman's body.

The storm eventually passed over the top of this mountain and the sun peeped through the low clouds, heating things up again. My red headed companion said we were now going to camp here until morning to give my foot a rest. We still have about another 800 feet or more to go to the tower at the top, but I was still in pain with my foot feeling twisted, so she took off my shoes and made me comfortable on some pine branches she cut with her hunting knife. She began softly rubbing my bare, sore foot as I felt myself drifting off to sleep, almost as if she put another spell on me.

When I awoke, it was near dark and I was lying naked on a small blanket, and Angeline's and my clothes were covering me. There was a small fire going in a makeshift pit, and I heard footsteps approaching into the light of the flame. It was Angeline, still topless, wearing only her short terry cloth shorts that hugged her butt, and holding a live and kicking jack rabbit, upside down in her hand.

"Dinner," she said smiling at me victoriously over her prey, and holding it by its legs she slammed the poor creature's head on a rock, causing it to let out a quick squeal, then it went limp. She began cutting into it, using her sharp hunting knife, cutting away the furry skin and exposing the fresh meat in the glow of the fire. "How's your foot feeling?" she asked while continuing her flaying. "It's a little better thanks to you," I told her. Then she told me, as I watched her leaning over the rabbit between her long, outstretched legs, wearing only those short shorts as she pulled the creature's skin down off of its butt and legs like a tiny pair of pants, "Stan, I had to slip you're pants off of you while you slept, so I could properly massage that foot of yours." I just shook my head, wondering how she did that without me noticing, even in my sleep.

She has always had this way of talking that was slow, and definitive, almost like each word, large or small, was calculated; Very sure of herself. She grinned and looked down at her now skinless rabbit saying, "It was getting too late to continue our hike so I figured we'd give your foot a rest and continue in the morning." I thought that was a good idea.

Just then Angeline said, "Oh shit!" Then I heard the high-pitched squealing of our poor dinner as he somehow came back to life. "I hate when that happens," she said as she wrestled to grab and hold this now panicking, slippery and skinless body down between her legs as it somehow tried to run from her. "I'm sorry buddy, but you're not going anywhere." She gave him a quick cut to the throat and held him down until he stopped moving, and it was all over for him. "I don't know," she said, "Sometimes a good club on the head only stuns them without killing them I guess, poor thing. That's only the second time that's happened to me . . . with a rabbit anyway," she said winking her eye at me.

I wondered what she meant by that, but I didn't want to think about it, as she then artfully butchered it into tender pieces, which we cooked on sticks she had cut, placing them over the flames. With her survivalist skills, this woman never ceases to amaze me, so, I had to ask her, "Do you enjoy killing?"
She looked right into my eyes and answered, "What do you mean?"
"What do I mean? I mean I've seen you kill a lot of things, lobsters, fish, squirrels, I guess I'm asking if you enjoy this?"
"Do I look like I enjoy it?"
"Yes," I told her, "I believe you do."
"Then why ask?" she said, "Besides," she added, "I only kill things I'm going to eat, and by the way, I noticed you seemed to be enjoying it too." I remained quiet as she continued fixing the sizzling rabbit pieces.
"Stan, remember those girls at the bar? The Siren's Coast?"
"Yes," I said, "How can I forget them? 'Some of the most attractive women I've ever seen."
"You're right," she said, "I agree. Well we're all sisters in a cult; A witch's cult."
I looked at her with what must have been a cynical glare because she followed up with, "You don't believe me and I can understand that, but I'm telling you, we belong to a coven." She was slowly turning and roasting the rabbit meat. "There's things I can't tell you about it, but the belief in what our religion is, goes way back thousands of years. Did you know that certain covens of witches used to eat human flesh?"

"No, I did not."
"Well, It's true. It was their way of taking the soul of a victim, a person they didn't like. But if there was a person who the witches thought was vile, to the point of being almost inhuman, they would gather together to roast the infidel alive, and have a feast fit for goddesses. It would be like a pig roast gala for all of the witches, or the sisters. Some just simply do it raw, you know, take a heart or liver, or other part of the body and devour it that way."
"No shit?"
"No shit," she said back at me adding, "Tastes like chicken."
"What, human flesh?"
She laughed while picking a cooked piece of the rabbit and putting it up to my mouth said, "No. I mean our rabbit! But it doesn't really taste like chicken. That's what people always say about something they've never eaten before, you know, the cliche, 'Tastes like chicken'?"

I chewed slowly on the morsel she put in my mouth and it was pretty good, the best, (and only) rabbit I've ever eaten. We ate and talked by the fire, overlooking the spectacular clear view of the night lights of Flagstaff, Arizona. Up above, every star was out, as they even pierced proudly through the one Ponderosa Pine tree we were nestled beneath. We were at the beginning of the timber line that eventuate these amazing confirs, and this is one of the few states that has Ponderosa Pines. Angeline pulled out a joint from her backpack and lit it, then passed it to me as we mellowed, and she began talking. "Remember that night at the Siren's Coast when we first met?" I asked her.
"Of course, I do, why?" she asked.
Do you know why the cops were there? You didn't finish telling me if I remember right. I mean did it have anything

to do with those two lobsters I took home?" I asked her point blank.

"It was a pre-empt of the upcoming sting set-up. The feds were casing the place for a week because there were diamonds being smuggled in from a heist in Vegas. No one could figure out where they went. The real value of them was estimated to be about 1.5 to 2.5 million dollars. These diamonds were hidden glued to the shells of the lobsters you caught from that tank, and I'll admit, you were set up by Snake and me. We stole the diamonds from Marco and Balance and they've had no clue about where they were, but suspected that we had a hand in lifting them. They were either patiently waiting us out, or for the diamonds to surface somewhere."

She took in some more meat, chewing it and continued her story, "Well, Balance was patient, and Marco, as you saw at the bar that night, was not. Anyway, as you remember, I had to have those lobsters, but not just for the diamonds." She took a long toke of the joint and handed it to me as we sat in silence for a moment.

"That night we spent together Stan," she said halfway whispering, "you know I'll never forget." I looked at her and a warm feeling went through my bones. "What happened that night Angeline? If you really are a witch did you really put some spell on me?"

"What do you mean? What were you feeling?" She asked.

"I felt like I couldn't take my eyes off of you," I was telling her, "I was watching every detail of your cooking, your movements, your hair, eyes, what you were wearing, I don't know, I guess I'm just being silly. 'Spell', Hah!"

"Don't laugh," she said, "It's not silly, feeling the way you did. You were all caught up in every detail of your feelings and other senses due to the mescaline you were on, not to mention the greens I fed you. I wasn't tripping but I was feeling a lot of the same as you were."

I thought for a second and said, "That's pretty much what Nancy told me, regarding mescaline. It warps your senses as you zero in on details and it can distort your feelings."

Angeline responded saying, "There was no spell, at least not one put on you, yet I may have had somewhat of a manipulating upper hand, as I was sharing your experience. If that's putting a spell on you, well, then I guess I did, but I really enjoyed every moment of being with you. . . and of course those last two sacrificial lobsters," she said laughing." She took a drink of water and continued, "That evening, while tripping, you saw my past and future in a vision on the beach, but you've not deciphered it yet," she took a toke and continued, "For the real spell, I had to have control of your heart and soul, even at the risk of you falling in love with me, and our souls had to touch, in order for myself, and my center, to be empowered enough for that conjuration, the real sorcery on the beach that evening, to be done successfully; and that began when we met at the Siren's Coast, when I realized you were the one, at Woodstock. That spell performed on the beach, back then, was not for you, but solely for this next upcoming full moon, the night when the universe will administer justice; judgement day,"
"I don't understand," I said, confused.
"You will," she answered, with a grin.

I took another toke, and looking at the Flagstaff night lights I took a chance and asked her, "Why did Nick tell me you were killed and Lila's out getting revenge for your death?"
"He obviously lied," she said, "That's what Nick wanted you to believe at the time. He wanted to distance you from

me for your own good, because I asked him to. You already must know that Lila and I are one in the same; we're what doctors call a split personality." Angeline's eyes were watering as she continued, "I went through some bad shit growing up and it messed me up mentally. I love Lila as another person, and as a part of me, as I talk to her, and she to me. She's my evil twin, and I guess she and I are both seeking revenge together."

She dropped her head and cried a bit and I held her, but then, very quickly she pulled herself together, and after blowing her nose said, "I want you to know, that I do not talk much to Lila anymore. I think she's gone . . . or at least we're not separate entities anymore. Stan, I want to tell you that I have you and Nick to thank for that. You guys were a pleasure to talk to, and open up to. I still have the anger, but I'm at least facing it, and dealing with those feelings as one solid individual . . . I hope." Then she smiled and said, "The sorcery we were involved in on the beach that night helped a little too."

What I remembered about the beach just then was a vision of her being a giant, and saving someone smaller, who looked like her, from Tony and Marco. It came to me like a surreal profound revelation as I smiled.

I felt a bit more comfortable with her and said, "You're a great person Angeline."
"Evangeline," she said, "Please call me Evangeline from now on. I'd like that."
"OK," I answered, "Evangeline it is." She wore a sweet smile that made her look like she was at peace with herself, and taking a toke on the joint said, "Not to change the subject but are you aware that Nancy has an enormous crush on you?" For a moment, I said nothing, and just basked in these words from her. Although I know Nancy's with Nick in a relationship, there's a sense that what I was feeling for

her lately was real, but I wasn't sure. Evangeline telling me this to me certifies these feelings . . . or maybe it's simply the high off of this Jamaican red we were smoking, but no matter, this makes me feel good. "What's that? Is this some kind of girl talk?" I asked her. Evangeline looked at me in the glow of the fire and said, "What? I don't even know what that means," she said, "All I know is that Nick told me that she feels real close to you, and that she thinks she's in love with you. I thought you would have picked up on that in the way she took care of you when you were inebriated your last night in Winslow. Boy, I'll tell you, you and Nancy kept a few of us up all night with your moaning and screaming!"

Flabbergasted, I sat in silence for a long time. So, it was Nancy who was in the sack with yours truly, and I was too drunk to remember it! All I knew was I had gotten laid, and thought it was that long-haired groupie girl hanging onto me all night. I now remember Nancy glaring at us from across the room. As much as I wanted to enjoy the moment of Evangeline telling me this, I couldn't, as the situation was that Nancy, Cuz, Derek and Al were taken somewhere and possibly in danger. Nick's girlfriend, Nancy, who he'll kill for, is now, I'm told, in love with me! And I'm sitting on the side of a mountain, in pain, with a woman who, not only I have some feelings for, but who's also diagnosed as a potential psycho! To say this is a little awkward would be, simply one more understatement.

Maybe It's me who's psycho, so I'll just take another toke and try to sleep on this flat rock, but I had to ask her, "What did Nick say about that?" She smiled at me and answered, "Nick had no idea, I had already taken him into the other room to fuck him, and that's why Nancy approached you. By that time, he wasn't paying any attention to anyone, but me. . . and he passed out right after he and I did it."

Then, after stoking the fire a bit, Evangeline said something else that got my attention. "Jackie's dad 'Marco' is out of the slammer, somehow escaped and he's directly involved in all of this," she said, "We'll probably see him when we see the others." Taking another toke and handing the joint to her I said, "I wish I knew what the hell was going on around here. All I wanted to do was play bass in a band." She shook her head and said in a calming whisper, "Stan, Stan, Stan . . . Why don't you mellow and just roll with it?" This is all exciting . . . don't you think?"

I took the joint she handed back to me and she continued, "Marco wants the stash; which is the money, and the pharmaceutical patent info, also other items, or so I was told, which are priceless only to him. That's what Jackie hid in Lake Nockamixon, and Marco will kill for it." She put another log on the fire which was reflecting off of her face, naked shoulders and breasts, which her red hair that she had let down, didn't completely hide, as I try not to stare while she continues her thought, "Marco made a few million a year easily, with that bar alone. Besides being in a cult, the women were high priced hookers involved in all kinds of high end style fetishes, such as foot fetishes, dominatrix fetishes, giantess fetishes,"
"Wait," I said, "Stop right there. What the hell is a 'giantess' fetish?" Evangeline smiled and looked like she couldn't wait to tell me.
"Giantess fetish is fantasizing about being dominated by a very large or very tall woman. Marco has a few of these fantasies, and more, as he likes watching a woman kill something to eat it, like a fish," Evangeline looks at me with a sly grin and adds, "or a lobster . . . " still smiling at me hands me the joint. "He also fears large women will eat him. It comes from when he was a boy on an island of tall women, a story for another time. Most women are tall compared to

him anyway, and that was his attraction to 'Snake,' if you remember."

"Strange fantasies indeed," I said, "but who am I to judge?"

"The thing that makes Marco a sick bastard," she said, "is that he himself enjoys killing people, really enjoys torturing and killing. He has a talent for keeping his victims alive while he mutilates them, but regardless, he's a fucking butcher. When Snake or I get hold of him, it won't be fantasy role playing for him, or a dream come true. We'll be his worse, nightmare; and it will happen before the full moon this month, and that's a witch's promise!"

"He is a sick bastard," I said. I lit up another joint and asked her, "Did you ever get involved in that role play stuff?"

"Yes," she said, "When I was a teenager, Marco was the one who got me into killing and skinning animals. He would watch me do the dirty work, and I had a feeling back then, that it was turning him on, as it also started turning me on, becoming my own little fetish. I was also sexually abused, as I told you earlier, by both him and Balance, and that's what tore Lila and I apart." She looked at me while saying this, and I got a chill down my back as her eyes looked right into my very soul, like she was crying out to me, as if to let me know the exact moment that her personality split right down the middle into Lila and Angeline. "I've never killed people for him though, that was Balance's job. He murdered people for a price, and also when the odds weren't on Marco's side . . . like if the man or woman were too tough for him. Marco is more of a coward and likes to hurt or kill people when they're either tied up, or down, or just plain helpless, or weaker than he is. Did Nick ever mention anything about his sister to you?"

"No," I said, "I don't remember him mentioning much about his family."

"Well, then forget I said anything about her. Nick and his family suffered enough. If Nick wants to tell you, he will. Just don't ever bring it up . . . to anyone."

She kicked her foot at the fire, sending up sparks into the starry night sky and continued. "I heard that he's holding 'Snake' up there with them. Marco thinks she knows where the stash is, but he's wrong, and only you and I know. He also thinks that Cuz and the others might know, so he'll attempt to use methods to extract the location from them."

"Methods?" I asked.

"Torture," she said, "Marco has no conscience and will resort to his heinous methods."

I got pissed and said, "Nothing better happen to Nancy!"

"Just keep holding that thought and you'll be fine with this," Evangeline said with a grin, "so will Nancy, Cuz, and the others. By the way, I've got Balance's number," she said, "and as I said before, I've got a plan."

I took one last toke, and once again, laid down on the flat rock and felt myself drifting off to dreamland. Angeline cuddled naked next to me, and we slept against each other under her blanket in our own platonic warmth.

"Pssst, it's time to get up. 'Your foot feeling any better?" Evangeline whispers in a soft tone awakening me from a deep slumber. My foot was a hundred percent better, and I told her so as I dressed. She packed up her things, put on her shorts and halter top and we started for the top. "I need you to listen to me," she said, "I've got a plan and we cannot deviate from it, or we'll both die. Understand?" I looked at her and was silent as we kept walking. "UNDERSTAND??" she repeated.

"YES!!" I said. "What's the plan?"

I'll let you know," she said, "but for now we have to get to that little trailer building unnoticed." She pointed through the darkness of early daylight to the tower and trailer amidst those sparse pines, as it was silhouetted against the dawning sky. The unmarked cars were there, in the twilight of morning, at the end of the steep road that apparently lead them there.

We hiked what was left of the steep incline of Mt. Elden until it tapered through the pines, and past a small helicopter. We made it to the tall, modular building wall undetected and heard some talking by a window, so we listened. The unmistakable voices were that of Marco and Tony, aka Balance. They were discussing the hidden money that Evangeline had mentioned to me earlier. I heard Marco say to Balance that there was something else in the stash that he wanted, more than the money. It sounded like something about a gold ring, but I couldn't quite make it out. They seem to think that Nancy or Cuz know where the chest of goods is hidden. Balance is saying that he certainly could get it out of them if he's given the chance, and they commented that the other bitch' might know.

Evangeline was already walking to another window, which the four men out front were just out of sight of, and she looked into what seemed to be another room in the building. I followed also, and we both saw Snake, who was that giant pretty and scary belly dancer woman from the Siren's Coast club with the unusually long tongue. She was tied up with her hands above her head, standing tall and naked. She just looked bored and sure of herself, with no fear; as I said, scary!

Just then, Marco and Balance walked into the room. Marco had a bull whip, and gave it a loud snapping crack, but Snake didn't even appear to wince. He asked her where the stash was, and of course, Snake remained silent. He flung the whip at her bare back and I think she squinted with the snapping sound of leather on flesh, as the cord sliced across her back. "I've seen enough," Evangeline said, "follow my lead."

She removed a .357 Magnum handgun from her pack and pointed it at me. "Just keep walking to the door," she said pushing me ahead of her. "What the fuck?" I said, as she just yelled, "SHUT UP!!" Just then the four guys standing around the front came running up, and she communicated to them that she found 'this cocksucker' (apparently meaning me) sneaking around."
I just stood there, offended and confused.
"Where's Marco?" she demanded.
"He's inside." said the big blonde dude, and he opened up the door. I led them in, with the gun at my back and walked down a hall to an opened door on my right. There was Balance, with a big grin, grabbing me by my collar, pushing me against the wall. "Runt!" he said. "Lay off asshole," Evangeline said to him, taking the words right out of my mouth. "Where's Marco?" she asked with a firm tone, as she displayed her natural strong female alpha demeanor, like a lion. He stepped aside with the same smirk and pointed to the door behind him. She made me open it and there he was, little Marco, with a bull whip and ready for another strike on the now bloody back of Snake.

Snake was, as we saw from the window earlier, stripped naked and now appeared like she was in some sort of trance, but unmoved by the wounds. She was even grinning. It was frightening enough to send a chill down my spine. "She doesn't know," Evangeline said adamantly. "Know what?" Marco asked. Balance followed up with, "Yeah, what doesn't she know?" The room got suddenly quiet, but then Evangeline squeezing my arm and shoving me forward said, "Here's the asshole who's been sneaking around outside. He's also the fuckhead bassist for the Lost Marbles."

"Easy there, I have feelings . . . " I whispered to her.

Just then, Marco smiled, seeming to know me and said, "Stan," setting the whip down in a chair. "I'm pleased to make your acquaintance," he added extending his sweaty hand to me in mock friendship. "Untie her," he then said to two of his goons entering the room, as he walked me over to a wooden chair and pushed me down into it.

The goons released her from her scourge bonds, and tied Snake's hands behind her back, making her sit next to me, still naked. Her legs were muscular but very feminine, even though both legs were entirely tattooed with scales. It looked like a thin, tight pair of pants from her hips and ass right down to her bare feet. Her feet both had tattooed faces of snakes, making her feet look like snake heads.

"I haven't seen you in a while," Balance said to Evangeline, putting his arm around her.

"Let's go," she said to him, "I've got something to show you."

Balance, with a wink, told Marco he's taking Evangeline and that he'll meet him at Sky Harbor airport tomorrow. They left together on the small helicopter that was sitting outside. I was left, again, to wonder about my present situation, this time, with the incomparable 'Snake'.

Then it happened, in walked Cuz, Nancy, Al, and Derek, with hands tied, and they sat them down in some extra chairs while the goons tied them quickly to the chairs, with each of them remaining silent as they did so. One big unhappy family! Nancy just stared at me the whole time, she looked worried. Derek and Al just grimaced as they observed the room, the goons, and little Marco.

"Get on up here bitch!" Marco said, grabbing Nancy by her arm.

He and the blonde goon tied her hands to a chain hanging from the ceiling. Marco had to stand on a chair, and then ripped off her top, exposing her naked back. Nancy started crying as Marco asked where the stash was.
"I don't know what you're talking about," she was saying to him with her extended arms shaking and her tears flowing. In walked Dallas, the guy that was giving the band all the coke in Winslow.

Dallas turned out to be one of the henchmen, or rather goons for Marco and them. Anyway, he was with the bull whip now, lean, muscular, and naked, and looking to give Nancy one hell of a beating and whatever follows. Marco was giving Nancy to him to do what he wants for not telling where this presupposed stash was. Dallas's mouth was watering at the prospect, since he had eyes for Nancy ever since he met her, but either Nick or I were always in the way.

Now, Snake, sitting naked next to me, had a pen knife in between her toes, and was prodding it past me, into Derek's foot, using her long legs. (I can guess where she had been hiding it) Derek picked up on this immediately, and in seconds, somehow, it was in his hands behind his back. I could sense something going down. I yelled to Dallas, "Wait! She doesn't know where the stuff is. But I do!"
"You do?"
"Yes," I told him, "I do!"
"Too late," Dallas tells me, with a big smile and laughed as he started pulling back his arm to strike the first scourge on Nancy's bare back. My fists were clenched with anger, as I was irate and fuming, barely sputtering an emotional growling, and loud "Nooooo!" All I knew is I wanted to see him dead, immediately, this instant, but I was tied tight. Just then, Derek and Al stood up miraculously, and both smiling, with their arms and legs free, and with Derek

saying to Dallas in his deep voice, "You're right, it's too late . . . for you!" Dallas' smile left his now ashen face in total shock, as he appeared to be scared to death, since there was brown running down his naked legs.

Before he could do anything else, Derek grabbed him and with one snap, broke his neck. Crazy Al plunged the pen knife they used to cut themselves free, directly into the eye of the blonde goon and snapped his neck also. Al and Derek then kicked the other two goons in the face, almost in unison and killing them instantly but never quite made it to Marco. Little Marco gunned them both down and the rush was over as quickly as it started.

Poor Al and Derek, it was a tremendous effort and now Marco has only one of his guards left to watch Snake, Cuz, Nancy and me. . . and he's pissed. I'm of course as shaken as the rest of us are, and trying not to piss myself. I've never seen anything like that, unless it was on TV, as Al and Derek had to be the toughest dudes I've ever seen, next to Nick. They were funny at times, great guys, and now, that quick, they're dead heroes! That's the best eulogy I can muster in this situation as they echo respectfully in my thoughts, while lying dead on the floor.

Marco walks over to them and kicked them each once, then walked right over to me. "I already know you know," He said, "That's why she brought you here."

"Yes," I said, "I know where the stash is but you'll have to let Nancy down, or so help me I'll kill you myself!" Snake let out a belly laugh and Marco followed with a loud snicker. I glared right into Marco's eyes until he stopped his jolly chuckle, and got serious.

"We'll all go together," he said. "We'll all go to where the stash is, and when I see it; Then, and only then will I let you and your friends go."

Snake let out another belly laugh, causing her shoulders to bounce up and down to the rhythm of her laughter. "You can count on that honey," she said facetiously to me, holding back the laughter just enough to get those words out.
"Put some clothes on her," Marco said to the other goon holding the gun on us. He untied us and threw Snake the top and jeans she must have had on when she was first abducted. We exited the building and we were escorted to the back of a van. "Stan, you drive, and Snake, you ride up front with me. The rest of you get in the back. Bob, keep them cuffed and keep an eye on them." We drove down the dirt road switchbacks, descending Mount Elden and onto route 89 to route 40 east. Then across country toward Pennsylvania. We were headed for Lake Nockamixon and the sealed chest of millions that awaits Marco.

Chapter 16

Back in Pennsylvania

After miles of driving and quite a few stops, and some sleep with Marco and Bob taking turns guarding us, we were in Pennsylvania. I look over at Snake, who's been pretty quiet. "A penny for your thoughts?" I ask her. She looked back at Marco who was nodding out as it was Bob's turn to watch us, and she grinned and said, "His days are numbered. I'm going to roast him alive."

A chill went through me, as it was the way her sexy eyes penetrated right through me, and I almost felt sorry for Marco, but then I welcomed the thought of someone hating him as much as I do now. Then she said, "He's a selfish, narcissistic, murdering coward, and I'm going to enjoy killing him slowly." I admired her confidence, since things don't look good for us right now. Snake comes across to me as being a little insane, but I can tell she's very intelligent, and I wouldn't want her as an enemy, but it sure sounds like she's on our side.

We reached Lake Nockamixon by 11 am on a Tuesday and turned into the park, taking a fenced off dirt road down a semi-steep grade and just within sight of the big lake. Bob put on some diving gear and we all walked, cuffed and at Marco's gun point, to a hidden 15' boat with an outboard motor. The lake was not crowded with fishing boats by any means today. There were a few sailboats out in the middle, and more to the other side, but they had no idea what we were doing in this cove, nor did they care.

Bob and a guy named Fred Simms, who met us there at the boat, took it out to the spot on the map I had pointed out to them. It was only about 50 yards out in a deep area, and the spot, that was told to me by Evangeline to be the place. Bob had his diving gear and flippers on to take him 20 feet down to unhook the weighted down sealed chest. In about 10 minutes after diving, he surfaced with the chest, and dragged it across the top of the water as the boat propelled them both to shore.

Marco waded out to them, to help Fred and Bob drag the chest onto the gravel and rocks of the beach. The padlock still looked new, but with no key, they took hammers and pry bars to open the metal chest, and had fresh empty containers there and ready to transfer the loot neatly, as they seem to have thought of everything. When the clamps and lock were off, the lid was lifted, and all of us were aghast.

The chest did not contain any money, but it contained the naked body of a man. The man was skinned, castrated, and probably still alive when he was placed in there, from the way his eyes looked, according to one of the goons. He's good and dead now, and the only one to scream was Marco, screaming like a little girl, because the man in the box was what was left of Tony Balencia. Balance!
"NOOOO!" wailed Marco, as most of us stared silently at the body, which tumbled from the box as Marco flipped it in an emotional rage. Snake, however, started laughing, and kept it up like a crazy person. Marco stomped up to her in his tearful rage and pointed the pistol against the side of her head; point blank, and looking up at her said, "You fucking bitch! You fucking, fucking BITCH!"

Instantly, to our surprise, she kicked him in the groin as her cuffs, just fell off of her; like a Houdini magic trick. She took his gun from his hand and pistol whipped him across the face, causing him to fall onto his knees. She pointed it at Bob and shot once, putting the bullet between his eyes. Fred just put his hands up and froze while she slipped the gun into the back of her tight shorts, and grabbed Marco's head in both of her hands as if getting ready to twist it off like a top. I thought this was it for Marco, but then, she leaned into his face and said, "This would be too easy. I've got better plans for you dear . . . before the next full moon. It's a witch's promise." Then her long tongue slipped out of her mouth and flickered into his ear, relentlessly, like a snake as he squirmed, causing him to pee his pants, as he did before. Then she threw him down, and laughing, took off into the woods like a deer, and she was gone, as we just stood there quietly, for a while.

    Balance laid on the ground, completely skinned, with the exception of his head and face, and dead on the gravel and grass with the distant look of death and fear in the stillness of his open eyes. He also had what appeared to be a very large knife up his ass, what a way to go. Evangeline, and the remnants of her alter ego 'Lila' had repaid him for the years of torment she had suffered at his hands. I wish I could have been there to see her overtake him, as I had wondered how she did it. She probably overtook him while having sex with him, just like the black widow spider. She once told me that she found out he was claustrophobic, so I'm sure she played that aspect into it, along with beating then skinning him. Poor bastard. The devil got his due. I remembered the spell, and those two lobsters that Evangeline named Tony and Marco before cooking them. Now it would appear to be Marco's turn.

    Almost immediately after her exit, about five of Marco's goons came running down to us from the trail. One of them was a big, piggish looking man they called Yo-Yo the butcher. Marco stood up and said as they approached, "Get him into the crate and out of here," pointing at Balance's lifeless body. He told Fred Simms and the goons to walk with him back to the van, as he grabbed Nancy by the arm and marched her with them, pointing the pistol to her head. He left with the goons, the bodies of Balance and Bob, and with Nancy. He also left the big guy, Yo-Yo, behind with us, and with clear instructions to dispose of us however he liked and to meet him at Rocky's tavern right up the road.

    Now Yo-Yo stood big, with a large hunting knife sheathed at his belt. He had a sweaty, pale complexion with greasy, dirty blond hair. He had an eerie high-pitched girly giggle coming from his smile that was short a couple of teeth, and it was a giggle that made my skin crawl. His face was round with about a week-old beard, and he had a big gut stretching from his stained white t-shirt. He held a pistol on us and told us to start walking. I went first, and Cuz of course right behind me, both of us still hand cuffed with our hands behind us, and we were off and walking into the oaks and maple trees of these lakeside woods. Yo-Yo was right behind Cuz.

I heard Cuz say, "What do you think you're doing?"
I turned while we were treading down the path, and saw Yo-Yo poking his finger hard into him, giggling, and then shove him hard into me, knocking us both down.
"Get up!" He snorted.
Cuz and I stood and we were instructed to walk further yet. He then started to poke Cuz in his sides as if tickling him and continued his nerve-grating giggle, then he shoved Cuz once again roughly into my back causing us both to tumble once again.
 Cuz blurted out, "What the fuck is the matter with you?"
Yo-Yo giggled harder saying, "I'm gonna cut you up, then fuck you both. . . in the face and in the ass."
"That's . . . pretty specific," Cuz responded with some of his wry humor.
Yo-yo giggled that high-pitched giggle again, and added, "Then I'm going to join the others in gang banging that sweet bitch of yours."

All I knew was that I had to act immediately, and act fast. The thought of Nancy at the mercy of these animals was too much to bear, so if I'm going to die anyway, I'll die trying. I'll tell you what, the size of the guy didn't matter, and the situation we were in did not stop me. I dropped, and rolled myself around on the ground like a crazy man and into a pretzel, until I was able to squirm my handcuffed arms to the front of me. The big oaf threatened to shoot if I didn't stop what I was doing, but I didn't care. I then jumped up, lunging at Yo-Yo, grabbing his hand that was holding the gun, and simultaneously head butting him on his nose once, twice . . . while kneeing him as hard as I could in the groin, as he raised the weapon, breaking my grip; then I gouged my thumbs into his eyes before I heard a shot from his pistol. I grabbed his hand once again, and bashed it against an old oak, causing him to let go of the gun.

His screams were loud and girly, like his giggling, but I didn't have the time to let it grate on my nerves. I now had him down on the ground and I was on top of his round belly banging my cuffed hands into his bleeding face, over and over as he screamed, and if he hit me, I sure didn't feel it. The blood was pouring from his eyes, nose, and mouth as I jumped up from his now limp form. While he was moaning, I reached into his pockets for the keys.

Just then, his hand grabbed mine firm, and his grip was hard to shake, as he was giggling that giggle again, peering at me through his bloody eyes. I was afraid he was starting to get up and I yelled for Cuz to help; then I saw a bare foot, that looked like a snake's head stomp onto his wrist, causing his grip to fail and I pulled free. Then the foot stomped him in the face, quieting him as he went limp again.

Looking up, it was Snake smiling down at me saying, "Very impressive, go ahead, get the keys." I picked them from his pocket and unlocked Cuz and me from our shackled hands while Snake took Yo-Yo's knife and began cutting his clothes from his back, arms, and legs, rolling him over systematically like it was nothing to her and cutting until he was totally stripped of his clothing. "You put up a great fight with him Stan. You should have been a woman," she was saying to me while trying on his shoes which were a close enough fit for her. "I'll take that as a compliment," I told her.

"You two better go now if you want to save your friend," she said rolling the rest of his clothing into a ball and tossing it behind a stump. There was a set of car keys on his key ring and I told Cuz we were heading out.

"What about him?" Cuz inquired, "Are we going to leave him to follow us?"

"Look at his eyes," I said, "I'll be surprised if he can see much of anything, much less follow us." His huge nude form started crawling away and crying like a baby, but Snake slammed her foot onto his back pushing his face into the dirt. She smiled and mockingly asked him, "Going somewhere?" Then she looked down at him as he wept, then at me saying "He's a bad dude, really bad. There's a reason they call him the butcher you know. Two of my closest friends aren't alive today to talk about it, but I'll take care of him for them. I'll take care of him really good." Then she looked at him and added, "Won't I love?" She was grinning and sharpening the knife on a piece of sandstone in her palm while pressuring her foot up and down on his back.

"Mmmm, you're nice and tender, and I haven't eaten a thing all day," she said tormenting Yo-Yo, then said to us:

"You guys better get going now and leave us be. We want to be alone." Then patted his butt and said, "Don't we dear?"

Yo-Yo looked like a beached whale laying in the dirt and rocks within this rarely traveled forest of oaks and maples. Almost pitiful.

"PLEASE DON'T LEAVE ME ALONE WITH HER," Yo-Yo whimpered, as she removed her foot, then stripped

herself completely naked. Turning around she threw her long, tattooed legs over him and straddling him, sat on his naked ass while she cuffed his arms behind him, then spinning around on her bare ass reached out and cuffed his kicking legs. I looked at Cuz to prod him along, so we could get going, but he was just standing, staring at her, paralyzed, with his mouth open in a trance, watching her flip Yo-Yo over onto his back, then squatted her ass back down onto his thighs.
"Well?" she said to us, sitting on Yo-yo with a determined look in her eyes and pointing the shiny, sharpened knife, "Get going!"

We high-tailed it immediately down the trail to a Chevy pick-up parked where we came in.
Cuz said between breaths, "She's beautiful but crazy, ain't she?"
"At least she's on our side, I'm glad for that," I said increasing my gate.
On our way out, we heard Yo-Yo's bone chilling shrieks of terror and pain in intervals, which doubled our pace. The haunting screams continued endlessly as they echoed through the woods, but the faster we ran, the more and more distant they became, as we saw the pick-up and we ran towards it. The key fit and we were in, starting the thing up.
"That tavern's right up here ain't it?" I asked, as we drove like a bat out of hell to Rocky's bar, an old hangout of mine, and where Marco was to meet Yo-Yo.
"I couldn't take my eyes off of her," Cuz was saying, "she had a strange, mystifying beauty or something about her; very erotic . . . don't you think?"
"I think you need a cold shower . . . with your wife Stephanie to take that spell she put on you away," I told him jokingly as we were driving the pick-up about 80 mph.

We arrived at the bar, and there we saw the parked van. Marco and the others were probably in the bar. We were able to sneak up behind it and unlock the back with Yoyo's keys, where we found Nancy unharmed; but bound and gagged and curled up on the floor. I was able to free the ropes and with the keys, quickly unlock the cuffs. She hugged me like she was never going to let me go. As we held each other, it felt like an eternity and I didn't want to let go, ever, but I had to. "No time for this, " I said pushing her back and grabbing her hand, "let's get the hell out of here."

We got into the pick-up and drove off, down Old Bethlehem pike and to a cabin I knew of, where a friend of mine lived. It was off of the road far enough to hide out as we made our phone calls. My friend who lived there was Bird, the conga player we knew. He always offered us his place anytime when we jammed with him and today we took him up on it. We didn't tell him any details, of course, and he asked no questions. He let us use his phone while he passed the 16 oz. bottles of ice cold Ortlieb's beer out to us with a welcoming grin. The first thing I wanted to do was reach Nick.

After a few hours and a few calls, we found out Nick was back in Warminster at the house. We called and arranged a meeting with him at a tavern in Hatboro. We didn't want to go back to the house, knowing that we were probably being sought by Marco and company. Nick did inform us however that Marco and his henchmen were there, but disappeared, and he told us to stay put for the night and he'll come up here to Bird's cabin to meet us sometime tomorrow.

While we waited for Nick, we kicked back a few more beers and watched some TV while Bird pulled out his con-

ga and acoustic guitar. Cuz and he jammed to some tunes while I sat quietly with Nancy when the news came on:
"This is a breaking news story from Bucks County, Pennsylvania. A body was found by hunters less than an hour ago by Lake Nockamixon near the outskirts of Quakertown. The body of a man, in his 40's was found cuffed and mutilated in what is believed to be, or at least in appearance, a homicide in a satanic style ritual. The body appeared to be skinned and disemboweled when the hunters stumbled upon it, as they heard what they thought were the victim's screams for help. Police are now investigating and asking for anyone to come forward who might shed some light on this gruesome slaying."

Nancy squeezed my hand and quietly leaned onto my shoulder as she reached out to change the channel. After another beer, and another song, we asked Bird if we could stay the night. He spoke not a word, but went into the back to bring out some sleeping bags and blankets. "I only have the one bed," he said, "but you're welcome to the couch, the chairs, or the floor." Thank God for Bird!

Nancy and I cuddled, fully clothed, under a blanket on the sleeping bag across the floor. Cuz got the couch, and Nancy laid right in front of me on our sides in a spoon position. She turned her head around and gave me a kiss on the lips and pulled my arms around her as she turned her head back, giving me the hair on the back of her head. I was real comfortable here, as we dozed off into a peaceful oblivion.

The morning came fast and we heard Nick pull up. All he said was:
"Thanks Bird, but we're all in a hurry and we can't stay. Hey guys, come on!"

Bird said nothing but handed us a six pack of a different beer in cans and told us to be good. "Let me know when you're playing next," he said and we were on our way.
"He doesn't know anything?" Nick asked.
"He didn't ask, we didn't tell," Cuz said.
"Well, I'm asking. What the hell happened?"
"Is this a rented car?" Cuz was asking.
"Yes," Nick told him, "It's rented! Now are you listening to me? What the hell happened? I was worried sick about you guys." He looked at Nancy, "Especially you!" He gave her a big hug, shed a small tear and we all got into the vehicles. "We're going to have to do something about that asshole's truck you have. He's all over the news. Follow me," Nick said as we drove off north on route 611 to an auto salvage place that Nick's old army buddy owned.

We were able to get rid of the vehicle, no questions asked and we continued north in Nick's rented car. As we drove we unfolded the whole ordeal we went through to Nick, detailing everything that happened to us after we were abducted in Flagstaff, and about the death of our two friends.

Soon we pulled into a Greyhound bus depot in Easton and Nick put Nancy and Cuz on the bus home. "Go home to your wife Cuz, Nancy will keep you company on the way while Stan and I have a few things to take care of."
"Are they going to be safe there?" I asked.
"Safer than you and me," he said, "they'll be OK."
We headed north to an airport in Scranton where there was a big Learjet waiting. I didn't get it. Where were we going?

Chapter 17

Heading Out of The Country

"OK Stan we're here. Let's go."
I looked at him puzzled as we started across the runway to the jet plane and he said, "Confidential, just trust me!"
We got to the jet, climbed the stairs and entered, and the person helping us in was a familiar face, my old girlfriend Barbara, who was also wearing a uniform like she was possibly the pilot!
"Barbara, you know Stan. Stan, you know Barb. She's going to be flying us to a place you won't believe!"

"Hi Stan!" she said giving me a big hug and a wet kiss. "Sorry, here, wipe the lipstick off," she said handing me a handkerchief. "Make yourself comfortable," she added, "it will be a long flight. Maybe we'll catch up later." I got in and sat down in a roomy seat and put on the seatbelt. We were off.

    We flew westward across the U.S. for a few hours before reaching the Pacific. In those few hours Nick and I talked.

"Marco's got Flash," Nick said.
"What?"
"Marco's threatened to kill Flash if we don't cooperate."
"Where are we going now?" I asked.
"We're going to meet with Marco and get our boy back."
"Okay, so where are we going? Geographically?"
"They're about two hours ahead of us on another jet. Are you familiar with Fiji?"
I looked at him in disbelief and said, "Yes, I'm familiar with Fiji. Is that where we're going?"
"Not exactly. But we are going to a small uncharted island about 800 miles east of it."
I sat for a few minutes before asking, "Is it a private island belonging to the creep Marco?"
"Not exactly private, although Marco owns the only ten million-dollar estate on it. The rest of it is smaller houses, huts, and fishing villages."
"Are we just walking in and taking Flash?"
"Yes, we are. Stan, these are all good questions," he said sardonically.
"Are we going to die?"
With a big smile Nick answered, "Absolutely not. Trust me."
"How did Barbara get here? It can't be just a coincidence."

"It's all part of the plan," Nick said. "I chartered this craft we're in and she's in the deal." Then Nick started outlining everything.

"Marco has his estate, and he has his goons, the guys surrounding him. He also has his beautiful tall women on the island, who have been catering to his every need. Money and power is all you need to have what he has. The box of cash, the seven million that Evangeline took from him is in the back. He doesn't need it, but he can't stand to lose it. That's why I'm bringing it to him, to trade for Flash."

"Will Marco accept that as a trade?"

"He said that's his plan. But it doesn't matter, I have an alternate to his plan. I don't trust that little pig and I'm not satisfied with his plan anyway." Nick leaned in towards me saying, "There's another Learjet about an hour behind us carrying some people of interest. I won't say anything more." Then Nick opened up a cola and asked me if I wanted one. I preferred a small bottle of scotch off of the tray. He continued to talk, "I need you there, Stan, for support because you're one of my best friends, and Nancy loves you. And I love you for loving her Stan, you guys are good together, trust me on this one. We're all going to be okay and I will never let anything happen to you." He took a sip and said, "Marco's going to wish he was never born for abducting you, Nancy, Cuz, Derek, Al, and now Hank. Derek and Al are dead because of me, and it's eating me up. All of this shit is happening to you guys; the band; because of me and my stupid obsession!"

Nick put his head down and was fighting back emotions. He was being tortured inside as if he wanted to tell me something, and it showed. I've never seen this man like this before. After an awkward pause in conversation I said, "You want to tell me something Nick? Tell me what this is all about." Nick opened a little bottle of scotch and gulped it down. Then he began his story.

"Stan, did you know I had a sister?"

"I think I remember you mentioning something about a sister at Woodstock," I said, "now that you mentioned it. You never talked much about family."

He began telling me, "Back at Woodstock, when you and I met, I didn't get the chance to introduce you to my little sister who was with me. She was only 15 years old. I called her 'Marbles' ever since we were little because she always could beat me at playing marbles."

"Marbles? Really?" I asked.

"Yea, I know, like our band, 'Lost Marbles'. That was an odd coincidence for me when Jackie accidentally coined us with that name. I kept my mixed feelings about that to myself."

"Now I remember," I said, "that you told me then that she was the only one who ever calls you 'Franky'."

"Yeah, that's right," he went on, "Anyway, as we grew, she always loved being with me. It was embarrassing sometimes with my friends, like Hank and them because she would cling all the time. But I really didn't mind because secretly I enjoyed her. She was so alive, and full of life and energy, and she could always make me laugh.

I was always her protector and she knew it. In shop class I made her and I two rings." He showed me the one on his finger. "See this jagged edge? This is half and her ring is the other half. They started out as one forged piece and I cut the jag in it to separate them, giving her one and this one. This means we were joined together. Anyway, she had gone with me up there that summer of '69 to the concert. I told my folks I'd take care of her, you know, be the big brother and look after her. The first night and day we had a great time with everyone. We were all so loose and carried away with the music and the festival and all, that I kind of lost track of her.

    To put it short, I lost her. I never saw her again, alive anyway. The rest of the concert I was searching, asking questions, annoying almost everyone I've talked to, but to no avail. She was gone." Nick poured a strong cup of coffee from a canister he had and I just sat and listened, surprised and captivated.

"What do I tell my parents?" he continued, "What do I tell myself? I went right to the police and they said they'd 'get right on it.' After a week, I went home and told my folks. You can imagine the heartache and worry. I was going fucking crazy searching and still looking for some sign that she was still alive somewhere."

"Holy shit Nick!" I said, "And she was never found?"

Nick took another sip of coffee and said, "She was found alright. Her nude body was found in the woods near the concert site in New York, beaten, raped and strangled! Even the ring I gave her was never found".

"Oh my God!!" I gasped.

"Oh my God is right. I thought I was going to lose my mind. Worst of all, my folks were devastated. These were people who depended on me to keep her safe. I love my mom and dad as I do my sister, and I was so afraid that this was going to kill them both. They say they don't blame me, but how could they not? All I knew at the time was that I let my sister and my family down. I wanted to find the murderer or murderers at any cost. So, I began by returning to Woodstock. That's when I met Evangeline, and that's where the search began. She knew who the bastard was who did this to my sister. It was one person. Marco."

"Marco?" I said, "You know that for sure?"

"I have a witness, Evangeline Helwig, who once was known to you as Angeline or Lila."

"She saw what happened?"

"Evangeline heard a girl meeting Marbles' description screaming 'Help me Franky' and trying to fight off Marco. She ran to her, and tried to get Marco off of her but Balance grabbed her. They were both then beaten and raped, but Evangeline as usual survived her ordeal. Balance stayed with Evangeline and didn't do anything with my sister according to her, it was all Marco. Evangeline was used to the abuse for years she told me, but she always tried to fend off any abuse she would see them do with other girls if she could. Sometimes she was successful with clocking Marco or Balance in the head, but that one particular time with my sister, she failed. Until I talked to her, she had no clue who my sister was. She only told me that the girl kept screaming for me, calling the name 'Franky' to help her. And as you know, Marbles was the only one to ever know me as Franky."

"I'm getting chills just thinking about it Nick," I told him with a tear.

"I knew, that because of who these people were, I had no immediate way of getting to them. I was smart enough by this time to think it through.

I joined the service right after that. with the help of Derek while Evangeline enlisted in the military also. I was more familiar with her 'Lila' personality and I never let anyone know I was aware of her DID. By the way Stan, I'm calling her by her given name because with your help, and mine, she thinks that her Lila personality is gone."

"Lila has left the building?" I said trying to have an 'Elvis' witticism.

"It's not funny Stan."

"I know Nick, I'm sorry."

"But yes," Nick said, "she's felt that talking to you and me, has been very good therapy for her and she swears she's cured.

By the way Stan, I'm sorry for telling you a while a back a lie, that Angeline was dead, and that Lila was avenging her. It was Evangeline's own plan to distance you from her. She made me promise. She wanted you to figure her out on your own, how unstable her mind was, and you did so. I could see it made you less drawn to that phantom ghost of Angeline. Evangeline really liked you. I mean still really likes you, but she also played you, and didn't want you to fall head over heels for her. She knew you would."

"That's pretty damn presumptuous of her," I said.

"Presumptuous indeed Stan, but true."

"I know," I mumbled, disappointed in my own transparency.

Nick then said, "She really didn't know you were in the band, when she first started to play you. That coincidence really shocked her, seeing you in the studio when Jackie first brought her in. Consequently, her fuck up, with you, and you being so ignorant to it all, turned out to be the coincidence that inadvertently put everything on a positive spin for her plan to fall into place.

"Hmmph. 'Glad I could help," I replied sarcastically.

Nick paused, after his grinning at my comment, and continued to reflect, "But way back then, Evangeline had opened herself up to me about her issues. With her high I.Q. and some creative bullshitting, she was able to mask the problem during the Vietnam era and enter into the military. Since then, I had eventually hooked up with Nancy and protected her with my life. She promised never to mention to anyone about my sister, or ever bring the incident up."

Nick looked at his sister's ring again and continued:

"Flash was devastated over her death too, and felt like blaming himself as I did, and we never mentioned it again. Now, I was on a personal mission, or vendetta, that was so secret that I never told anyone, until now Stan; I'm on a mission to get this clown Marco and wipe him out. I've been very selfish and putting my friends and loved ones at risk, and I am real, sorry about all of this; like what happened to 'Marbles,' I realize it's all my fault."

"Stop blaming yourself," I told him, "This bastard has to be stopped, we all know that."

"I know," he continued, "but I was too blind with personal rage and selfishness to see that I was putting everyone at risk, and for that I'm sorry."

"My only dilemma," I asked, "is why didn't they blow Evangeline away at the tower building on top of Mount Elden in Flagstaff if she testified against them?"

Nick grinned and said, "Evangeline knew about something that was in with the stash that Marco wants, something about a gold ring. It's some sort of an island witch, voodoo thing that he's obsessed with getting returned to him." Nick said taking another sip then said, "Besides, they were all in the same boat by then, and Evangeline knew exactly how to play Balance."

"She certainly did then," I told him as I listened.

He paused for another sip of coffee and then continued, "Flaming Flash Hank is going back with us, and I need you to know that I have it under control because if there are any doubts, it may jeopardize the plan. When this is done, it will be done."

"Nick," I said sarcastically, "When did I ever doubt you? You've always been my hero!"

There was a pause as we looked right at each other. Then we both started laughing so hard I thought I was going to piss myself. "You are so funny," he said, "I'm really glad you said that. Your sarcasm saves the day again" he added, "I'm so heavy sometimes, ain't I?"

"You are," I said, "and let it be known Nick, you are, and always will be my friend. Just know that I'm with you."

Whatever Nick's plan is, I feel we're both good and ready for it now.

We had landed to gas up and I got to chat with Barbara. She told me she's been a pilot for years now, ever since her Golden State days, doing these private charter flights. She's been in touch with Nick and Nancy off and on through the years, letting them both know her progress, and that's how they managed to hook up over this flight; It wasn't coincidence, as Nick is a very smart guy, dumb like a fox, and arranged it somehow that Marco would book her as the pilot to this island that only he himself knew the co-ordinates, so Barbara's working for Nick as well, unbeknownst to Marco.

Something else I noticed, is that Barbara and Nick appear to be very close; not that it matters to me, other than I wonder how close Nancy and he are doing anymore. It's sometimes hard to read Nick, and I know I'm having feelings for my best friend's long-time flame. I know now how Eric must have felt with Patti and George.

Barbara was back in her seat at the flight controls and we were off and over the blue Pacific Ocean. The new co-pilot we picked up here was a pretty blonde, very tall, and large breasted, so much that she had to have her top buttons unbuttoned. She looked familiar but I couldn't place the face, as she wore lots of makeup, but tastefully. She had the dark red lipstick, like Barbara had, and the long, downward pointed thin eye brows, and the eye liner . . . almost like the style of someone playing Cleopatra in a movie. I guess this was all part of the uniform these female Learjet charter pilots wear, as I remember stewardesses wearing makeup in the same manner, making me glad I'm a man. "This is 'Ginger'," Barbara said introducing her friend, "She'll be hangin' out with us." Now I remember, this was her friend Ginger, with the bullfrogs at our farmhouse from years ago.

As we flew over the deep blue Pacific toward our destiny, Nick told me that he and Nancy are not the same anymore. He looked at me and said, "Stan, I know that Nancy really likes you, and I have the feeling you feel the same about her."

"Nick, I don't think . . . " I started but Nick interrupted saying, "Just let me talk," and he took a sip of strong coffee, then said, "I'll always have feelings for Nancy, but I'm not in love with her." He looked out at the ocean then back at me saying, "You really know how to treat her, and I admire that."

"Come on Nick, you treated her very well for all these years. . . and she loves you."

"She loves me," he said, "but we're not in love."

I sat for a minute quietly and said, "Hey, I'm not good at this kind of talking, nor am I comfortable."

"I know," he said. Then he added, "I'm just saying, whatever you and Nancy want to do, I'm alright with it. I mean it."

There was a lull in conversation before Nick grew a smile and said, "Remember when you tried to date Stephanie before Cuz moved in on her, stealing her from you? You thought she might be the one?"

"Yes," I said embarrassed, "I remember."

"What was that she said to you Stan? When you were seriously asking her to go with you to the shore for, what was it you said? Oh yeah, for a 'lost weekend of lust, decadence, and irresponsibility'?"

"I don't recall what she said . . . " I told him frowning now, and looking up to the front of the plane.
"She said, 'You know what Stan? I've never seen you with a girl."
Then she said, 'I wonder why that is Stan?!?'
Do you remember what happened after that Stan?"
"All I know is that I was drunk," I said.
"Do you remember?"
"Okay, okay, I threw up on her shoes!!" Nick and I laughed so hard that the co-pilot opened the door to see if we were alright, then smiled and closed it again.
"I was never lucky with women like you were Nick," I told him with a smile. "I don't have that kind of confidence."
"Stephanie's one of the many who weren't meant for you. She has no clue who you are. I'm sure you know that now," he said, "I think you've done alright for yourself, I've seen it. I've seen you with the ladies, and now you've even won Nancy's heart."
There was a pause, then Nick snickered and said in a soft, low voice while shaking his head, "So come on, Stephanie. . . were you kidding me Stan?"
We both broke out in laughter.
Nick and I just sat quietly for the longest time. Then I asked him what he knew about Snake.
"It's funny you should be asking me about her," He said, "This whole trip wouldn't be happening without her help, and influence."
"Snake?" I asked.
"Vanessa is her given name," he said, "She has a big part of this plan because she was actually originally from the island we're heading to right now. Years ago, Marco exported her, and quite a few young girls from there when he was building the mansion on the island, and his empire in the states. He took them from their families promising them

fortune in the U.S.A. but it was never to be. He got them into prostitution and drug dealing, telling them that their families would be killed if they did not cooperate, subsequently, the families never heard from their daughters again.

Marco lied to them saying that their daughters had gotten killed in a plane crash, and he gave their families some compensation for their grieving. With that, he harvested some admiration from these same families for himself.

The young girls, of course, had no way of knowing and no way or means of ever contacting their parents or families on the island. As far as the U.S. knows, the island doesn't exist.

Well, Vanessa, or 'Snake', found out through Jackie and Evangeline that Marco had personally murdered her father and mother, making the other women wonder about their own families. This, and the sting operation I initiated, really made the shit hit the fan for Marco."

Nick pulled out a folded paper and while unfolding it, continued talking. "So, he started turning in his own men, ratting out some high-end drug dealers to save his own ass. It got to the point where he wasn't safe in prison and the government granted him a pardon and asylum, in trade for enough information to undo nearly 50 percent of the country's heroin and cocaine operations, but the bastard ran out on them from their sanctuary, to his own island, where he can never be found."

Nick had this map now opened to what he said were the exact coordinates of the island. He then said, "This is the main reason, along with the mysterious golden ring, why Marco wanted what was in that chest at the bottom of Lake Nockamixon. The map locates his island. It had nothing to do with patents, or even the money, although he wants the money too. The feds, however, already know about the murders he committed, and Barbara, working incognito for Marco's personal airline, (and undercover for us) already knows the island's location. Anyway, Jackie always had this hanging over him, so he would feel somewhat more secure in his own well-being, and within his dad's operation. Now we, or at least I know where Marco is, with Flash. He knows we're on our way."

"So," I said, "we're going to get him?"

"We're going to get him." Nick answered.

"Seat belts on," Barbara yelled through the opened door from the cockpit area, "We're getting ready to land in about ten minutes."

I looked out the window, but observed only blue ocean, and the sun low in the sky in front of us. We're still heading west and noticeably closer to the water. There were what looked like a scatter of fishing boats and sailboats, separated in a sparse void of open sea. Nick and I sat tight waiting for the jet to touch the ground. We were almost touching the water, or so it seemed, until as quickly as I saw beach and dry ground, we landed on a strip with palm and coconut trees on either side of us, slowing down past the windows as we were taxiing to a stop.

"We made it," Barb said as she and her co-pilot walked out past us and said, "Come on, time's a wastin',"

Nick and I left the plane, and I couldn't help but look around as we walked. There was a shack, a rancher style structure that was apparently the airport's main building. There was a jeep waiting for us in a car port and the four of us got in. "Are we going up right away?" said Barbara, speaking of the mansion we were to meet with Marco.

"Nah," Nick said, "Let's get a place to sleep for the night. We'll head up in the morning."

Chapter 18

The Islands' Story

    We stopped at a rancher style adobe house with a terra cotta clay roof where Barbara said she knew the family. They spoke English, which only some of the islanders, not all, learned from the sailors on Australian ocean freighters for trade to and from the island. Australia is the only continent that deals with, or knows about these remote islands, though their visits are quite rare. The family called themselves 'Kita'. Jun, was the father of the three children. Jun stood about four and a half feet tall, like most of the men here on the island, and was about my age. He had long dark hair tied in a bun on top of his head. He wore a Hawaiian shirt and baggy long pants that looked almost like painters' pants. The children, one boy and two girls were ages ranging from 3 to 6, the boy being the oldest. The mom, who was Jun's wife is Luka, and she was still out on the boat bringing in the dinner, but we saw her coming into the dock with her catch. Jun invited us in and he sat us immediately at the table. The house looked bigger on the inside than it looked from the outside. They had family pictures on the walls along with oil paintings from Jun himself. The paintings were brilliantly done, depicting the morning and evening landscapes of the island, his children's portraits, and a beautiful portrait of his wife. The colors were spectacular within the lifelike pictures. I complimented him on them and he was very modest.

"It's just paint," he said, "The real beauty is in really seeing what's around you."

"I agree." I responded to his profound statement, and smiling at the rest of the room. The furniture looked handmade and everything seemed to be in its place. Just then in walked his wife.

"This is Luka," he said with a big smile. She returned the smile, kissing him and giving him a great big hug before she even acknowledged our existence. She was a young, beautiful woman in her mid-twenties, standing at about seven feet, with long sun bleached blond hair, and a figure of a model. She was wearing short denim shorts and a bikini top, and was holding a live squirming eel she had just skinned.

"I brought some pan fish and flounder for dinner, I hope you can all stay," she asked with a nod of her head as if signaling us to say yes.

"Yes," we all said in unison, and she asked Jun to clean the fish and prep them so she can start. "The dinner will take a half hour. Sit and talk," she said placing the writhing eel on the hot grill, poking it into submission with a fork. We were within sight of them as we told them about what was happening in America and traded their stories of fishing and the island gossip.

"So, you folks know the festival is on tomorrow night, don't you?" Jun asked. He had just cleaned the fish and Luka had them on an open grill. "Yes," Nick said, "We're actually going to help you with some of that."
"That's great," Luka said adding, "Jun here is going to cut my hair for it."
"You're going too?" Nick asked.
"Yes, I wouldn't miss it for the world. It's a once in a lifetime opportunity. Jun is going to stay here with the kids. I'll be going with my neighbor Sundra, and I'll be helping her with a surprise feast. This festival is a once in a lifetime feast, for women only, and will never come again. The plan is to cleanse the islands for good from the evil, that was brought from the east by one of our own."

The kids were sitting at the table with us now. The little boy was showing me a little tiny crab he had caught, and he then showed it to every one of us. His dad said to him, "Put it outside Tam, he wants to go home to eat too." So, little Tam followed daddy's instruction and placed it in the sand outside. The little girls kept laughing at us. Then I saw Nick making faces at them while they, quite successfully, duplicated his facial stretches.

The food was ready, and we ate heartily, as we were pretty hungry from the trip. We drank a mango and moonshine drink, but I only needed one before I said enough, because I knew we were heading out soon. This family was in complete harmony. It was hard to tell if anyone of them was the head of the family. But if I was to guess, I'd say the roles were reversed compared to the standard American living I knew of at this time.

She was the boss, sitting at the head of the table as he stood behind her with his hands on her shoulders waiting for her next request, but he had everything under control, and he had a creative touch, as I once again stared at the paintings. I really liked his beach landscapes of sunsets, or sun rises.

While he was showing me a landscape after dinner I became aware of a strange ring on his third finger. It was golden and had unusual engravings on it. He picked up on it right away that I was curious about it.

"All married men on the island wear this style ring to show devotion to wife and family," he said answering my unasked question. "Wearing it brings continuous good karma and luck. However, when the spiritual bond between husband and wife is broken by the man wearing the ring," he continued, "it is believed that he must never take it off, lest his luck will diminish. Once he has the ring on his finger, he must keep it for life unless his wife removes it from him. If he tries to rid himself of the ring, it will come back to him as death." He took a sip of wine and said in a softer voice, as if he didn't want anyone but me to hear, "However, if it comes off of him, and his spouse then places it on her own finger, he will die a thousand deaths for deceiving her, as she will then have the power to keep bringing him back from the dead to torture, at least until the following sunrise."

"Wow," I said. "Do you really believe that?"

"It's the legend of the island, from the ancient ones.

Then I asked him with some skepticism, "What about the females, you know what I mean, like if THEY break the spiritual bond? Do they have a ring?"

"It's never happened," he said, "but the women here have such a tight bond between themselves that if anyone of them would go against the cult, they would be roasted alive and eaten, according to legend, as a special cleansing ritual." He gave me a pat on the back and said, "That would be rare though. The men don't even screw up like that, unless you're someone like that 'Marco' character."

Just then Luka came up to us and asked us if we wanted any more wine. I declined. She smiled, and leaning down gave Jun a peck on the cheek, then softly and slowly ran her tongue across his ear as she placed her arm slowly and sensually around him, pulling him into herself tightly and delicately; burying his shoulder under her large, soft bikini covered breasts. His facial expression changed to a zombie like blank stare, with a boyish grin. Then turning to us she said, "You folks could stay if you want. Jun and I are going to lay down for a while if you don't mind. It was a long day for the both of us." We understood completely and decided to head out. She picked him up in her arms and cradled him lovingly, in the manner a man from our country would carry a bride over the threshold, and she carried him to their bedroom.

With full bellies and a friendly feeling of our new friendship we bid our goodbyes to the Kita family as we piled into the jeep and headed out. We drove down roads made of sand, and cobblestone, and roughly kept macadam. As we drove along the coast and inland, I was observing the people.

The people here were of mixed races, with a touch of Asian, white and black. It appeared to be predominantly women, who were on average almost twice as tall as the men; Almost like the fictional amazon race of women. The men, on average were four, four and a half, to five feet tall, while the women stood between seven and eight feet, and there were quite a few at eight feet. The couples and families seemed to work well together on the fishing boats, and in fields where there were crops. We came upon a little village where we stopped and checked into what was considered a hotel. It was a large building that looked as if it was built in the 1700's. It was stucco on the exterior and had clay terra cotta roofing tiles. The interior was like something you would see in the Florida Keys or New Orleans. The wall pictures were original paintings of local artists from the past, and the portraits were island life, farming, fishing, and market places. There was one that seemed unusually detailed which caught Nick's eye, as he brought it to my attention. It was this one of a pig being slaughtered and butchered by a group of naked women. Barbara walked up behind him and said, "You really like this one huh?" Nick said he'd never seen anything like it and inquired what it was about.

"It's based on a local ritual that takes place here every year," Barb said. "The native people here call it "Kung Jaadaa Taagang Iihlangaa," which is an ancient festival. It's said in their native Athabaskan language. It basically means "Moon Woman eats Man."

"That sounds pretty scary to me," I told Nick, but Barbara answered, "It would be for you as a man, if you lived here on the island about a thousand years ago. The women have become moderately tame since those days."

Nick was looking transfixed on the portrait and inquired, "What exactly is this 'Moon woman eats man' story? What's it about?"

Barbara smiled, poured us a glass of wine, and began the ancient tale:

"It goes back about a couple of thousand years ago, when these islands were threatened by warring people from the other local islands. There was a king, a man called 'Ptu', who was a notorious murderer and pillager. His people were like that of the reign of Genghis Khan, but worse. Men, women and children were being murdered almost every day for years. The peaceful island people and their villages were disappearing.

The women, who were always a little taller than the men, eventually grouped together (against the wishes of their own men) in a union with the purpose of opposing the order of Ptu and a nation grew within them, with the females having the upper hand, and making the decisions. This happened due to all of their men on the scattered islands being wounded and/or crippled from their forced battles during this reign of Ptu.

A much stronger retaliation eventually ensued with the female uprising against the regime, driving both sides into near extinction. The women dominated in the end, and when they captured Ptu alive, it's said that to make an example of him for the men under him, and for any man that would want to war against them, the women, as a sacrifice cooked him alive over an open fire and they all partook in the eating of his flesh."

"Holy shit," Nick mumbled as we listened.

"I know," Barb went on, " It was an old custom from their forbearers, who were believed to be witches. It was a custom that was abolished with time. They felt the need to revive it I guess."

"That's fucking brutal," I said.

"Although this made them cannibalistic," Barb continued, "it signified a triumphant victory for them. That was when the original festival was born. Legend has it that for years, they'd go once a year, at the same time, which turns out to be the last full moon in August on our calendar, to the island of the savages that killed their men and children, and capture one of these male natives, while luring their females to join with them, and they'd have the same festival with the new meat. They would simply bring him back to this island in a cage, skin him, and cook him; Usually 'alive' if he was a known murderer. They took things personal from what I was told of the lore."

"Wow."

Sometimes, it was said, that they could lure the men from that island by singing a chant, like the old Greek myths of the sirens."

"You sound like you're enjoying talking about this women domination stuff Barbara," Nick said.

"Cannibals," I said.

"Of course," Barb answered. "Through the years it was their way of keeping their people protected, in their minds anyway. Ever since those days, the women maintained control in a peaceful way, over the men. As a matter of fact, the course of evolution made them almost twice their size."

"Why the pig in this portrait? Where do the pigs come in?" Nick asked.

"After about a few hundred years or so, after the original celebration, the generations of women to follow made peace with all islands and people, but kept the annual festival using pigs as the meal and sacrifice instead of humans. They became somewhat civilized."

"I guess that means men are pigs," Nick said, then grinned and shook his head.

Barb laughed and said, "Don't take it personal, they get along fine with their men." Then she looked at him with a sardonic grin and added, "As long as they know their place."

Even I laughed at that. Nick just kept shaking his head, but he too was laughing.

"Does this so called "savage" island still exist?" I asked.

"Yes, it's the one where Marco built his mansion. It's out there, about fifty or so miles with a group of other islands," Barbara said pointing in the darkness toward the sea.

"When Marco came back to the island about 10 years ago, he had millions of dollars behind him from his successes with the underworld and the pharmaceuticals. He had the mansion built to his specifications, and gained respect from the locals, with his donating to the families of the women he said were lost in a plane crash. He lied to the parents about their daughters, which he actually kept as prostitutes in the states."

As she told the story, I was remembering Nick telling me about some of this earlier. Barbara took off her shoes and slipped into her sandals and said, "You see, living here as a boy he knew the language."

"You're saying he lived here as a boy?" I asked taking off my own shoes.

"Yes. No one but Marco knows the whole story. What I know is he ran away as a child, by stowing away on a boat to Fiji, and somehow made it back to the states. At least that's the story from Evangeline, who got it from his son Jackie." Just then, there was a voice from behind us saying, "Did I hear my name mentioned?" It was Evangeline. She was accompanied by a middle aged, or older native American looking guy who stood about 5' tall and a stocky build, with greying long hair in a single braided ponytail. He had high cheek bones and deep grayish green eyes that seemed to pierce the soul, but with an aura of peace.

"Hi Evangeline," Barb said with a big smile and giving her a hug. Evangeline was wearing the bigger smile as she introduced everyone to her father.

"This is my father, Erik."

"Hello Erik," we all said introducing ourselves and making the both of them feel welcome in our temporary abode.

Erik, it turns out, is a born-again Christian, but he doesn't dwell on talking about it. He's a man who shows it through actions such as diverting away from negativity in conversation, and realizing we are all brothers and sisters under the skin. We're all capable of mistakes and entitled to forgiveness. However, he's aware of what happened to his daughter through Marco and company and wants justice.

THE LOST MARBLES STORY

After making our acquaintances, we sat with wine and beer and an unexpected story began to unfold and it took the most of us by surprise. Evangeline said that her father was born on this island, and left it when he was about eight or nine. When he left this island, he was with a friend about the same age. The friend was who we now know as Marco.

Eric used to look up to Marco, because Marco was tough and fearless. Marco hated the women because they were too dominant in their ways. Although they were both rebellious, Marco was the one who developed a mean streak.

Erik was telling us the story, "One day he was being punished by a teacher after school. He was incorrigible and she was just trying to get him under control. She slapped him silly and eventually sent him homeward. Well, she left the school later and found her own house burning to the ground when she got there. She never said who it was, but she knew, and I knew it was Marco who lit the match. He eventually told me he did it, and he swore that she was seeking vengeance. He also told me he heard enough about America through the talk of the fishermen and the merchants, who were bringing goods to the islands, and he wanted to go. I was not getting along with my parents either, so I decided to join him.

I waited for him by one of the empty sail boats used for fishing, and when he came, we jumped onto the boat and we stole the damn thing. We piloted it across the sea for miles from island to island until we reached Fiji. When we got there, he showed me a bloody knife, and I immediately knew that he had murdered that teacher. My heart was heavy and I felt sick, but by now, I knew there was no going back. I also felt as if I was an accomplice, even though I had nothing to do with it; It was Marco's way. He had a way of manipulating people, even at an early age.

We managed to get into one of those Australian freighters that was headed to Hawaii. We already knew some English from hanging out with the merchants on our islands so were able to talk our way onto another freighter to the states."
"Wow," Nick said, "that's an incredible story."
"It's all true," Erik said, "By the time we were stateside, we were just a couple more orphan kids in the mass of immigrants entering the U.S.A. It was around 1929 and it was the last time I saw Marco, until he managed to look me up, where I was living on a farm near the town of Woodstock New York."

   I was hesitant on asking either Evangeline or he any questions about the farm, and what went on there with Marco. But Evangeline, once again, read my mind.
"Daddy knows about them being predators, but we're not going to talk about any of that," she said looking down.
"I certainly didn't know about any of that at the time, "Erik said, "and I'm about to make up for lost time. I cannot undo anything, and I'm a peaceful man, but I want to see justice!"
"You will, Daddy, you most certainly will."
   I know that they must have been on that jet an hour or so behind Nick and me. No doubt that they had a nice long daughter to father talk on the way here. I wonder who else came with them? I'm starting to feel really good about all of this.
    Erik and Evangeline said good night and retired to another area of the hotel. The four of us, continued to talk, drink our wine, then Ginger stood up and said she's turning in. She apparently went to another area of the hotel on her own. The three of us continued talking until Nick finally said, "We need to go to bed. Daylight comes early." Nick and Barbara went to their room and I laid back in a ham-

mock in the corner of the veranda listening to the ocean and thinking about Nancy. I slept like a baby.

PART THREE

Chapter 19

The Island Mansion

I woke up to a storm, and the rain was like a quick monsoon that lasted for about twenty minutes or so, as the winds swayed the palms, pineapple and coconut trees. Of course, this short outburst from the clouds, which just as quickly disappeared into the horizon of the early morning blue sky, did not stop the islanders from their daily chores of getting fishing boats ready, or setting up markets in a cobblestone square. Nick and Barbara came over to get me moving on our quest; To free Flash.

Barbara had shaved the hair of her head above the ears, forming her long mane into a wide mohawk. I noticed that the island women I see this morning have all done the same, and I'm assuming it's for this big moon festival for this evening. She looks good, and it's actually very sexy looking in the way she wears it. Anyway, I also became aware that the women were all gathering into this big clearing by the beach, complete with a number of barbecue pits, tents, blankets, and palm canopies. It seems as if the large part of this festival is taking place here. It looks like a beachfront "Woodstock" style gathering, only it appears to be all women attending. Tall women. The gals on this island average between 7' and 8' and incredibly built, from what I've seen so far. The men are like Marco and Erik. As I found out before, the women call all the shots in this part of the Pacific, but the men don't seem to mind. Apparently, this is their festival; Their day. "There will probably be about five hundred to a thousand attending this shindig tonight," Barbara said as we got into the jeep.

    We drove to a pier where a small boat took us to an anchored sailboat. We boarded and two very tall women in bikinis, and of course, long and thick mohawks, one of them blonde and the other a redhead, piloted us out to sea, I presumed in the direction of the island where Marco's mansion from what I was told, overlooked the sea. From below deck came Evangeline. with the sides of her head also shaved, and her long red hair pushed over her back. She looked great. Her dad was already out by the front hatch, climbing back from under the jib sheet to help one of the ladies with the boom on the main sail. I guess he knows his shit regarding sailing. I on the other hand know nothing, but it was a nice ride though, as we skimmed through and across the waves. The island wasn't within sight, but we were headed eastward in the right direction. I asked Nick if we had everything, like the chest of money in trade for Flash.

"Don't worry about it," He said, "It's under control."

"How long," I asked, "will it take to get to Marco's island?" We left early at about 6.

"We have a very good tail wind," Erik said, "We'll be there in three hours, so about 9:00."

I kicked back, and Evangeline gave me a few tablets to take. "What's this?" I asked.

"Don't worry, it's not mescaline, or anything like that," she said, "It's to prevent motion sickness . . . 'so you don't get seasick." I took them with a swig of some fresh water. I thought it was a good idea since I'd never sailed at sea before. It worked I guess, since I never got sick.

After about an hour of sailing I could see the island in the distance. When I tried to go below to use the facilities Nick stopped me and encouraged me to go off of the stern.
"You only have to pee, right?"
"Right."
"Just be careful," he said, "sharks like jumpin' out of the water at whoever's waving little tiny things at them."
"Hardy har har . . . " was the only comeback I could think of at the time.
Evangeline winked at me and yelled to Nick on my behalf, "Well, it had better be a great white with a big mouth."
"Knock it off Evangeline," her dad Erik bellowed.
Nick broke into a big laugh and threw Evangeline his knife in the sheath and said, "You heard him. Here, knock it off while Stan still has it out!"

I was done though, and I made my way to the bow while Evangeline followed. We both laid on our sides and felt the wind. She looked better than ever. Her bikini top and sarong were the same color as her pink skin. She asked me to apply some sun block lotion onto her back and shoulders and I obliged. We talked.
"What's going to happen when we get there?" I asked.
"You'll see," she said. "We're going to drop anchor in a lagoon at a pier and we'll be met by his goons. He'll be expecting us."

She gave me two small, green leafs, that looked to me like that of a deciduous tree, like the White Oak, but considerably smaller, about an inch long and wide.
"What's this?" I asked.

"These are from a special tree," she commented, "that can only be found on this island. It's hidden in the high mountain. The tree is said to be over a thousand years old and only produces leaves once every hundred years. This present year of the cleansing festival is its year. There was a procession of people hiking the mountain yesterday to get to it, and my dad and I went with them. The tree was picked clean of the leaves; It's the only way the tree survives. They call it a 'prayer tree'. The tree occasionally generates lightning bolts from the tree to the sky by some strange quirk in the laws of nature within this hemisphere; with respect to this exact latitude and longitude. I do, however, believe it's a miracle of mysticism, or God."

She rubbed some more lotion on her arms and continued telling me about it.

"You have two wishes, one for each leaf. You make a wish with the leaf in your right hand, and it will come true."

She must not have liked the look I gave her because she said, "I'm dead serious! Don't throw them away either. Wish for something that will mean something to you." She then added, "Selfish and avarice wishes of greed, or wishes of grandeur won't come true because the wish can't possibly be originating from your universal 'center' on those requests. They must come from your 'center', or 'spiritual core'. Don't just test them; but believe it. I'm not asking you to do it now. Save them for something you really want. . . but know what you want." She leaned to her side then rolled onto her belly. I looked at the two leafs and I put them carefully into my wallet. I thought about Nancy.

I also thought about how there were no telephones on the island where we were, and I wondered how people communicated. I did see a lot of towers, and windmills mounted on some of these towers. Nick and Erik told me that these towers were ham radio transmitters and short wave. The windmills are how people generate electricity to the small homes and work places. They're a pretty resourceful community of citizens. I continued to inquire from Evangeline what she knew about our plan.

"Once we get Hank back. . . " She stops me and says, "Hank? Don't you mean 'Flash'?"

"His name is 'Hank', but yeah, we call him Flash. Anyway, when we get Flash back, what happens to Marco?"

"Does it matter?" she said sitting up and facing me. "As long as Hank is back safe and sound, isn't that all that matters?"

"Well, yeah," I said, "but we shouldn't just let that asshole get away with all of this, should we?" I was looking into her bright green eyes with the bright sunlight reflecting off of her face as she was grinning back at me, never blinking, and she answered, "Hell no. He's toast"

As the island, that we were heading to seemed to grow upon our approach, we were told to move our asses to midship. We followed the order as the boat glided into the lagoon to the pier. Dropping anchor, we were met by two muscular dark-haired men who had assault rifles pointed at us. We were encouraged to disembark, and we did so. They walked behind us as Nick, Barbara, Erik, Evangeline, and the two lady sailors, Maggie the redhead and Shauna the blonde trekked up the sandy path to a wall with a metal gate. We saw other soldiers in the palm trees, also with rifles, and I was hoping we knew what we were doing. The gate slowly and automatically swung open to let us in. We walked up marble steps to the door of the mansion and we were told by the goons to wait. The door was opened by a scantily dressed tall woman who looked very familiar. It was our co-pilot Ginger. Only Ginger now had red hair, shaved in a mohawk, and was acting like she didn't know us, but with a wink of her eye encouraged us to do the same. "I'm

Ginger," she said with confidence, "I'm the masseuse, Marco is expecting you. We're in the middle of a session." She peers at each person. "You're all here it looks like, just follow me up."

The place was almost like a castle, but with adobe-like terra cotta plaster walls, stained glass windows, and dark brown beams of wood that couldn't have possibly come from this island. We entered a large room with ten-foot ceilings and a large 8'x16' picture window looking out over the ocean. And there, near the far wall, on a table face down naked with a towel over his ass was Marco, awaiting the return of his masseuse Ginger.

"Come in! Come in!" he said with his head peering sideways at us as Ginger walked over to him and started pouring oil onto his back. He had a great big smile, showing off his golden teeth as Ginger told us earlier, that they were all solid gold implants. 'Must be nice to be that rich.

"Where's Hank," Nick said immediately as Ginger began Marco's rub down.

"In due time," Marco replied grinning and feeling the flexing fingers of his masseuse and adds, "Where's the money?"

"In due time," Nick responded. Nick and I both noticed the ring from his sister on Marco's finger. Nick nudged me and whispered, "ring".

Nice friendship ring Marco. Where did you get that from?"

He had a few rings on his fingers, like he was a collector of them, but that one from Nick's sister stood out because of the odd shape. He raised his hand to look at it and said, "Yeah, it won't come off. I had it on since 1969 and I got it from some hippie bitch at the Woodstock Rock Festival," he paused, spinning the ring and said,

"Those were the days, boy."

Nick was shaking ever so subtle because of his amazing self-control as he looked at his own ring, spun it a few times and said with a poker face, "My sister lost one exactly like it at Woodstock."
Marco started to laugh, rolled right past it and said to Evangeline, "Speaking of rings, I want what was in that chest from the lake."
There was a chilling silence as he then followed up with, "I see you brought my old friend. Hi Erik. Your daughter here is a real hellcat. It took both Balance and I to hold her down, so we could get it on, you know, get it done." Then Marco snickered.
Erik was silent. Marco's words fell on deaf ears as Evangeline answered,
"Where is Balance these days?"
Marco impulsively started to push himself up at her remark regarding his old friend Balance, but Ginger forcefully pushed him down saying,
"Relax, Mister Clark, you're too tense. I'm trying to do a job here." Then she kept massaging him.
"You're right Ginger," he said, "Just don't ever do that to me again."

The two gunmen just looked on as one cocked his automatic as a reminder that he was there watching. Marco has no idea that Ginger knew us and at this point I was just watching, because I don't know what Nick's plan is.
"So, you took care of Balance, didn't you?" Marco asked Evangeline.
"Did I? Why yes, I guess I did. He was good too." She patted and rubbed her tummy, which indicated to Marco that she ate his flesh.

Since I knew he was castrated, I can only imagine what she meant by that, but Marco knew. Then she said, "I guess you're going to ask me about your son Jackie too?"

"I don't care about him," Marco bellowed, "because he was ripping me off all my life, so 'good job there Evangeline, a job well done." Marco paused and continued, "If you wouldn't have done it, someone else would have." Marco then let out a loud laugh and added, "And if they didn't, I eventually would have. He took a single valued possession of mine, and I want it back. You know what I'm talking about too."

Besides the money, I had no clue what he meant, and I wondered if anyone else did. Then Marco lowered his voice and said, "My fucking son Jackie, he was an asshole."
"Like father like son," Evangeline said, almost under her breath but loud enough for him to hear.
As Evangeline responded Nick, who was listening patiently became infuriated.
"Where's Flash?" Nick demanded.
"I haven't seen any money, or the contents of the chest," Marco replied and added, "This can go on forever if we'd let it." After a moment of silence Marco directed his attention to Erik.
"You could have been my partner Erik. The island has the mother lode of mother lodes in diamonds. I have the mine."
"You mean you stole the mine," Erik said.
"I obtained it in a business deal," he said, "So that's not stealing."
"You're right." Evangeline responded, "It's more like murder!"
"I can't help it if some undesirables get killed in the process," Marco answered, "They had no Idea what they had, or how to use it properly. This is business."
"The mine belongs to Vanessa and her family," Erik said firmly.

An angry Marco then said, "I call her 'Snake', like everyone else. She's a snake and not worthy of the diamonds. Neither were her substandard parents with their ancient beliefs. The mine must belong to someone who can appreciate its value. The mine belongs to me!"

Nick said, "So, that's what this is all about! That's why you came back here to this island. You wanted control over a stupid diamond mine? You murdered innocent people, her parents, over diamonds? Well, counting all of your malevolence in the states, with the murders, the drugs, the torture, the rapes, I guess this low-life move of yours doesn't surprise me or anybody else here."

"Not just any stupid, diamond mine," Marco said, "but a mine that makes me rich beyond anyone's wildest dreams. . . and it's mine. So, I don't give a flying fuck about what surprises you or anyone."

"So," Erik said, "If you are rich beyond belief, what the hell do you want with the measly millions from the lake?"

"I was going to ask that same question," I said.

"Who asked you?" Marco said looking at me, then said, "But I'll tell you. I just wanted what was rightfully mine. My son, rest his soul, stole it from me."

"It's nice to see you have values," Nick said sarcastically.

Marco, now laying face up on the massage table started laughing. Ginger continued massaging his chest but Marco asked her to go lower toward his groin area. The obedient goons guarding us were ready at any time to fire their weapons at the slightest sign of trouble on Marco's command.

"It doesn't matter to me anymore," Marco said, "I have enough riches here that I could easily change my identity, my appearance, and no one would know."

"I'll know," Nick stated adamantly.

"Yes," Marco replied, "But you're as good as gone on my command. What I'm going to do is kill every last one of you. What if I told you your trip was in vain, fools, and you're never going to see your friend Hank . . . " Marco got distracted by how Ginger was softly rubbing his erroneous zone. . . "Oohh, right there, Ginger . . . that's the spot . . . "

About that time, two big 6' goons grabbed Barbara by each arm and a shorter one, just under 5' stood in front of her, looking her over. He had a full head of dyed purple hair, wore a ripped t-shirt above his worn-out jeans. He was eyeing Barb's figure, but also her tattoo of the black widow on her belly. He turned around to Marco and said, "Can I have her boss? Please?"
"No, Peter, I'm still negotiating." Then Marco asked one more time about the money and the contents of the chest saying, "Please don't make it hard on yourself or your friends Nick. Just let me have what was in the chest and we can go our separate ways peacefully."
Nick's answer was still the same, "Where's Flash?"
Marco was obviously perturbed, and getting irritated, then looked at Peter.
Peter asked Marco again, "Oh please, she's pretty boss, can I please have her? I really like her."
Marco, frustrated, said to him, "Okay Peter, take her in the other room. If Nick wants to be an asshole, I can be one too. Just be careful taking her tattoo, Peter. You don't want to damage it." Peter let out a crazy laugh as he faced Barb, ripped off his own shirt to expose his own tattoo on his hairless belly, which was a tattoo of a man with a fish tail holding a trident. They then muscled her into an adjoining room, and with her struggling, they disappeared as the door closed.

"I have to please the help you see," Marco said smiling while looking up at Ginger, who was now going to town on his private area, massaging him thoroughly and relentlessly, causing him to be even more distracted.

Just then, another door opened, and another of Marco's goons was standing in the threshold. Marco looked up at him, obviously surprised and said:
"Lance! Get back in that room you fool! What are you trying to do?"

The goons behind us raised their weapons but were hesitating, I guess they were wondering like everyone else what was going on. This guy Lance, appeared to stagger, like he was propped up by something, then fell on his face, with what appeared to me to be a broken neck. Then after what seemed to be an eternity, but was only a split second, Hank emerged from the doorway with an assault rifle, blowing away the two goons behind us with two quick shots before they ever got the chance to point theirs.
"FLASH!" Nick yelled.

Marco quickly pushed himself up once again but Ginger, squeezing his nuts and causing Marco to wail, dominated him. Through his screams she pinned him down, cuffed him, and started tying him up like a roped calf with Maggie and Shauna jumping in to assist her. We heard a few more shots from the outside and within the room where Barbara was taken, then silence once again fell onto the compound grounds. More shots were coming from outside on the grounds when the doors from the outside of our area and where Barbara was, flew open, and tall women with guns and crossbows entered with about five of Marco's goons in front of them, with their hands held high.

Maggie and Shauna walked up to the prisoners and started stripping them naked then cuffing and tying them as well. Barbara was walking with that goon called Peter. She had him in a headlock and pushed him onto the ground, sat on him, and tied him up. "He ran like a little rat when his big boys were shot," she said. Nick greeted and hugged Flash, and the rest of us walked onto the balcony overlooking the ocean, leaving the women to do what they wanted with Marco and his men.

Flash told us that he was in a room with three goons guarding him and going through alcohol withdrawal, since he had not been that dry, for that length of time, (which was only a few days) since he could remember. The goons figured he was a wimp, and weak, but said he heard them talking about how Marco was going to give them Evangeline. While their mouths were watering over the prospect he managed to deceive one of them by earning his trust. He had quietly eliminated all three using his latent marine guerilla warfare training by the time we arrived, but he waited for an opportune moment before making the wise move that he did. We laughed and Nick hugged him again. "There's hope for you yet," he said. Just then, a familiar voice from behind us said,
"It is done. Nice work."
We turned and saw Snake, in a mohawk, and in her glory, half naked wearing almost nothing, except small furry animal skins as pasties and a thong, which is how the other women were adorned.

It turns out that this was an ancient warring habiliment that distracted their male enemies. It works for me. Evangeline walked up to her and gave her a long, long hug. Then Snake greeted and thanked us all before she and Evangeline walked back inside the room.

I found out that the plan was a long time coming. Barbara had been in communication to the women on the island about Marco, his vicious crimes and his deceit to the people. Snake and Evangeline and the women from the Siren's Club teamed together over a year ago to put this together. Nick was in on it but knew not of the specific details. He sidestepped the government, keeping them in the dark as the plan unfolded.

The festival for the full moon was planned since the night Evangeline and I had our date at the beach in 1977. That particular ritual, with those exact crustaceans on the night I was with her tripping, was a religious conjuration that brought forth the outcome of Marco's demise, and the diamonds attached to the shells of the lobsters were the crystals needed for channeling some mystical energy for their sorcery. . . according to Snake and Evangeline. Balance was not in the equation of needing to be here because he was not originally from the island; so, he was just simply eliminated.

The festival tonight, will be the last true cannibalistic festival for all time. It's a sort of religious 'clean-up' of the existing threat to their present culture, which has worked for them successfully for hundreds of years. There will be no more after this one, except the continuation of the annual pig festival celebration, posing as a reminder. They will, however, keep cannibalism on the table as a form of capital punishment, if needed, or so I'm told.

As Snake and Evangeline walked into the room we followed, and there, on the floor lined up, tied, blindfolded and gagged were the six male captives. Some of them were from the states as loyal bodyguards, the others were the island followers of Marco's ideas which, of course, is taboo to the islanders, especially the female population, who frown heavily on anyone turning away from their way of life. These male outlaws, according to Snake are still being rounded up. They expect to have them all by tonight for this island cleansing celebration.

The smallest of the present captives was Marco. He was sniveling, shivering, and whimpering under his blindfold and gag. Snake bent over top of him, keeping her athletic and tattooed legs straight, like a gymnast, grabbed his head in her hands as she had done before, almost like her playful ritual with him, and turned it to the side, and with her long tongue, flickered it steadily into his ear until he peed himself. This made him scream through his gag, as he realized who it was, his worst nightmare. She then removed the blindfold, revealing her smiling face, showing him her fist and said to him, "Look what I have!" He immediately froze in fear, and his face became ashen as he trembled and moaned, then vomited.

 I myself didn't see, but whatever it was she just showed him, made him think she was the devil from hell. He screamed, and it was unbearable to me as he wriggled and squirmed hopelessly. She picked him up like he was a small fatted pig; cradling him in her arms, and as he continued writhing and squealing, she calmly, and without expression, carried him out and down to the boats. I watched Nick smile as he said, "Poor bastard!"

 The others were carried by the women as well, to cages on the boats, and there, they were untied and put into the separate 4'x4' pens. The prisoners were hauled to the island for their destiny, which was tonight's beginnings of the festival.

"What's going to happen to them?" Erik asked.

"They are substitutes for the pigs," Evangeline said, "This is to be their justice."

 Erik seemed to be fighting with his conscience. Even though he knows they did unspeakable things, especially Marco, he thought originally that maybe we were going to take them back to the states, where their punishment would be less brutal, or at worst, a merciful death. He then got the notion that because he had some connection with Marco once, he can save him spiritually now, especially since

Marco is seeing no hope for his present situation, or so it appears.

"That's nonsense Dad, just don't think about it," Evangeline said trying to comfort her father.

"I can't help it," he answered, "It's wrong."

"It's justice," said Barb, who's been somewhat quiet. "It's also their way. I wouldn't try to argue their religion against yours if I were you. Not here, not now."

"Barbara's right Dad. They have their beliefs, you have yours. Didn't you kill people in Normandy?" Evangeline asked.

"I did. That was different."

"You shot German prisoners, Dad. I remember you telling me about that."

"They killed Americans," he said, "They killed friends of mine."

"I rest my case," Evangeline said.

"It's no different. No different at all!" Barbara replied.

Erik sat in thought while our boat took to sea, back to the main island.

Chapter 2

Ladies Night
(Boundless Beauty with a Diabolical Edge)

By the time we got back to the main island we were tired, as we watched the cages with the captives being unloaded and carried to the festival grounds, where there were about five hundred or more women, adorned in skimpy skins like Snake. They were milling about, setting up pits, and butchering some hogs. There were baskets of fruit, and vegetables, and fish freshly caught from the sea, all done in their festival's sacred custom of nudity, handed down from their ancient ancestors.

Besides the captives, Nick, Erik, Flash and I were the only males in sight. I didn't know if I felt lucky or uncomfortable. Barb walked over to us wearing the same customary garb that Snake and the other women were wearing, and she really looked good in the furry skin pasties and loincloth skin thong. Before she got to us I heard Nick say under his breath, "She wouldn't be caught dead wearing that back in the states, I'll tell you that right now."

"You guys can head over to that grove of palms," Barbara told us, "There's a building that was set up for you with real food, water, beer, whiskey, wine, and whatever you want. I don't think it's a good idea, you're standing around here.

No men are ever invited, and you won't like what we're eating tonight anyway," she said with a wink. She was sipping a concoction of root tea, which all of the women drink at this festival. It's supposed to increase their aggression, stamina and appetites. She turned toward the cages and yelled "Hey, Wait for me!"

We watched as she rushed over to where the first naked goon, who was one of the shorter men, one of the island natives who became a Marco loyalist, was being pulled out of his cage and wrestled down by Snake, Evangeline, Ginger and a few other women to the ground. It was that one that wanted his way with Barbara; Peter was his name. It wasn't Marco, and I'm getting the impression they're doing Marco last.

Barbara knelt there right with them, holding Peter down and preparing him, or whatever it was they were doing. The guy managed to get up, frightened beyond description, and he was all slick and greasy and started to run and kept running. Barbara took off after him while the others watched and laughed. She ran like the athlete she was, like a gazelle or a deer. Flash even made a remark, not surprising for his juvenile humor, referring to her pasties bouncing, as she quickly caught up to Peter, tackling him, then physically dragging him back to the group by his legs as he shrieked. The laughing women once again enveloped and retained him. Barb's back and arms were moving the most over him, as she was the one chosen for him. Occasionally we saw his feet kicking in pain, so whatever they were doing, the guy was definitely not enjoying it, however, the women most certainly were.

"Boy, Barb's really getting into this ain't she?" Nick said, "I've never seen this side of her."

"Me neither," I said, "Except once . . . with a bullfrog." Erik just sat and remained quiet through it all, not wanting to watch.

The poor bastard, Peter, then let out a shrill scream, then another and the huddled ladies chuckled even louder and harder as Barb stood holding his bloody pelt in one piece over her head victoriously, whooping and hollering like a Banshee!

"You go girl! You're doing fine, he's dinner anyway," came Evangeline's voice from the group, directing it to Barbara.

"You know what they say about a woman scorned," Nick said.

Right next to the ladies was a large fire; and sitting on it was a big steaming metal cauldron with a lid, and full of sea water, apparently coming to a boil. It reminded me of those cartoons I saw as a kid, the ones about cannibals and big black pots. Snake and Evangeline rose from the circle, and with two long sticks lifted the lid, pulling themselves back from the billowing mist and smiling towards the huddle of ladies. We all knew what was about to happen here, and so did Peter, still alive, and the poor guy's pathetic shrieks were getting even more desperate as he continued fighting in vain trying to free himself.

"I've seen enough. Let's get the hell out of here," Flash said.

"Amen," I answered, and we ran to the jeep before we had to hear anymore. My stomach would never tolerate me being witness to what was to be a gruesome execution of a human being.

We drove across the sand in the jeep, to the trees a half-mile away. This was our refuge for the evening, I guess, until we can get back to the jets. We need Barbara to fly us out of here and she's obviously predisposed in the partaking of this festival.

"I thought Erik was with us in the jeep," Flash said.
"So did I," I said looking around.
"Look, he'll be back," Nick said, "Here's that shack with some real food, and some beer.
"I just want to get out of here," I said.
"Relax Stan," Nick said, "We're in another world. Let the women do their thing. Just roll with it."
"Don't you miss playing music?" I asked him.
"No," Flash said as he started banging on a pair of congas that he found in the shed.
"Twang, twang." Nick was walking with an acoustic guitar and strumming it.
"Groovy," Flash said as they both immediately got a rhythm going.
I sat with them, drinking beer and singing, and we found yet another old guitar. Flash decided not to touch a drop as he seemed to really enjoy his new sober attitude towards life. Nick was smiling and jamming to a great rhythmic groove. It was like old times again, as we were doing old blues and country standards, Hank Williams, Willie Dixon, Merle Haggard, Robert Johnson, Howlin' Wolf, and a few of our own. I guess we were celebrating too, celebrating the end of the Marco regime of terror.

   After a while of jamming there was a knock at the door and it opened. It was Evangeline and Snake.
"Nick, we're going to do Marco now. I know how you feel, so I wanted to know if you wanted to come and watch this bastard get his?"
"No, thank you though," he answered, "Will you do one thing for me though?"
"Anything love," she said, "What do you need?"
"Will you please get my sister's ring back from him?"

"Consider it done. I'll see you in a while. I'm really looking forward to this one!" she said smiling and she looked right at me and winked her eye.

We all continued jamming, eating real pork sandwiches and drinking beer, all but Flash. He ate, but of course, drank not a drop of beer, or liquor. We were all making the best of it when Erik came in with a new friend who joined us. He jammed and played guitar rather well, and he was also a native of the island who spoke English, and called himself Lon. Lon stood about four feet, was barefoot, and wore a loudly colored Hawaiian shirt and shorts. Flash commented on what a great shirt it was. As Lon jammed with us, there existed a sort of new energy. It was like the music lifted and drew an aura from beneath us, so we rode on this for a while, changing chord patterns and harmonics. We went from minor to major and back to minor chords. I couldn't get Nancy out of my mind since the beginning of this trip, and I exploded into lyrics when the next major change came around as I sang,
"Long as I could be with you tonight, it would be alright.
Long as I could be with you tonight, it would be alright.
Let the fires burn out the day.
Let the waters wash us away,
Long as I could be with you tonight."
The jam was good with our new partner. We stopped and laughed at how much fun we were having.

So, I asked Lon what he was doing on this side of the island tonight. He said he's hiding from his wife 'Sundra', because she just found out he was working for Marco. It appears that Marco ratted him out, thinking the women would promise him some kind of pardon from the evenings' festivities, but he was wrong, and they already knew about Lon. Lon said he should have known something was up when his wife asked him to drive her to this shindig, but he figured it out, and he slipped away from her.

This was bad news, because even though we previously bonded with Lon musically, that news put us on alert, and you could hear a pin drop after that. Tonight, is the festival of the cleansing of anything 'Marco'. That means they're looking for Lon, who's on the lam, and we're potentially appearing to be hiding him.

My instant thought is a little self-centered. Why can't I be somewhere playing music like I was intended? Why am I in the middle of all this? I'm supposed to be in a band for crying out loud.

"I want to sneak Lon back to the states with us," Erik said meekly, "He's a nice guy and made a few mistakes. But now Lon says he wants to become a Christian."
Nick and I couldn't stop ourselves from laughing at that one.

Just then the door flew open, it was Marco, without a stitch of clothing, as when we left him with the women. He was a bit pudgy from an easy life of riches and crime, but not too bad for being in his sixties, and pretty muscular. He had a desperate look of panic on his face and said, "You've got to hide me! Please!" He went toward Lon who was backing away in fear and said, "Lon, please help me! I'll give you jewels, and money!"

Poor Marco was also covered completely in greasy pig fat or something that smelled like a barbecue. Then he grabbed at Erik and said, "They're animals! Evil bitches from hell! They want to skin me and take my soul!"

Erik just stood there, and a frightened Lon ran to the back room, out of sight. Marco jumped behind a wall partition and crouched down, cowering and shivering like a trapped rat.

Through the opened door came Evangeline. She was completely naked and covered with what looked like the same oily substance. She did however wear a thin leather belt supporting a large hunting knife.

"Where is the little piggy?" she asked, standing tall and shiny with her hands on her hips and that sanguine, determined look in her face and eyes.

We all just stood quiet, in disbelief of the whole scenario. Moments ago, we were all jamming and having a great time avoiding all of these festivities, and now we're in the center of it. I have to say, I do not know how to deal with this abhorrent, ritualistic behavior of the ladies, I mean, like I had enough trouble as it was watching lobsters being cooked. Anyway, she stood there scanning the room, and the only one sitting was Nick, who with his foot pushed the thin partition that was concealing little Marco over, and revealing his cover.

Frantically, Marco jumped up and ran past us. Evangeline grabbed him, but he slipped right out from her gripping arms. "Look at her bounce," Flash whispered, once again into my ear smiling, as we watched her move from side to side blocking Marco's escape, then grab and tackle him again. Then laughing she said, "Gotcha, you, asshole." But Marco was too slippery for her and slipped out of her grip again as she was trying to regain her clutch on the poor bastard. He then, in desperation, dove out of the large opened window.

We immediately heard a shriek from Marco, as Snake was right there to catch him in her arms, like an acrobat in the circus. We looked out the window to see her naked, and oily form in the bright moonlight, holding her screaming and kicking victim, who was only half her size. She was however able to maintain her greasy grip on him, with one hand gripping his hair and the other one clutching his tub-

by belly saying, "Mmmm, tender, but juicy I bet!" Then with a cheerful smile glanced at Evangeline and said,
"I win!"
"I know," Evangeline said smiling and patting her on the back, then giving Marco a hard spank on the butt as Snake was now raising him like he was nothing, with her one hand holding him up by his leg.

"We'll share, you can help me skin and cook him," Snake said to Evangeline, talking like two chefs on a TV cooking show. "I'm right with you," nodded Evangeline, as Marco's wailing got louder.

Snake then cupped his big golden toothed mouth to stop the yelling and once again, with a laugh, stuck her very long tongue into his ear and said, "Let's go piggy." Then looked back at us and said, "You guys can go back to what you were doing, but I'd stay away from our festival if I were you."
"Yeah," agreed Evangeline, and teasing us added, "You guys don't want to end up in the wrong hands." Then they laughed, restraining Marco as we watched them both walk toward the ocean surf, with Snake carrying him high in her one hand, that was big enough to now wrap around his wrists and ankles, holding them together so he hung like a large tear drop.
"The whole thing is scary and provocative, isn't it?" Nick said.
"They're going to flay him. That's what they're going to do out there," Lon was telling us after coming out of hiding. Then he added, "They were chasing after him, like the women here have done with the greased-up pigs at the annual festivals. The winner gets the pig to cook it."

Flash was watching the women walking away in the full moon toward the shore saying, "Damn, Marco should count his blessings. That's some fine-looking females right there."

Nick laughed at Flash, and said, "You never surprise me, Flash, your ignorance is your best quality," as he started strumming his guitar.

Then we heard a shrill long wailing scream coming from Marco, but it became muffled in the wind, and the roar of the ocean. Then there was yet another scream from him, much louder and shriller.

"Some set of lungs on that guy eh?" Flash said, as he peered out the window, drumming a beat on the windowsill with his hands, and observed the two shiny and bare silhouettes of the ladies in the distance, the witches crouching and bending over, eventually sitting on their fighting victim in the surf. We shut the door and closed the window hatch.

"Scary and provocative," Nick said again, still strumming his guitar.

I sat by Nick and said, "Am I the only one that thinks that this is all insane? Is everyone considering all of this normal?"

"It's normal to them, and it's their island. Lighten up Stan," Nick said, strumming a tune.

Nick was right, because some of these ladies, like Snake and Evangeline, have experienced seemingly endless suffering and betrayal, not to mention rape and torture, originating from this narcissistic, poor excuse for a human being, and his goons. They've lost family, and friends to his trust, and now want retribution. I wish I was as strong as my comrades-in-arms here, and able to handle the primal vehemence of the feminine brutal justice. Or, I could just avoid getting near any of it.

"If my wife gets her hands on me," Lon said, "I'm going to be just another roasted pig at the festival."

He handed me a gold ring with a strange inscription on it. It looked like writing, but like no other writing I've ever seen, other than on the ring I saw our friend Jun wearing when we first arrived on the island.

The print looked like letters, but like no letters I'm familiar with.

"Here," he said, "If something happens to me, if she catches me, don't let Sundra get this."

I looked into his eyes and he had a deep, dark stare when he said:

"If she wears this ring, I won't die only once. She'll keep bringing me back to life with its spell to torment me again and again, until I'm part of their sunrise breakfast feast. It's an ancient spell included in the sacred wedding vow, wife to husband. You see, I'm married to a witch."

This was of course one of the legends of the island's witch cult. Other than what our friend Jun, Luka's husband relayed to me, I don't understand it completely, but trying to be a friend to this lost soul, I held onto the ring for him.

One of Lon's mistakes is that he sold his teenage daughter to Marco's goons last year, but he didn't know Marco was doing what he was doing. He just wanted the money, but unfortunately, his daughter was never to be seen again. Not cool, and now his wife, Sundra, has become aware of his deception, that her daughter didn't just disappear.

This was a bad situation for us if we got caught with him . . . or tried to get him off of this island. Even turning him over to them would be risky now, so the plan was, we were going to try to get him onto the plane tonight. The good news was that this side of the island is kind of barren of people due to the festival. The men of the island took the children to the other side for the evening, leaving the women to celebrate. The bad news is that we're going to be the only men in sight, easy to spot. Suddenly, there was a knock at the door and it opened.

"Evangeline," I said, "How's everything at the festival?"

"Just great," she said darting her eyes around, and scanning the room as if looking for something. She wasn't naked anymore but was wearing fresh tiny skins on her breasts and a fresh skin loin cloth.

"We finally have everything cooking," she said, "Marco put up a good fight, which made it a lot of fun, but now he's roasting on the spit."

"I'll bet," I said as a chill went through me reminding me what the ladies were doing out there, "and I'm glad you're enjoying yourself."

I turned around and Lon was completely out of sight. I wondered if she saw him, but she didn't say anything. She walked over to Nick and held up a dismembered hand. Nick pointed at his sister's ring on the middle finger and Evangeline used a cleaver to chop it off. She removed the ring he asked for and handed it to him.

"Sorry, your ring's dirty," she told Nick.

He dropped it in a glass of grain alcohol and said, "No worries, Thank you."

Nick dried the ring off and put it together with his matching mate on his finger, with a tear in his eye. Evangeline also dumped from her hand his gold teeth onto the table and said, "These are on the house." Then she waved her hand for someone else to come in.

"This is Sundra," Evangeline said, "she's looking for her husband Lon."

Sundra was a very tall blonde goddess, with blue eyes and well-endowed with perfect physical attributes. Unlike the others, her beautiful long hair wasn't shaved into any kind of a Mohawk, but naturally long. She was wearing what everyone else was, the tiny skins. Her stature looked strong, but at the same time soft, and very feminine. She spoke English and said assertively, "I'm looking for my husband. He's about this tall, dark hair, and calls himself 'Lon'."

"We'll keep an eye out for him," Flash said.

As she walked away, we were all sweating, not because of fear, but because of how sensual and beautiful she was, and the way she carried herself. I guess we've never seen physical beauty like this where we come from, and the attire they wear doesn't hurt any either.

Flash, of course, had to comment:
"Did you see those jugs? They were large, firm and jutted out perfectly!"

Still, I did not envy Lon, who actually took offense to Flash's comment. Nick and I stopped him short from lunging at Flash, and Flash, having his back turned, didn't even notice the near skirmish. I felt we needed to get Lon out of there, if not for him, but for our own safety. The ladies would shish kabob us for thinking we're hiding him.

When we were sure the ladies were gone, we took-off into the night. It was Flash, Nick, Erik, Lon and me. The plan, like the jamming, was formed out of boredom. We ran down the beach in the moonlight and around the peninsula to the small airfield. The top of the Learjet shone silvery in the moonlight as we carefully looked around to see if the coast was clear. Then Nick ran with Lon to the door opening, and to manually put the steps down. He then flagged us to come over. We ran and went up the few steps into the fuselage. Lon jumped through the dark into one of the seats, as I did. Nick turned the lights on and we were all mortified. Especially Lon.

There stood the voluptuous Sundra, tall, with all of her sensuality and beauty, with those piercing blue eyes of hers. But now she was naked, except for war paint, in all the right places. I can't imagine her hurting anyone, but I've been wrong before about women. She was wearing one of those hunting knives used for skinning, positioned in her bobbed up hair like a beret. Evangeline was behind her, shaming her finger at us.

Lon, frightened, jumped up from the seat to run, and a leg came out of another seat to trip him, causing him to fall flat on his face. That leg belonged to Luka, the woman whose family we had dinner with yesterday. Totally nude also, her hair was shaved on the sides just like the others. Flash, noticing her seductive curves, had another remark: "Oh my God, her too. I must be in heaven," as he watched Luka turn and squat on Lon, pinning him down as he flipped and squirmed under her like a landed fish. "Jam-patchkol!" Luka commanded in her native tongue, causing him to mellow, temporarily.

"Thank you, Luka," Sundra said as she picked Lon up by his hair and half dragged him out the door, kicking and screaming again, into the moonlight. Then she held him up by one leg like he had no weight whatsoever and with the assistance of Luka stripped him completely naked, using her other hand, saying, "Let's get this done clean and easy, into the salt water, mister."

Luka just laughed, pulling the last bit of clothing off of him saying, "Lon, the piggy." Sundra and Luka each had a leg now, holding him upside down high in the air between them, as they sashayed together toward the wet sand and surf; with Lon wriggling, howling and wailing all the way. Evangeline shut the door so we couldn't see anymore and said, "You guys should be ashamed of yourselves, interfering in family matters."

"Family matters?" Flash said, "Isn't she going to kill him?"
"Of course," Evangeline said, "Lon sold her only daughter into prostitution. The other woman, a neighbor, was in fear

for her daughters. They're going to flay him in the surf by moonlight; before she contributes him to the feast. I think she's entitled."

None of us said a word except for Flash:

"Are they going to eat him?"

"Yes," Evangeline said.

"Can I have his shirt?"

Barbara was with us on the plane too, standing with her hands on her hips. We all noticed that her two covering pasties were now skins with purple hair, and her loincloth was a new skin with a tattoo of a man with a fish tail holding a trident.

"Didn't Peter have purple hair like that? And didn't he have a belly tattoo of a man with a fish tail holding a trident?" Flash asked. She looked at us and did the "tsk tsk tsk tsk" shaking her head at us, then said to Evangeline, "Should we leave right now?"

"Immediately! If you want them to get out of here alive," Evangeline said to her looking at us.

"I'll think about it," Barb said with a mocking grin.

Then Evangeline said, "I am grateful to you Nick, and Stan for all of your help." She peered into my eyes from inches away and said, "I'll never forget you." Then she turned to Erik and said, "Dad, you can come with me. You'll be safe. I need you here." Then she looked at each and every one of us saying, "Flash, and everyone, Thanks and Good Luck . . . and Good bye!!" We all hugged then Erik and Evangeline left the plane. Before the hatch door closed we heard one last long and lengthy shrill but distant scream from poor Lon through the sounds of the surf, as if he was saying good bye. I guess you can say he was.

"Almost sounded like Jackie's singing, didn't it?" Flash added. Always with the comments. Nick was the only one who laughed at that one, as he walked into the cockpit. Then

THE LOST MARBLES STORY

there was another issue. Nick couldn't get the jet engines to fire up. He checked the fuel, then went outside to check the fuel lines. With some searching he noticed that an igniter plug was missing. Evangeline returned, realizing we were having trouble and said that in order to get a new plug, it will cost us a gold ring.
"A gold ring?" Nick asked.

She went on to say that Lon had a gold ring from their wedding that Sundra needs in order to complete a spell that will guarantee the return of her daughter. "It seems to be lost," Evangeline said, then she looked straight into my eyes. "You haven't seen it, have you Stan?" I reached into one of my pockets and went to hand it to her, but she said, "Sundra has the igniter plug. I want you to hand it to her yourself." I was concerned for our safety, mainly mine when Evangeline said, "Don't worry, you're safe. . . as long as you hand it over to her, but you can't go like that."

She made me strip my clothes, and she and Barbara covered me completely with a red oil, rubbing it on me from head to toe, and told me that because I'm a man, this is the only way I'm aloud to walk on the sacred festival grounds, without being cooked! It felt more like a practical joke, but I went with it anyway, anything to get us off of this island. I put the ring in a string pouch that they hung around my neck.

I walked, by myself, about a quarter of a mile across the sand, and through some palm trees between the moon shadows to where the ladies were. All I wanted to do was feel safe around here. I did not want to be a shish kabob. Also, I declared myself squeamish, and I didn't want to see anything that would nauseate me, please.

There, in the light of the fires and lamps was the beautifully bewitching Sundra, perfectly naked, except for a fresh human skin tied as a skimpy apron around her waist. She was standing over a large pot with a large flaming fire beneath it. Her war paint was gone and she looked like she just stepped out of the shower, but I know she just stepped out of the surf. There were other fresh skins drying over the fire next to the large kettle, which was big enough to fit someone my size, although I tried not to think about it. Lon was nowhere to be seen, and I noticed she didn't appear to be killing anything.

Sundra was bending over the pot, that had just begun to steam, adding spice and seasoning when she became aware of my presence. "Why hello handsome, you look good in red. You're Stan, right? I was waiting for you," she said with a big perfect smile. Her teeth were perfect and white, with a slight sexy overbite. She turned away and leaned again to stir the brewing stew, which made me somewhat nervous, considering what I'd seen earlier, but then returned her gaze toward me.

"Don't be afraid. You've got something for me?" she asked.

I answered with a question, "'You've got something for me?"

She smiled, put the spoon down, and walked over to me, enticingly and slowly. As tall as I am, I was still looking up at her alluring face as she placed her one opened hand flat on my red belly, then took my hand with her other; calmly squeezing it, mercilessly, until my hand felt like it was in a vice. The brute strength of this soft spoken tall goddess was indescribable!

"Um, I believe you're hurting me," I said nervously.

Then sensually licking her lips, she said, "I've got your life at hand. Do you want it back?"

I remembered Lon's insistence on her not getting the ring, lest she'll be owning, not only his body, but soul until

the morning light . . . thus I'm to not ever give it to her; but I'm not a total believer in legends and wanted all of us to safely get out of this place. Besides that, my red hand was turning blue. Under the existing circumstances, I pulled the ring out of my neck pouch, and handed it to her without any regrets, and she let my hand go, thank God.
I figured Lon was long gone by now anyway.

 She took the ring, smiled, and handed me the igniter plug, and a wire. "You'll need both of these. Nick will know what I'm talking about," Sundra said with a sly grin. She set a plate, with some kind of raw meat onto the table, then sat down in front of it, like she was going to eat it and invited me, but I demurred.

 I then watched Sundra slowly slip the golden ring onto her finger. Almost immediately the meat in front of her started pulsating, causing her to smile. I realized then that this woman is really a witch, and that this meat appeared to be a human heart. Then there was movement coming from within the now steaming kettle that was over the fire. Two hands, then arms, then a screaming face emerged from the brewing broth. A whole body grabbing at the air, then at the rim of the pot. It was Lon; skinned, disemboweled, and coming back to life! And honoring the curse; screaming its head off, it tried to climb from the now stewing infernal soup!

 Sundra, calmly sashayed, almost erotically, to the cauldron and stood over what used to be Lon, and simply grinned as she grabbed at its arms. "Jambaka tanda!" she asserted in her native tongue; in a commanding tone, as she shoved its head and the rest of it beneath the surface. It emerged again, apparently aware I was there.
"STAAAANN! HAAAALP AAiieEEEee . . . " it shrieked as it struggled hopelessly against her stronger and overpowering feminine physique. In its desperation, its fighting

hands were randomly slapping at, but slipping off of her abundant and bare busts. Sundra once again, unmoved, grabbed its wrists but burned her arm on the flames that were now welling up from beneath the pot.

"Ouch, that's hot, you burned me you bastard!" she said wrestling it back into the simmering cauldron, uttering what sounded like another command to it, "Jumbaka ta Plenksta!" and with her free hand, commenced putting the big heavy lid on the kettle by herself; weighing it down with rocks as the steam plumed from the creature's pathetic failing efforts to lift it. She then grumbled in her native language, shaking her head.

Smiling at me with a wink and wiping her hands with a towel she applied some ice to the burn on her arm as she sat back down at the table, over the disgusting and still beating heart; with a knife and fork in her hand.

Then, as if nothing happened, and without any concern for its continuing muffled shrieks from within the cauldron she casually asked me: "So handsome, are you staying? Or what?"

I then felt every hair on my body rise, just like when I was tripping a few years ago. I realized now that these women were real, honest to goodness witches. They dehumanized their victims, to the point where this brutal punishment really was the 'norm' for them. This was all too horrifying to me, and I turned and ran as hard and as fast as I've ever run.

Unfortunately, I ran in the wrong direction, to another group of ladies. It was Evangeline, turning a roast on a spit. Leaning over the spit was Snake's shiny body glistening in the light of the fire, naked except for a skimpy apron made of human skin supported on the front of her, with a thin string around her neck and around her bare back, which had the healing slice wounds from that recent scourging from Marco's whip.

She was brushing barbecue sauce on the roast, while Ginger was on the other side poking it barbarically with a fork. This would have looked like a normal barbecue pig roast except that the roast was human, a flayed and disemboweled human! And to my disbelief still moving, frantically. It was Marco! It began screaming, then it would stop. Then scream once again as Evangeline continued slowly turning it over the fire. Its shrieks were eerie as it rapidly kicked in vain, sending more chills up what little spine I had left. I actually felt like I was witnessing the bowels of hell, as it was explained to me in catholic school by my second, third, and fourth, grade nuns.

Snake was chewing on some red meat she had taken a bite out of before handing it to Evangeline. She smiled at me, wiping fresh blood from her mouth and showing me her fist with a golden ring on her finger, while Evangeline took a bite of the raw meat and handed it to Ginger to finish.

My first impression of Snake, when I first met her a while back was she seemed quiet and reserved within her evil appearance, however now, she was somewhat talkative.
"Stan, you look good in red, and I'm glad you're still here" she said, "You've been a good sport about everything, and I have to tell you something I've been ashamed of. This is Marco's and my wedding ring on my finger."

As she held it out to me, I noticed it was like the others I've seen worn by our friend Jun and the other island guy Lon.
"Marco and me", she continued, "were married about ten years ago, right here on the island."
"Really?" I said.

As you might guess, I was surprised, and mortified, as I watched her continually brushing barbecue sauce on the unfortunate soul, totally unconcerned regarding its flinching.

"I know," she said, continuing commiserating about her contrite and compunctious feelings of marrying him, "I was younger, and I was stupid. It also pissed his son Jackie off something awful. Marco, here, married me to get to my parents, and their diamond mine; My parents . . . whom he eventually murdered; burning them both alive in a fire he set to their own house."

Just then their roast, on the spit with its handless arms tied in front of it and legs straightened, but slightly spread, let out a long inhuman growl and then a very loud, high pitched shriek as it squirmed. She bent over and stuck an apple into its mouth to quiet it down. "I got it," Ginger said cramming the thing into its toothless maw. Then continuing, Snake said, "Jackie stole the sacred ring from him, and hid it in the chest with the stash of money, and that's why Marco wanted to find it. It really wasn't the money, as he said. I yearned for, and nurtured the stricken, pathetic look on Marco's face when I showed him I had it on my finger. The poor son of a bitch should have killed me when he had the chance, but his own greed stopped him . . . and I'm not complaining in the least. I kept my promise, 'Didn't I darling'?" she said, directing her attention to the roast again.
"No complaints here either," Evangeline said, high fiving Ginger and Snake.

I then remembered once again, about the legend of those wedding vow rings and deduced her intentions. He's apparently going to die a thousand deaths before sunrise, according to the ancient folklore, and it looks to me like he's gone through at least a hundred of them already!

Snake again showed me the ring on her finger saying, "He was more afraid of me finding this, than me catching up to him, 'Right darling?'" she said, directing her attention again to the roast. Then she quietly hummed a melody, brushing its rump, then its front again as Evangeline turned it. Ginger on the other side just kept poking it ruthlessly with the fork and kept the flaming coals and fire burning evenly.

As I observe the poor bastard now, I think to myself 'No wonder Marco was always afraid of her. So, they were married! Holy shit!'

By this time, it would be safe to say I was becoming very uncomfortable with all of this, these witches, (as they declare themselves) and I'm in no mood to remain around this succubine circle of horror. These women were high and insane on that intoxicating root drink, that makes their appetites strong and their moods aggressive. I broke into a cold sweat, and felt the unavoidable need to vanquish my presence, or better yet, get the hell out of this crazy, god-forsaken festival.

So, I ran again, without stopping, with every hair on my body standing on end through this red oil covering me, and this time I ran all the way to the plane; and hearing the three of them breaking out in a reverberating, witchlike cackle as I exited. I was wondering once again if this was all a hallucination; all a dream. The more that I hoped it was, the more reality set in confirming this was all very real. I was so filled with horror at the unbelievable scenes I just witnessed that I actually felt like I was high myself, on some drug. This was a way of life that was supposed to be far, far away . . . and as of now, 'far, far away' is my goal, and where I want to be.

I returned to the plane and handed Nick the plug and the wire and stood there trembling and catching my breath.

Nick looked at the wire and said, "Why, that bitch." Then he looked at me and asked, "Wow, look at you. What the hell are you on?" Then calmly shook his head saying, "Wash that shit off of you and go put some clothes on," and casually went to work repairing the engine while I tried to regain my composure. I jumped into the ocean to rinse this red crap off of me, then found my clothes and dressed.

Nick got back into the cockpit and the engines were firing like nothing ever happened. We were all in and ready to go. I was trying to forget what I just saw at the festival site. Barbara got into the cockpit with Nick, but Nick held up Barbara's flight uniform and said, "Here, please put this on, I don't want anyone I know to see you wearing that," regarding her garb of human skins. Barb gave him a grin and a cold stare, then obliged, and within minutes we were airborne. I must say, it was an adventure, and I am probably the happiest of all of us to be out of there. That was stranger than any trip I've ever been on, physical or mental! What's the name of that island," Flash was asking," or those islands Barbara? Do you know?"

Barb's voice came from the cockpit saying, "They call themselves 'Jaadaa'. They say it means 'Woman'." Flash, now laying back comfortably in Lon's Hawaiian shirt was quiet for a moment before saying, "Man, how about that Sundra and Luka? I mean, Holy smoke, talk about the absolute perfect breasts, Wow."

Barb then said with some annoyance, "I didn't say anything about breasts. I didn't even mention anything remotely relating to breasts, you perfect ass."

"Perfect ass," Flash answered Barbara, "You're right! That too was perfect."

Barbara then let out a barely audible groan revealing her disgust.

Nick then responded to Flash, making sure Barbara heard him, saying,
"Hey Flash, that woman Sundra is available now. You might want to look into that. It's said that those women on the island want sex all the time."

An irritated Barbara remained quiet, and now somewhat sullen, as Flash thought about it for a second before answering:
"I would, Nick, except that I know I wouldn't be able to keep up with a well-endowed woman like that without getting myself a mild heart attack; becoming somewhat useless to her. And then where would I be? I'll tell you where. Looking up at her perfect breasts, from a skinning board or from inside of a cooking pot someday!" Barbara couldn't take anymore and said, "ALL RIGHT! KNOCK IT OFF!!" Then I heard Nick say sarcastically and melodically, "Sounds like someone didn't get enough to eat today!"
I heard what sounded like a loud slap come from inside the cockpit. . . then Nick's voice saying, "Not the face," then Barb saying, "It's not, that's an ass."

    As we climbed in altitude over the gleaming ocean through the moonlit night, I thought about the balance of the universe. I wondered about karma, the prospect of good and evil, and the insanity of punishment.

    For years, people have balanced their off centered emotions by getting back at whoever they blamed for throwing them off center. People have cast fear into the hearts of others through acts of terror and torture to gain power, or through rumors and gossip to create paranoia and acquiring these same results. Power through mind games.

    Native Americans were being invaded by countless invaders, who tortured and raped them, and when they returned the same acts, they were demonized by the multitudes who veritably were the originators of these acts. A specific example is what Custer and his men did to Chief Black Kettle's camp. Some of the men reportedly cut the vaginas out of the Native American women and wore them as hat bands after they raped them. When white men were captured alive by Sioux, or Cheyenne, it was the women of the tribes who handled the torture and slow deaths. Retribution.

What we witnessed on the island was horrific, but I asked myself if it was any more horrific than our own capital punishment? Was it any more horrific than a hangman's noose? Or a firing squad? Or an electric chair? Or a gas chamber?

No, I say, I believe it's less horrific, because the idea of the latter is too organized, too systematic, too controlled, too orderly . . . which to me makes it too frightening. Does any of this make it right? It's become too much like buying meat in the market. No one sees it being killed, because it's just bought and eaten as if it never lived before. 'So and so' went to the gas chamber. Oh well, out of sight, out of mind. Or it's like the ignorance of sending soldiers into battle because it's what we've always done, "Send them over there, out of sight, out of mind," but no one ever thinks about the outcome, except the families of the dead and the wounded.

The women and men of the island where we were, have lived in peace for hundreds of years until Marco stuck his evil hand in to stir things up. Are these natives considered "savage"? It depends on who you ask. Are the people they've killed tonight who've invaded their way of life considered "savage"? In my opinion, Yes.

I took a few gulps of wine, went to the bathroom, and while I was here, I took a shower. Yes, this plane has everything. After that, I didn't want to hear or talk anymore about anything. I know I'm going to sleep well, presumably without any nightmares.

Chapter 21

Nancy and Me

Flash and I nodded out in our separate areas on these fold out beds, and although I don't know how long it was I slept, it was around 2:00pm and daylight when I woke up, California time. I ate steak and eggs prepared by Flash.

"Hey sleepy head," Flash was telling me, "you missed our stop. We picked up some supplies and I made these for you. Tell me how you like it?"
"It's great Flash. It's fucking fantastic!"
"That's what I want to hear," he said with a smile.
"Where are we headed now?" I asked.
"We'll be at the Scranton airport in about an hour. That's where Nick's rental car is. We're going to drive home. Home sweet home!"
"That sounds good to me Hank. Has anyone contacted Cuz or Nancy yet?"
"No, Nick wants to just drive home and surprise them."
"We should have called to let them know we're alright," I told him.
"They know we're alright Stan. Nick sent a telegram saying that we're on our way home and we'll be pulling into the driveway any minute."
I enjoyed the meal and sat back with a beer. Then I thought about Nancy and couldn't get her out of my mind. Not that I wanted to, it's just that I missed seeing her and it was kind of hurting.

I remembered those two leaf wishes from Evangeline and pulled one of them out. I remembered that it's one wish per leaf, and thought: 'Why not? Everything about that island was magical'. I squeezed the leaf my right hand and wished that Nancy would be there at the Scranton airport with a separate car, for just her and I. This would solidify my feelings and I'll know for sure she feels the same. I felt a sensation in my right hand like heat. I slowly opened my hand and in a puff of smoke, the leaf was gone. I looked all over the floor for it, but it literally disappeared. Oh well, maybe that means my prayer will be answered.

After a few minutes, I nodded out again. The next thing I heard was "Fasten the belt Stan. We're getting ready to land." In about ten minutes we were touching down on the landing strip in the Scranton airport. We taxied in, and we stepped down from the plane. We said so long to Barbara as she headed into the building like nothing happened. She however was folding her collected skins and put them in her flight bag. It was like this had all been a dream. Flash and Nick and I walked to the gates where the cars were parked and where his rental was waiting.

Before he touched the door, I felt a hand on my shoulder. I turned around and there she was, looking straight up at me. Nancy!

She jumped up onto me, and wrapped her arms and legs around me teary eyed and trembling, squeezing with all of her might. I couldn't hug her back hard enough. We stood entwined for what I wanted to be forever before we heard Nick's voice say, "Break it up." I had to pry her off of me to face the reality of the airport parking lot and Flash laughing aloud, who also gave her a hug, and so did Nick. They didn't get the same greeting from her and I'm not sorry to say that it made me happy.
"What the hell are you doing here?" Nick asked.
"What the hell do you think?" she said, "I'm helping out with the rides. Come on Stan." I shrugged my shoulders and she pulled my hand toward a Jeep that she rented and had running.
"I'll catch you guys at home," I said, smiling and waving.
Nick said, "Wait a minute." And he ran over to us. He got within inches of my face and smiled saying, "See, I told you it would all work out. You're one of the good ones, Stan. Thank you." He gave me a kiss on my forehead and then a hug, and I saw a tear which made me produce at least one, maybe two. He patted me with both hands on my shoulders and headed back to his rental car.

"I want us to go to a motel," she said. I looked at her, and thought about that other leaf; and then thought that I'm just going to save it. Then I answered her. I said, "Okay."

We drove south and stayed in a nice hotel right in the Delaware Water Gap. It was about 4 o' clock in the afternoon when we arrived. We showered, separately, and we stood naked to the world in front of each other. We looked into each other's eyes, as she took my hand, and placed it onto her breast ever so delicately as I wrapped my other arm around her, pulling her into me as we kissed. We spent the next hour and a half laying naked in the sheets of a soft king-sized bed, rolling and tumbling.

Making love to her was so erotic, as we constantly looked into each other's eyes and talked softly sometimes. Other times our voices were silent, until we screamed in our euphoria. She'd glide her fingernails across my chest as my hands caressed her soft breasts. On my back and looking up at her, she looked like the inimitable, consummate goddess, as I lay beneath her in her upright position, with her open hands on my abs sliding up and down, and my hands stroking and embracing her every curve from her front to her back, as we conducted our experiments in perpetual motion. We felt each beat of our own hearts together, pounding ever stronger in a steady rhythm, until the rhythms seemed to pass each other as we both exploded into interminable ecstasy, and lay simultaneously exhausted and refreshed within it's inevitable aftermath; spooning; Spooning our sugar over a satiable nap.

After the nap, we showered again. In order to save time, we showered together. She actually had brought a change of clothes for me. She said she went into my closet and chest of drawers at home before she came to Scranton, knowing I'd be ripe in these old duds I was wearing. We

dressed and we sat in the dining room of the old hotel and had a dinner of prime rib and my favorite, Lobster smothered in butter.
"I told you before Stan, I'm going to cook this for you sometime."
"That would be nice," I answered.

She gave the sexiest smile, winked and we both chowed down and talked. I told her some of the island's adventure but I wanted to be careful not to awaken some abeyant bad memories of her previous experience being kidnapped. I did however want to assure her that the danger was most certainly eliminated, for good. She was extremely happy about that prospect, and she began telling me about the band, and Cuz and Stephanie. Because of the incident in Flagstaff, the rest of the summer bookings were cancelled. There was nothing else she could do. There are radio stations in L.A. and Houston playing our songs, but a good deal of the country has never heard them, or us for that matter.
"We don't have a big-name label," Nancy said, "We're our own commodity. It's tough to push these songs and the band any farther on our own."
"Nancy, you took us pretty far just on your own," I said.
"I know, but we seem to be dead in the water now. Besides, Cuz is not into all of this touring anymore. He's happy just to keep everything local, you know, just Philly, maybe New York, Baltimore . . . He and Steph have a kid on the way and playing on the road could prove to be disruptive to their auspicious relationship."
"Are they getting along okay and everything?" I asked.
"Everything seems promising," she said, "If Cuz holds up alright anyway."
"What do you mean? What's the matter with Cuz?"

Nancy and I are on our second glass of wine and we both pause to drink a mouthful before she tells me. "Cus has been doing speed and Demerol. He's been shooting the stuff up, you know, using needles. Stephanie has no clue, but I caught him with it. Crystal meth. He said he's been doing it since that first concert with Jackie."
"I don't believe it! That's absurd! I would have known about something like that. We're with him all the time," I told her.
"Well, it's true. He told me himself. He's been hitting up right before the gigs, and taking to hitting up Demerol afterwards to mellow, so he can sleep."
"I did notice that he seemed more 'up' for the shows now that I remember," I told her, "but I would have never guessed . . ."
"He wasn't doing it much at first," Nancy said, "but he developed a habit of hitting up a gram each time, then he actually hits up the Demerol."
Nancy and I were quiet for a few minutes as we finished up our dinner.
"Nancy, let's talk about something else, okay? This subject just depresses me."
"Awww," she said standing up and coming around to my side of the table. She bent over to me and giving me a hug said, "Let's finish up and go back to the room."

Back at the room, I undressed and crawled under the sheets and watched Nancy sitting at the vanity in the nude, slowly and softly brushing her long brown hair. She was beautiful. She was talking to me, but it was just small talk about hair, tan lines, eye makeup and a new dress or something. I guess that's why they call it a vanity. She asked me about Evangeline and if I'd miss her. "Evangeline who?" I said returning the question. She stood up in all her beauty with a laugh, then a smile, and walking over to me said,

"That's the right answer." She then preceded to jump onto the bed, and me. We savored every moment of the next hours in the sweat, and the smells of unforgiving sex and deep, deep love making. Once again, we fell asleep spooning. My new favorite position.

We awoke to the rhythmic tapping of the pouring rain on the balcony gutters and the windows. Thunder and lightning storms were brewing and we went back to sleep. When we awoke to the same dark weather at around noon, we laid back in bed, skipped lunch, and rolled around again to the lightning and thunder of our own making, until Nancy and me, in unison, cried out a final climactic thunderous roar in complete euphoria. We then slipped soundly into a peaceful, restful sleep once again.

Needless to say, we stayed another night and checked out before 11am, showered and tired, but refreshed. It was sunny and looked like the rain had never happened, except for some puddles and debris where streams of flood wash from Mount Minsi had left their legacy across route 611.
"This part of 611 always reminds me of our trek to Woodstock in '69," I said.
"Mae and I were sleeping through here I guess," Nancy answered grinning and continued, "I really miss Mae. What happened to you two?"
"We were young," I said, "Like you and Cuz were."
"Isn't it funny how life just goes on, and keeps changing things?" Nancy asks as she looks out at the spectacular views of the hills and river from this northern section of route 611.
"That's life," I said, "Always changing." I drove and we both talked as we continued toward our home in Warminster.

Chapter 22

Intervention and Togetherness

Time marched onward into autumn, and we managed to acquire a nominal sum from the records and the tours we did before it all came to a grinding halt. We also acquired, thanks to Nick and Evangeline, a good part of the money from the stash that was in Lake Nockamixon. We split it up evenly and had more than enough for Nancy and me to buy a house on Valley road, right by Neshaminy creek. A handyman special.

We also did an intervention with Cuz. Nick, Flash, Stephanie, Nancy and I sat with Cuz at the Warminster house, which Nick recently bought off of Nancy, and talked Cuz into going to a rehab in Doylestown. This came after he asked me to drive him to a buddy's house where he said he was getting some money back that he owed him. When he asked me to walk in with him I was dubious, or a bit hesitant to comply, but I agreed after his insistence, and we walked in together. This was in Lacy Park, which was a low-income development right around the corner from where we were.

Anyway, inside I saw a rat scurry through a hole in a half-painted fiberboard wall. This was someone's living room, where there was an odor of urine and the pungent bouquet of garbage; but the people sitting in the worn-out chairs and sofa didn't seem to mind. Cuz told me to have a seat, but I declined. He went with a tall Hispanic looking dude into another room while I was left looking at these bozos sitting around me. They were heating up spoons with meth mixed with water, filling syringes, and getting off, right in front of me. One of the guys sitting across from them asked me, "Who the hell are you?"
"I'm Stan. Who the hell are you?"
"Are you a narc or somethin'?" he asked.
"If I was, do you think I'd tell you? I'm just waiting on a friend."

These were not responses that were welcome here. It finally occurred to me that my asshole friend, Cuz, used me for a ride to get him here to cop some dope. The fool who was asking my identity then said:
"See this? This is for blowin' people away."

He was holding up a bomb device that was made to be mounted to a vehicle of whom these people call 'undesirables'. I kept looking him in the eye and said, "That's nice. Where's your car? I'll help you install it."

"What? Waddeya mean?" he asked with a genuine blank expression. Just then Cuz came out and said, "Come on Stan, I got it. Let's go."

"The money he owed me!"

Through his resistance I rolled up his long sleeves to see many needle marks, and two very fresh ones still bleeding.

"You are a fucking asshole!" I told him. "You will never, ever drag me or anyone of us into a place like that again!" I literally threw him into the car and drove him home disgusted.

So, we took Cuz to the rehab to get clean, get treatments, and become healthy and Stephanie played a big part. She was pretty far along in her pregnancy, getting very big and as I said before, she's already big boned, but she looked great as a mother to be. At this time, we were told that the baby is really Nicks'. Nancy knew this, and this was the final driven wedge between her and Nick. When Cuz found out, he was devastated, and it made him more vulnerable to his addictions. But in spite of this, Cuz wanted to raise the baby as his own, with Stephanie, and keep on loving her. She did seem to love Cuz and they're intentions were to work everything out.

Nancy and I bought a 'handyman special', to be our own house on Valley road between Furlong and Jamison, Pa. It was a rancher, which we fixed up in our own time, to our own needs. When we weren't working on the house we were hiking and fishing together, traveling to different areas of the U.S.

We sort of distanced ourselves from everyone, living off of a nest egg we've developed from our previous adventures, and funds from my part-time construction business, that kept me somewhat busy when I wasn't working on the house. On some days, when I'd come home from working a hard day, I would hear her voice say, "Stan, Is that you? I know you're home. Get your ass in here and come dance with me!" And we'd dance to the Temptations' song, the one we danced to years before and we'd just hold each other for a while. We knew how to give ourselves those moments.

I still played my bass guitar a few times a week but was not as involved in music as I was before I started living with Nancy. Everything felt perfect once again in my life, but for obvious and different reasons.

Sometimes, Nancy and I would climb up onto the roof of the garage and just lay together, sometimes naked, sometimes not. There were no houses or people within viewing distance of this secluded spot of ours. Here, we sometimes made love in the sunlight, or in a warm summer rain, or under the stars. But most of the time we would simply talk, and direct our thoughts into deep conversation, that took us even deeper into each other. It was almost as if it was us against the universe, but there was no negativity or darkness, because we converted everything to be positively brilliant, and everything remained absolute. Perfect.

Once, on one of our road trips, we ended up sleeping out in the woods in the Bitterroots, somewhere in Idaho. The tall ponderosa pines surrounded us, but we could see the stars against the border of treetops. It was another beautiful view of the universe, seeing her naked form against that backdrop as we made love, taking turns looking up into the cosmos at night. We were responsibly insightful, regarding the laws of the wilderness, but both of us ig-

norant to any knowledge of bears; so, following our passionate evening, we subsequently slept peacefully, fearlessly, and soundly within the womb of our sleeping bag. The following morning, we walked about a half a mile back to our jeep, and it was turned onto its side. The canvas top was gone, along with our picnic basket cooler of fried chicken, fruits, and tomato sandwiches. Other than some remaining tattered canvas shreds, the jeep appeared to be in good health. Nancy stayed completely calm as we approached it, but I, on the other hand, was terrified.
"Give me a hand," she said laughing at our situation, as she started to push the vehicle over, back to its natural position, onto its wheels.
PLOMP! Then, still laughing she said, "We'd better get the hell out of here."

We drove away, continuing our camping at a few more nicer areas, as we made our way back to our home in Pa; That is after getting a new canvas top installed onto our jeep in Missoula, Montana.

After about two years of not playing, we were all getting antsy. The songs we had on some of the charts to no surprise disappeared. We became old news rather fast. Nick had actually gotten married to Barbara, who continued her career as a pilot, flying charter flights and making good money. Nick continued working for the government doing who knows what, working his own hours and getting paid generously for it. Some of the work had Barb and him working together which makes for a good team, I guess. They call it "Marital bliss." Cuz ran a successful landscaping business and was totally clean. He does drink but has total control since this was never a problem for him.

The big news was Cuz and Stephanie were married. Yes. They became Benjamin and Stephanie Unkelheyer!

Stephanie had the baby, a little girl they named Susan Unkelheyer. Cuz is a great father to her and is the only father, as far as Susan will ever know. Nick had no problem with that and is still in doubt that Susan is actually his. The Unkelheyer family, with all due respect to Nick, denounced him as the father and continued on as one happy family.

Flash stayed clean of alcohol through the years and had opened up a roofing business: *Henry Zeke Roofing,* which kept him busy and also hooked up with a lovely woman named Wanda. They never married but lived happily in their home they shared. He even wrote a song about her with his own lyrics and we all helped to put it to music.

This is what lit a fire under our butts to bring the band back together. Not necessarily the song, but the getting together of the band and the camaraderie we shared, and I was ready for it. Nancy and I were married, and very happy, living on Valley road in the rancher by the creek, but we were opened to new adventures. Nancy and I also had a baby, a boy we named Abraham. Abraham Cactus Stephens. She always loved the name Abraham and so did I. The middle name, Cactus, was because we knew he was conceived under the stars beneath a very large saguaro cactus near Tucson, Arizona.

Nancy also got into the role of being a true home maker, and a home body. Long before our boy was born she made our house the home that it is, while I worked my construction business. She was happier than I've ever seen her. Not only is she a great mom to Abe, but Nancy could make curtains on the sewing machine, mix and match paint for the wall and ceiling cracks she spackled, then paint the walls to look like a pro did it.

She even took on some farming. She brought home some egg-laying chickens and a rooster. I knew this was coming when she had me help her put up the chicken wire around the previously unused half of the old barn, which she fixed up rather nice with straw and new wood framing. She also had a garden with tomatoes, zucchini, squash, green beans, romaine lettuce, and even corn.

Her long brown hair would be braided from the front and the braids pulled back across the top of her head like a crowned queen, while the rest would be two braided pigtails coming down over her shoulders. She would dress like a Daisy Mae farm girl in the summer with a skimpy halter top exposing her strong, but very feminine sexy shoulders and back. Or sometimes she just had her sexy shirt tied like a halter top above her belly button and her denim shorts would always be cut right at the crest of her cute ass.

I loved working in the garden with her, as we'd be mulching and digging and getting all dirty. We had an eighth of an acre of just tomatoes. She would sell them from a little produce stand she and had I built together at the side of our road, along with the other veggies she grew. We had so many tomatoes one summer that we couldn't give them away.

It was that particular summer we were working together when out of the blue, 'whaaaap!' a tomato hit me square in the top of the head. I looked up to see her smiling and throwing another. This was war! We only destroyed about two dozen of them but we both looked like we'd taken a blood bath. She insisted I won, but I knew better. We must have spent an hour in the shower together washing the tomato and dirt off of ourselves, then another hour totally naked checking each other for ticks. Any excuse to be naked together.

Anyway, we had plenty of tomatoes left over for canning and Nancy had all of the mason jars she needed to can the tomatoes, the squash, and the zucchini. She even canned the tomato and zucchini together in about two dozen jars as a nice winter stew. There was even room for habanero and jalapeno peppers to be put in with some of them, and When the baby came, she didn't let up with the housework. She always had young Abraham with her in the garden, in the kitchen, in the chicken coop, and hanging the clothes up to dry. She showed me how to properly change the cloth diapers, and how to rock him to sleep.

One day in the summer, we discovered that one of the hens, we named 'Dolly', wasn't laying anymore. We got the bright idea that we needed another rooster, but that was a bad idea! Both roosters had to be separated and Dolly still wasn't laying eggs. One morning before I went to work Nancy came walking in with Dolly in her arms, holding and petting her under her Daisy Mae haltered bosom saying,
"Stan, she's done laying, and we can't really keep her."
"I don't know what you mean," I said.
"I think you do. It's time to say good bye to her."
"Are you going to call a butcher?" I asked. She just smiled and said, "No, I'm not going to call the butcher. I know how to do this." She grinned and with the deep look into my eyes she kissed the side of my face and whispered directly into my ear like it was a secret, "I'm making chicken for dinner tonight." I shivered as I watched her walk with Dolly outside, and I went the other way to work.

When I came home at lunch, she was holding a plucked 'Dolly' over the opened gas flame on the stove, burning off what was left of the pin feathers on the deceased and decapitated fowl. She was flapping the wings, then turned it upside down flapping the legs, looking like she was born to be a farmer, and a very sexy looking one at that. "Actually Stan," she said, "Evangeline was the one who told me how to do this stuff."

She walked to me with the knife and held it out to me saying, "You want to do the old rooster? He has to go too."

I declined, and she smiled, saying "sissy!" and we both laughed in agreement. I don't have that in me, but I'm glad she does. She walked outside and grabbed the rooster, like a pro, and it was over in one quick squawk. By the time I was leaving, she had him tied upside down on the clothesline plucking him for dinner.

As my eyes drifted, looking past her perfect figure cleaning the rooster, in those tight shorts under that strong bare back of hers, I saw how the garden we've worked on within our yard was growing. I noticed how everything she touches does so well. The house she's painted and fixed up, the eggs we're getting; even the chicken and rooster for dinner had the best life it could have possibly had with her. I realize I'm blessed to be with her, more now than ever. I also wonder what I could have possibly done to deserve her. Or better yet, I wonder what the hell she sees in someone like me. It makes me think, I must be doing something right.

Anyway, by now I was working as a full-time contractor doing small jobs with masonry and drywall. I had a few people working for me and we were doing well, but I was hungry for playing out again. We were all ready. The plus side was we all had money in the bank thanks to our previous endeavors.

Chapter 23

Lost Marbles are Back

One day we were all invited to an outdoor spring concert. All of the Lost Marbles attended. We were not scheduled to play, but we were invited by a few friends who were putting it together, invited to attend, listen, and enjoy the day. We were also told that all of the acts were local, but one act from New York was supposedly huge.

"The Mollusk People", from New York, were an act that was new wave, and popular. They were the featured band, and we were looking forward to hearing them. Nancy, little Abraham, who was in what some mothers call the terrible twos, and I had a blanket in the middle of the field surrounded by others with the same mind set.

Sharing our big blanket were Cuz and Stephanie with their little girl Susan, who was now about 3. Flash and Wanda were about ten feet away with their cooler of iced tea and non-alcoholic beers. I saw them pull up in their '70 VW bug. Flash seemed to always have this vehicle, and he's managed to maintain it throughout these years, but not without heartaches.

Once, back in the mid-seventies, Flash had the VW running and was driving Cuz and I down a long winding hill in a rainstorm. We were all drinking beers of course. The radio was blasting, and we were all singing a Grateful Dead song, but I can't recall which one. Anyway, Flash lost control of the vehicle and we spun, and somehow, we flipped the VW onto its left side then skidded about a hundred and fifty feet, stopping in the middle of the macadam country road. I was in the back, and all I remembered seeing was the back of Cuz's head through the whole ordeal, and that I never spilled a drop of my beer! We rolled down his passenger window and we all climbed out of it one at a time after Flash turned off the engine. Yes, the engine remained running until he turned it off. We stood around the steaming vehicle and decided to flip it back onto its wheels. We then bent a fender out from scraping the tire and we were even able to open the driver's side door for Flash to get in. He started it and we were on our way, to the all-night party we were invited to, and we even played at it.

Flash, however needed body work to get it through inspection, so he also tried to get the insurance company to pay for it, but they didn't buy the fact that the vehicle was side swiped by a big semi. "I never heard of a semi made of road tar and gravel," said the insurance man. Flash put it in storage and restored it after his Buick was stolen and trashed, that night driving home from a Center City gig. Anyway, it was good to see them.

Cuz had a six pack of beer and some quarts of malt liquor in his cooler, with Stephanie handing these to him. He's been remaining clean of dope, even pot. Nick was with our old friend Gus, as they both came walking over to our blanket. Gus had his flute, and as soon as we made eye contact with him, he put the flute up to his mouth and started blowing into it wildly, dancing all around like he was Pan, or a dancing hobbit, and he was going wild. Little Abe and Sue stood up; and looking right at him started to bob up and down like they were dancing too. He had the face of a madman, as he brought it down to them closer, then pulled back, as he didn't want to frighten them, and soon mellowed.

Lowering the flute from his mouth he extended his hand in greeting.
"Remember me?" he asked still wearing his Cheshire grinning perfect teeth through the full beard. "Yes," I answered, "I see you made it Gus."

Gus then wandered off to talk to other folks in the growing crowd and the kids both sat facing each other. Nancy nudged me to watch them as little Susan crawled out to the padded down grass to find a flower, then stood up, and walked with it, bringing it back to Abe. Abe stood up, received the token of generosity, and said, "Ba Ga", then began to devour the petals.
"Ew, he's eating it," Suzie's baby voice blurted out.

Nancy immediately answered the alarm and grabbing Abe, pulled the petals from his mouth. "No!" Then she smiled at me saying, "I don't think it's poison, but I don't want him making a habit of eating flowers."

Nancy is a fantastic mom to Abe. She breast-fed him until about a month ago and Abe has gotten pretty independent. The bond between them is so strong that sometimes I feel like an outcast. That is until he climbs up on me when I'm sitting in the chair reading the paper. I always put the paper down when he does, and I listen to his babbling, which only he and Nancy understand. Nancy also has him wearing real cloth diapers, none of that plastic shit. I don't mind changing him with these cloth and safety pin diapers. I got so good at it that Nancy keeps handing him to me when I'm home and she's actually fooled me into really believing this. But I know now that it was a ploy to make me feel useful with him, and to give her a break.

I watched this little son of mine at the festival, and I see me in him, but just as much of Nancy is observed in him. He has not just her eyes, and good looks, but every bit of her determination. I don't think he gets any of that from me. Abe saw me looking at him and he sat down right next to me. I look at him and hold him, then I look at Nancy and catch her smiling at me. Life is good.
    Nick sat down with us and he told us we might be playing here today if a band cancels. I looked at him as Nancy punched my shoulder in disbelief, and said, "What do you mean Nick? Who's canceling?"
"I don't know," he said smiling, "You never know about these things."
"But we're unrehearsed, and our equipment isn't here," I told him as Cuz sat up attentively. "I brought our guitars," Nick was saying, "they have the amps, cords and Flash can play the drums that one of the bands here has already set up. He already talked to the band and their cool with it. We're going to use those Marshal amps you see right there. They're already hooked up through the board."
"It sounds like you already have it planned," I said pointing at Nick and tapping Cuz to see if he's catching all of this. "I just heard that 'The Mollusk People' cancelled. Actually, I heard from a reliable source that they never intended on showing."
    "Well," said Nancy, "I think that's pretty rude of them, and pretty fucked up, if you ask me."
"How do you know this?" Cuz asked.
"I hear things," Nick said, "Just be ready." And with that he got up and walked to the back of the stage.
    The first act was two people, a guy and a gal calling themselves 'The Jersey Drivers', singing and playing acoustic guitars. In a half-hour, the next band came up. It was a four piece with drums and a bass, and a keyboard, and a

guy doing the singing. They were okay, but nothing that got the audience in any kind of a tizzy. The whole show went on like this and I told Nancy I was thinking about leaving. I wasn't having a good time, and neither was she. Cuz started packing his stuff in frustration when the emcee announced that the Mollusks we not coming.

The crowd started to go nuts, until it was added, "Would you, nice people like to hear a huge local band who recorded 'Sing Those Blues'? And 'Rock and Roll Radio'?" To our surprise, the crowd actually started to hoot and holler.
"We have as a treat for you today, 'The Lost Marbles!' Let's have a nice welcome for this blast from the recent past, 'The Lost Marbles'!"

The entire audience stood up. Why not? Most of them were friends of friends and a lot of them attended our County Theater concert a few years back. We walked to the stage and Nick had everything ready. We went right into 'Sing Those Blues', then 'Rock and Roll Radio', and then we went into 'Zenith', a long jamming instrumental with Cuz really ripping it up on the leads. I stood right next to Nick and we did our customary syncopated riffs, weaving our intricate sound grooves in and out of each other. Flash tied it all together with his solid rhythm, like that of a of a concrete mixer, pouring a foundation that couldn't be compromised if we wanted to.

The song seemed to go on for hours but in reality, it was about fifteen minutes. Cuz was doing the female vocal on his guitar with his unusual bending of the notes and some effects. We of course couldn't do the harmonies but Cuz and Nick faked those parts ingeniously with their guitar work. The whole front herd of people were dancing, some getting naked. It was a sight to behold from our perspective because it was like we had the power, or something.

Gus was in with the dancers playing his flute. It looked like he was leading them around as they were certainly following him. Some young lady ran up on the stage and threw panties around the neck of Cuz's guitar as he kept playing, not losing the beat. Stephanie saw this and immediately appeared and removed them from around the machine head of his Strat, and flung them back into the audience, then surprisingly smiled. We did a few blues standards and then closed out with a classic, "Johnny Be Good." The whole show seemed flawless.

Except for a bad clam, (mistakes) here and there, it all went over pretty well. Nancy came up to us all and told us we were fantastic. She pulled me aside and said, "I've never heard you sound better Stan." She gave me a big hug and discretely grabbing at my crotch said, "I'm hot. Let's get you home." The audience wanted more but we knew we needed to pack it in for today, and for obvious reasons I knew I wanted to go home, right now! We all now have, the musical bug back. We're all itching to do something with what we have, and Nancy even said, referring to the band, "The time is now, Stan. It won't last forever."

It was now the spring of 1984. We rehearsed as the original members of Lost Marbles and we managed to put many blues and rock standards together, along with the few originals, including "Wanda" on tracks. We made a 45 rpm of Wanda on the A side and we put a song we wrote called "Lila" on the B side. Notwithstanding the formidable lyrics of the latter track we called it the 'dark' side. The words were customized to our recent experiences with a strange, but compelling woman:
"LILA"

"You stand with him on forbidden shores. I can see him in your shadow.
To be in love is to be with only one. Within your lie are you aware?
Your eyes say you're the woman of my dreams. A taste of honey from inviting lips.
Appearing soft and white you're far from pure. Within your lie is he aware?
And like the sirens you will call,
and put our backs against the wall.
I watch the men around me fall. You can't have us all.
Oh Lila, you're missing me.
Oh Lila.
Oh Lila, you're missing me.
One seductive smile could start a fire. With just a wink you hypnotize.
A language mastered through the ages. Within your lie are they aware?
And like the sirens you will call,
And put our backs against the wall.
I watch the men around me fall. You can't have us all.
Oh Lila, you're missing me.
Oh Lila.
Oh Lila, you're missing me.
Someday the truth will come to haunt you. Like a chilling ocean wind
blowing through a lonely winter. Within your lie are you aware?
And like the sirens you will call,
And put our backs against the wall.
I watch the men around me fall. You can't have us all.
Oh Lila, you're missing me.
Oh Lila.
Oh Lila, you're missing me."

There was a lot of cutting and editing for this track to fit, but we managed a short version. We had about 1000 copies made of a 45 containing side A and side B and once again we were our own producers. We were learning that high tech standards were graduating into the recording industry. What little we knew about analog, was converting slowly to what we knew nothing about, which was digital. We had our own studio for rehearsing and recording in Jamison. Nancy was not as involved but she showed us the ropes as far as the booking and promoting.

We had pictures taken of us in front of mine and Nancy's house, down by the big rock in the middle of Neshaminy Creek and formulated a promotional package that was sent out saying to the music world we were back, live and kicking. There was so much excitement and enthusiasm within our circle that we couldn't contain ourselves.

We managed to book a few gigs, and by late summer, we were playing a few bars in the neighborhood and in Philadelphia. However, the record we were pushing, floated like a lead balloon. It sunk like a stone actually, but we continued to play the songs at the bars and sell the 45s right there. We would arrive at the gig, set up, tune up, and play. Cuz and I were doing the singing. Nick could harmonize along with playing his solid rhythm on his Les Paul. Flash pulled the rock-solid beat in with his perfect timing while I wove the bottom into the continuous current pulse of the song. Cuz intricately floated his lead guitar notes between the grooves, as if searching for answers from us, and we responded with a syncopated climax of solidarity that couldn't be denied. We were hot as a band. No question about it, and we knew it.

THE LOST MARBLES STORY

Sometimes we'd get a request for 'Wanda' and I'd look at Cuz, with his brand-new Fender Stratocaster guitar and count the song 'Wanda' off:

"She works behind the bar, Bermuda's tight and blue.
While looking at her legs, I noticed her tattoo.
It said 'Wanda'.
I had an empty glass. I started getting loud.
I snapped my fingers once, then Wanda turned around.
I yelled Wanda, oh, Wanda, I want you Wanda.
Don't you know she looks alright?
I asked her if she's free tonight.
She looked at me and she didn't speak.
She shined her knuckles with my teeth!
Wanda Wanda Wanda Wanda.
I told her she was wrong to put me in my place.
She filled my empty glass, she splashed it in my face!
Oh Wanda, I want you Wanda.
Don't you know she took my heart?
I had my finish from the start.
Now at least she knows I'm here.
I wish she'd just bring me my beer.
Wanda Wanda Wanda Wanda.
I patronize that bar, and now I'm never blue.
Because across my heart, I wear a new tattoo.
It says, 'Wanda'."

The song always got applause, no matter how many people were at the bar we were playing. Unfortunately for us, there was no radio airplay, except for the very local stations such as Warminster and a Jersey station. To top it off, no one remembered us from our known songs from the past, "Sing Those Blues" and "Rock and Roll Radio." Although we played these at our bar gigs, got great feedback and sometimes a standing ovation, but this was like starting all over again. Maybe we weren't as well-known as we thought we were. We know we were at one time, but that was over four or five years ago, and the popularity was short lived.

I guess it's like going back to a high school reunion if you've only attended the high school for a single year. No one recognizes you anymore. To top it off, the industry is growing, and the new and diverse musical acts are as talented as they are technically superior, to anything that we could create within our own comfort zone. In other words, the competition is infinite and we're feeling left behind.

Nevertheless, we continued to book the band, getting weekend gigs and working our day jobs. We actually played a gig, a bar actually, where only twelve people showed up all night. We played our hearts out as usual and we kept those twelve people there, drinking, and dancing all night. Then we would play a club where a hundred or more attended and we did the same with them. We were consistently good, only not popular. The fact of the matter was, along with the frustration, that we were playing as good, if not better than we ever played before, and we absolutely knew it. This gave us the confidence to continue and to enjoy what we were doing. Our individual home lives were still fulfilling, and we were energized to rehearse after a day in the work and family life, practicing two nights a week.

The irrefutable fact was that music was changing, and we, as The Lost Marbles, were not in synch with the great 'musically hip' pendulum swinging to the side of eighties style rock, big hair, and the glitter and glamor that was required to portray and grandstand the newer sound that rivaled our echoing attempts to remain in the outdated sound of the seventies; Timeless, but unfortunately in the slowly disappearing limelight. In short, our new songs sounded like oldies to the younger generation.

As time went on, we continued playing the local scene from Jersey and back to Pennsylvania. We stopped the New York and the Delaware tour scene because it was wearing us out. We did a gig in Delaware where a guy just kept harassing us to play 'something good,' (he kept saying). He wouldn't let up. Then he walked up to Cuz and tried to take his guitar off of him, telling him, "Here, let me show you," and Cuz was trying to shove him away. Nick, acting like his body guard stepped in front of him and told the joker to 'beat it'. The guy grinned at Nick and picked up a beer bottle by the neck as if picking up a hammer, and before he could get it into throwing position, Nick had the guy in a headlock and was hustling him out of the bar. Nick threw him down on the ground and started punching until we were able to pull him off of the poor bastard. We were fired from there, and Nick was sent a dental bill, which he subsequently trashed.

Another time, in Philadelphia, Stephanie, Nancy, Wanda and Barbara were all sitting in a booth in front of us, watching us as we played to another smoke-filled bar. Some guy went up to Barbara, who happened to be sitting on the outside of the booth and asked her if she wanted to dance. She declined, and he asked each of the others who demurred.

Feeling rejected, the dude then kept looking at them, staring at them from the booth behind them. This same jerk then began flicking lit matches across the booth at them. We were in the middle of a song, and we saw the girls looking at him and saying something. He then threw a shot glass, hitting Stephanie in the head, and before I could do anything, Cuz was off of the stage and was on top of the guy, pounding on him mercilessly while the girls tried to pull them apart. Nick and I did nothing as we played out the rest of the song. The owner told us to go, and we did so without getting paid.

That was the last time that the girls ever came to any of our gigs. By the time 1990 came around we were playing against more changing sounds. Alternative Rock was the new sound. Grunge rock, as it was labeled, was reaching its peak and we were stubbornly billing ourselves as classic rock, refusing to conform, or modify our sound to the beat of the new era. We were only booking and rebooking about ten of the same bars and clubs a year. The money was fair at best, but it wasn't what it used to be. Through the 90's we had a good time playing, but we lived our own separate lives. We didn't write anymore tunes and we seemed to be going through the motions rather than living the music.

My son Abraham was growing fast, and Nancy was getting back aches while having a heck of a time keeping everything together. I kept working my construction business and continued to play music, while Nancy kept the home fires burning. The Lost Marbles continued playing a drone of these same clubs over and over up until now. The past ten years of playing was the same every night, but it remained a positive outlet for our energies, at least until recently.

I've been feeling a dark cloud of gloom hanging over me that I can't explain. I can't think about it, for it throws me off center sometimes, and into deep depressions; so, I just keep burying myself in music to sublimate my negative deliberation. I'm finding myself questioning the existence of the only positive outlet in my life (besides Nancy) which is, The Lost Marbles, at a bar room gig in 1998.

Chapter 24

Catching up to the Beginning of My Story

1998

After reflecting on the past, and how we all got to this point, from Woodstock to this dive, I finally come back to the reality of the present, 1998; and back to the smoke-filled bar from the beginning of my story; my ongoing saga of our band's awkward silence. While packing up the equipment from tonight's show, and after reflecting on the past for what seemed to be months, but was only minutes, I looked at the guys, my comrades in arms who I've bonded with through the years of good and rough times and wondered, "What the hell was going on with everyone?"

Maybe we're just stale? As I said before, when we're playing the music together, we're so spiritually and emotionally in tune with each other. It's like an auto pilot comes on generating good vibes, and emotions, but when we're done, we're like zombies programmed to be rendered emotionless, until the next time we're jamming. This happened tonight, even more so than the past month or so. It's like we're all drifting apart from each other, not liking each other, or something. Men without faces; Souls without purpose.

I'm not sure how to talk with these guys anymore, as a darker cloud keeps looming overhead and as I noted before, it's unexplainable, at least by me. All I know is I'm incapable, in my present state of being, to analyze or scrutinize it. Could it be that every thing's coming to an end? I can't explain my reasoning for my present depression and unhappiness, and I want it all to be over.

Before we headed in our separate directions, I saw Nick talking to Cuz, who called Flash over to him. They were standing on the other side of the wet lot from the recent downpour on this warm summer night, but there's not a cloud in the sky now. I wondered what the discussion was that they were having, and I'll admit, I'm a little paranoid as they didn't include me.

Maybe someone's going to break the ice on this estranged behavior emanating from us, or maybe they're going to kick me out of the band. Maybe once again I'm merely thinking too much, but just then, all three of them start walking over towards me. I finish loading the car up and by then Flash, Cuz and Nick had me surrounded.
"Stan," Nick said, "Are you alright?"
"What?" I ask.
"Yeah Stan," added Cuz, "We're concerned. We want you to be able to talk to us."

Hearing this I was now even more confused. What are they getting at?

"Talk to you about what?" I said, "You guys haven't talked for the last ten gigs or so."

There was a pause and Flash said, "We didn't want to interfere, but we want you to know you can always talk to us."

I started getting a little more confused and now aggravated at this. This was crazy talk, as I started to feel rather intimidated.

"What the hell are you guys talking about?" I kept asking, "Where the hell is this coming from, and what's going on?"

Nick nodded his head and said, "Stan, you don't have to keep it a secret about Nancy, we know, and we care."

There was a silence, and my mind went blank for what seemed to be forever, but I know it was only a second. The dark cloud that was looming in my head finally burst into a veil of tears from my eyes. Then I remembered, and my mind was clear once again.

"Oh my God!" I said as I whimpered like a baby, and the three of them huddled around me in a group hug. They somehow now know, as well as I have; for a while, that my Nancy has been battling stage four cancer in her spine. I didn't want them to know, for Nancy's sake. They've been wondering why I've been more and more distant from them.

I was unaware I was being so isolated, or I didn't care, as I've been blocking out the very thought of it from myself, and not telling anyone, thinking I was protecting her, or something. It had gotten to the point that I was putting it completely out of my mind on nights we were playing, like tonight, and it was unconsciously destroying me.

About a year ago Nancy was dealing with back problems, and we noticed a lump on her spine. The doctor thought it was a slipped or herniated disk, but when she went in for surgery, and upon opening her up, they discovered it was cancer. They were not prepared to operate on cancer, and they closed her back up, but unfortunately, the air supposedly hit it, causing it to spread like wildfire. "Like rolling a ball of string" one specialist explained to us in his "layman's" term of description as we were subsequently told our options. We were nothing short of devastated, as Nancy and I have tried chemo and radiation treatments, as ordered by specialists, but this proved to be fruitless.

Nancy lost her beautiful hair and was covering her bald head with a bandana when she would go out from the house. Surgery at this point was no longer an option and now, the doctors told her last month that she only had about three more months, at best, to live. We've decided we're going to spend that time at home, not in a hospital.

Nancy and I spend time together trekking to the creek, only a few hundred feet in front of the house and we'd fish. We also take drives to the shore, and another weekend to the hotel in the Delaware Water Gap, where we were even able to do a couple miles on the Appalachian trail. That was a weekend I cancelled a band engagement, telling them I was with the flu.

Our son Abraham is now 16, and he's there with Nancy when I'm not, and our family is on an all-natural diet of beets, garlic, capsaicin, turmeric, cinnamon, ginger root, tomatoes, eggs, and also things she likes, as long as she eats the before mentioned. She's been up and around, but mostly tired, and insists that life goes on, that she doesn't want things to die around her, saying she wants me to continue playing music. I did stop my business, well, I delegated the work so I could spend more time with her. She didn't want me to stop playing, but most of all, she didn't want anyone to know what was going on with her, and that part was tough.

THE LOST MARBLES STORY

I wanted to tell the guys, but I respected her wishes, and once insisted on me taking a hiatus from playing, for just awhile anyway, but she had gotten irate; and her blood pressure went sky high. The decision was made then, to honor her wish, even though it made me uncomfortable to do so.

God, I love her so much, and she's the whole reason I've existed on earth for this long; or made it this far. Anyway, I've managed to block her situation completely out of my mind, at the last few gigs, just so I could exist, and it worked for a while, but I don't know how healthy that is mentally for me or for anyone concerned. In the meantime, it seemed to me as if everyone was being distant or removed, but I was simply rationalizing, by thinking it's the repetition of the band's ongoing drone of playing the same places, and doing a lot of the same songs, as a mental defense to keep me grounded, I guess. But today, when I spent all day with Nancy, I couldn't figure out how to leave her side. She's in pain, and I didn't want to disappoint her at the same time by not playing tonight.

Well, now the guys know, and the burden is shared, but Nancy is number one and I want her to be comfortable. Abe tells me she sometimes cries and that she misses me when I'm not there, and that breaks my heart. I guess it's time to be honest with her, that I need to be with her as well, even though she's already aware of that. She's the strongest person I know, and the strongest person I'll ever know. The boys in the band did mention that they wanted to take a break for a while anyway. The guys also said that Abraham was the one who let them know, as he had told them about Nancy because he was worried about me, but he gave strict orders that they're not to visit or talk to Nancy until she feels comfortable talking.

Abraham is the best, and I couldn't be any prouder of him than I am right now, as I learn from him, and I'll add that Nancy did a great job being a mom to him. But she was too worried that if people found out about her illness, they would do what she would do; which is drop everything to help someone out, and she couldn't accept the thought that this may bring people down or put them out. It's her way of dealing with it for now, but I'm going to change that tonight if I can.

The guys and I talked and commiserated for a few minutes before we said our 'so longs' for the evening. Thanks to them I feel much better about everything now, and I guess it is better to let it out among friends. These guys are the best friends anyone can have!

Anyway, I steer my way home from this Philadelphia bar, which is about an hour drive without traffic. I stop on the way at a convenience store, well, all night market to get her some apples and avocados.

I was sitting in the driver's seat with the groceries, and still parked on the lot of the convenience store, when before I start the vehicle, I saw a bolt of lightning directly above, in the clear and starry sky; very unusual. Then a leaf from a White Oak landed on the windshield just long enough for me to identify it, then flittered away on a summer breeze into the darkness. It reminded me of something, something special I was given a while back.

I looked in my wallet, and sure enough, there it was, in between my social security card and my voter registration, the two cards I haven't removed from my wallet in years. Between them was the tiny prayer tree leaf that Evangeline had given to me almost 20 years ago. It's still intact with the perfectly rounded edges, and oddly enough still green and fresh as if it was picked today, and that in itself sent a chill through me. (The heebee-geebees, as my mom used to say.)

The island that this came from was so mystical that I thought, 'What the hell,' so I put it in my right hand and made my wish. My wish was so ridiculous that I started to snicker. It was so ludicrous that I rolled on the ground of the lot after opening the car door, laughing so hard at myself, for thinking that I could believe that a wish such as this could ever come true. But I did it, I sat back in the driver's seat and I wished that Nancy would be cured of the cancer by the time I got home this morning.

It's not like I was wishing for her to be cured this instant; which would be totally preposterous. My wish was less preposterous, which made it more tangible, and laughable, giving it time to do what it had to do until I got home. Less unbelievable can still be called believable, so clenching the leaf in my right hand, the wish was made; and as before, the smoky, steamy mist came from my hand as well, and upon opening my hand, I saw the leaf was gone. As before, I looked for it, this time on the floor of the car, but it wasn't to be found. I started the car and made sure I had the avocados and apples before driving home.

I got to Valley road in about 50 minutes, and in another half minute I was turning into our driveway. It was about 3am and the lights in the house were on. Abraham was still up and standing tall in the front door entrance waiting for me.

"Uh oh," I thought. The thought of reality hit and instead of miracles, I was expecting the worst. He was standing in his jeans with no shirt, a strapping young man like his father, I thought vainly, and I saw he was sobbing. I started to get sad too, as young Abe said to me in a trembling voice, "Mom's been sick for so long, and now it's hard for me to believe, it's finally over, Dad."

Now I was trembling. Did I have too much faith in a prayer and a wish? Was my wish more for myself than for

her? I didn't think so. Was the wish for cancer to be gone a death wish? I was starting to cry when all of a sudden, I heard the beginning of the Temptations song "Just My Imagination" coming from the living room stereo. Then Abe said with tears and an emotionally high vibrating note in his voice, "She's waiting for you. She wants to dance with you! Do you believe it?"
"What?" I asked.
Abraham, containing himself for a moment continued, "She got up, and started running around like she was in the Olympics, doing vacuuming, and singing that song that's playing now, since about an hour ago, until you pulled in . . . " Then a familiar voice interrupts us, with a familiar phrase:
"Stan! Is that you Stan? I know you're home. Get your ass in here and dance with me!" By now I wasn't sure what to think, but I was certainly starting to feel better about all of this.

    As I walked in, she was standing in the middle of the living room with her hands on her hips, bald headed as ever, but wearing her same style Daisy Mae halter and shorts. She looked thin still, but very healthy; and the smile, the smile she was wearing cancelled the memory of a year of illness. She had that same fire in her eyes, and upon seeing me, threw her arms open in outstretched silence, maintaining her illustrious smile, as if to say, 'look at me!' or 'TA DA!'

    You better believe I ran into those arms, and I picked her up in the air, banging her poor bald, but beautiful head lightly on the ceiling and gave her a hug as we spun around to the music. She was as I said, still thin but wiry, and stronger than the devil!

I knew what had happened here and I was in complete awe! Through tears of happiness, we began slow dancing to the Temptations.

"I was lying in bed," Nancy was telling me while we were dancing and holding onto each other tightly, "and a voice said, 'The illness has left you. Rise and walk!' But I thought, 'Yeah right,' you know, like I was dreaming, so I rolled over to sleep on the other side. But Stan, you know what? My pain was completely gone! Then I stood up, and once again I thought 'I must be dreaming'. I felt more energetic than I had in years! What's happening Stan? I know, maybe it was the beets, and the garlic, and all of that ginger . . ."

I loved hearing her talk, but I interrupted her.

"You're not dreaming," I said. "It's one of life's miracles. One of God's miracles. Don't question it."

The record was finishing, starting its inevitable fade when Nancy said, "Stan, remember the first time we danced together to this song?"

"I will never forget it Nancy. I'm impressed you remember that."

"Oh, come on now," she said, "you know me better than that, please put it back to the beginning and hold me." Then she stopped me, saying, "Wait!"

She then had Abe put the speakers in the open window, pointing outside and said she wanted to dance in the moonlight. She took off her clothes and made me do the same. Abe just turned his head away, giving us some privacy and cried happy tears.

The song started, and we danced in the moonbeam of a gibbous moon, naked on a sandy patch near her garden and softly swaying to the rhythm of the early seventies, and to our favorite song. Abraham was watching his mother and father dancing in the glow of the moonlight, as it cast our shadows onto the ground beneath the clear skies. He watched through the blur a young man's tear, at least until the chorus, but I wasn't looking at him anymore. No matter, we're all happy now. When the song ended, Abe appeared again and put the song back to the beginning for us without anyone asking.

"You guys are on your own tonight. I'm going to bed," he said.

Then Nancy asked him to put on "Dream" by the Everly Brothers before he leaves, and to put it on automatic replay; and with that, we continued our embrace. Nancy is so beautiful, and she never felt better than she does in my arms right now. The light and aura of love is strong and warm in the yard, and in our home.

The following week, we went to the doctor to run tests, which confirmed that the cancer was gone. The newspapers wanted to publicize the news, but we demurred to comment, while the Catholic Church wanted to spread the word that it was a supposed miracle for some proposed saint we've never heard of, so they can be canonized accordingly, but we ignored the religious press. We basically stayed out of sight for the next year, enjoying our freedom of living. The band stopped playing anywhere with smoke-filled rooms, and that cut our gigs in half, but no worries, as we were having a great time just playing together.

At one of the gigs, in Center City, a tall woman approached us with her card, saying she was with a recording company called *Ladynight Records*. She was drooling at the prospect of our song "Lila," and with the CD market at a high point, she thought this was an opportunity for a band like ours to get on the band wagon. No pun intended. She had looked up our other songs and decided that if we wanted to, we could call our own shots and record with her company. She wanted to redo our original recordings of Sing Those Blues, Rock and Roll Radio, and make an album in CD form.

Everything is CDs now while vinyl has been disappearing for years, and this offer couldn't have come at a better time. Her second option was having an all-girl group she had in mind to perform our songs on her label, and we'd get royalties on their success. The Lost Marbles unanimously agreed to have the all-girl group take on the project, since we figured that with our lives already full, we were happy just playing places of our choice and living our present lives to the fullest, with our families, and counting our blessings.

The all-girl band, who will remain nameless here, turned out to be very successful and we did pretty well through them with our songs. Our old friend Runx, as per our promise to him, even got his cut for writing some of the songs.

Anyway, we did so well on this that Nancy and I took an early retirement. Her hair had grown back long and full, and she's as healthy as she was in her twenties, or so she says, but I'll swear by that because she makes me feel the same! We bought an old, classic VW van, removed the seats, with the exception of the driver and passenger seats, and we toured America, including Canada, involving ourselves in hiking, camping, fishing the mountain streams, crabbing the bays, and even pulling lobster traps, which included Nancy, as promised, doing her special; A romantic home-cooked fresh lobster boil dinner, her own way as she always has done with our lobster boils since we were together.

It's always done like a beach party, with me wearing my cutoff jeans and she, good to her word and loving it, in her ravishing red slingshot bikini. Just her and I and the unfortunate lobsters, which on occasion we'd subsequently name after politicians we didn't like, as I watched her toss them remorselessly into the boiling pot to meet their inexorable demise. The lobsters weren't the only ones hot and steamy on those torrid nights to be sure.

The amorous memory of the lobster boil with Evangeline didn't exist since I've been with Nancy, and that's exactly what Nancy wanted, just like her loving memories of Nick. All still there, but as prudent thoughts, or sober memories of times past, with 'past' being the key word of existence. Like Nancy said to me once, "Memories are a big part of our lives, if you delete items of your past, you shorten your lifespan. So instead of trying to forget, it's better rather to rationalize and nurture the memories you still have." She also added that it's probably better to think, but not tell all; Good advice.

Between the long trips, we'd work together in the garden and on the farm, never getting tired of each other, reflecting sometimes on the old days when we first met, and how we secretly had a crush on each other even through our other relationships. Once we finally got together, on that first night in the hotel in the Water Gap, we've never strayed from each other. We had bonded somehow before that, to cliche a phrase, it's like we were meant to be. To put it into words, I've never been more in love with her as I am every day of my life with her.

We would let Abraham know where we were, at intervals on our excursions, and he'd sometimes meet us for dinner at a restaurant, or for a hike in the mountains. He'd occasionally bring his girlfriend, who coincidently ended up being the bassist 'Lizzie', in the all-girl band doing our songs. Abe was over 18 by this time and was taking over the contracting business. The rest of the Lost Marbles went their separate ways and into their full and happy lives, sober and clean. We do however get together religiously once a year to play and jam and catch up. Life is Good!!

Chapter 25

Epilogue

Evangeline and Vanessa (A.K.A. Snake) made it back to the states for a visit. This was in 2003. They, like us, were older but they were well and healthy. They stayed with Nancy and I for a few days and with Nick and Barbara for a few. Nancy really enjoyed their company, and anything that once distressed or annoyed her about Evangeline and myself is long gone, which goes the same for me regarding Nancy and Nick.

As a matter of fact, Evangeline and Vanessa are now living together as partners on Jaadaa, having a home, and enjoying their lives fishing the ocean and farming their own crops. Evangeline's fair skin even developed a tan, with more freckles through the years. They own their own private jet and both know how to pilot it, and even have their own island airstrip fifty feet from their back door by the ocean. Vanessa said that the festival we attended on our last day on the island lasted about a week, and that the island people subsequently lived happily ever after.

Sundra's daughter, who was previously sold into prostitution by her late husband was found and returned to her by Evangeline. Most of the other women from the island who were deceived into that lifestyle were returned to their parents and families by either Vanessa or Evangeline. Unfortunately, some were never found, as they were murdered by Marco, or Balance, or some of the other henchmen, of which are also not alive anymore.

Vanessa's family, in the memory of her murdered parents of course, had their land with the diamond mines reclaimed and have used their wealth to profit the island for the inhabitants. Marco's mansion was torn down, and that particular island in the chain restored to its original natural beauty. Guests are welcome to camp and live off of the natural resources of the islands, while paying guides to help them with anything they need, but the islands are not advertised. Only by word of mouth is the island accessible, and it's 'who you know'; The natives prefer it that way.

There hasn't been any cannibalism on the island since the festival, although Vanessa said she missed it a little, but the yearly pig festivals satisfactorily fill those yearnings. Other than that, the island people are a very friendly nation. A society of united families and joyous, gregarious folks.

Nancy and I won't ever go to those islands, like Nick and Barbara do. There's something about it that bothers me still, even though I know that the people are happy and friendly, despite the fact that Evangeline's father Erik is spreading Christianity to anyone who'll listen. I guess that because we're just happy the way we are, alive and well, we're easily pleased in whatever we're doing within our normal day to day lives, as long as we're together.

We're planning to hike the Appalachian trail within the next year and we're going to go all the way, from Georgia to Maine, but we may be doing it in sections, state by state because Nancy's been doing her volunteer work with cancer patients and at a children's hospital, thus, she doesn't want to stay away from that for too long. It's her way of giving back she says, but in all honesty, I've never seen her happier working with the children and the terminal patients.

I help her where I can, but I don't have the knack she has, as her social skills are outstanding and her accomplished attitude in any given situation is nothing short of magnificent. She's always had exemplary people skills which is why she did so well managing our band. As she said before, she wants me to keep playing music, which brings me to mention the band.

We play more now, at places of our own choice, non-smoking venues, about ten or twelve gigs a year and that suits us fine. We're all kind of retired and doing what we want and living off of royalties and fringe benefits. Cuz, Stephanie, Flash, Wanda, Nick, Barbara, Nancy and I, all get together from time to time for parties and barbecues, like one big happy family and talk about our lives, our kids, and our memories.

We also have a big outdoor concert in a big field on Valley Road every July with the Lost Marbles, featuring assorted local bands. Lately we've even started featuring an occasional big-name act, but we'll see where it goes from here.

Nancy and I are very happy, and it's hard to imagine now, that we were ever apart. That's what our friends say when they see us, but a part of me felt I've always known her, always. Probably because of the story she told me the other day, which she never mentioned it until then.

Nancy and I were laying on the roof of the garage together, as we've always done, looking up at the sky and remembering Arizona and Clear Creek near Winslow where we were laying back and making clouds disappear, and we were now looking at our own blue sky and witnessed a hawk flying far above. Then we saw a crow rapidly flying in another direction, far below the hawk, with two smaller birds tormenting and chasing it. "That crow probably invaded the momma bird's nest," she said. Then we'd get lost in thought before we both tried to evaporate yet another small cloud on the horizon using our concentration, and had some success, then she held my hand.
"Do you have any regrets?" she asked me.
"None." was my immediate answer. She rolled over to me, and wrapped her arms around me, and we held each other for a long while, when out of the blue, she recited a poem I had written years ago.

"Center of the Wheel," she said in a mild whisper near my ear, and continued:

"Faces puncture closing curtains on the set of yesteryear,
When ghosts performing godlike gestures stormed the stage, ignoring jeers.
Like puppets looking out the window, through the glass partition know
The glass is only half a mirrored one-way ticket to the show
of dreams to be constructed solely for a storage bin beside
a toolbox purchased for a purpose. Destructive instruments reside.
And both are closed and locked outside a room inlayed with begging doors.
A one key fits all proposition when assumed the choice is yours.

Searching finds, and having loses. Winter springs, and summer falls.
Failures congregate in circles, come to emulate the walls,
Ionized in magnetism, drawing passion effortless,
Until a weary traveler's left subdued in seas of haziness.
Which cannot seem to undertake the emanating smile so real
From deep within the inner circle at the center of the wheel.
Which runs on infinite propulsion, and perpetuates scenarios,
To conquer serpentine reflections on this shroud of punctured glow."

She continued to the last part:

"As the captain of the vessel dawn's the evening sea,
sailing with the inner star revealed,
Takes the turning in his stride, constitution verses tide.
Steering on an even-tempered keel, I climb behind the center of the wheel."

She laid back silent and I asked, "Wow, how did you remember that?" She gave me a smile and said, "When I first met you through Cuz, you handed me that poem on a piece of paper, asking me to tell you what I think. You were drunk on your ass, and flirting with me, though I never told Cuz; and you handed me the poem, then fell asleep on the floor." She then unfolded it in front of me, a wrinkled and faded piece of loose leaf paper. "I'm going to keep this forever," she said, "And to answer your question about what I think about it, I think you wrote what you had foreseen as an equation, or premonition of your life; and that you're a deep solid soul and were very easy to fall in love with."

    I was shocked into silence over her remembering and memorizing that poem. It was one of my earlier literary works, forgotten in the annals of time.

Then she asked me if I remembered anything about my childhood. "Of course," I answered, "I already told you about Mary and the lobsters." Then she went into detail about her own childhood, about a summer in 1958, in Beach Haven, New Jersey.

She was about six or seven when she and her folks came down from New York for a week's stay. She said she was playing in the surf; and filling a bucket with wet sand. She saw a little boy about the same age, building a sand castle with the dryer sand further from the surf. Nancy said she kept bringing him sand from the surf, and it made him smile the cutest smile, which made her really like him.

Then a nearby transistor radio, played her favorite song at that time, "Dream," by the Everly Brothers. She said she took the little boy by the hand and started slow dancing with him, while he just stood there, blushing, but not backing down. He lifted his arms, put them around her, then danced with her regardless of the teenagers, who owned the radio, laughing and applauding. When the song was over, that little boy took his shovel and bucket and walked out to the surf and started digging for sand crabs. Just then someone grabbed her arm. It was her mom. "Where were you?" she asked her. It seems that Nancy had wandered too far down the beach from where her parents were. Nancy said that it was the last time she ever saw the little boy. Now here's where this gets scary.

In the summer of '58, I was a little boy, about six or seven, maybe, and I was actually at Beach Haven, New Jersey. I clearly remember a girl, about the same age as me, approaching me with a bucket of wet sand while I was building a sand castle, and bringing me more as the castle got bigger. I remember seeing two teenage couples dancing to "Dream," which was a hit that summer. One of the teenagers was my babysitter Mary, wearing her red bikini, and

Mary grabbed me to dance with herself, with my face pressed into her belly button. Then she said, "Aww, how cute," and turned me around to see the little girl, who had extended her arms out to me. Mary pushed me into the little girl's arms and laughed, saying, "Oh my gosh, they're so cute." I began dancing with her while Mary went back to her boyfriend and we finished the dance.

When it was over, Mary kissed her boyfriend, and the other dance couple kissed each other. I looked at my little partner to find her head tilted back, lips puckered, and her eyes were closed. So, I did what any red blooded American eight-year old boy would do. I picked up my shovel and bucket, and went on the hunt for sand crabs, and I never saw her again, but was looking for her the rest of the day, and virtually the rest of my life. As I grew older I wondered what she looked like, and where she might be, and who she might be; almost like I was searching for her.

So, there you have it; that little girl I met on the beach at Beach Haven was Nancy, many years ago. Coincidence? Who's to say? So, we have met, and danced before, and I'm not searching anymore.

Nancy told me on the garage roof that day, that she always knew it was me, but figured that I knew too. When we met again as teenagers, it was because she was dating Cuz, which was long before Woodstock, and I felt some kind of weird connection with her, a subconscious knowing. I don't like trying to analyze it, all I know is it's like it was meant to be, but as I said, who's to say? It's like that feeling when we're slow dancing to "Just My Imagination" or "Dream," I feel as if we've always danced together on an endless sandy beach under an eternal moonbeam, without a beginning, and without an end. I know, I'm corny, and although it might annoy the reader, it doesn't bother me at all that I am, because love does that. Nancy and I were like two lost marbles in the sands of time, coming together in the bottleneck of time's own hourglass, as we now hopefully and graciously pass through the coming ages, healthy and happy.

"They danced around on the virgin crust, naked feet in their naked lust,
Their own place, their own trust. A lonely cloud becomes moon dust.
Within this dream they waltz on the sand. They feel forever as one hand in hand.
They never met, for they always knew, each other's footsteps beneath the same moon . . . as they danced on a moonbeam."

- Tom Rukas

ABOUT THE AUTHOR

Tom Rukas is a musician and a songwriter residing in Bucks County Pennsylvania. Along with some poetry, he has produced and recorded three albums containing some of his original music: "Forgotten Words and Rumblin' Wheels," "The Possession of Abraham Cactus," and "Watching the Wagons Roll." In his leisure time, Tom plays bass guitar in a local classic rock band.